THE CHANGED

Book 2 of The Taken Saga

AVERY BLAKE
NINIE HAMMON

STERLING & STONE

THE CHANGED

PART I
In The Mothership

Chapter One

YOU WERE NAMED Falling Star to fulfill the prophesy made about you by your ancestors who sit beside the Great Spirit and the White Giants in round lodges on the other side of the moon.

PAPA EAGLE FEATHER'S words echoed in Star's mind, as if her head were inside an oil drum and the syllables were bouncing off the metal, repeating.

Falling Star ... *star ... star ...*

Ancient name ... *name ... name ...*

Great Spirit ... *spirit ... spirit ...*

And the White Giants.

Falling Star Yellowhorse had dreamed about the white giants, huge and bald, with blue eyes and expressionless faces, wearing those dress things like you see on statues ... togas, the short ones that didn't go all the way to the floor. They weren't scary looking, just horrifying in their strangeness, the way they looked like people, sort of, but distorted people.

She'd dreamed about the silver balls hanging in the sky, too. And the others, the monster creatures with too many bug legs and razor teeth that looked like they'd been invented just to scare people, like for a horror movie.

But *this* wasn't a dream.

Star kept her eyes shut, resolutely refused to open them. Even as she thought that, squeezed her eyelids so tightly closed it wrinkled up her whole face, she understood it was being a baby, like hiding under the covers. She was blind — couldn't have seen anything if she *had* opened her eyes, but there was a symbolism in keeping her eyes closed that she intuitively understood and acknowledged.

Still — *not* seeing something didn't make it go away.

And Star wanted this to go away. All of it. Every single day since the Astral Telescope spotted the little white spots lined up in neat rows out by Jupiter. After that, everything was ruined.

Cities burned, governments collapsed and people — that was the most horrible part of all — *normal people changed.* Uncle Clyde would probably say they hadn't changed, they'd just became who they'd really been all along. Either way, the result was the same. You couldn't just assume that people would be good and kind and decent anymore. You were in danger … everywhere.

Oh, how Star wanted a do-over! Wanted to wake up in the morning and smell bacon frying, and hear

Pumpkin whining because he needed to go to the bathroom really bad and the littles squabbling over some toy.

Life. She wanted it *back.* Life where she wasn't so scared she was nauseous, trying not to throw up. So scared her heart wasn't beating at all, it was humming in her chest.

Could you die from that? From your heart beating too fast, from the blood squirting around so fast it didn't have time to do whatever it was blood did that kept you alive?

Pumpkin was leaned against her leg, trembling. No, *vibrating.* She dropped to her knees, threw her arms around the dog, buried her face in his fur, so soft he felt like a stuffed animal, and wanted so badly to cry.

Her knees had landed on something hard. It wasn't sand. She'd been standing in sand and she wasn't anymore, which meant she wasn't where she had been, on the mesa that looked out over the Sangre de Cristo Mountains of New Mexico.

She was somewhere else. And she knew where else, the only *where else* she could be. That understanding scared her so bad she couldn't even cry. She stopped in the middle of a sob and sucked in a trembling gasp of air, clinging so tight to Pumpkin she was almost choking him.

What was she going to do?

No, that wasn't the right question. The right question was what was she going to *be?* Papa Eagle Feather had told her she had to be brave. Uncle Clyde would want her to be brave, too. Only she couldn't think about Uncle Clyde. The image flashed on the screen in her mind, anyway, showed up hot and stinking and it was too powerful to resist.

She's cuddled up beside Uncle Clyde under the trailer house, her arms around him, hugging him, but he isn't hugging her back. He isn't moving at all and as she lies there she feels the wetness on the front of his shirt dry and grow stiff, feels his body grow cold.

Star pushed the image and the wave of overwhelming grief away with a shuddery intake of breath. She didn't cry, though. That was something, made her feel a little like the brave girl Papa Eagle Feather had told her to be.

Thinking about Papa Eagle Feather didn't hurt like thinking of Uncle Clyde because he wasn't dead. Just gone. She felt loss, of course. Loneliness. But mostly what she felt was confused. He had taken her and Pumpkin up to the top of the mesa and told her that she was standing in the Taking Place, that the gods had foretold she would one day stand there, and that they would take her away.

And it had happened. She had been *taken away.*

All those thoughts — dozens of thoughts! — flew through Star's head in seconds. Either that, or time stood still long enough for her to think them all slowly, ponder each one, and she didn't believe that was it. She had thought it all — about the dreams and the giants and Uncle Clyde and the mountaintop —

between the time her grandfather let go of her hands and stepped away and the beam had enveloped her in golden light.

She *saw* the light. She was blind, but she saw it. It was sparkling, like it was made of gold glitter. But it had texture somehow, which made no sense but it was true anyway. It felt like you could reach out your fingers and rub it between them and if you did, it would feel like velvet.

And then the golden light was gone but there was still light. She was blind, but not black-dark blind. She saw lights and blobs of shapes and bright colors. What she saw now through her closed eyelids was not warm, golden light. It was white light, bright and sterile, the kind of light that might shine down on an operating table so some surgeon could see where to cut you open.

It was cold light, too. And it didn't feel like it was coming from above, like the golden beam had felt. It was from all around, from everywhere and nowhere.

But she didn't open her eyes to see because she'd finally gotten all the way out to the end of herself, out to the boundaries you set up so you don't have to know a thing if you don't want to. And she didn't want to, not yet. She wasn't ready yet.

Her grandfather had taken her and Pumpkin up to the top of the mesa, said a bunch of weird stuff and then stepped away. Then she'd felt/seen the golden glow. And after that, harsh white light.

And silence.

All sound was suddenly gone, too. Gone was the gentle rustle of the sagebrush and the lonely cry of a chicken hawk high in the sky.

No smells, either. The scent of the flowering cactus and the leather of Papa Eagle Feather's vest, and the horse smell that was just a part of who he was. Every smell was gone.

Like maybe she was in a test tube.

She forced herself to loosen her strangle-hold hug around Pumpkin's neck. He was trembling but he wasn't whining like he did during thunderstorms, which terrified him. He wasn't afraid. He was … something else. Confused. Disoriented. Bewildered, maybe.

Star knew why. He was trembling because he could see what she couldn't. He could see *where they were*, while she was just guessing. But it was a pretty safe guess even if it was crazy, bull moose crazy.

Mescalero Apache Indian girls from Roswell, New Mexico, didn't get abducted by aliens! Not in real life. In stupid science fiction movies, or in the minds of wack jobs who believed there were little green men living in Area 51.

But not for real.

What were you supposed to do when "for real" was impossible?

She bleated a burp of some sound that was almost like a laugh. It wasn't, not a sob, either. Something in between. She put her hand on the surface where she was kneeling. It was cool and smooth. If she'd had to guess, she'd have said it was plastic but she didn't imagine Astral spaceships were made of plastic.

The last wall fell then, with the feel of that smooth, cold surface, and terror gripped her chest so tight she couldn't get her breath. Crazy or not, impossible or not, this-doesn't-happen-to-real-people or not, Falling Star Yellowhorse was up in one of the alien spaceships, the silver balls she'd seen in her dreams hanging over cities, suspended in space. Up there with the white giants. And the black lizard things with razor teeth.

Pumpkin might not be afraid, but Star was *terrified*, so frightened it felt like there were leather straps around her chest so tight she had trouble drawing in a breath.

She had never in all her eleven years been as frightened as she was right now. Oh, she'd been scared when the crazy man who'd killed Uncle Clyde came back to kill her, too. She was afraid to die. Everybody was afraid to die. Now, though, she was afraid to *live*. Afraid of what the white giants and lizard things were going to do to her. They were *aliens. Things,* not people. And they'd taken her away, kidnapped her, brought her here — for *what*?

Whatever they intended to do to her, it wouldn't be good. It would be horrible, maybe so horrible she would wish Papa Eagle Feather hadn't saved her from the man who was trying to kill her. It might be so terrible that being dead was better than being alive … here.

A full-body shudder wracked her like a seizure and

she clung to Pumpkin. But she *wasn't* crying. It wasn't crying if you didn't make any noise. Her shoulders shook and tears somehow found a way to run out of her eyes and down her cheeks.

She didn't open them, though. Kept her eyes squeezed tight shut.

Chapter Two

Noah Matheson looked down at the rock in his hand. It was flat, round and smooth, smaller than his palm — the perfect rock to skip across the water. That's what he'd intended to do with it. His father had just shown him how. He had held up a similar rock and signed "hold it like this," then he'd gripped the rock with his index finger and thumb, in the shape of a C. He'd fit the rock into that.

Noah had nodded.

His father had signed something to Gretchen Hampton, too, but he didn't see all of it, something about snapping your wrist to put a spin on the rock when you threw it.

Dad was teaching him and Gretchen how to skip a rock across the pond behind the tenant house on their farm that was empty because the couple who'd been living there left on Astral Day. Noah dug around on the rocks on the shore beside the water, looking for a rock the right size and shape. They were getting harder and harder to find because he and his father had spent a lot of time by the pond, skipping them. Well, his father'd been skipping them. Noah had been throwing them out with the side-arm swing his father had demonstrated and then watched them plunk once and sink.

He'd been searching for the perfect rock for one more try because the sun was setting and it'd soon be too dark when he'd unearthed this one. It was perfect. Gretchen's mother, Ellie, and Gretchen had started into the house and Dad had followed along behind. Noah was turning to get his father's attention, wanted him to stop and watch this last throw because Noah was sure he'd get it right this time and the rock would skip across the water, at least once, before it sank.

But he hadn't made it all the way around. He'd been turning. And then he wasn't. He wasn't moving. He was standing frozen in place on the shore of the pond with the rock in his hand. He felt like he was stuck in cement. He'd always had a secret horror of that. Back in the old house, when they'd had a real home, Dad had laid out a sidewalk from the driveway to the porch, poured wet cement, smoothed it out and said it'd be dry by the next morning and they could walk on it. And it had been dry the next morning. But during the night, a toad had hopped out onto the wet cement and had gotten stuck there. When they found it, the toad's feet up about two inches were incased in cement and it couldn't move. That had struck Noah as such a horrible sight at the time — even though his father busted up his brand new sidewalk to free the toad. After that, Noah was horrified of being frozen in something, unable to move.

And he was now.

But he wasn't standing in cement. He was standing in a beam of golden light, shimmering gold, like he was standing in the shower and all the drops of water were made of gold, shiny gold. Thicker than the droplets of water in a shower, though. So thick he could only barely see through them to the other side of the pond, not to the house. Because he'd been frozen in the act of turning around.

It was crazy, stuck in a beam of light!

He wondered what was *really*—

And then he'd looked up at the source of the beam of light and his heart had stopped moving along with his muscles. He stopped breathing, maybe the blood stopped flowing through his veins, even. The sight was that arresting and terrifying. He was standing under a silver ball that was hanging in the air with nothing holding it up. It was one of the little silver ships they'd seen on the juke, the first news footage of the Astral ships that had been broadcast on every channel all day to a world holding its breath.

The one hanging over Paris was so close to the Eiffel Tower it seemed to be touching it. The one over Shanghai was the creepiest. It had other little silver balls around it. Not just balls, but all kinds of shapes, some of them like the flat rock he was holding in his hand. And the news anchor had said the big silver ball was the "mothership" and the little ones, in different sizes and shapes, were "shuttles." The man speculated that the aliens got into the shuttles on the mothership and used them to travel around in, maybe to land, although nobody had seen one land yet. They called them "Astrals" and Noah didn't get why they needed a whole new word. Alien had worked fine until now, but they called them Astrals all the same, and the world was still waiting for them to land a shuttle and get out so humanity could have a look at them.

Noah had already had a look at them. He'd seen them in dreams for a month before they spotted the little white dots flying in formation to Earth from Jupiter. He knew what the aliens looked like because he'd been dreaming about the silver balls and as soon as the ships got close enough to Earth for telescopes to take detailed pictures of them, he'd seen they were the balls from his dreams. So the rest of the dreams, the part where there were white giants with bald heads and blue eyes and the lizard creatures with razor teeth must be true, too. That's what the Astrals inside the big silver balls looked like.

And inside the shuttles, too. Like the one that was hanging above him right now, shining down a golden light that froze him like concrete.

The light grew brighter and brighter. It was beautiful, scary beautiful, but beautiful, sparkling droplets of gold that got thicker and thicker a until he could no longer see through them at all. For a time, he didn't know how long, seemed like only seconds, he could see nothing but golden light all around him, warm light. Then golden light began to fade.

That's when his heart started slamming into the

walls of his chest so hard he was afraid it would burst from the impact. As the golden glow grew dimmer, he could see through it again as he had when it first enveloped him. But what he could see through it wasn't what had been there before. There was no pond, no trees on the other side, no golden pink sunset sky. All that was gone. It had been replaced by white, and during the time it took him to think that thought, the white light replaced the golden beam of light and the golden light vanished.

Noah was standing on … it wasn't the creek bank. It wasn't rocks and dirt. It wasn't even outside. He was in a room with a floor that was shiny white and it led to shiny white walls except the floor didn't stop at the wall. The wall didn't sit on top of the floor. The white floor bent, curved and became the walls, which curved and became the ceiling. There was no seam anywhere. Just white, all around him, in glaring white light that seemed to come from everywhere and nowhere. There was no source for it — like a lightbulb overhead or a lamp or track lighting on the floor like in a movie theatre. It was just there, all around, and the light cast no shadows.

As all of that slammed like a wrecking ball into his awareness, reason spoke remarkably calmly in his head. He was in one of those shuttle things he'd seen on television. The golden light had … *transported* him here from the bank of the pond.

He was on an alien— an *Astral* spaceship!

That was ridiculous. Absurd. Unbeliev— but it was real. Real! Noah was filled with equal parts terror and wonder … no, not equal parts. He was so afraid he thought he might wet his pants.

That's when he saw her. And felt her. Okay, that was certifiably crazy, but it was true. She was *warm*.

He was in a white room, but he wasn't *alone* in the white room. There was a little girl here, too, on her knees beside a dog. She was hugging the dog and crying.

Noah instantly knew two contradictory truths. He had never met this little girl. But he knew her.

She was *real*. How could that possibly be?

It had never occurred to Noah, in all the years she'd occupied the background of his dreams, that she might be a real person and not just some figure his mind had conjured up. Like some little kid's invisible friend, except she wasn't invisible and she only came to him in dreams. Every night since … for four years. Black hair in braids, a happy, engaging smile. He hadn't dreamed *about* the little girl. She was just in them, there in the background. The dog was there, too.

Noah was propelled toward her. Not by some alien — *Astral* — power ray or anything like that. He was propelled by his own wonder and curiosity. No, more than that. He was drawn to her in a way he didn't have words to explain.

The little girl he didn't even think existed, the girl from his dreams, she'd been kidnapped, too, and taken up into a spaceship.

Chapter Three

As soon as Noah started toward the little girl, her dog turned and looked at him. He was an adorable dog, with soft apricot-colored fur that made him look like a teddy bear. The dog wasn't wagging his tail. He was just sitting beside the little girl, who was clinging to him, leaning against him sobbing. Noah didn't know much about dogs, he'd never had one, but surely if the dog was vicious, had planned to lunge at him and bite him, he'd look more menacing somehow.

The little girl's lips moved.

"Who's there?"

It wasn't a what-is-your-name? kind of question. It was a who … or *what* is out there? What awful thing is out there in the darkness that I can't see?

"I'm … my name is Noah Matheson," he signed.

She gasped.

"*What?*"

He couldn't think what else to say, so he signed, "I live in Kentucky." Except he didn't live in Kentucky, not anymore. He'd been kidnapped from there — by Astrals.

"It's *you*," the little girl cried and turned her head in his general direction. But her eyes didn't focus on him. It was obvious they couldn't, that she was blind.

An irrational thought popped into his mind. Maybe she didn't participate in what was happening in his dreams because she didn't know what was going on, couldn't see.

"Wait … you mean, I was in *your* dreams?"

"Yes!" he signed.

"You were in *my* dreams. I thought I made you up. You're *real*? A real person?" Excitement and wonder colored her words. "You're blond, right? Like *really* blonde — almost white, kind of. And your eyes are blue."

That's when it hit him. And he suddenly felt dizzy, disoriented in a way far more profound that being kidnapped by Astrals.

They'd been having a conversation, but she couldn't see what he was signing and he couldn't hear what she was saying.

"You can't hear? You're deaf?"

He didn't sign this time. Didn't speak out loud, either.

"Yes, I'm deaf. And you … can't see, can you?"

"I can see some things, blobs, shapes, light. But I need Pumpkin to keep me from running into stuff."

She reached up and began wiping the tears off her face, babbling, clearly relieved that she wasn't alone and stunned by his presence.

"My name's Falling Star Yellowhorse. Kind of a

mouthful, I know. Just Star's fine. I'm Mescalero Apache."

Noah's heart took up that woodpecker-trying-to-peck-its-way-out-of-his-chest banging again.

"How did you hear me ask if you were blind? I didn't say anything out loud."

A look that was equal parts shock and terror washed over her face, with a side order of confusion and wonder.

"I don't know." This time, her lips didn't move when she said it.

"I think I do." He only thought the words, neither signed nor mouthed them.

"No," the little girl cried. She was speaking out loud. He could see her lips moving. But he was hearing the words in his head as clearly as if … as if he *could* hear.

"No, no, no. I can't do this. It's all too weird. I can't be here!"

She leapt to her feet as if she intended to run away, but of course, she couldn't see where to run. Even if she'd been able to see, she couldn't have escaped. There wasn't so much as a seam on any surface — no door, no window, no source for the light that was nonetheless there. Like being inside a test tube, and Noah did not like the image that conjured up.

She took only one step, then stopped and all the purpose and tension drained out of her body. "Do you know where we are?"

Her back was turned to him, but he heard her question.

"We're in—"

"We're in one of those things, those shuttles that fly around the motherships. I've seen them, in my dreams."

"Me, too. And they're real. They showed up today, the Astral ships. There were pictures of them on the juke, hanging over cities — New York, Paris, Shanghai. They look just like what I dreamed."

She turned back to him, and he watched her open her mouth, then purposefully close it.

"Can you hear me?"

"Yes."

"No," she said, out loud, her lips moving, shaking her head back and forth, denying what it was too obvious not to see. "Please, I can't …"

"I can hear what you're thinking without you saying it." Noah thought the words.

"How is that possible?"

"I don't know, sweetheart, but the same thing's happening to me and it's scaring the holy shit out of me!"

Star's head snapped to the right, facing something, someone behind and to Noah's left. He must have spoken out loud and Star heard him. Noah heard him, too, though, and not with his ears.

He turned in that direction and stood staring at the boy who was standing there. He was Hispanic, taller than Noah, older. A teenager, maybe sixteen or seventeen, with shaggy black hair. But the boy didn't feel warm, as Star had felt. He felt … not cold, but cool, the way it felt when Noah stepped from the sunshine into a cave. The boy was barefoot, wearing only sweatpants. So his bare chest was visible. The tattoo on his chest was visible.

Fear as real as an icy wind passed among the three of them.

They stood, facing each other, too shocked and frightened and confused and — every other emotion you could pull out of that *tararus* book or whatever it was Noah used to look up terms when he was labeling the schematics of a building.

Then they all started thinking/talking at once. Noah saw that the boy's mouth was moving, he was speaking, even though Noah couldn't hear him. But the girl was just standing there, her face displaying the emotions in the words she wasn't saying aloud.

"I've been dreaming about both of you," the Hispanic boy said. And *thought*.

"The ships, the round balls, have you dreamed—?"

"I've dreamed about *you* for years, ever since … the wreck." That was Star. He didn't need the sound of a voice to tell the difference between the two people's thoughts. It was like the thoughts themselves … *sounded* like a voice.

"That thing …" Noah pointed to the tattoo on Paco's chest. "I dreamed about that, too."

"What is it?" Star wanted to know.

"It's a skull, with a spider crawling out one eye socket—" Noah began.

"And a snake out the other," she finished for him.

It was more than that, though. More than a tattoo. The tattoo had been inked on top of scars, heavy bands of scars. The picture itself had been *cut* into the boy's chest. The tattoo just filled it in with color.

"Don't ask, man! Ain't none of your damned business where I got this tattoo!"

There was force in the thoughts. If the boy had said the words aloud, he would have shouted — no, not shouted. He'd have said them slowly. Menacingly.

Star looked suddenly pale. "How can this be happening? It can't. It can't be …" She swayed a little and he and the other boy instinctively stepped forward and took her arms to hold her upright.

POP!

The instant the three of them were physically touching each other, there was a pop, a snapping sound. No, not a sound. Or maybe it was a sound the other two could hear, but Noah couldn't. But he was almost sure they hadn't heard it, either. It wasn't something you heard with your ears. It was something you felt. A *shock*. Not like electricity, though. It wasn't painful like touching a frayed lamp cord, or even like static electricity. It wasn't electric at all. It was just … *power*.

And it was familiar power. He'd felt that power, that SNAP! before.

It was clear from the shocked looks on the faces of the other two that they'd felt something, some force when they touched and they let go and stepped back from each other.

When Noah had touched Star, an image appeared in his mind. She was in the front seat of a car, looking out the passenger side window at a truck, coming right at her, and Noah was instantly terrified. At the same time, an image flashed out from Paco. He was standing in a hospital room, looking down at a blond boy lying in a bed. Noah felt a wave of grief and pain wash over him.

The images and feelings came in an instant and disappeared the second he stopped touching Star and Paco.

For his whole life, Noah had been able to … it was hard to describe, but sometimes when he touched people, an image would appear in his head, something about them. Not just some random thing, though. It was always something emotionally painful, some sad or bad thing that'd happened to them and for a moment, he'd feel what they'd felt — scared, angry, shocked. He'd figured out as a very small child that he couldn't tell people about that because when he tried they just smiled and acted like he was playing pretend. So after a while he *did* play pretend — he pretended it wasn't happening, that he hadn't seen the image, felt the feeling, ignored it so maybe it'd go away, but it never did.

"You're on a bridge, the two of you," Star said/thought. "We all are. It's a rope bridge and beyond it is … there's nothing. We walk into … nothing at all."

"Paco," the boy said, in answer to the question Noah had thought but hadn't asked.

"I'm—" Noah began.

"I know. You're Noah, as in Noah's ark, and you climb around in caves," the Hispanic boy said. "And you're Star. You used to pretend like you could tell people's fortunes by touching glass rocks but that's not really how you did it."

"I think … I'm going to—" Star said, and she put her hand over her mouth.

"I wouldn't throw up if I were you," said the Hispanic boy. "Swallow hard, 'cause I ain't seen no bathrooms around here, not even any doors. If you're gonna puke, tell me. I'm barefooted."

They both looked at his feet, and an image formed in Noah's head of a laundry room, and this boy standing there, pulling his pants slowly down—

Bam! The image vanished.

"Keep your nose out of what's none of your business!" The threat and menace in Paco's thought appeared in Noah's head as clear as the words.

"I didn't mean to—"

Star sank back down to the floor beside her dog. "They've made it so we can talk with our minds." She somehow managed to color the simple word "they" to sound like the most vile obscenity. And in her mind, it was.

"Maybe," Paco said.

"*Maybe?*" Star and Noah thought the word at the same time.

"I mean, how do we know they made this possible? After all, we've been hanging out in each other's heads, in a manner of speaking, for years. They didn't cause that."

"What did?"

They all were silent.

"It started when ..." Star didn't finish, but emotions — fear, loss, pain — pulsed off her, and an alarm was buzzing in her head, and *Noah wasn't even touching her*! The alarm was like the alarm on his phone that had sounded when ... he didn't let his mind go to the fire. But when he was in the hospital, after that was when he'd started dreaming about Star and Paco.

He felt a wash of intense emotions from Paco, too, but no images accompanied the feelings.

"Do you think being able to talk to each other without speaking is just ... you think if we'd bumped into each other on the street, it would have happened?" Star asked.

"I don't know for sure what I think. Maybe if we'd met, we wouldn't have felt anything. Or maybe just being here in the ship is making it happen. But I'm not sure it's intentional, that it's happening because *they* want it to. I just think ... maybe it's more about us than it is about the aliens."

Then she shook her head, tilted her face up toward them and would have looked earnestly into their eyes if she hadn't been blind.

"Is this real? It can't be. We can't possibly be ... up in a — *no!*" She shook her head savagely. "It's too much. Meeting you, finding out you're real. And then talking in each other's heads. It can't be happening!"

"Maybe it ain't happening to you, but it's happening to me," Paco said, didn't even bother to move his lips. "You can pretend you're not here if you want to, but it doesn't change nothing." Then the thought became fierce again. "And it's real that I can see what's in your minds and you can see what's in mine — and I'm warning you both right now, don't you go poking around in my head! I can feel it, and if you start nosing—"

"We can just … *talk*," Star said. "When I touch people — it's been this way all my life — I can see things. But I *don't* see them. I taught myself not to … oh, it's hard to explain. But you can *decide* what you pay attention to and what you ignore. I think … if it's like how it is with me … I think we can talk to each other, just not out loud, and hear each other. *And ignore everything else.*"

"Just talk, yeah." Paco looked from one to the other. "Deal? 'Cause I can feel it, feel you in there, and if you go digging around in my mind—"

Then the white wall beside them melted.

Just … *melted*. Like it turned into water and the water drained away from the center to the sides, making a hole that became an opening, a doorway. On the other side of the open space were people. Humans! Maybe thirty or forty of them. Standing, sitting, pacing. Some crying. They all looked every bit as scared as Noah felt.

"Misery loves company." Paco didn't say the words out loud.

"They've been abducted, too." Noah didn't speak the words either.

Chapter Four

THE GOLDEN LIGHT that had engulfed him changed
into a white light and Paco Salazar found himself in a
white room with two kids. He was behind them and
they didn't see him at first. A girl, maybe eleven or
twelve, dark, a Native American, and a blond boy
about the same age.

But he didn't just see them. He *felt* them, a gentle
warmth pulsing off them, not like a roaring fire, more
like a shirt feels when you put it on right out of the
dryer.

The sight of them was almost as stunning as the
sight of the white room and the understanding *where*
the white room was. The two kids — they were the
ones he'd been dreaming about ever since he got back
from West Virginia four years ago. He'd always just
assumed he was making the two kids up. It annoyed
him that they were there every night as soon as he
went to sleep. They never said or did anything, just

stood there, watched the rest of the action of his dream alongside him, so after a while he learned to ignore them.

About a month ago the ships and Astrals put in an appearance, previews of coming attractions — dreams of silver balls and white giants and needle-teeth monsters. Every detail he'd dreamed had been true. The needle-teeth monsters could rip a man to pieces in seconds. He knew. He'd watched them.

An arm, just an arm with a bloody stump, flies through the air and slaps into the wall behind Paco's head. Almost hits him in the face.

He shook the image off, stared at the for-real kids.

What did it mean that his mind had … found real people out there and hooked up to them somehow? Why? No, how? He hadn't just made somebody up, and not just one real person, two.

Bigger question: what did it mean that the Astrals had brought those two for-real people from Paco's dreams here, to a shuttle, and put the three of them alone in a room *together*?

People who believed in coincidences were idiots. Everything happened for a reason. The fact that the three of them were here in the same place, the same time now — it wasn't an accident.

He knew it was totally irrational, but he couldn't help being glad to see them, like meeting an old friend. Somehow, this alien space shuttle didn't seem quite so horrifying with the friends from his dream to face it with him.

Friends from his dreams?

Seriously?

That was lunacy.

He wasn't so crazy he was imagining the ship, though. It was *real*. And apparently, so were the terrified kids. Paco was scared too, scared shitless. Still, he figured he was the only one of the three of them who would rather be here than where he'd been before he got kidnapped. The golden beam that froze him in place in that alley had rescued him from … well, whatever happened to him on this spaceship, he'd been running away from worse. And if that beam hadn't come down and shined on him when it did, he'd probably be dead now, because he'd have died rather than let them take him alive.

He had survived and he was here, and he knew quite a lot about *here*, at least what humans thought about the ships and the Astrals who piloted them. He'd sat in the visitation room of Radcliffe Correctional Facility for a week. Day after day, he'd watched news broadcasts about the approaching alien armada, had been forced to watch — the juke was on in the room and they couldn't turn it off. Consequently, he knew way more than he wanted to know about the silver marbles that'd been spotted this side of Jupiter on Astral Day. After which the whole fucking world had fallen apart, not just his part of the world. He'd been trapped in hell, and the Astrals had rescued him. Literally. He'd still be stuck there if that shuttle hadn't landed in the prison yard, *a shuttle like the one that had brought him here.* That shuttle had been full of monsters that had weighed into the inmates in the yard, just *killing.* Indiscriminately. Ripping men apart, blood flying everywhere, and he'd run and run and …

Then the golden light had taken him away. But the golden light had done more than that. Either the golden light or being here had … healed him. He had been injured, hurt and bleeding. But not now. He looked down at his bare feet and they were dry. He'd been standing in a puddle.

He was dry and healed.

Not totally healed. The scars on his chest still protested when he moved. The burning pain of stretching scar tissue had become such a part of his life that he only noticed it when he attended to it instead of ignoring it. When he paid attention, there was pain associated with every movement that pulled at the scars on his chest. That was pain he didn't mind, though. It was a gift from the best friend he'd ever had and he was glad the Astrals hadn't taken it away.

What had happened to him in the prison, though, the emotional repercussions and fallout from that, the mindless horror and revulsion — it should be fresh and raw in his mind. It had happened to him only a few hours before the alley and the golden light. It should be consuming his mind. It had been as he ran, but now … Now those memories were foggy, without sharp edges, formless. The emotions — rage, horror — even as he thought about them, they slipped away. It occurred to him that since the aliens had healed him physically, they must have healed him mentally as well. Which would imply one of two things: they were kind and compassionate and wanted to relieve his suffering, or they needed him to be whole for some purpose. The safe money was on door number two.

"Who's there?" the little girl asked.

"I'm … my name is Noah Matheson." The little boy moved his hands, sign language, didn't *say* anything. But Paco *heard* him just the same.

Noah was from Kentucky, went to a school for deaf kids called Zion Academy. The girl was Falling Star Yellowhorse. She'd been snatched up from a mesa near Roswell, New Mexico.

Good information to know, and even better to know that even though the Astrals were doing weird shit in his mind, they hadn't taken away his "sight." He'd always known things he couldn't know, just did. Apparently, he still could so maybe he could still do the rest of it, too.

The little girl and boy had been "talking," carrying on a conversation without speaking, trying to understand what was happening to them. The whole thing was seriously freaking the little girl out.

"How is that possible?" the girl thought and Paco decided it was time to try his hand at the *mind talking* thing.

"I don't know, sweetheart." He said the words out loud and the little girl heard. So did the boy and he was deaf. "But the same thing's happening to me and it's scaring the holy shit out of me."

As they *thought* a conversation, Paco considered

how being able to get inside each other's heads was both amazing and dangerous. He had lots of things in his mind he didn't want anybody else knowing, private things. And painful things. He drew the line in the sand when the boy started looking around in his head for how he'd gotten the tattoo. That was nobody's business but Paco's.

And he told the boy so.

Bam, slammed the mental door in the boy's face.

And it worked. He had shut the boy out. Yes, the Astrals had left all his mental gifts in place, the mental power he'd used to stay afloat on the streets of Los Angeles. The power that had deserted him when he was locked up for days with men more animal than human, left him because … Because he'd been too freaked out to focus on it. Too rattled. Too … admit it, *too afraid.*

And that fear had left him vulnerable. He'd paid a horrific price, paid with his body, his mind and his soul. But Paco would rise above the horror of what had happened to him in the dark when a human monster attacked and brutalized him. He would go to school on it, learn from it, *use it.* In the week he was locked away, he had let himself get so knocked off center that he couldn't concentrate, couldn't focus, couldn't use his "edge." And without his edge, he had become a victim. He would *not* let that happen again.

Actually, it wasn't as hard for him to accept the "talking inside each other's head" thing as it probably was for the other two. He had shaken hands with the "unexplainable" four years ago when he'd visited his aunt in West Virginia. He had seen the impossible happen. It had happened to him. He'd paid a horrible personal price for that knowledge, but he felt like what he had done that summer had earned him admission to a special space where most people never went. A space where not everything had a reasonable, rational explanation. Where maybe lots of things didn't. A space where the unexplainable happened, and where you might just be able to figure out how to "make" the unexplainable happen.

He had confidence in his own mental strength. He believed he'd be able to keep others from seeing what he didn't want them to see, and might even be able to peek into their private places whether they liked it or not.

But right now, all that was secondary to the situation at hand — that he and the other two had been abducted by aliens, brought together just the three of them in this room all by themselves.

And Paco was pretty sure he knew *why* that had happened.

Then the wall melted away. He'd seen that trick before. The door on the shuttle that landed in the prison yard had melted like that — not opened, melted.

On the other side of the door was a group of people, looked like a random-grab from a Walmart parking lot. Men, women … no kids. The only kids he could see anywhere were right here in the white room with him. But they were people of every other age, every size and shape. The Astrals had snatched up a handful of everybody.

That confirmed what he suspected about what they'd all been seized for.

Chapter Five

"MISERY LOVES COMPANY," Paco said inside Noah's and Star's heads.

"They've been abducted, too." Noah didn't speak the words either.

"There are other people?" Star sounded thrilled, and Paco supposed it felt comforting not to be the only bug on a pin.

"Let's go make nice with our neighbors."

Our neighbors.

An instant understanding passed among them, from each to the other two. It was a knee-jerk response. Unspoken but absolutely clear.

"We" is the three of us and we're set apart from all these other people.

They fit together like puzzle pieces somehow. It seemed so natural that they were a unit, a team, that it was hard to believe they'd only met a few minutes ago.

The three of them walked into the room … if you could call it a room, where the other people were milling around, clearly as confused/scared/angry and every other emotion as they were. As soon as they stepped outside the room where the door had opened in the wall, the wall melted back together and they couldn't return. Paco exchanged a look with Noah, who shrugged.

"You think they can do what we can?" Star asked.

"What, you mean talk inside each other's heads? Why couldn't they?" Noah said.

"A better question is why *can* we?" Paco said.

"Do you think it's just what happens to you when you get here?" Star said.

"I think we brought something to the party nobody else did, but let's find out." Paco turned his attention to a man who clearly worked a desk job somewhere. Or had until the world ended. He was mostly bald on top though he looked to be barely thirty, had a mustache and what had probably once been a neatly trimmed beard that was quickly going to seed. He was wearing a white shirt and dress pants and expensive shoes.

"Hey there," Paco said to the guy, but he didn't say the words out loud. "What'd you have to pay for those shoes?"

Silence.

"If they're real Italian leather, you're talking five hundred, a thousand dollars."

The guy had looked at Paco at first, had been looking at all three of them. But he turned then and began to pace, or to continue pacing because it appeared to be an activity they'd interrupted and he needed to get back to it.

"Those shoes," Paco said to the man, out loud. "They real or knockoffs?"

The man looked at Paco like he was a cockroach that'd run out from under the baseboard in the kitchen when he turned on the light. Then some kind of realization hit him, like maybe he didn't have society to back him up anymore in his natural superiority over the Latino kid, because he jammed a smile onto his face that looked as artificial as a stick-on black mustache.

"Fake. They're fake. Did … did you just get caught in a golden light … and then suddenly you were here? I was in the back yard putting up a fence, you know, a security fence, and then all of a sudden …"

"The golden beam, yeah, that was my ticket here, too."

"Where are you from?" Paco asked, but not out loud.

"That's what the others are saying, too," the man said, indicating the other people in the room. "Just poof and you're here."

He returned to pacing.

Paco said inside his head to Noah and Star. "It's just us."

"Why us?" Noah wondered.

"Better question: why have we been populating each other's dreams for — how long?"

Noah and Star answered simultaneously. "Four years."

It had been four years for Paco, too. *Exactly* four years. He even knew the day. They'd given him a 'sedative' after what happened and Noah and Star had shown up in his dream that night.

"Four years ago … on …" He didn't want to finish it because beyond the words were all sorts of strange possibilities. He'd never imagined they could be real, the bookends in his dreams — he thought of them that way because in their absolute oppositeness they were a matched set. A blond and blue-eyed boy. A black-haired, brown-eyed girl. Bookends. "… the day after Halloween."

Star looked like he'd slapped her. The color dropped out of Noah's face so fast the veins in his temples suddenly became visible, like streaks of blue Magic Marker.

Paco instantly let it go. He wasn't ready for what he might find if he kept picking at that scab. When it did come off, it was likely to be painful and bloody. He steered the conversation in another direction.

"And then, about a month ago, I suddenly started dreaming about the spaceships and the Astrals in them — just like you two did." Then he leaned forward, as if getting closer would actually make his "voice" louder. "And that was when the ships were way out there in deep space, before the Astrals even got as close as Jupiter."

"How'd they make us see images of them when they weren't here, not even nearby?" Star asked.

"Maybe they didn't. Maybe it didn't happen from their end; maybe we made it happen on ours."

"How?" Noah asked.

"Maybe we picked up images from them the same way we picked up images of each other." Paco wasn't really sure what he was thinking, only began to unravel it and figure it out as he heard his own words form in his head. "We were connected somehow before the Astrals showed up. I bet that's why we could see images from somewhere else, too, from the Astrals — whether they sent them out or we just ... picked them up, somehow. I think it's why we can talk inside each other's heads now."

"Talking in each other's minds when we're awake, that's kinda dreaming about each other turned up real high," Noah said. "Amplified. Being together ... or being here—"

"Or being *here together*—" Star said.

"Turned it up really loud," Noah finished for her.

"And ... I think the Astrals want to know what our connection *means*. We're different from other people and the Astrals want to know how being connected changes us. They abducted us to find out."

"You think they want to do experiments on us?" Then Noah made a wide gesture to indicate all the people in the room. "On all of us?"

"That's what all the scientists have been saying for a week," Paco spoke aloud. "Trust me, I've been listening to news broadcasts twenty-four seven for six days and I know everything they have to say."

The man in the knockoff Italian shoes was passing by close enough to overhear.

"I've been watching the news, too," he said.

"They've been digging up all the Looney Tunes who, it turns out, aren't really Looney Tunes after all. All those scientists who've been saying for years that there have been alien visitations to Earth in the past. They're called Ancient Aliens experts. They were the lunatic fringe of the scientific community until the white dots out by Jupiter. Now, they've got a leg up on everybody in understanding what's going on. And they're the ones who're saying the aliens want to study humans."

"Study us?" Star spoke aloud. Paco could feel the terror in her voice and he wanted to comfort her.

"No, not that," he told her, speaking aloud, too. By unspoken agreement, the three of them had begun speaking aloud as soon as there were other people around to hear it. "Not like probes and things like that." Noah looked a little confused and then Paco realized he hadn't heard what Italian Shoe Man had said. "They don't need to find out about how we work biologically, but they do need to understand the rest of our shit."

"What do you mean?" asked a woman wearing a red uniform with the words "Harper's Cafe" stenciled on the pocket. She'd been seated with her back against the white wall a few feet away and she stood and came forward.

"This one guy, his name was Dr. Benjamin Bannister, and he's some expert who has a lab in Moab, Utah," Paco said. "He said that the aliens have been here before lots of times. He said they seeded humanity, started us as sort of a science fair project."

"Aliens didn't start mankind," the woman said. "God did."

Paco blew by her remark. "He said that the aliens put us here, then left. And they come back at intervals to see how we're doing. They're collecting data, figuring us out. I'm betting that's what we're all doing here."

"To study?" asked Italian Shoe Man.

"I think they want to experiment on us — not cut us open like frogs in science class, but study our behavior."

A bald man with a bulbous nose, wearing a New York Yankees tee shirt, had stopped to listen, too.

"Looking for what?" he asked.

Paco shrugged.

"Dr. Bannister says they are a hive mind."

"Hive mind?" It was the first time Star had said anything, and the others turned to look at her. She and Noah had been so quiet, no one had noticed them.

"They aren't individuals. They all think with one mind."

He cast a look at Star and Noah. "Which means they don't need to talk to communicate, not if they're all just one mind."

Italian Shoe Man took the thought and ran with it. "They hear each other's thoughts, sports fans, so it's not much of a leap to suppose they've turned that microphone on us."

"You mean, you think …" The waitress didn't like where this was leading.

"I think their collective hive mind is listening in on our thoughts right now," he said. "If they can hear each other's thoughts, you can bet your sweet bippy they can hear ours."

The man then realized he'd collected an audience and either felt self-conscious, or didn't want to be singled out as a leader, as in *take me to your leader.* He hunched his shoulders, tossed out a parting "… but what do I know? It's just speculation, pure speculation." Then he shuffled away.

"I think he's onto something," Paco said to the other two without speaking. "I think the Astrals are listening in to the thoughts of *all* the humans, including us."

Paco might be able to keep Star and Noah out of his private affairs, but the Astrals? Could he keep them out of his head?

~

STAR SAT ON THE FLOOR, feeling the plastic that wasn't plastic beneath her. She could tell there were lots of other people near her. Noah sat beside her, almost felt like a part of her. Paco was nearby. She could sense his presence.

She had no idea how long they had been here. Long enough for her to calm down. When she first arrived in the room, the horror — *I'm up in a spaceship!* — and the added horror of knowing what was in that ship, the reptars with their needle teeth, was just too much. She had cried, hadn't wanted to, hadn't meant to, but the tears came.

But that had been … how long ago? Paco said time wasn't the same thing to the Astrals as it was to humans, that they could bend it — whatever that meant. So was an hour here a day on Earth? Or maybe the other way around? Though the Astrals probably didn't even measure time in hours or days.

A sudden flash of light so bright even Star could see it brought cries of terror from the others in the room and Star reached over, trying to find Noah's hand to hold.

"What the fuck?" Paco said, out loud.

"What is it? What happened?"

"Boxes. There are boxes on the floor," Noah said.

He described a stack of white boxes, about the size of shoeboxes that had appeared in the middle of the room, seemed to be made of the same material as everything else they'd encountered — white plastic. They had no lids, no fasteners, no apparent way to open them.

Star could hear the crowd talking about them, moving to pick them up and examine them. Noah handed her one and her fingers felt all over it, trying to find the catch or latch, some indention or crack that would indicate how to open it. But there was nothing, it was as smooth and seamless as the floor and walls of the room.

"Oh, my God," a woman's voice cried, and suddenly Star could smell … roasted turkey?

"That lady got one of the boxes open and there

was food inside," Paco said. "Like Thanksgiving — turkey and dressing."

Star suddenly realized how hungry she was, like she hadn't eaten in days. And maybe she hadn't. She scratched around on the box, trying to find a way to get to the turkey and dressing inside. But there was no—

"Damn, look at this." It was a man's voice this time. "Kung Pao chicken. My wife made the best you ever tasted, but I swear this is just as good."

"Hey, you got to share. We're all hungry."

"Like hell, I'll share. I got the box open, you didn't."

Arguments broke out all around her, she could see the blobs of people forms moving, probably shoving each other.

"There's salmon in this one," a man cried. "Baked. Just like I like—"

Then another cube opened, and another.

"Stop fighting," called a man's voice, deep and authoritative. "I get it. The boxes are individualized. There's one here for everybody and it'll only open for you. So stop shoving."

She heard the sounds of boxes dropping and imagined people picking them up and then dropping them until they came to one that would open. Apparently, what they found inside was exactly what that person wanted, their favorite food.

Noah handed her half a dozen boxes before one opened in her hand. Inside was … she could smell it, could it possibly be … a juicy cheeseburger from

Burgatory. There was bacon on it, too, which she always had to order separate, and extra pickles. The fries were crisp, just like she remembered them, and the vanilla malt — not a milkshake, a malt — that accompanied it was so cold it hurt that tooth in the back that was sensitive.

Paco's box contained some spicy Mexican food, just like 'Mama Rosa' made for him.

When he smelled it, Star saw the image that formed in his head — a large Hispanic woman bustling around a table, singing some haunting melody, but the words were in Spanish and Star couldn't understand them.

Noah opened his box to fried fish. He and his father caught the catfish in the river when they went fishing.

Star saw the image of Noah's father, Sawyer, taking a squirming fish off a hook and grinning.

Chapter Six

THE QUEEN WAS WAVING.

Sawyer Matheson picked up the figurine and turned it over in his hand, noticing then the photoelectric cell on the little figure's purse that propelled her hand, half-orbiting back and forth on the end of the wrist, in a perpetual "royal wave."

"Got her at Covent Garden in London when I was a student at Oxford," Garson said when he saw what Sawyer was holding. He hadn't just been a student. He'd been a Rhodes Scholar. "At the time, Queen Elizabeth was still alive, ancient and *revered*. Possessing a disrespectful effigy of the grand lady could get you castrated. Had to sneak the old girl through Heathrow security in my jock strap."

Sawyer shot the man a glance. He had said it with a straight face. Still …

Dr. Mikhail Ziegelman Garczonski, Ph.D., known to his friends as Garson, was a conundrum to all who knew him. The man seemed to have been assembled out of leftover appendages bought at a garage sale. His arms were long, his legs short. His head, covered in curly white hair, was too big for the rest of him and it sat on a skinny neck with an Adam's apple roughly the size of a tennis ball. Sawyer sometimes got distracted by it, watching it bob up and down like the little red-and-white cork on a fishing line when you got a bite. But Garson's hound-dog-droopy eyes were crystal green, a bright, *alive* green that somehow transformed the rest of his face so you forgot about the mismatched pieces parts of his body.

Many an errant student in one of his classes had felt the full force of that green-eyed gaze, which, it was rumored, had been known to cause internal bleeding.

"Surely, that's not the whole story," Sawyer said, setting the little statue into a box with the other contents of the lone shelf in the professor's office not jammed with books that had titles like *Welcome to the Universe: An Introduction to Practical Astronomy, Analytical Techniques of Celestial Mechanics, Galaxies and Cosmology,* and *Space Physics Parameter Estimations and Inverse Problems.*

Sawyer suspected there probably didn't exist an *Astrophysics for Dummies* book, though he'd never asked.

"Oh, my, no indeed. The incident involved a nasty cavity search, during which they threatened to shove her majesty's crown, pointy side up, through the southernmost aperture of my body into a portion of my anatomy 'where the sun doesn't shine.'"

Sawyer looked full at him and said, "And if that story's not true, it should be."

"Ah, you know me too well, my friend."

In truth, Sawyer didn't know the man nearly as well as he would like and he suspected the complexities of the old man's personality and intellect were far too extensive for any one person to master them all. But he would get a chance to try now that the professor had finally listened to reason and agreed to move out of Danbury before another shuttle showed up at Hillsdale College like the one last week that deposited half a dozen white titans to lumber around the astrophysics lab looking for *something*.

The old man had barely managed to grab the files — hardcore old-school: everything on paper — of his correspondence with Dr. Benjamin Bannister and chuck them into the dumpster behind the building for safekeeping. In their last communication, Dr. Bannister had described in detail the mothership that was hovering over his lab in Moab, Utah — just hanging there in the sky.

As the McClintock County sheriff, Sawyer had used that point to hammer home the reality that unless Garson wanted his own personal mothership guard dog, he'd best vanish now while vanishing was still possible, and nearby Zion Academy, home to more than a hundred deaf children, tucked into a secluded hollow in the Kentucky mountains, was at least in the same area code as "vanishing."

Sawyer looked around.

"Appears we got about everything," he said. They had already packed up the meager possessions the professor kept in his tidy apartment in the historic Faversham Rooming House on campus.

"Oh, not everything," the old man said. He opened his bottom desk drawer and took out a small, oddly shaped geodesic dome, and Sawyer felt like he'd been kicked in the belly.

It was the scale model Noah had built for the old man only three days before Astral Day, when the apps on the whole world's phones had reported the presence of an invading armada of spaceships that would land on Earth in six days. They'd shown up right on schedule. And the next day, one of the alien shuttles had abducted Sawyer's son. He had watched Noah vanish in a beam of golden light.

Garson saw the look on his face and was instantly contrite.

"I'm sorry, Sawyer. I didn't mean to—"

"It's alright, Garson. I understand."

"Well, no, actually you don't understand what I was … but I do understand why you don't understand …"

He stopped and began again. "They're saying now the total is twenty thousand people the Astrals abducted from all over the world but they've been sending them back, hundreds every week. Well, except Noah. And I understand you must be scared that they're doing something horrible to … not that they *would*, of course …"

His voice trailed off and there was an awkward silence.

"Sawyer ... do I have your permission to open my mouth and remove my foot?"

That coaxed a smile, a small one.

Garson was undeniably off-the-charts brilliant. No one ever disputed that, even when his Ancient Aliens theories had made him a laughing stock in the scientific community. But there were different kinds of intelligence. Garson might be a giant in astrophysics, but he was a titmouse in interpersonal relationships.

Noah, just twelve years old, had an affinity for people, a gentle touch and an uncanny kindness. Sometimes, he was so compassionate it almost seemed like Noah could actually feel the pain of those around him.

The boy was special. Was that why they kept him up there, wherever he was?

"The others coming back just makes it harder," Sawyer said. "You keep wondering, if they let all those other people go, thousands and thousands of them, what in the world do they want with one deaf twelve-year-old? He's just a little boy ..."

He had meant to hold onto his emotions, but despite his control, the last word came out as a strangled sob.

Garson was across the room in two gangly steps and reached out ... maybe to embrace Sawyer, but thought better of it. Maybe he intended to put his hand on Sawyer's shoulder, but he didn't do that either. He just stood there, too close, awkwardly invading Sawyer's personal space.

"It'll be … he will come home, Sawyer. I believe that. I really do."

Sawyer believed it, too. Not to believe would kill him. The boy *would* come back.

But when he did, would he even be Noah anymore?

Chapter Seven

A PART of the wall a few feet from Noah — not the same part as where he and Star and Paco had entered the room — melted and a giant white creature entered through it. It resembled a human, a giant human, had arms and legs, fingers and toes and a face with eyes, ears, nose and a mouth. But its skin was as white as a piece of parchment and it was totally hairless.

Its eyes were huge and bright blue.

The waitress screamed, let out a single shrieking wail when she saw it and then she fainted. No one went to her aid. The whole room full of people stood dumfounded, just staring, seeing in the flesh a creature from another world.

Noah was as overwhelmed as everyone else, though maybe slightly more prepared. He had, after all, seen this creature in his dreams for a month. He saw that Paco wasn't even looking at the titan. His eyes were trained on the melted portal through which the creature had entered.

"That dude isn't the meanest dog in the Astrals' junkyard," Paco said.

The gigantic blue eyes of the huge white Astral scanned the crowd of people until he spotted, Paco, Noah and Star. He advanced two steps toward them and made a come-on gesture. The words *come with me* appeared in Noah's mind as clear as if the thing had spoken them. But the creature's lips never moved.

The three of them stood rooted to the spot, unable to move. The Astral made no effort to force them to follow him, appeared to assume they'd do what he told them, because he turned and started to lumber back out of the room.

"It's one of them, isn't it?" Star asked in Noah's mind. "The white giants?"

"Looks just like it did in my dream," Noah replied. "It's called a titan." Noah didn't know why he knew that, he just did.

"Then that means the *others* …"

She didn't finish the thought but Paco finished it for her.

"Are just like in the dreams, too — yes, they are. I've seen them."

Noah reached over and took Star's hand. He liked to think he did it to reassure her, but he needed the reassurance as bad as she did. The Hispanic kid started off behind the titan and the two of them, and Pumpkin, followed.

As soon as the titan appeared, the dog had bared its teeth and Noah was sure it was growling. Noah hoped the dog didn't decide to attack. He suspected the titan would make short work of the dog and he knew Star would be devastated if anything happened to it. But she patted the dog's head and he seemed to relax, at least slightly. He didn't lunge at the white giant, so that was something.

The titan led them down a long hallway as white and featureless as everything else had been and the farther they went the more it became apparent to Noah that—

"We're not in some shuttle," Paco said inside his head, picking up on his thought. "Unless they're a lot bigger on the inside than they are on the outside."

"We're in … one of those motherships," Star said, "one of those silver marble things, the ones as big as as—"

"The one over Paris, I saw it on the juke," Noah said. "It looked like it was bigger than a battleship."

The shuttles were like cars, or airplanes, Noah supposed, that the Astrals used to travel around from the motherships to the earth, or maybe between motherships. The motherships were—

"Where they *live*," Paco again finished for him.

Noah couldn't even begin to get his mind around that. Beyond these endless plastic white walls, any one of which could melt and become a doorway, were the living quarters of the white things. Where they ate and slept— Did they eat and sleep? And if there were titans living here, then—

"Yep, the others, the nasty ones called reptars are in here somewhere, too."

They rounded a curve in the hallway — not a

corner exactly, he hadn't seen any sharp edges on anything — and approached a solid wall that Noah assumed would—

It melted away and revealed another white room exactly like the one they'd left.

Wait here.

The titan gestured toward the room and they crossed in front of him and entered it. The doorway immediately reformed into a wall.

"I'm sure it wasn't lost on the two of you that out of all those people, they took us, the three of us together," Paco said.

Then the light went out.

Noah understood absolute dark. He'd spent his life exploring the caves that formed the massive Matheson Caverns with his father, uncle and cousins. Dark in a cave was *dark*.

This dark was like that.

And then the light began to return, but it wasn't the white light from before, emanating from nowhere and everywhere in the white room. It was soft light, that grew out of the darkness slowly and as the light grew, Noah saw mist swirl and dance, realized that he was in fog.

His mind was as foggy as the mist he saw around him. He had trouble focusing, like he had just awakened from a sound sleep and was having trouble coming fully awake.

He looked at Star beside him. He had never let go of her hand, but she was kneeled down with her arm around her dog and he didn't remember her doing that.

Then he turned toward Paco and took a step back.

"What—?" Paco began, then realized what had startled Noah. Paco had on a tee shirt now, covering his chest and the tattoo. It was just a plain white tee shirt, similar to the one Noah was wearing that said Zion Academy, and bore the seal of the school underneath. Paco also had on jeans — like the ones he and Star were wearing. Old jeans, worn. Shoes, too. Star was wearing leather sandals that looked handmade, but new, not like the worn ones she'd been wearing before. Paco had on Champion running shoes, like Noah's. His father had gotten them for him for his birthday, so he wouldn't look so out of place at the academy with all the rich kids.

"Check out the Champions," Paco said, but he didn't speak aloud. "Never had a pair of these. Only way I could ever come up with something like this was to mug some white kid."

He seemed to realize what he'd said, almost looked chagrined, then didn't. His face wasn't defiant, but it was resolute. It proclaimed: that's who I am. Deal with it.

"Noah!" Star cried out in his head. He could just make out her form beside him as the light grew. Now she was standing beside him, not kneeling with Pumpkin. He reached out and took her hand, and he squeezed it. Paco had stepped closer to the two of them, but he hadn't reached out to take either one's hand and Noah didn't know if that was because he was trying to be macho and brave or because he didn't want the sensation they'd experienced the last time they all three touched each other.

The light grew. They were no longer in the white room.

"I don't think we're in Kansas anymore, Toto," Paco said.

They all had stopped speaking aloud.

Noah had no idea what Paco was talking about but apparently Star did because she said, shakily, "Are we on a yellow brick road?" Which made even less sense.

He and Paco strained to see through the fog, but it was too thick. The forms of leafless trees appeared around them, dark and twisted. At their feet, tangled and gnarled tree roots spread out into the path.

He looked around them and then pointed down the trail. "The light's brighter that way, on the other side of that weeping willow tree."

Paco turned and headed that way and they followed.

"I hear ... what is—" Star began, but she didn't finish. Just froze and turned back the way they'd come. She and Paco heard something and whatever it was, it terrified them.

Paco grabbed Noah's shoulders and shoved him down the path toward the willow tree.

"That's a reptar. *Move!*"

Noah pulled Star along with him as he ran from the sound he couldn't hear and Pumpkin never left her side.

The tree suddenly looked crisp and clear, close, appearing out of the mist like some tentacled monster in the gloom. The trail circled the edge of the tree and continued and Noah dashed headlong down it, his heart hammering, a cold sweat breaking out on his brow. The hand that clutched Star's was clammy.

About fifty yards past the tree, the mist cleared enough to see a bit farther and Noah stopped so abruptly he had to yank on Star's arm to keep her from continuing. Paco almost ran into him, and cried out, "What the fuck—!"

Then Paco saw what Noah saw.

He stopped running and repeated, this time in an awed voice, "What the fuck—?"

Stretching out in front of them was a rope bridge. It had a wooden floor and a thick rope railing that was affixed to the floor with the web of rope rigging you'd see on the mast of a ship. It was a ruin, looked ancient. The floor slats were rotted and decaying and there were huge gaps where they had crumbled away completely. Vines tangled and wound up the rope railing, and through holes in the decaying floor. Whatever it stretched out over was lost in the mist. And the bridge itself was lost in the mist ahead of them.

"What is it?"

"A rope bridge."

"It's old and falling apart with broken floor slats," she said. "I saw it, remember, I told you. When we all touched that first time, I saw an image of us on it."

Star had seen them on the bridge *before it happened.*

Paco suddenly tensed and looked back down the trail.

"The reptars are closer! We need to get across that bridge."

"Cross it — are you serious?" Noah asked.

"It's either that, strike out through the woods, and in this fog we'd be lost in seconds, or back toward the reptars."

"It's some kind of test," Star said. Noah sucked in a gasp and didn't breathe it back out. "Isn't that what you said, Paco, they would run experiments on us, tests?"

"What are they testing?" Paco asked. "Whether or not we have the courage to cross the bridge?"

"Or the common sense not to!" Noah said.

Then Paco jumped at whatever he heard behind him. It was that close.

"This bridge looks dangerous, but it's *survivable*! Reptars aren't. I've seen what they can do. You can stay here and make nice with them if you want, but I'm crossing." He stepped around Star and Noah.

"Or are they testing whether or not we'll stick together?" Star said.

That stopped him.

"Come on!" he commanded, turned back and grabbed Star's hand. When he did, the three of them were connected again. It wasn't a *Pop* this time, though. But the power was there. Noah felt it and so did the others. He could tell by the looks on their faces. This time it was a *hum*, almost like the vibration you could feel on the transformer box of his father's antique electric train set. Only much more powerful. *Much* more.

"Come on," Paco said, quieter this time, and he turned and began to make his way over the gnarled tree roots toward the bridge, pulling Star along behind him.

Chapter Eight

With Paco in front holding her hand, Star approached the hanging bridge. She could picture it in her mind as she'd seen the image and it terrified her. If she wasn't blind she would have squeezed her eyes tight shut so she wouldn't have to look. Everything around her was a gray blur, no blobs of light or blobs of substance. A uniform gray, with a few swirling variations of white and dark.

The mist was cold and clammy, and smelled of mud and decay and other things … unspeakable things.

Pumpkin had growled when he saw the titan, and Star was sure if the titan had tried to touch her, the dog would have attacked, and would have died. So she'd calmed him, had to keep control of him, as she had done the day she sat on her front porch and the men who had killed Uncle Clyde came.

He was in total attack mode right now, too, growling low in his throat, his hackles raised. He could sense/see/smell some threat the humans couldn't and whatever it was, Pumpkin was prepared to rip its throat out if it got near Star.

She reached down and patted his neck, could feel every muscle tensed.

"It's okay," she told him, wondering even as she did why she bothered. He knew better.

"Is he growling at the reptars?" Paco asked. "Are they *that* close?"

"Maybe. Or maybe there's something *else* around that's … dangerous that we can't see. "

Paco let go of her hand.

"We gotta boogie." His voice was urgent and breathless as he described the bridge for her. "There are slats missing on the floor and the ones that are still there look like they'd crumble away if you stepped on them. I'm going to go from plank to plank, one at a time and you follow me. I'll tell you how far to put out your foot for the next plank. Okay?"

"Okay."

"We can't stand on the same plank together. There's not a board here could hold the weight of any two of us. Shit, I'm probably going to fall through the first board I set my foot on."

Paco took Star's hands and placed one on each of the rope railings.

"Hold on tight and scoot your hand along as you go. If a board gives way under you, you can catch yourself on the railing before you fall."

"What's down there, under the bridge?"

"Fog," Paco said.

Then she heard him step out onto the first board of the bridge floor. It creaked and groaned beneath his weight. She thought to wonder what they would do if they got half way across and the whole floor was gone, but it only scared her to think of that and she was already scared enough so she pushed it out of her mind.

The bridge swayed slightly, moved when Paco stepped on it.

Star pictured the bridge, felt the rough texture of the ropes beneath her fingers.

"Okay," Paco said. "Put out your foot and start feeling around for the next slat, but don't put your weight on it until you're sure I'm not still on it."

She had already put out her foot and found the next step and was starting to shift her weight.

Noah was behind her, still on the trail, not yet out onto the bridge. The sounds on the trail behind him were getting louder and louder. Something was coming that made a lot of noise, certainly wasn't trying to sneak up on them.

In fact …

She dismissed the thought as soon as it formed. Still … there was so much noise behind them, it was almost like the reptars wanted to make sure the three of them knew they were coming, were herding them along.

"Next step," Paco said, and she bent her concentration to making sure her feet were the right place on the boards.

One step, then another. Then another. The boards

creaked and whined and protested. The farther they went, the more the bridge swayed back and forth whenever any of them moved on it. As best she could tell, they were about four feet apart, and Paco was making sure she didn't catch up to him and put her weight on a step the same time he did.

The reptars were still coming.

NOAH STUDIED the bridge as Paco and Star started out across it. Pumpkin had skipped ahead of Paco and was waiting out there in the mist, still close enough to see. But he wasn't on the other side yet, he had just stopped to look back at them.

No matter how hard Noah tried to peer through the soupy grayness of the fog, he could make out no discernible images in it. What they were crossing could have been a mile-deep gully, or a creek three feet below the bridge. There was no way to tell. And he wasn't looking forward to getting to the point where they would not be able to see anything but bridge, where this side of the bridge was shrouded in mist and the other not yet visible. It would seem like they were suspended in time as well as in space, from nowhere going through nowhere to get nowhere.

He was looking back over his shoulder at the vanishing trail behind them when Star fell.

It happened without warning. She had put her foot out on one of the boards. It looked rotted and rickety, but no more so than any other board on the bridge. There wasn't even a crunching sound of it giving way. It just suddenly let go beneath her, like the trap door beneath a gallows, and she dropped like a rock, would have vanished into the mist below them if Paco hadn't been as fast as a snake. He reached out and grabbed blindly for her, got a handful of her shirt and her upper arm and yanked her toward him. He fell backward with her as he pulled, a purposeful motion, so his body would be stretched out across the boards, not concentrating his weight on any one of them.

Star cried out in terror. He could hear the sound in his head and he could hear Paco spewing obscenities.

Paco landed on his back with a firm hold on Star's upper arm. Star landed on her belly, with her feet from the knee down dangling into a mist-filled nothingness.

"Are you alright?" Noah cried out, without words.

"Hell no, I'm not alright. Would you be? Shit, that scared the … shit out of me." Paco was babbling in his mind and in Star's and Noah's minds, too.

When Paco finally got his breath, he told Star to belly-crawl as he pulled her up beside him.

Then the two of them were lying side by side, gasping, on the far side of a three-foot gap in the boards on the floor of the bridge. A gap Noah was going to have to cross.

And he couldn't figure out how. If he jumped, and he could probably leap that far, he would land hard on the boards on the other side of the opening and they didn't look any more stable than the ones that had fallen away.

"There wasn't any sound," Star said.

"What?" he and Paco thought at the same time.

"When the board fell away … it never hit anything below."

"Shit, it must be a thousand-foot drop below us. Or maybe there is no bottom at all, maybe—"

Paco's thought cut off. He was focused in rapt horror on something on the trail leading up to the bridge.

Noah turned to look over his shoulder. Less than ten feet away from him, still standing on the pathway, were four reptars, their blue eyes flashing, their teeth looking as sharp as the knife his father used to fillet the fish they caught in the pond. He sat for a moment, transfixed in horror.

One was as big as … as a moose, the others smaller. But they all moved so quickly size didn't matter, the big ones as agile as the panther-sized ones. Covered in something like armor plating, ebony scales, the skin giving off a blue glow from underneath.

Even a nightmare couldn't make them as horrifying as reality, their faces a horror too monstrous to look at and still breathe. Dual sets of eyelids over eyes with irises that shifted from yellow, to green, to blue, to brilliant red. And their mouths. Teeth like knives and jaws that looked like they'd unhinge, like they could swallow something as big as they were.

They made slurpy, sucking sounds and a kind of purring, like a gigantic cat.

Noah couldn't breathe. The images of these beasts had terrified him so badly in dreams he'd awaked in sweat-tangled sheets, a scream on his lips. But *reality* … The real thing was so much more terrifying than the dream images that he literally could not move, could not breathe, would have wet his pants if he'd needed to go.

For a moment, it looked like the reptar was going to walk out onto the bridge. But it didn't. It just stood on the edge, glaring at him, seeming to consider its options.

"That dumb fucker's planning on trying to cross. You got to get over here, Noah!"

"How?"

"Okay … I'm going to lay down on my belly and crawl out as close as I can get to the broken slats and hold out my hands. You lay down on your belly and do the same and I'll grab you."

Noah couldn't even articulate all the reasons that sounded like a horrible idea. He was standing on the last board before the broken one, and he was only ten feet from the nearest reptar. If he lay down on his belly and stretched his feet out behind him, he'd be … maybe within grabbing range. Depended on how far a reptar could reach.

"Yeah, the idea sucks. You got a better one?"

Noah did not, so he crouched down and carefully lay down on his belly with his knees bent so his feet were in the air above his butt. He only glanced, because he really didn't want to get a good look, but it appeared that if he lowered his feet to the floor of the bridge, a reptar could grab him around the ankle.

Paco lay down on his belly, and inched toward the opening in the bridge floor. He had scooted over to the side, so he could grasp the rope rigging below the rope railing for support. He held his weight on the rigging and began to extend his hand. Noah grabbed the rigging on his side and began to extend his hand. Then the board beneath where his upper body was stretched out began to creak and crack.

"Go back!"

Paco pulled away just as the board beneath him gave way and fell into the abyss.

Star screamed in Noah's head. She had scooted on her back away from the opening, was about ten feet from Paco, leaned back on her hands. Suddenly, the board beneath her hands began to come apart. Star shrieked in terror, and Noah was sure it wasn't just a sound inside his head. Paco reached back to grab her, but she'd felt the board beginning to give way and lurched forward, and now she lay on an expanse of bridge directly behind Paco.

One second. Two.

They all three were panting, terrified. Waiting for the next piece of broken bridge to drop them into the abyss.

None of them said anything, in their heads at least. Noah was sure that the reptars only a few feet from him were making all manner of threatening noises, but gratefully, he couldn't hear them.

"This couldn't be any worse." Star gasped, panting, and both he and Paco looked at her. "We can't go forward because the boards will give way. You're trapped between two holes in the flooring and Noah's trapped between an opening and the reptars."

Then Noah thought he got the point she was making.

"So this is some kind of test, right?" he said. "A test of what?"

"What the fuck difference does it make? If we fail, we die."

"We don't fail. I saw us on the other side."

Noah looked off into the swirling mists around them, then focused in nearer. The railing was attached to the floorboards with rigging, like a ship's rigging. He could see now that the rigging was affixed to the ropes with fasteners. Those babies wouldn't let go for anything. The rope was stable.

"We can't walk on the floor, but we could climb across on the ropes."

He didn't wait for affirmation, just inched his weight over to the side of the bridge and used the rigging to pull himself up. With his feet in the rigging on the bottom, he began to move sideways toward Paco, going from one rope hold to another, like a sailor high above the deck of a ship at sea. The rope felt as solid as the floor had felt insubstantial. In seconds, he had crossed beyond the opening on the boards of the floor and was coming up beside Paco.

"Can Star …?"

"Can Star what?" she asked.

"Picture a ship's rigging, you know the spiderweb

of ropes on those old sailing ships," Noah said. "Scoot over to the edge of the bridge and grab the rigging, climb up it."

She was already moving off the boards.

"No, the other side," Paco said. "Noah and I both are on this side."

She slid carefully to the other side and climbed nimbly up off the floor and into the rigging that went up about four feet from the plank flooring to the rope railing.

"I'm going first," Paco said. "Star, you follow. Let me get a long way off before you start, Noah."

But weight didn't seem to be a problem. For all the frailty of the rotting boards on the floor of the rope bridge, the ropes themselves were strong and steady. Noah was glad he couldn't hear the monsters barely out of arm's reach, kept his eyes resolutely forward on Paco and Star, who were climbing sideways in the rigging like monkeys.

In no time, Paco and Star were sitting in the dirt of the trail at the end of the bridge, panting. Pumpkin had leapt like a ballerina from one piece of planking to another and was waiting for them there, his tail wagging.

His tail wagging.

Noah didn't know much about dogs, but that seemed … odd. A few minutes before, he'd been ready to attack anything that got close. Now …

Noah collapsed in the dirt beside them. He looked back across the bridge, but the far side was shrouded in mist.

Chapter Nine

Sawyer coughed to cover up his emotion, turning to busy himself folding down the top of the box he had just filled with the last of the professor's office belongings.

"Sure, Garson," he said, "Noah will be returned. It's just hard … to wait."

Sawyer headed out to his cruiser with the box. Tall and lissome, Sawyer moved with the assertive gait of an athlete out into the sweltering Kentucky summer, into the raucous cry of cicadas in the bushes, the haze of humidity hanging over green velvet mountains against a sky a turquoise shade of blue that looked rubbed on, stepping on hot sidewalk that felt like the hard crust of a loaf of freshly baked bread.

He'd vowed to hold the lid on his little corner of the world — while humanity spun out of control all over the planet — and even the time he'd spent coming to get Garson in neighboring Westlake County, was time he couldn't genuinely afford to spend. But Garson had been such an unexpectedly good friend, particularly in the first days after Noah was taken when Sawyer was almost out of his mind with worry.

The two had met years ago when Sawyer was at Hillsdale teaching a self-defense class offered as part of the physical education curriculum. Sawyer chanced to be passing in front of the science building and ran into Dr. Mikhail Garczonski, Ph.D. Literally *ran into him*. A sighted Mr. Magoo, the man ping-ponged through his world, bumping into walls and door frames and shelves, leaving behind a trail of lost belongings. He'd plowed into Sawyer on the sidewalk, dropped an armload of books and as Sawyer stooped to help him pick them up, Garson had led with what Sawyer soon learned was his customary method of introduction — a non sequitur.

"You do know, don't you, that descriptions in the Bhagavad Gita and other ancient texts sound suspiciously like a nuclear holocaust."

Sawyer allowed as how he did *not* know that particular factoid.

"Come along with me, son, and I'll explain."

And the friendship had developed just like that — with Garson expostulating on one Ancient Aliens theory or another and Sawyer following along, physically as well as metaphorically, picking up whatever the other man dropped. He had liked Garson, had actually *believed* him. He didn't think the old professor was a crackpot even before Astral apps across the globe showed the cluster of white specks that appeared out of nowhere just this side of Jupiter.

Lifted from obscurity and ridicule to the position of prophet overnight, Garson had done his dead level best to keep a low profile, deflected all questions and media attention, and there was tons of both, to his esteemed colleague, Dr. Benjamin Bannister in Utah. In truth, the men had worked side-by-side together in an international community of Ancient Alien theorists — scientists who believed that alien beings had visited Earth in the past — each leap-frogging over the other with one theory or another for half a century. Bannister looked better in front of the cameras, so Garson and the others deferred to him, though he was every bit the expert on ancient alien theory that Bannister was.

Ever since he'd watched his little boy … disintegrate in a beam of golden light from a shuttle, Sawyer had been picking the man's brains about the aliens — and there wasn't much the old man had to say that was easy to hear.

Actually, nothing he had to say was easy to hear.

As he loaded the last of the professor's belongings into the trunk of his cruiser, he remembered the day the old man had removed his spectacles, cleaned them absentmindedly with the end of his tie, and told him the Astrals were actually mankind's ancestors.

"It's really very simple, Sawyer. This alien race seeded the planet. The evidence is everywhere if you have eyes to see it, and they have returned periodically over the millennia."

"So this is just a check-in, how-ya-doing, anything-we-can-bring-you-from-home visit?"

"Hardly."

"Then what *do* you think they're doing here?"

"They're doing what they have done every time they have returned. They are judging mankind."

"On what criteria?"

"That's ... not clear. There is much speculation, but we aren't as certain of that as we are of other things."

"What other things?"

"That whatever the criteria, mankind has always failed the test."

"Failed the test?"

"My dear Sawyer, the aliens would not likely have wiped the planet clean of humanity and started over if we'd been their star pupil. We failed and they destroyed us."

"Destroyed us?"

"You have but to look at the historic and geologic record to see proof of it, that our shortcomings earned us extinction."

"Extinction."

"Stop repeating everything I say, my boy. You sound like a parrot."

"But how ...?

"Look in Genesis. The world was destroyed by a flood and only a handful of people were left to repopulate the globe."

"You think that was ...?"

"I think they come, they find us wanting in some

fashion I could guess at but haven't quite pinned down in my head, and so they start over."

"Start over."

"You're doing it again." He paused and sighed. "Look, Sawyer, don't make me draw you a picture. They started a species — us. They come back every so often to see how the species they started is faring. They don't like what they see, so they wipe out the species, leaving only a few to repopulate, and start over, hoping, I suppose, that we won't make such a mess of things next time."

"So they've come here to what — nuke the earth?"

"It is clear after what happened in Moscow they don't need nuclear power for destruction."

That was clear. A few days after the Astrals landed, somebody in Russia got trigger-happy. Nobody was sure whether it really was the Russian military in a planned response or just some jackass with access to codes he shouldn't have known. And nobody would ever know for sure which it had been because the mothership that was hanging suspended above Moscow, that wasn't even dinged by the nuclear warheads fired at it, destroyed the city. There was video footage, the most horrifying footage Sawyer had ever watched. Far, far worse than the films of the airplanes flying into the twin towers in New York City on 9-11. In Moscow, fifteen million people had been disintegrated. Nothing was left but black ash.

"So that's it, the whole world is going to get a taste of what they delivered to Moscow?"

"That's how I see it."

Sawyer felt like all the oxygen had been sucked out of the room.

Garson finally must have noticed how upsetting his pronouncements were. That was the thing with Garson. He missed body language cues. He would have dumped the whole *we're-doomed* load on a roomful of people and never noticed that, oh by the way, women were fainting in the aisles and small children were screaming. When he finally did see Sawyer's response — though clearly it puzzled him, after all, it was just simple truth — he had moderated it a little.

"Before you get your panties all in a wad, Sawyer, remember that even if we do believe they have already written our destruction on their day-timers, *we don't know the date.* We don't know how long they have stayed in previous visits. Do they come and destroy the world in two days? Clearly, the time frame is at least slightly longer than that. Do they come and destroy the world after a year, a decade, a hundred years, five hundred? We have no idea. Remember, time is irrelevant to them. They have harnessed time. They transcend time. They couldn't have crossed multiple galaxies to get here if they didn't know how to manipulate time, fold and bend it to make it sit up and do tricks for them. Yes, I believe that ultimately the Astrals will decide that we have flunked whatever test they set for us and they will wipe us out. But that destruction could very well be five hundred years in the future."

"And what will happen during those five hundred years or five hundred days or whatever it is?"

"My guess — they'll spend that time studying

mankind. We don't know the criteria on which they judge the progress of humanity. Clearly, they didn't know as soon as they hit our atmosphere that we had failed or you and I wouldn't be standing here having this conversation. So will they have to stay, watch us for a millennium or two before they reach a decision? Nobody knows, my friend."

Sawyer felt impotent rage swell in his chest.

"Who do these motherfuckers think they are to set themselves up as the judge of all humanity?"

"Maybe you could go out to one of those stone circles and ring them up and ask them."

The stones had appeared about the same time the Astrals did. Parallel lines of giant stones stretching out for hundreds of miles crisscrossed the globe, connecting circles of stones. It was quickly discovered that close proximity to those stones granted mind-to-mind communication. Or so those who'd ventured close enough to them to find out said. Sawyer did not number among those adventurous souls.

"That's what you think those are, the stones? You think they've been dropped out there to allow humans to communicate with the Astrals."

Garson made a "humph" sound in his throat. "Hardly. We've talked about it on our network." That's what he called the group of scientists all over the world who'd spent their careers amassing information about previous alien visitations to Earth — that the world had scoffed at until now. It gave them quite a leg up on their naysayers where understanding the aliens was concerned. "Dr. Bannister believes the stones aren't there for us at all. They're there for the Astrals to 'take the temperature of humanity.' So they can eavesdrop on our thoughts, collect information, you see. Always collecting data on us."

Sawyer turned and spotted Garson tottering down the steps of the science building with a large box that didn't appear to be heavy but was unwieldy enough to upset his delicate sense of balance. He rushed to steady the box just as Garson was about to go down.

"I said I'd carry this stuff."

The old man didn't respond, just stood looking up wistfully at the building. Garson had spent the majority of his career in this small college, forty-five years of his life climbing these steps every morning and descending them every evening. He'd lived almost every day of his life in the rooms behind those walls.

And now he was leaving, never to return.

Sawyer saw emotions flit across the old man's face but couldn't read them. He put his hand on Garson's bony shoulder, patting him gently.

Garson reached up and squeezed Sawyer's hand affectionately. Sawyer thought he was going to tear up, but he didn't, just shook his head sadly.

"It is what it is," he said and sighed. "But red brick would have been ever so much more attractive than gray slate."

He turned and walked down the steps toward the cruiser with Sawyer hauling the box along behind him.

Chapter Ten

"Oh, shit!" Paco said. He was looking back out across the mist-shrouded bridge.

Star looked suddenly terrified. She'd heard them, too.

"Are they coming?" Noah asked, his heart in his throat.

"The motherfuckers!" Paco spewed out other obscenities. "They're like, bugs, those legs, like bugs."

And they did look like bugs. The reptars making their way slowly across the shattered bridge looked something like spiders with too many legs. They were clinging to the rope railings on both sides of the bridge and delicately making their way across without ever touching the planks that were rotted.

"Let's go," Paco said. He grabbed Star's hand and took off down the pathway that led away from the bridge, with Noah right behind. Pumpkin trotted along beside Star.

The woods and the path were swaddled in thicker

mist than before, soupy. It swirled around them in little eddies like water in a pond when they passed through it.

They were literally running off into nothingness. They couldn't see anything more than a few feet in front of them. And they couldn't see the reptars anymore either, but they could hear them, that odd purring sound and the sucking noise, the clatter of the armor plating on their sides.

Noah was looking back over his shoulder into the nothingness behind and he almost ran into Paco and Star, who had stopped in the middle of the trail. When he turned around, he saw why they'd stopped. The mist had cleared away, suddenly, inexplicably, to reveal a house.

A haunted house.

Yeah, like right out of a horror movie or a fairy tale.

About fifty feet in front of them was a house, two stories tall, but the pointed roof had windows so there must be an attic up there, too. Wide stairs lead to a porch with a railing. There was a balcony on the front of the second floor, too, and it had a railing with spindles. The front door was flanked by two huge windows, and the door on the second floor was as well. The windows in the roof were the kind that stuck out. Maybe they were called dormer windows, Noah didn't know.

What he did know was that the house was in at least as bad a shape as the bridge had been. Maybe worse. The steps leading up to the door had holes in them, broken boards. All the railings on the first and second floors had posts missing, making them look like the rotted teeth in a witch's mouth.

A light glowed in the attic window on the left side, a flickering light, a candle, maybe, but otherwise the windows were dark holes. Eyes looking out at them.

A black cat walked gracefully across the porch railing in that way cats have of looking like they're tiptoeing. Its tail was stuck straight up into the air. It jumped gracefully off the railing onto the porch, turned and started toward the door. As the cat approached, the door slowly opened inward, its hinges protesting with a horrible screech. The interior was a black maw and when the cat entered, the darkness gobbled it up and it disappeared. Then the door slammed shut with a resounding bang.

Noah spotted a cat on the railing on the second floor, too. No, two of them. The one in front of the window on the left was just sitting, licking its paws, the other walked across the railing, turned, and walked back the way it had come. Almost like a sentry standing guard.

But the most impressive thing about the sight in front of them was what was in the sky behind the house. It was a moon. A gigantic moon, took up almost the whole sky. The kind of moon you'd see in creepy movie posters behind a haunted house.

They all three exchanged a glance.

Then Noah pointed up into the sky. "Look … bats!

Flying in lazy circles around the chimney of the house was a flock of bats.

Then a black bird fluttered down and came to rest on the railing on the first-floor porch.

"A raven," Paco said. Then he quoted, "and the silken, sad uncertain rustling of each purple curtain …" He saw that the others weren't following. "Edgar Allen Poe. It's a classic. I read it in English class in West Virginia when …" His voice trailed off.

Behind them in the mist, they could hear the purr and burble of reptars.

"Do you hear that?" Star asked.

"That's the sound reptars make, the purring, and then later, when they attack, it sounds like they're sucking—"

"No, I don't mean the reptars. I mean everything else."

"What everything else?"

"That's my point. There *isn't* anything else. There's not a sound here, not a bird, not a leaf rattling. When you're blind, you listen really hard to what's around you. And there isn't anything."

"This is like a cartoon!" Paco said. "Every awful thing you could imagine in a haunted house — presented here for your viewing enjoyment."

"Why?" Noah asked, trying to drag his eyes away from the bats circling the chimney. "What's the point?"

"Another test," Star said. "Something's weird. Look at Pumpkin."

The dog wasn't in attack mode anymore, but neither was he the relaxed dog with the wagging tail that'd been waiting for them at the end of the bridge.

He was whining and had pressed himself up against Star's leg.

"That's his confused, I-don't-want-to-be-here whine." She paused. "Smell that?"

"What?"

"Nothing. Before, back at the bridge, I could smell mud, and like decaying leaves, and other — I don't know what, but it was *something*."

The door began to open again. Slowly. Star put her hands over her ears and shook her head so the sound must have been an agonizing squeak.

When the door was wide open, a voice echoed deep in the bowels of the blackness. Noah *heard* it! He must have merely heard through the minds of the others what they heard. But it didn't feel like that.

"Star," the voice said. It sounded like it had been produced by a sound echo chamber, an enhancement of a real voice with an exaggerated creepy quality.

"I *heard* that," Noah said, but not aloud. "Or I heard you two hear it."

Paco wasn't paying attention to Noah.

"Come inside," the voice purred.

"Fuck that," Paco said and might not even have realized that he'd instinctively moved his body between Star and the house.

"Come inside now, or you all will die."

They exchanged looks, totally confused, trying to puzzle it out. This was undoubtedly the single most scary place Noah had ever been. The black, bare trees, gnarled and bent out of shape, the ridiculously huge moon, the house and it's gaping front door, the cats and the bats and the raven, all of it shrouded in the cold mist — wait a minute, the mist wasn't cold. It wasn't … anything. You could see it but not feel it.

"I don't want to go in there," Star said, cringing back.

"Duh!" Paco said.

"It's almost like …" Noah couldn't quite put his finger on it, but everything was just … too much. "It's everybody's worst imagining of a haunted house."

"We have to get out of here, but where can we go?" Paco said. "Off into the mist? It's like before. There's only one way to go and that's forward. They've herded us here and either the reptars will get us or we go in there."

Noah looked at Pumpkin, who sat on the ground huddled against Star's leg, looking totally out of his element. Maybe that was because there was nothing for Pumpkin to smell. Dogs didn't see very well, he didn't think, but their sense of smell was like ten thousand times better than a human, so they got most of their information about the world from their noses. If this place wasn't real, was somehow made up, it didn't smell like anything at all. And Pumpkin was left without any sense to use to investigate his world.

"Come now, or you'll be eaten alive," the voice said and laughed. Like the *bwa-ha-ha-ha* of a wind-up toy.

A lone reptar emerged from the mist behind them. A big one.

Paco bolted up the broken the porch steps. Star

stood with Noah as he stared in horrified fascination at the reptar.

"It could attack, leap on us," Noah said. "Why doesn't it?"

"Come on!' Paco cried, and they followed him onto the porch and through the open door. As they did, a second reptar that looked just like the first one appeared out of the mist behind them.

Exactly like the first one, as a matter of fact. An identical twin or a clone.

Paco reached out and took Star's hand. She took Noah's, and it happened, what they expected would. There was a hum, a surge of some kind of power, a kinetic energy that ... it made a glow!

The darkness leapt back away from the glow of their presence, which had a greenish tint, like the illumination of a glow stick. What was revealed in the glow was ... nothing. Bare floor. No rugs or furniture. What they could see of the walls was bare. But it looked odd. Noah couldn't have described how, but it looked more like a photograph than reality. They took a couple more steps, far enough into the house for the door behind them to suddenly slam shut. The bang shook the whole house.

Then it was quiet. The room grew lighter, but there was no source for the light. No lamp or overhead fixture. The shadows merely receded and there was no longer a need for their green glow to illuminate their surroundings.

The spooky sounds started then, like a recording of weird sounds, creepy music, faint maniacal laughter, the sound of chains dragged across a metal floor. Noah heard what the others heard, but didn't know if the sound was coming from his ears or his mind.

The room grew lighter, but there was no source for the light. No lamp or overhead fixture.

"You smell anything?" Star asked.

Noah knew what she was driving at this time. He sniffed the air. Nothing.

She let go of his hand and took a tentative step forward. "Old houses stink. They smell like old plaster, and decaying wallpaper, dusty and musty and … this place smells like the white rooms, like the inside of an envelope."

Then Star screamed.

Chapter Eleven

STAR COULD SEE! Star could *see*!

Between one heartbeat and another, she'd been given back her sight.

And what she could see froze her heart. It appeared in the shadows, a small movement, at first. Maybe nothing. Then it boldly walked out into the light. It was the size of a chest freezer, maybe four feet tall and equally as wide. Each of the eight hairy black legs ended in a claw the size of a grappling hook and together they held its bulbous body swaying between them, where Star could see a snapping mouth, a horror with something like a pointed beak.

Star could see the spider!

Star had been terrified of spiders her whole life and suddenly being able to see — and see a monster out of a nightmare, the most horrifying spider imagin-able stole her breath and turned her knees rubbery.

"What?" Noah asked. "What are you screaming at?"

She backed up. Noah still held her hand and wouldn't let go of her hand so she dragged him backward the few steps to the closed door and her back banged into it.

"Don't you see it?"

"*See?* You can see?"

"What do you see?" Paco asked.

"The spider, the giant spider."

"I don't see anything," Noah said.

"It's right there," she cried, so horrified she barely had the breath to speak at all.

She was pulling away from Noah, trying to pull free so she could turn and open the door and run. But he held her hands firm.

"Let me go!"

"Go where? Back outside with the reptars?"

"But the spider …"

"There is no spider," Paco said.

But of course there absolutely was too a spider! It was right there in front of her. She could *see* it, could take three steps and touch it!

It suddenly lifted up onto its back legs, like a horse rearing up, the two legs in front clawing at the air while the six behind held the body in place.

She screamed again, tried to yank herself free from Noah's grip, take Pumpkin and …

Pumpkin.

He stood next to her, his body touching hers in a gesture of dependence and uncertainty. But he was clearly not terrified. And he should have been. They all should have been. There was a spider …

That the others couldn't see. That Pumpkin couldn't see — or smell.

She stopped trying to yank her hands free of Noah's grip and forced herself to look away from the monster in front of them.

"You don't see a spider?"

The instant she looked into Noah's face, she recognized the truth.

"I don't see anything but darkness," Noah said.

She glanced to her right, at the spider, pawing the air, its beak mouth opening and closing, drool oozing out of it and dripping on the floor.

"How can you not …?"

"It's not there," Paco said.

Then Noah sucked in a horrified gasp and his eyes grew huge.

"You see it now, don't you? You see the spider!"

He shook his head, was so frightened he was temporarily breathless.

"I … not a spider. It's a snake."

THE COBRA COILED on the floor not ten feet away from Noah rose up so its hooded head towered in the air three feet above him. It was probably fifty feet long, and a foot, maybe two feet in diameter. It swayed there in the air in front of him, its hood four feet across, its snake eyes the size of baseballs, its forked tongue licking in and out of its mouth as it swayed.

Back and forth in front of Noah. Its eyes never left his.

He could hear the hiss.

How could he *hear* the hiss? But he could, he could hear it, a sensuous wheezing noise that sounded like death itself. He could also hear, in his ears and in his head, Star's and Paco's voices. They seemed to be coming from a long way away, but he could hear them.

"It's not real." Star said. "I can see a spider, right there where you say there's a snake."

"Look away," Paco commanded. "Look at me!"

The force of his words was powerful. Noah had never heard Paco sound so commanding before and he was compelled to turn his head to the left where he met Paco's eyes. They were such a dark brown they were almost black and they were mesmerizing.

He could see the snake out of the corner of his eye, sensuously bobbing and weaving, flicking its forked tongue in and out of its mouth.

He shuddered.

Never in his life had he ever seen anything more horrifying, more real than that snake. The ends of its forked tongue wiggled, as if sniffing the air. He'd seen on *Animal Planet* that the tongue was a snake's nose. Its eyes darted back and forth with unreserved hatred and aggression. Its body was coiled like a spring, instants away from launching itself at him, burying its fangs in his chest.

Paco suddenly turned away from Noah, dropped

his gaze, looked instead at something that cramped his features in pure terror.

"What is it, Paco? What do *you* see?"

GRINNING, his face only a few feet from Paco, he looked deep into Paco's eyes, then threw back his head and laughed, a full, rumbling, roiling laugh.

Mr. Jinx. The original Boogie Man.

He had no hair. What was on the top of his round, grayish-colored skull was more moss than hair. Paco was a city boy; when he'd visited West Virginia, Vincent had taken him into the woods looking for ginseng, which grew wild there and Vincent said you could make a lot of money selling it. If you could find it. Paco thought he had struck gold when he found a green, fuzzy, slimy substance on the base of a tree.

Until Vincent told him it was moss.

Paco hadn't wanted to touch it, because it looked soft and silky and gross all at the same time, completely covered the back of the tree in a way that made Paco think of some kind of infection spread out over the tree's surface.

Mostly he hadn't wanted to touch it because the moss had looked just like Mr. Jinx's hair.

Mr. Jinx had shown up in Paco's closet when they lived in the apartment above the pizza parlor when his mother was still something approaching a functioning parent, before the crack ate her brain and then her soul. She invited men home sometimes … actually, she invited them home a lot of times, and made Paco stay in his room and not come out no matter what. He heard sounds coming from outside and they scared him, so he sat up in bed, shivering.

Then the noises had started coming from inside his room. From inside his closet. And one horror-filled night when he awakened from a monster-filled nightmare, Mr. Jinx was looking out of the darkness from the depths of his closet.

He vaguely resembled a character out of a superhero animated video Paco had seen a couple of days before.

Mr. Jinx had green silky hair, like moss, soft-looking. Spongey. And Paco knew without knowing how he knew that if he touched that hair, if he allowed the hair to touch him, it would begin to grow on his skin, too, like it grew on Mr. Jinx's head, only it would grow all over Paco, cover every bit of his entire body, including his eyes so he couldn't see and eventually his nose so he couldn't breathe and he would die.

Mr. Jinx's eyes were red. Just red, no black centers. But the color only had a little white around it and there were no eyelashes, just black circles all the way around. He had no eyebrows, and most horribly, no nose. Where it should have been was a hole, a nasty, oozing hole where green phlegm and snot and yellow pus oozed out. His lipless mouth had two huge teeth in front, like rabbit teeth, but the two of them ended in a single point that was as big as his big toe and looked to be as sharp as a butcher knife. The other teeth were pointed, too, and blood dripped off them, off all of them, and pieces of flesh from whatever it was he had just been eating.

"I am Mr. Jinx," the horror had said, in a raspy voice that sounded too dry to come out of any throat, so dry it was like sand scouring a rock, or scarab beetles scratching away in a tomb. "I have come to eat your soul."

And then he would come out of the closet — Paco didn't remember his body, just his head, and shuffle toward his bed, his mouth opening and closing and blood oozing off the sharp teeth.

Paco thought he saw Mr. Jinx in his closet every night for years, was terrified to sleep in the dark, pleaded with his mother, and then Mama Rosa, to leave the light on. He had nightmares about Mr. Jinx his whole childhood. In fact, they didn't stop until … until Vincent. And then Star and Noah had come into his dreams and there were no more nightmares until the Astral spaceships and the reptars showed up in his nighttime world a month before Astral Day.

Mr. Jinx breathed on Paco out of the darkness and his breath smelled of corpses mouldering in the grave.

"I have come to eat your soul," he said, in that rattling dry voice.

The horror that rose up in Paco's chest was as elemental as it'd been when he was just a little boy, trying to huddle under the covers of his bed so the Boogie Man wouldn't see him. He couldn't get his breath, couldn't—

"It's not real," Noah said beside him. "Whatever it is you see, it's not real."

And Paco knew that it wasn't, understood on an intellectual level that everything they were seeing had been conjured up for them to see. But it didn't make Mr. Jinx any less real.

"Not real," Noah said again, and touched his arm. Noah had hold of Star's hand, and when he touched Paco, the power surged again. It didn't form a green glow this time. It merely froze the image … *images* in front of them.

Paco could see the spider now and the snake along with Mr. Jinx. But they were frozen, not pictures exactly, but not as substantial as mannequins. Clearly not actually what they appeared to be.

"What is *that?*" Star cried, pointing at Mr. Jinx.

"It's what I'm afraid of," Paco said. "Like the spider and snake are what the two of you are afraid of. But we blocked them." He took Noah's hand, then he lifted up their clasped hands, like a referee raising the hands of a prize fighter who has just won his bout. "With our hive mind, we stopped them from manipulating what we saw."

Paco didn't like the thought of his mind being tricked. In fact, it pissed him off. Who'd these fuckers think they were? Maybe Paco ought to flip the script and trick the trickster.

He didn't know what he was doing, didn't know how to do it, just concentrated, the way he did when he was trying to get somebody to do something he wanted them to do, when he wanted to know someone's name before he met them. He squinted, and rose up with a mental force, as much power as he could muster. He stared at Mr. Jinx. Glared at Mr. Jinx. Willed Mr. Jinx to be gone.

And the image began to falter. It shook, trembled. Not like the creature himself had trembled but like the image before Paco was shaking. He tried harder, concentrated with all his will. He felt a headache bloom in the center of his forehead when he did that. It blossomed out across his skull in an ooze of red-hot pain that made him slightly nauseous. But he didn't give in, didn't quit. He pushed out with all the force of his will … and Mr. Jinx blinked away.

Then he was back.

Then gone again.

Then Mr. Jinx stood before him and slowly turned to smoke and drifted away.

The headache slammed into his skull full force then, and he almost staggered.

"What did you do?" Noah asked, but his voice came from a long way away, from somewhere hollow. "How'd you turn that monster to smoke?"

Paco dropped to one knee.

Then everything went black.

Chapter Twelve

THE DARKNESS HIT with the suddenness of a clap of
thunder. The absolute lack of light. Paco took three or
four ragged breaths, wondering if he had been struck
blind like Star, and then the light began to return, a
bulb on a dimmer switch. In the growing light, he
realized he wasn't where he'd been, down on one knee
in front of the spider and the snake — with Mr. Jinx a
puff of disappearing smoke. He was sitting down on
the white plastic-like substance and he knew what he
would see when the light returned fully. He felt dizzy, a
little foggy, like maybe he had brought some of the
mist back with him in his head. And then he opened
his eyes to the white room. Maybe the same one,
maybe a different one. It was impossible to tell the
difference.

Noah was sitting, leaned up against the wall,
looking at him. Star was lying on her back. When
Pumpkin began to lick her face, she pushed him away
and rolled over on her side.

"Back home again," Noah said. "I wonder if they missed us."

Paco looked around, studied the walls and the floor and the other two.

Star sat up. "And I can't see anymore," she said, and he could hear the disappointment in her voice.

"I can't hear, either."

"I don't think you ever could see," Paco told her. He turned to Noah. "They needed you to *hear* the creepy shit and Star had to *see* the spider. It's all part of them fucking around in our heads."

It made sense, a horrible sense that Paco didn't like one bit, but there really wasn't any other explanation for his white tee shirt. The Astrals could make them see … a reality that wasn't really there at all.

A part of Paco was so horrified at that prospect that he could barely get his breath, felt unclean almost, knowing the Astrals were rummaging around inside his mind, looking at things, knowing all of it. but another part of him was … impressed, no, *awed,* that the Astrals could perform such a feat. It was, after all, an extension of the kinds of things Paco had been doing his whole life. Paco couldn't rummage around in the minds of others, but he could see some things, know things he could only have gotten out of their minds. Making somebody see something that wasn't there — no, Paco couldn't do anything that amazing. All he could do was persuade, maybe manipulate; maybe the fact that he could usually talk people into almost everything was him bending their minds to his will.

But today, he had banished Mr. Jinx. Had beaten him — after the three of them had called a halt to the Astrals' little puppet show.

The wall beside where Noah was sitting suddenly did that melting thing again. The people from before were in the room the door had opened into, along with some other people who hadn't been there before.

Paco got to his feet and the wave of dizziness passed. He stepped through the doorway into the room with the other people, looked around for a familiar face and found one. The waitress was there, the one in the Harper's Cafe uniform. She was sitting on the floor, leaning up against the wall and she looked exhausted. Her uniform was filthy and torn and there was an angry-looking scratch that ran from her elbow up into the sleeve of her dress.

"I wonder what happened to her," Noah said in his head.

"Whatever it was, it *really* happened," Paco said. "It wasn't some simulation in her mind. She really went somewhere and did something."

"Yeah, and got hurt doing it."

Making his way through the throng of people milling around in the room, Paco went to the other side where he sat down on the floor and leaned against the wall. As with the others, these people looked as if they'd just been sucked out of their everyday lives, which they probably had been. A teacher out of a classroom with chalk dust still on her hands. A fisherman who smelled of fish. And the dude in the

Italian shoes. Paco looked around for him but didn't see him.

Noah led Star and Pumpkin to where Paco sat and they plopped down on the floor around him.

"She went somewhere real," Noah said, nodding to the waitress. "And after the bridge, they sent us — at least we thought they did — somewhere … *stupid*."

"Like a bad fairy tale," Star said.

"No wonder they have to study humans," Noah said, "if that's the best they can do … find some creepy old movie to scare us with."

"The shit out of our own minds was pretty hairy," Paco pointed out.

"Why did they want to scare us at all?" Noah wanted to know.

"Maybe because we're just kids," Star said.

"If it was an experiment, what were they trying to find out?"

"Duh," Noah said, "what we'd do when we were scared."

Then Paco got it. "When we were cornered, without even a rope bridge to escape, what we did was … *fight back*." That had to be it. "They pushed us — using stupid things, but I don't think they knew they were stupid — to see what our 'hive mind' would do. It took us a little while to figure out how, but we responded by using our hive mind against theirs."

"But why do we have a hive mind in the first place?" Star bleated. "I don't even understand that part."

Paco decided it was time to pick at that scab.

"It has something to do with what happened to us on the day after Halloween four years ago."

Star's hand flew to her mouth. Noah turned the color of a new gym sock.

"If you don't want to talk about it, fine," Paco said. "But we're never going to figure this out until we know how we got here."

There was a long silence, then Star said, "Okay, I'll go first."

She took a deep, shaky breath and let it out slowly.

"We were in Cincinnati, my Mom and me, visiting my uncle. I was just seven. And my mom ..." She stopped and gathered herself. "She used drugs. Lots of drugs, all the time. Bad ones."

"Been there, done that," Paco said.

"She'd stayed clean the whole visit until the last day when we were on the way to take the rental car back to the airport and she took something. Metha-trexadone, I think."

"What's metha-trexadone?" Noah asked.

"Makes you see the world like everything's a cartoon image," Paco said. He'd tried it once and did not enjoy the trip. He did not like losing control of himself like that and he never took any of the illegal drugs available on every street corner in LA.

"She had to have the car back by eight o'clock or get charged an extra day, so Mom set the alarm on her phone for eight. But after she took the drug, she wouldn't let the car drive us there. We had plenty of time, but she took over control, kept making wrong turns, giggling like it was all a joke, driving crazy, all over the road. We came to an intersection; the light was red but she blew right through it. There was a truck coming, a big one, an eighteen-wheeler. I watched it …"

She didn't go on, but she didn't have to. The horrifying image was in the front of her mind. A truck roaring toward the passenger-side door, getting bigger and bigger. Star screamed, "Nooooo!" and there was a buzzing sound, her mother's phone alarm, and then blackness.

"I hadn't thought about it since that day, hadn't even remembered … but … when I screamed, I felt a SNAP. Like when we touch each other. I'd forgotten that part." She stopped again. "When I woke up I was in the hospital. My mom was … dead. And I was blind."

Paco knew then, knew for certain, because he'd felt that power surge before, too. When the three of them touched the first time, he'd almost remembered but not quite. He did now, though. He'd felt it that day in Vincent's room, the day he …

Noah reached over and put his arm around Star. When he did, his face changed, looked as frightened and grief-stricken as Star.

Then slowly, both their faces relaxed.

"You're next, kiddo," Paco told Noah. "We'll save the best for last."

"Me, too," Noah said. "The snap. I felt it, too, when …"

Noah couldn't seem to find a voice, then said

simply, "I like to build things. I'm really good at it, like ridiculous good."

Then he told the story of the first thing he ever built when he was not yet three years old, how he didn't really remember the event, but had heard it described to him so often it seemed like a real memory. His family always spent Christmas in the home of his father's brother, Taylor, who had two sons, David, who was ten at the time, and Samuel who was eight. David had gotten a model kit of the Eiffel Tower with hundreds of small, fit-slot-A-into-hole-B pieces. His uncle had been reluctant to buy it, in fact, because it was so complicated, said he'd looked at the assembly instructions and didn't think he could figure them out if he had to assemble it himself.

Christmas dinner happened. Cleaning up dinner happened. Watching the football game on the juke was in the process of happening when the adults missed Noah. He had just vanished.

They found him in the entry hall outside the den, where he'd dragged his cousin David's Christmas present. While the family had been cleaning up after Christmas dinner and watching a ball game, Noah had opened the box and assembled it! Without benefit of the instructions, because at two and a half he couldn't read them.

"On my father's desk at the sheriff's department, there's a framed picture of me sitting next to the completed tower."

"What does that have to do with what happened to you four years ago?"

"That's why I did it, because I was building a model and it was so cold the glue wouldn't dry."

Then Noah opened his mouth to continue, but couldn't speak. He dropped his chin to his chest and tears began to roll down his cheeks. He didn't have to tell them the story then. It bloomed so crisp and clear in his mind it was like watching a movie.

Chapter Thirteen

An EIGHT-YEAR-OLD NOAH leaps off the bottom step of the school bus to the ground and lets out a whoop of delight. It had started snowing right after he left for school, had snowed all day and now it lay in an eight-inch blanket on the ground. Tomorrow was Saturday. He and his father would build a snowman for Rosie-Posie. He'd make a snow fort and have a snowball war with his cousins.

And he still has time today to finish his project — if he hurries.

He rushes into the house, plants a little peck on his mother's cheek and gives Rosie a hug. That can't be hurried, though. At three, Rosileigh rules the Matheson household with an iron fist, a tiny one, but iron all the same. And when she wants a hug ... you don't let go until she lets you go. That's just how the world works.

"Kiss Osie," she cajoles after she releases her strangle-hold on his neck. "Osie needs kisses up to the bean cloud!"

Making the rounds of the neighbors last night trick-or-treating, Noah had dressed as Jack from Jack and the Beanstalk.

He'd told the story to the little red-haired Tinkerbell with aluminum-foil wings at his side over and over, like five times.

Noah obediently kisses her nose, her chin, both cheeks and her forehead.

She beams, which means that her majesty has dismissed him so he is free to go about the rest of his day.

"You remember the wood, right, Noah?" his mother reminds him. He doesn't but acts like he does. "The first fire of the season — with the first snowfall." That's the family tradition. "I'm about to light it, but I'll be out of wood by the time your father gets home." Dad is supervising second shift, so he probably won't make it before Rosie's bedtime at nine o'clock.

"I'm on it." He gives her a thumbs-up.

Noah steps out the kitchen door into the one-car garage that no longer has room for a car — even a small one because it is piled high with Noah's building projects and dominated by the big work table in the center of the room.

Sometimes, when he looks around, it's hard for Noah to remember building all the structures sitting on shelves, benches and on the garage floor. When he goes there, to that place where he gets lost and loses track of time and his fingers do the bidding of his mind without him willing them to, he is often a little surprised himself by what the final building looks like.

Noah glances at the Eiffel Tower, in its place of honor on the shelf by the kitchen door. It is only one of dozens of structures he has made over the years, and only the first few started out as 'kits' with the pieces pre-cut to the proper shapes. Big Ben, the Taj Mahal, Notre Dame, St. Peter's Cathedral — the greatest architectural feats of mankind.

By the time he was five, Noah had graduated from precut pieces to BrickDough, a product similar to the Play-Doh his father described playing with when he was a little boy. Brick-Dough came in a chunk six inches by eight inches, was soft and spongy, you could pull off big or small pieces of it and form it into any shape you could imagine. Once you'd fashioned a shape you wanted to keep, you let the pieces dry and they became as solid as a brick, almost unbreakable.

His eye scans his BrickDough structures — tall buildings, geodesic domes held up by pillars that shouldn't have supported their weight but did. Fantastic, futuristic-looking structures that sometimes looked like they couldn't possible remain upright, but somehow he had intuitively figured out what engineers and architects spent years of sketching out schematics and working complicated math programs to figure out.

He's working right now on his most complicated building yet. It's for the science fair at school — which his buildings won every year. It's a building with a daring archway and a peaked roof held aloft with the weight distributed so that it only requires a single rafter rather than a configuration of them. He picks up the BrickDough and begins to imagine a strange-looking, might-not-work archway and gets lost in the images in his head. Hours pass but he doesn't notice until he eases the last piece of the intricate framework carefully into place, squirts out a gob of GooGlu and sets the alarm on his watch-phone for twenty minutes to let him know when the glue's set and he can start adding the tricky parts.

Twenty minutes is straight-up eight o'clock. He's been at work for more than two hours.

It isn't until that moment that he realizes how cold it has grown. It's dark outside now. His breath is frosting. He crosses to the heater his father set up against the wall to heat the building so he could work in the wintertime. The heater is cold.

He flips the switch on. Nothing. Tries again, plugs and unplugs it. Still nothing. The old thing has died before and the last time it did his father said they'd have to replace it.

Then it occurs to him that the glue on his project probably won't dry properly in the cold. If the framework comes apart later while he's building the roof …

His leg bumps something covered with a small tarp beside the heater and the idea forms a millisecond later. He pulls the tarp off the fire pit, the one his dad set on the deck on cool autumn nights, and the family roasted hotdogs or marshmallows over it, making sticky s'mores as they huddled under wool blankets.

He can build a fire in the fire pit in the garage! The coals in the pit don't make any smoke, and he won't die of whatever it is you died of — lack of oxygen, maybe — from an indoor fire, not if he leaves the door to outside open a crack.

His mother opens the door a crack and calls through it.

"Wood, Noah — remember?"

An instant cold shiver works its way down his backbone, like ice from a melting icicle dripping from one vertebra to the next. He thinks at the time it's from the cold. He wonders later if somehow he knew those would be the last words he would ever hear his mother say … the last words he would ever hear, period.

"Yes, ma'am."

Pulling the fire pit out into the middle of the floor, he fills it with charcoal, squirts lighter fluid on it and drops in a match. There is that satisfying "whump" sound as it catches and blue flame races across the surface of the charcoal. The garage will be toasty warm by the time he goes to the shed behind the barn, gets the wheelbarrow, loads it up and pushes it back across the snow-

covered yard to the back porch where the wood box sits beside the back door.

As he trudges across the yard, the snow reflecting the big floodlights so it's almost as bright as day, he can hear his mother upstairs, playing the piano and singing to Rosaleigh. Oh, how his father had complained about having to haul that thing up the stairs! But the "music room" his mother'd made up there under the eaves is her favorite place in the whole house.

Noah turns behind the barn and the house is lost from sight, though he can still faintly hear his mother's voice.

"... wishing on the same bright star. Soooooomewhere out there ..."

It's more trouble than he thought it'd be to get the wood in the pile onto the wheelbarrow. It's darker here in the shadows beyond the backyard lights, harder to see. The snow covered the pile and he has to dig it out. As he does so, he fashions some of the handfuls of snow into snowballs, amassing an arsenal of them to use when his cousins come over to play tomorrow.

The pleasant aroma of the fireplace smoke wafts to him as he works.

He lines his ammunition up on the edge of the bin, stands back and smiles. Yeah, he'll ambush David with these. Dave's the oldest and he always wins snowball fights, but this time Noah will hammer him before he has a chance to make any snowballs of his own.

Imagining nailing his cousin in a hail of snowball bullets, he grabs the handles of the wheelbarrow and starts pushing. It is heavy now, filled with wood, will barely move, and he considers whether he should have made two trips.

He rounds the corner of the barn toward the house and a

warm wind, filled with the aroma of the fireplace moves over his face. He's looking down at the wheels digging into the snow …

The snow looks red.

It's reflecting …

He looks up.

His mind stumbles, trying to make sense of the images he sees. It takes him a moment to form any thought at all.

The house is on fire.

It's … on fire!

Not just on fire, a blazing inferno.

The next thought that forms is so savage, so huge and horrible and unthinkable that it lands not in his mind but in his chest, like he's been struck by the business end of a sledgehammer.

The fire pit in the garage.

He hadn't set it far enough away from the workbench. Something, a piece of something, fell into it and …

Oh, dear holy God, he set the house on fire.

He forms the thought a heartbeat before he hears the first scream.

A wail, a shriek of terror … and more than fear. Coming out the same window as his mother's singing had come only a few minutes ago.

Mom and Rosie are upstairs, in the back room. The fire is between them and the stairs!

All those thoughts race through his mind, banging into each other, knocking holes in his soul.

He has to get them out. Has to—

Then he's running across the yard but it takes so terribly long to make it all the way from the back by the barn up to the porch. Just in that time, the whole roof has caught and a black snake of smoke licked by crimson flames vomits upward, sending bright sparkles into the night sky.

On the porch.

Smoke is pouring from the porch roof. He can't even see the back door.

He reaches blindly, finds the doorknob. Opens—

Hell has opened up a crack in the world right there in his kitchen.

There is nothing but flames. A red-yellow dancing wall of death.

He hears the screams from the window above then, has probably been hearing them all along, but now he hears them.

His legs give way and he sinks to his knees, unable to move or think. The heat from the burning kitchen scorches his face. He smells burning hair, his own.

The screaming is beyond description. Wretched, horrified, wailing screams of terror and pain that go on and on.

He shakes his head fiercely, puts his hands over his ears, stops his ears up so he can't hear them, muffles the screams, makes them gone, but not really. They're still out there in the world beyond his stopped-up ears, the screams of his mother and sister as they burn to death.

He hears a buzzing sound, the alarm on his watch, and he tilts his head back and joins his voice to the screams of his mother and sister that he can no longer hear, that he will *no longer hear.*

"Noooooooooo!"

SNAP!

Then the world goes black.

Chapter Fourteen

Paco was so stunned by the scene in Noah's head that'd been transmitted to him and Star that he didn't know how to react. Star was crying softly, her hand out, patting Noah's foot because it was the only part of him she could get to. As the images formed in his mind, Noah drew his knees up to his chest and clasped his arms tight around them, turned his face toward the white wall.

Time came unhooked from reality. No one spoke.

Finally, Paco let out a breath.

"That's really fucked up, kid." He was surprised that his voice was gruff with emotion. He pulled another breath into his lungs and forced himself to move, dragging the other two along with him.

"You were in Kentucky, right? That's where you lived when it happened?"

Noah said nothing, but he lifted his head and nodded, his almost-white hair falling over his forehead.

A random thought struck Paco — had Noah's hair grown? It had. It had grown a lot since … yeah, since *when*? Yesterday? It felt like yesterday that they'd been standing together for the first time in the white room. It also seemed like it had been years. How long had it really been, in Earth time? Were their body clocks humming along at the same rate as humanity down below? Or were they caught in some space/time-warp shit with the Astrals in the mothership?

He shook off the thoughts, tried to concentrate.

"And you were in Cincinnati," he confirmed with Star. "What happened to me" — he only paused for a beat, then moved on — "was just like what happened to you. It was the day after Halloween four years ago. And it was exactly eight o'clock."

An image bloomed in his mind, a clock on the wall above a hospital bed, the second hand sweeping up from the ten to the twelve, the hour hand on the eight.

"I screamed in my head, too, screamed, '*nooooo*,' just like you said you did. And there was a snapping sound."

Noah was looking intently at Paco, his cheeks slathered with tears he wasn't even bothering to wipe away.

"What *happened* to you?" Noah asked.

Paco ignored him.

"I was in Charleston, West Virginia." Paco paused, waited. "Do you see it — *Charleston, West Virginia*?"

Both of them looked blank.

"Imagine a map of West Virginia, Ohio and Kentucky. Can you see it in your heads?"

He imagined the map himself and knew they could see what he was seeing. He'd spent hours of boredom on the bus trip east from California, tracking his progress on a map and he had no trouble at all picturing it.

"Here's Charleston." He put an imaginary finger on the capital of West Virginia, a small city less than an hour's drive from the Kentucky border. Then he moved an imaginary finger across Kentucky to the northernmost point, just across the Ohio River from Cincinnati, Ohio. "Here's Cincinnati." Then he moved his hand downward into Kentucky. "Where's Jessup? About here, right?"

"Yeah, about."

"It's two hundred miles from Charleston to Cincinnati, and—"

"It's two hundred miles from Jessup to Cincinnati, too," Noah said. "My dad said—"

"So let's assume it's two hundred miles from Jessup to Charleston. Now do you see?"

"It's a triangle," Star said. The one who couldn't see saw it first.

"I can't prove it right now, but I bet it's a perfect triangle — two hundred miles on each side." He paused again. "So think about it … at exactly eight o'clock on the same day, something horrible happened to all three of us. We cried out and …"

He stopped.

"And what?" Noah asked.

"How the hell do I know! But I think … *something* happened. I know something happened. At that moment, we were … oh, I don't know, hooked up somehow. That was the snap, the surge of … power. Maybe because Star's … you know, can see things, the future. I can do things, too. I …" He couldn't explain it and didn't want to, but he believed he'd figured out the answer. Noah was special, too, somehow, had to be, because the three of them who were "different" … the power of their united pain had made something unexplainable happen. He didn't look down into his shirt at his chest, but he felt the scars there. He knew there were lots of things in life that had no rational explanation. "That night, the two of you were in my dreams for the first time."

"I was unconscious for two days," Star said. "But the first night after that, I dreamed of you." Her face was turned to Noah. Then she turned her blind eyes on Paco. "I didn't dream of you, though. I dreamed of your … tattoo. Why would I dream about the tattoo?"

"That's what I saw in my dreams," Noah said. "The picture on your chest."

He didn't say the tattoo. He said the *picture*.

The picture Vincent had drawn. The one Vincent had clawed into his chest.

"You haven't told us what happened to you that night," Noah said.

Emotion Paco couldn't tack words onto swelled in his chest.

"And I'm not going to tell you!" he yelled. He hadn't meant to shout, but the words had exploded out of him. All the other people in the room turned to look at them, at the three kids sitting off by themselves, not talking at all until Paco shouted.

"But you said—"

"Fuck what I said." Paco didn't shout, but he still couldn't control the words, couldn't keep them inside his head and they came out in a furious hiss. "It's none of your fucking business, okay? Butt out. You know all you need to know. We've figured out the puzzle. For some reason when something awful happened to the three of us at the same time, we … our minds were connected. We were in each other's heads in dreams. We weren't a hive mind then, but here … so close to the Astrals' hive mind … like you said before, Noah, it's like the volume got turned up on everything. Mystery solved."

"We told you what happened to us." Star wouldn't let it go, but he shut her down.

"Butt out! I mean it." Even in his head, the edge of menace in the words was clear. "My private affairs are not available for your viewing enjoyment."

The two of them said nothing, studiously thought nothing either, but Paco was sure if he'd nudged even a little bit, he could have gotten past the pitiful little barriers to their thoughts the other two had constructed so he wouldn't see they were pissed or upset or … *whatever* that he wouldn't share with them. But he didn't push because he didn't care what they were thinking. It didn't matter whether they liked it or not. It was what it was.

He scooted farther down the wall then, away from them. Lay down on his side and rolled with his face toward the wall as if he were taking a nap. It wasn't meant to be such a dismissive gesture, such a separating gesture, but he saw it for what it was and couldn't seem to make himself care enough to fix it.

After that, it was *different.* There was Star-and-Noah. And there was Paco. The three of them formed a hive mind when they needed to perform in some kind of dog-and-pony experiment for the Astrals. But it wasn't the three of them together anymore.

Paco couldn't help feeling isolated, even though the isolation had been of his own choosing. He could actually feel the combined … *warmth* of the other two whenever he was near. But the price of admission back into the mighty threesome was allowing the other two to see what had happened to him that night in a hospital in Charleston four years ago. And that was a price Paco wasn't willing to pay.

The white boxes appeared to feed them. Lights went on and off, like some kind of simulated day and night to help them sleep. Paco could feel the first roughening of beard stubble on his chin and cheeks. It grew out.

Noah's hair no longer just fell into his eyes. It was so long Star gave him one of the elastic ties she used on her braids to pull it back in a ponytail at his neck, and used the other tie on a lone braid down her back. Paco's hair now brushed his shoulders.

They got new clothes — clean ones, maybe the same, maybe different — when they soiled theirs on an adventure. The clothing just appeared on them. They'd open their eyes and there it'd be. But even when they weren't out slaying dragons, they got new clothing at intervals ... *because they had outgrown their other clothes.*

Chapter Fifteen

IN AN APPARENT EFFORT TO simulate waking and sleeping cycles for the humans, the Astrals turned down the lights every so often. Nobody knew how often because nobody's watches worked here. Paco had curled up on his side near Star and Noah, but when he opened his eyes, there was a titan standing in the center of the room and no other humans were there.

Fuck, how he hated the Astrals' control of everything! When they ate. What they ate. When they slept. Where they went, or didn't go. If, indeed, they ever went anywhere at all. One second, they'd be in a group in one of the "envelope rooms" and the next they'd be somewhere else entirely, and they had to figure out what was real and what was simulation and what was …

But the humans had no say over anything.

Being totally alone was new, though. Paco had only been separated from Star and Noah on one other occasion and it'd been brief. He had suddenly found himself sitting with Italian Shoe Man on a beach with sand that should have felt warm in the blazing sun but felt cool instead, one of the "sensory details" the Astrals missed that always gave away their little charades.

"I don't know why he'd do it, that Dempsey guy," the man sitting beside Paco in the not-right sand said, "why he'd take a drug like ayahuasca so he could communicate with the Astrals — who'd want to do a thing like that?"

And then the two of them spotted reptars in the distance, coming their way and they had leapt up and run. Chased down the beach by reptars — the ocean to his right with crashing waves surfers would have killed for. The horizon beyond ... it didn't look right. Too high in the sky, like the ocean went uphill toward it. Simulation fail. Only, maybe it had been real for Italian Shoe Man because he was actually the No-Shoes-At-All man now, barefoot, not even socks. And he looked like the shit had been knocked out of him more than once.

Paco rolled over and sat up. The titan just stood there with that maddening enigmatic smile on his face that looked like he'd taken Human Smiling 101 in junior college and flunked the course.

Then thoughts formed in Paco's mind.

The other two from your cell are gone now. You will remain.

"My *cell?*" he asked. He spoke aloud because he *could* speak aloud and he thought that was a skill the Astrals hadn't managed to master yet, so fuck them, he could do it and they couldn't. Childish, but any leg up was better than none. He knew the asshole was talking about Star and Noah but pretended he didn't.

Your unit.

That was apparently all the explanation that would be forthcoming.

"Gone where?"

They made an arrangement.

"Arrangement?"

We sent them back to Earth.

A fist of pain/loss/fear slammed into Paco's belly.

"They're gone … *home*?"

The thought of being *alone* here was suddenly so overwhelming Paco thought he might be sick. *Alone?* Without Star and Noah? All by himself.

"Why am I still here?" He heard the fear in his voice but couldn't control it.

That was the bargain.

"Bargain?"

Paco hated that any communication with the Astrals was laborious. You had to drag everything out of them. They offered nothing.

In exchange for returning them to Earth, they agreed to leave you behind.

If Paco'd been standing, he'd have had to sit because his knees would have folded up under him.

His mind was suddenly so full and so empty at the same time he couldn't think. So full of thoughts/questions/emotions. And so empty … alone … that he could barely get his breath.

"You're telling me you told them they could go

home if they'd bail on me ... and they did it? *Bullshit.*" He shouted the last part, not that volume seemed to matter here, since the Astral might not even be able to hear like humans with an organ that picked up auditory impulses from the environment. Maybe they could only hear words in their heads. But he yelled anyway.

"That's fucking bullshit! They wouldn't leave me here. You're a lying, motherfucking son of a bitch."

The titan's expression never changed. He turned in place. The titans were somehow graceful even though they were big oafs who should have lumbered along like mastodons. He left the room, stepping into a hallway where Paco caught a glimpse of two other humans he didn't know walking behind a titan in the other direction.

Then the doorway melted back into a wall and he was alone.

Really alone.

THE EXPRESSION of the titan standing before Noah and Star never changed. It was a female, small, so short, in fact, that her toga almost brushed the floor. Though the titans' facial features and body structure varied somewhat, their expressions were always the same. Like they'd been stamped on their faces. It was particularly maddening now not to be able to see any nuance, any "body" language to prove the lie.

"I don't believe you," Star said. "Paco wouldn't do that."

"He wouldn't agree to leave us here so he could go home," Noah said. "You're lying!"

The titan continued to smile her not-smile as she turned, walked back out through the doorway that reformed instantly into a featureless wall.

Noah felt Star's fear, disbelief — and her anger — even without touching her.

"You know it's a trick," she said inside his head. "It's another one of their stupid games, their stupid experiments."

Noah agreed, and felt Star begin to relax a little.

"They've decided it's divide-and-conquer time." Noah had a horrible thought. "In fact, they might separate you and me next time around. Might tell you that I—"

"I don't care what they tell me. They're liars. I don't believe Paco has gone back to Earth. He's still right here in the mothership."

There was always the *possibility* that he'd been sent back to Earth, but it wasn't possible that he'd made some kind of deal with the Astrals, agreed to abandon Star and Noah in exchange for a ticket back to California. Star was right about that part.

Then it occurred to Noah that if Paco was still here …

"Maybe we can find him," he said. "Reach out to him and talk to him. There are two of us, after all. That's two thirds of a hive mind."

"How?"

Noah shrugged, then took her hand in his. "Close your eyes and concentrate."

She burped out a small laugh. "That sounds as corny as the stuff I used to say when I told fortunes at Alien World."

He felt a wave of sadness wash over her as images of ugly orange buildings flashed through her mind.

"Maybe that's what the test is, the experiment," he said. "Maybe they want to know if we'll reach out to him. Or if we can reach out to him."

Then Noah held tight to her hands and tried to figure out how to make his mind go searching for Paco.

~

PACO'S HEART hammered like a lunatic woodpecker had gotten loose inside his ribcage. Alone. The word reverberated, echoed.

Alone.

Shit.

How was he supposed to … to …? How could he do anything here alone? Oh, there were other humans who came and went, cycled in and out. But he couldn't talk to them without speaking aloud. They weren't a hive mind.

Here … all by himself.

He grabbed hold of his emotions, clutched frantically to stifle them before he erupted in full-bore panic.

The titan had said Star and Noah were gone but

the Astrals were liars. They'd say anything. Just because the Pillsbury Doughboy said they were back on Earth didn't make it so. In fact, him saying it was just about a guarantee that it wasn't true.

His heart began to take up a more natural rhythm. That was it. Sure. Liars.

This was just another one of their dipshit tests. Telling him something like that was as stupid as the idiot tests the Astrals made them participate in, not-for-real situations. They'd proven over and over that they didn't know anything about people. They didn't know friends didn't do that to each other.

Friends.

Like Vincent.

The wave of grief, remorse/pain/anger/every-thing-else that rolled over him was almost overpowering. Either by lucky accident or design, the Astrals' putting them in stark white rooms was disorienting. Everything that happened was intensified because there was nothing for the senses to glom onto in a white room. If the external was devoid of life, the internal provided it, the mind was alive, colorful, real.

No, that hadn't been accidental.

He never allowed himself to think about Vincent, about the glorious time they'd spent together when he was visiting his aunt in West Virginia the summer he turned twelve years old.

Vincent Singleton. Paco Sálazar. S & S. The spider and the snake. That's what Vincent had dubbed them. Vincent who was sixteen but hung out with Paco because he wasn't like the other West Virginia teenagers who planned to drop out of high school before their seventeenth birthdays and would wind up dead, pregnant or hooked on Oxycontin before they turned twenty-one. Vincent was different. He had plans, was going to be a Navy SEAL. He would make it out of the mountains, had inspired Paco to get out of his ghetto and make something of himself.

The "Spider and the Snake" grew out of the single most glorious, colorful, convincing lie anybody'd ever conceived, the one Vincent told that church lady to get them out of trouble for spray-painting an "S & S" on the fence behind the building. He'd looked into her eyes all innocent and said that the wall had been defaced by the Spider and the Snake, a dangerous street gang whose logo was a skull with a spider crawling out one eye socket and a snake out the other.

Paco suddenly found himself sitting with his head in his hands on that white floor, the world around him populated with memories that, once set free, he couldn't gather back up and lock down, as he'd kept them these four years.

He and Vincent had been best friends, soulmates. Vincent had taught him how to thread a worm on a hook and steal a watermelon out of a field. They'd laughed together, gotten high together … and drunk together, but only that one time. So drunk they could barely stand, they'd decided to break into the change machine in the laundromat for money to buy dope. But they couldn't get the thing off the wall, so Vincent got another brilliant idea. He wanted to get inside a dryer and ride around and around. He'd done it, too,

Paco watching, giggling. But then Vincent wanted out, and Paco couldn't stop the machine because two police cars had pulled up and parked outside. After that …

Then the memories were no longer colorful. They were deadly black, glaring florescent white and endless horrifying shades of gray.

Working for a month to be selected for the trip to Charleston so he could sneak away from the school group and visit Vincent in the hospital there.

"Paco," Vincent had said as Paco finally stood by his bedside.

"Paco."

"Paco" was the only word he said, though. The only word he *could* say.

PACO STANDS *beside the bed looking down at his friend on the starched white sheets. Watches the pearl of drool escape the corner of his mouth and slide slowly down his chin. And he knows he can't leave him like that.*

He lifts Vincent's head and removes the pillow from beneath it. Then he places it over Vincent's face and presses down. Vincent fights back, claws with sharp fingernails, shreds Paco's chest. But he holds on. Watches the second hand on the clock over the bed swing up to the twelve as Vincent goes limp, stops fighting, and Paco screams inside his head, "Noooooo!"

HE KILLED HIS FRIEND VINCENT. But he didn't kill his friend Tiburón. A reptar did that. The reptar that had chased them both across the prison yard. Paco'd leapt through an open door into the safety of a building. Then he'd kicked the door shut in Tiburon's face.

If he hadn't, the beast would have killed them both. At least, that's what he told himself then. Still told himself now.

The image of Tiburon and the reptar bloomed in Paco's mind. He tried to turn away from it … and that's when he saw them.

Star and Noah.

They were standing in the background, ghostly figures in the shadows of his mind, just like they used to appear in his dreams. Standing there watching, seeing it all.

STAR TRIED to empty her mind, think of nothing but Paco. That was how she'd concentrated when she'd "read fortunes" back in New Mexico. But it didn't work. There was nothing but blackness. Even with the energy, the pulsing of whatever that strange "power" was between her and Noah, she couldn't find Paco. Searched, but couldn't …

And then there he was!

She found his mind, stepped into it.

And watched, horrified, saw Paco smother a blond boy lying on a hospital bed beneath a clock displaying the time: eight o'clock. She watched him kick a door shut, leaving another boy outside with a bloody reptar.

But she did way more that see, she *felt*, connected to the agony in Paco's mind.

Then Paco's consciousness became aware of her, of both of them. Noah was with her, holding her hand, and some part of Paco noticed the two of them, looked at them, though there were no eyes involved in the looking.

"Paco, I'm so … sorry."

NOAH WATCHED in horror as the boy on the bed clawed Paco's chest, ripped into it with bloody finger-nails. But Paco kept the pillow in place, kept it on the boy's face. Killed him. Then another image, a different boy running from a reptar, and Paco kicked the door shut in his face.

And in those images Noah felt so much pain wafting off Paco, it broke his heart. Paco hadn't wanted to do what he'd done. Killing the boy on the bed had devastated him, cut his soul to the bone. And left him scarred, literally — the scars on his chest, the skull, spider and snake. The boy on the bed had done that to him.

Paco saw Noah then, saw *both of them*.

Noah wanted nothing in the world so much as to comfort Paco, ease the pain in his heart. But he didn't know how. Instead, he said, "They told us you went back to Earth, but they lied. We're all still here, the three of us! We're still *together*."

Then Paco started to scream.

~

THEY SAW!

Star and Noah, they *watched*!

Nooooo!

Paco's whole mind was suddenly lit with a murderous red glow. Everything was the color of blood — his guilt, his shame, humiliation and …

Rage.

How dare they! He had told them to mind their own business, but they'd come here anyway. Tricked him, sneaked into his mind when he wasn't looking, when he was freaked out by being alone. And by their *betrayal*!

They'd left him here, cast him aside. Abandoned him.

But before they floated back down to home and hearth, they gave it one final shot, determined to get a peek into the darkness of his soul.

Their lips were moving, but like when they spoke in his dreams there was no sound. And that was a good thing, oh yes, indeed, because if he had heard their condemnation, if he'd had to listen to their self-righteous denunciation, he might have gone completely mad.

"Motherfuckers!" he shrieked, his whole being contorted in mindless fury. His face twisted in hatred, his teeth bared in helpless rage, so full of anger he could barely form words. "You motherfucking little bastards! Fuck you! Fuck you both!"

THE LIGHT WENT OUT, plunging them all into total blackness. The world around them vanished, leaving nothing to touch or see or hear. A void.

For Paco.

For Noah.

For Star.

Everything was gone.

Then light returned. Golden light.

PART II
On Earth

Chapter Sixteen

SAWYER DID A PRETTY good job when there were people around.

He'd had an early supper with his brother Taylor and his family — the boys, David and Samuel, and his wife Kelly Jo. Sawyer had followed his big brother around like a puppy when they were boys. Now, Taylor followed him around, or seemed to. When Sawyer's wife and daughter were killed in a fire four years ago, Taylor had been like an appendage, like he never left Sawyer's side. And after Noah was taken by the Astrals almost three months ago, every time Sawyer turned around he tripped over Taylor. Both boys had learned early and well that "family trumps everything." When family needed you, you showed up. You were *there*.

And Taylor was there, alright. Omnipresent.

In truth, there were days Sawyer might not have been able to hold it together if his brother hadn't been beside him, the glue that stuck him to the world.

But now, Sawyer was home — *alone*. And sometimes he went off the rails when he was alone.

This was one of those times.

He was in Noah's room. Not a good idea. But he had lost the battle to stay beyond the threshold of this room that he'd had to wage every one of the eighty-six days since the boy vanished — there by the pond with the warm spring breeze whispering out of the woods, carrying the scent of honeysuckle to sweeten the redolent black-mud perfume of the still water.

The sun had been sinking behind the mountain and Sawyer had been showing Noah and Gretchen how to skip rocks across the water. Gretchen's mother, Ellie, had returned to the house to re-make lemonade and Sawyer had looked at Noah there, standing on the bank of the pond with darkness settling in a veil around him, thought maybe he needed some alone time. So he'd left him there, started back to the house with the girls, when Gretchen turned toward him and screamed. It had happened so quickly, in an eye blink. A silver orb appeared above the pond. Out of nowhere, just there. And a golden glow of light melted away the darkness around the boy, settled over him and then took him away.

Noah's essence seemed so real here in his room. Even though he spent more time in the dormitory at the academy during the school year than he did here, this was still "home," a place for bedtime stories, where the boy's nearness afforded the luxury of standing in the doorway in the middle of the night and watching him sleep. There were a handful of

Noah's models sitting on shelves — unique structures so unlike ordinary buildings. Most of his models had burned with the house, and after the fire, the boy had lost interest in building things. Like he'd lost interest in just about everything else in life. His vellum lay on the floor beside the video game console that Sawyer'd intended to take to his nephew David to see if the boy could fix it. Several pairs of Noah's shoes lay in a jumbled, musky pile just inside the open closet door.

It was a sweet agony to be so close. And so far.

Sawyer understood that he needed to leave — now. Understood that you could go over the edge if you let yourself stray too close to the things that stabbed into you with such sharp agony you had to look down to be sure there wasn't really a dagger in your belly.

He had learned that lesson when Jessica and Rosileigh died.

He and Jessie and the kids had spent the week before the fire at Taylor's, housesitting and staying with his two nephews while Taylor and Kelly Jo took a fifteenth-anniversary cruise. They'd forgotten things, left some belongings behind at Taylor's — clothing, some of the kids' toys. After the fire, that was all there was, the only things left. Noah had had one change of clothes. That's it. Everything else had burned up. Sawyer'd had a clean shirt and a pair of boxer shorts and the work boots he'd taken off and left beside Taylor's back porch so he wouldn't track up the kitchen floor Jessie had just mopped.

Every breath after that taught him what he

couldn't do and remain sane.

He couldn't pick up Rosie's teddy bear, the one missing an eye, and feel its softness on his face, the way it had brushed against his cheek, back and forth, when she'd held it in her arms while he rocked her to sleep. He couldn't pick up the blouse Jessie had left hanging in Taylor's guest room closet. He'd found it there, yanked it off the hanger and buried his face in it and discovered he could still smell Jessie's perfume on it. Like she'd just taken the blouse off, was getting undressed for bed … and they would lie down together, touching each other slowly, a delicate dance, its rhythm faster and faster, making love so achingly beautiful the act seemed almost holy.

He had learned he couldn't do those things because when he did he began to lose his grip on himself and the world. On his very soul. The pain was so intense, he couldn't breathe. Literally. Could. Not. Breathe. The world would begin to gray out around him. He'd see the black shutters on the edges of his vision inching forward, getting closer and closer together. When the darkness on both sides slammed shut in front of his face, trapping him inside, he would die.

And he couldn't do that. He had to think of Noah.

Noah was how he got his breath back.

Noah was how he had made himself take Jessie's blouse to the big green Goodwill bin in the Baptist church parking lot. He'd done it at night, in the dark.

Had eased it gently into the slot, held it there, squeezed it and then let it slip out of his trembling fingers. He'd sat in his car afterwards, looking at the bin, yearning for the sweet release of tears that wouldn't come. He had taken Rosie's teddy bear to the hospital and snuggled it in bed beside Noah. But Sawyer never held the bear close, not even after Noah woke up and came back to him. Even then, he couldn't feel the softness of that bear on his face and keep his grip on his soul.

This was like that. He knew he shouldn't be here alone in Noah's room, knew that every sight, every smell and touch would create an agony of longing that could rip everything loose inside. Everything he was grasping with the fierce desperation of a man who knew if it came apart this time he would sink down into darkness and never find his way back out.

He felt an ache in his jaw from gritting his teeth, took a sip of air, a shallow breath, forced his reluctant feet to turn and his legs to carry him out the door and into the hall. He closed the door quietly behind him and leaned against it, gasping in the breath the pain in his gut had knocked out of him.

Noah would come back. *He would.* And when he did, Sawyer would be here waiting for him, strong and reliable, the rock the boy depended upon.

He drew in a shaky breath. And another. Then he walked through the house and out the back door to the porch. It was coming up on sunset, and sunset in the mountains was not the same as it was out there in the flatlands. In a few minutes, the sun would sink down below the wooded brow of Goose Creek Mountain to the west and after that the texture of the light would announce sunset by degrees. The sky would turn pink or gold or sometimes so red it looked like the mountaintop was on fire. But nightfall itself would creep in unannounced on little mice feet. The shadows would gradually grow thicker, darker, swell to meet each other to make solid black puddles of darkness beneath the trees. The sky's colorful dancing skirts would fade to blue, then a dark blue that would slip so seamlessly into black you couldn't mark its passage even if you were watching for it, and the black sky would break out in stars that looked as big and cold as chips of ice.

Sawyer rested his hands on the porch railing, looking out at the mirror of the still pond reflecting the dark shadow of the mountain reaching out to it. Pink edged the shoreline, doubled the number of reed stems with their shadows and—

A silver orb appeared above the pond.

Not there.

Then there.

Just like before.

Sawyer didn't gasp because he couldn't breathe at all.

Was he imagining—?

The bottom of the orb began to glow with a golden light.

Oh dear God—

Then Sawyer was running, stumbling down the

steps. He tripped, fell to the ground, scrambled up and kept running. His eyes never left the shoreline of the pond, gobbled up what he saw there in the orb's golden light.

The little boy in the light.

Noah.

Chapter Seventeen

Noah was there beside her and then he wasn't.

One heartbeat.

Two.

They'd been holding hands, searching for Paco's mind. They'd found it and had seen what he'd refused to share with them — and she knew why not. Of course, Noah hadn't just seen Paco put a pillow over the face of the boy on the bed. He'd seen/felt/understood what was going on inside Paco when it happened, how devastated he'd been. And Star had felt what Noah felt.

Then Paco had become aware of her and Noah. She saw an image of him turning toward them.

If she'd seen the face of the man who'd tried to kill her, maybe she'd have seen there what she saw on Paco's face. She hadn't, though, so nothing in her life had prepared her for a look of such pure rage and loathing. It stole her breath. For a horrifying moment he shrieked at them, but it was like in her dreams when she tried to hear what Noah was saying but couldn't.

Then all light vanished, and she felt that sensation she did when the Astrals were screwing around with them. Pumpkin whined pitifully and Star knew something was about to happen that the dog knew about, could sense, smell, feel — *whatever* — something she and Noah didn't know.

Then she felt the difference. The thing that Pumpkin had sensed/thought/smelled a few heartbeats before she did. The light was different. It wasn't the sterile, white, all-inclusive, from-everywhere-and-nowhere light.

The light was … *golden.*

She felt warmth on her face.

She smelled desert air with the scent of early morning when the flowers on the cactus hadn't yet withdrawn from the blistering heat.

A breeze that carried the aroma of sagebrush kissed her cheek and she could hear the lonely cry of a chicken hawk high overhead.

The light was *real*, too, from the sun instead of from some unknown source that sometimes tried to look like it was sunlight, but she, Noah and Paco could freeze the images and knew it was fake.

Her sandals crunched on sand and she put her hand out and felt the warm dirt. Pumpkin barked a single yelp of joy.

They were back. Falling Star Yellowhorse and Pumpkin had been returned to the Taking Place on the mesa. *They were home.*

Sinking down into the dirt, she pulled Pumpkin close to her and tried to orient her mind to the reality that it was over, that she'd survived a nightmare on an alien spaceship, that she'd made it back.

But not as who she'd been when she left — how long ago? In real time, she had no idea. For her, though, it had felt like years. Decades. When Star thought about the little girl who'd stood here with her dog in a beam of golden light a lifetime ago, it was like remembering somebody she had once loved who had died.

Star was back.

But Noah was gone, and the lack of him, his absence … it felt all *wrong*. It was like … a tooth missing and her tongue kept going to the spot that was empty and feeling around, wanting something to be there that wasn't. Noah's absence hurt with a fierce pain that stole her breath. The throbbing ache of the vacant space in her mind that had been occupied by Noah beat with a heartbeat pulse in her soul.

She tried to blank out all the painful thoughts, to concentrate on the single reality that she was home. She took one deep breath, let it out slowly. Then another.

Images formed in her quiet mind. A scramble, a jumble of familiar items — a jackrabbit and a chickadee, ants, lizards — and half-thoughts, incomplete, that she could make no sense of.

It felt like hearing Noah and Paco. But totally different somehow. This was foreign, totally *other*, but not in a threatening way. Different. Strange. Formless thoughts. Where could they possibly be coming—?

It was *Pumpkin.*

It was! Yes. Pumpkin.

She had heard murmuring in her mind like this when she was on the mothership. But she had taught herself as a child not to attend to the thoughts of family members, and on the ship the three of them had "agreed" to talk, to communicate with each other in their heads, but to go no further. And with Noah's and Paco's thoughts in her head she hadn't heard *this,* hadn't attended to this.

She was alone with Pumpkin now, though, here on the windswept mesa that overlooked the desert, and she could *hear* him. Hear *his* thoughts.

No, that wasn't it. Pumpkin didn't have "thoughts" like hers, just images. She concentrated on them, tried to make out what they were. What was her mind receiving from the dog's mind?

Well, it couldn't be what he was seeing, she didn't think. Dogs' eyesight was terrible, not as bad as being blind but not a whole lot better. They didn't see colors like humans, didn't see light and dark the same way or sharp edges. They saw blurry things, or at least that's what the Dog Whisperer Ramon Chavez had said.

She thought about the show called Man's Best Friend she had watched on the juke in Uncle Clyde and Aunt Mary Ellen's trailer house in Roswell a lifetime ago, remembered the part about a dog's sense of smell. She could picture the professor from some Florida institute on sensory research telling Mr.

Chavez that a dog's sense of smell was ten thousand to a hundred thousand times more acute than a human's.

"Let's make an analogy to sight," he'd said. "Say a dog's sight was ten thousand times better than a human's. That would mean that what you and I could see at a third of a mile, a dog could see just as clearly more than *three thousand miles away*."

Pumpkin's images grew clearer in her mind as she tried to concentrate on them, tried to "listen."

Papa Eagle Feather!

Papa Eagle Feather was here. Pumpkin saw …

No, he didn't see her grandfather. He *smelled* him. And the images he smelled were jumbled. He could smell Papa Eagle Feather here earlier today and yesterday. And other days. He had been here over and over in the past and Pumpkin could tell the difference between each visit. And Pumpkin could smell him in the future, too.

Pumpkin could smell him *approaching*.

She concentrated, saw an image that looked like a blobby Papa Eagle Feather. He was climbing up the trail that led here. He was at the bottom of it, starting up.

Pumpkin barked.

And the image of Papa Eagle Feather grew bright in Pumpkin's mind.

As if hearing the dog had caused something in Papa Eagle Feather to react and Pumpkin smelled the reaction. Had caused her grandfather to be happy and Pumpkin could tell.

"Star?"

She rose and turned toward the voice, pushing aside the images from Pumpkin so she could attend to the images her own mind created. The blurry form becoming larger as he approached. The smell of horses and leather and the clinking sound of his beaded necklace.

And then he took her into his strong arms. Star started to cry, hugged him fiercely, clung to him, breathing in the smell of dried sweat and the dust in his hair. Pumpkin barked again. He wasn't a yappy dog, only barked when he had something to bark about. A greeting bark. A warning bark. A frightened bark. A threatened bark. Usually just a yap or two and he was silent. He nuzzled his way in between her and her grandfather, wanting their affection.

The old man peeled Star's arms off his neck and put his hands on her shoulders and held her out away from him, looking her over, examining her.

"How are you?" The question had so many other questions in it she didn't know where to begin to answer it.

So she started talking, then found herself babbling, a streaming, nonsensical narrative she couldn't stem or edit.

"… white room made out of plastic … a burger from Burgatory with extra pickles … Noah, the boy I dreamed about, with blond hair and blue eyes who …"

"He was there, in the spaceship?"

"He had been dreaming about me, too … a bridge in the fog … white giants."

There were white giants. Tell me about them.

"When I dreamed about them, I also dreamed about this white skull and Paco had the skull on his chest and Noah described it to me. But not out loud, not with words. I could hear what he was thinking."

"Like you heard me, just now. I was starting to ask about the white giants—"

"And I heard your thoughts."

Star grew very still. Back here in the real world wasn't supposed to be new and different and weird. But, of course, it was — because she was different. This world would never be for her as it had been when she left it.

Star took a deep breath and tried to center herself.

"How long?" she blurted out. "How long was I gone?"

"One day short of three months."

Three months. That was both a preposterously long period of time and a ridiculously short one. Both at the same time.

Papa Eagle Feather put his hands on her shoulders.

"Are you hungry? Thirsty?"

She was neither, though she couldn't remember when she'd last eaten or what it had been or what she last had to drink.

"No, I'm fine. But Pumpkin might be …"

She found herself reaching into Pumpkin's mind as naturally and effortlessly as she would reach out and scratch him behind the ears.

He wasn't hungry or thirsty either.

"Is there anything you want?"

And there was. She hadn't thought of it until he asked the question.

"I want to visit … to go to——"

"You want to be near your Uncle Clyde. I will take you there."

He took her hand and led her like a little girl down the trail on the side of the mountain.

Chapter Eighteen

PACO COULD SEE nothing but light, white light. No, not white. Not now. It had been white, but now it was golden. Shimmering. Like the air around him was full of sparkling glitter that he could reach out and touch, catch a handful and it would run through his fingers like sand. He remembered that light.

And then the light was gone. There, gone. Blink. And with the light gone, his surroundings became visible. He sucked in a gasp, looking around, his eyes gobbling every detail, every tiny speck of visual information.

He was standing in … no, not in water. Not in a puddle. He had been standing in a puddle the day they … but there was no puddle here now. It had been raining that day. It wasn't raining now. In fact, the sun was bright, brilliant, hot on his shoulders, made him squint when he looked into the distance where the gigantic silver ball hung in the sky over Los Angeles.

He was back. This was real. It was *real.*

It was no longer springtime, though, with buds on the trees and a pleasant warmth to the air. It was dead-on summer, had been summer for long enough that the grass was dried brown and the crabapples on that tree had ripened and lay rotting on the ground. He must have been gone for months.

He reached up and felt the beard on his cheeks.

Or for five minutes in Astral time. Who knew? But however long it had been in real time, it had amounted to years of living. Noah'd grown two inch—

Then it all came back, slammed down around him with the sound of cell doors clanging shut.

Noah.

Star.

No.

No way in hell.

No motherfucking way in hell would he think about them!

They had seen!

A wave of horror washed over him.

They'd betrayed, abandoned him. How long had he been a captive after they bailed? Time there meant nothing. Neither did memory. He could have been there for—

No, goddammit. He was not going to think about them. Never. Again. *Never.* He would not let the conniving little motherfuckers rent space in his head. That was over. That was then and this was now.

And now was … what? Now was a little town in nowhere California located next to the prison where—

He had not thought those thoughts in so long he

expected the pain of the memories to knock him to his knees. It didn't. The Astrals had healed his body the instant he landed in that white room. And he'd believed at the time that they'd healed his mind, too, that they'd bathed the emotions associated with what had happened — what Spade Jackson had done to him — in a healing balm, as if years, decades had passed.

Now, he understood that hadn't been the Astrals. That had been Noah.

No.

Not. Going. There.

He shook his head as if literally flinging the thoughts away, then turned slowly in a circle. He was in a dead-end alley. He'd been chased here by the two cons, the one who only had four fingers, who'd mauled him through the bars that first day and Harris, the white con with the nightstick. They'd wanted to take "Spade's bitch" back to the prison. He had been standing here in a puddle, barefoot, shirtless, wearing sweatpants he'd stolen out of somebody's laundry room.

Now he wore jeans, a white tee shirt and — Champions. Thank you, Astral assholes.

He suddenly laughed. Not a full-bore belly laugh but a chuckle that left a smile on his face when the laughter was gone.

What must those cons have thought when the shuttle showed up over Paco's head and swallowed him in a beam of light? That must have scared the salt off their crackers.

"I ain't taking this shit no more, that's why I'm leaving. Anywhere's better'n here."

Paco spun around to see where the voice had come from, instantly alert. But there was nobody there. The alley was empty.

"You think nobody's going to notice you gone and come after you?" another voice said. *You dumb fuck.*

Paco froze. He could now hear the approach of footsteps on the sidewalk next to the street in front of the alley. Somebody was coming that way, two somebodies. He could hear them talking. But that's not all he could hear!

You planning on ratting me out, you motherfucker!

That was what the man was thinking!

A thrill of excitement and fear and anticipation rushed up Paco's backbone. He quickly moved behind a dumpster to stay out of sight.

"He won't notice if don't nobody tell him," said the first voice, full of menace.

"Why you say a thing like that, Santoro? Why you think I'd tell?" The voice was offended, aggrieved. *When you gone, I'm moving into yo room, and into that bitch's bed.*

"You tell and I'll come back, split you open at the bellybutton, leave your ole Eduardo's guts steaming in his lap."

Gotta be careful. Make sure they catch him, that he don't slip away.

Paco could hear the thoughts of the two men — Santoro and Eduardo — as clearly as he could hear what they were saying. The realization so stunned, surprised and thrilled him that he felt an anticipation he hadn't felt in … He had no idea when he'd had any feelings about the future, the next five minutes or five days except dread and fear.

He could hear what these men were thinking as clearly as ever he'd heard Star and Noah. *But they could not hear what he was thinking.* And there had to be something Paco could do with a thing like that. Surely that would give you some kind of edge you could use.

Use to what?

Yeah, to what.

What did Paco want? Now that he was back, now that he'd survived and been sent back, what did he want?

He wanted Spade Jackson dead.

He hated Spade Jackson.

He knew that the way he knew how bad it hurt to stub his toe. But he didn't feel the hurt.

Then he *willed* the hatred back into his heart.

He forced it to well up out of his guts. Welcomed it back, an emotion so pure, so blindingly bright it was like looking into the sun with both eyes wide open, seeing the power of it, knowing it was blinding you and not caring. One pure, simple, perfect emotion: *hate!*

Paco *hated* Spade Jackson.

Yes. And now he *felt* that hatred again, as he'd felt it standing in a puddle in the rain, prepared to die rather than go back.

That hatred had … faded … became a ghostly shadow while he was on the mothership. But he refused to think about what … no, *who* … had healed this mind as the Astrals had healed his body.

He summoned the feelings, relished the rush of heat as they surged through him and he was glad!

Paco *hated* Spade Jackson. He had sworn an oath, before the reptars had mopped up the prison yard with dead bodies — *including Tiburon's, no, can't think about that, won't think about that* — before the reptars had massacred half the inmates, that he would kill Spade.

And he planned to keep that oath. *He wanted to kill Spade Jackson,* would, in fact, do whatever he had to do, no matter what it was, to kill Spade. Hearing the thoughts of others … now *that* was a great first step.

He purposefully put a thought out there, searching for the one named Santoro.

You don't have to worry about him turning you in if you kill him. Dead men tell no tales.

One set of footsteps stopped, but the other continued another couple of steps across the entrance to the alley. Then the man stopped and turned around. He was wearing the uniform of a prison guard.

Chapter Nineteen

IT DIDN'T TAKE Star long to get on sensory overload, which was a strange thing for a girl who had spent the past four years of her life on sensory deprivation.

But it soon became too much, particularly the connection to Pumpkin.

As she bounced along the rutted road in Papa Eagle Feather's old pickup truck, the sounds and smells assaulted her senses and she remembered that smell was what the Astrals had forgotten when they had put her and the other two into first one environment and then another, that Paco had figured out didn't really exist anywhere besides in their own heads.

Smell was everywhere here, experienced in a way she never had before. The warm *smell* of the air. And the smell of ancient dust billowing up out of the old seat of the truck every time they bounced up into the air and bottomed out the almost nonexistent suspension system when they came down.

"Is this a road?"

"Define road."

"Where cars travel, vehicles—"

"No, this is not a road."

"So we're just—?"

"On a trail. Driving out across the desert."

That explained the collisions with yucca plants. She could hear them rattle when the truck grill hit them, the hard shells of their seeds like castanets in the hands of Mexican dancing girls. And she could hear the "cheeee-cheeee" cry of the prairie dogs, outraged by the truck tires' invasion of their burrows.

Tapped into Pumpkin's senses, the smells were so bright they might all be colored red and orange and chartreuse, everything so vivid, and her mind struggled to make sense of the images the smells produced.

Finally she had to shut it off.

With surprising ease, she purposefully did not attend to the images coming from Pumpkin and the tumult cycled instantly down to a background murmur. No, not surprising really. She'd taught herself when she was a little girl not to listen to the minds of her loved ones, and had done the same with Noah and Paco on the mothership.

Until the end, when she and Noah had reached out trying to find Paco … and stumbled into the nightmare he had never wanted them to see. Paco had screamed at them, but like in their shared dreams, the words carried no sound. But the rage on his face left no doubt what he was saying.

She'd wanted to explain, to comfort him. But the world had gone black.

And then it had gone golden.

Now Paco was … where? Still on the mothership?

No, he was back in California. He'd been sent home, too. They all had been. She didn't know why she was so certain, but she was.

Noah was in Kentucky and the throbbing ache of missing him brought tears to her eyes.

Papa Eagle Feather was quiet and they rode along in silence. He had never been particularly chatty. But she suspected he was being quiet now to give her space. Or maybe because he knew she could reach into his mind and was he covering up his thoughts so she couldn't.

No, it was consideration. He was giving her some reentry time.

She put her arm around Pumpkin, who sat on the seat between her and Papa Eagle Feather, and steadied him, so he didn't have to scrabble with his clawed feet on the old leather seat as they jolted along. And then she let the warm wind blow in her face and just was. Was back in her world.

Was home.

But it wasn't home. Home was where Uncle Clyde was and he wasn't anywhere in this world.

"You miss your Uncle Clyde, don't you?" Papa Eagle Feather asked.

Could he read her mind? No, her thoughts showed on her face.

"I never had a chance to …"

"To mourn."

She hadn't mourned, but she had been healed all

the same. Noah had done it with his touch. He hadn't taken the pain away — would never have done a thing like that because that would be ... what? Disrespectful? Would have discounted the importance of Uncle Clyde and how much she'd loved him. What his touch had done, instead, was grant ... distance. Space. Time. When in reality, there had been none of those. Though she'd never really grieved for her Uncle Clyde, the pain was like what she had felt for her mother years after she had been killed.

Noah.

At last, she let go and allowed her whole self to acknowledge that he was gone. The lack of him, his absence felt so very *wrong*. The presence of his absence was everywhere.

The bouncing pickup truck made one more massive lurch and then it stopped bouncing. They had come off the prairie onto a road and the riding was smooth.

"How far is it to Alien World?"

"There is no Alien World. It is gone."

Of course, she knew that, she hadn't been thinking. The monsters who had killed Uncle Clyde had burned it down that night. But somehow it remained in her memory as she knew it to be. The buildings, the petting zoo, the amusement park. The fact that it was gone would matter much more to a sighted person than it did to Star. She hadn't really "seen" it all the years she'd grown up there. And she would never see it now destroyed. So she got to pick. She chose the images of how it had been. She would cling to those in her mind as the reality of Alien World.

In the time it took to drive from the Taking Place in the mountains around Sedona to what remained of Alien World and Uncle Clyde's grave, Star talked a lot about Noah.

The longer she was away from him, the harder it was. She had last seen him only a few hours ago, in real time, when they had stumbled into Paco's nightmare. But instead of his memory fading in that time, it had grown more intense. In the beginning, she had likened it to a missing tooth, a gaping hole that you try to ignore but no matter how hard you try to ignore it your tongue goes there involuntarily, explores it, feels the pain of it.

Maybe she would dream of him. It was absurd, but the thought of seeing Noah in her dreams, even though that wasn't even real, was comforting in a way she could never have explained. But it wouldn't happen. Somehow she knew it wouldn't. She, Noah and Paco had been connected in their dreams before they became a hive mind on the mothership. They'd grown beyond that connection and wouldn't likely return to anything as simplistic as the background of a dream.

When they pulled off the highway, Pumpkin sniffed the air and the backwash of images sent Star reeling.

Fire, smoke, flickering flames licking up from smoldering cinders, burned wood, charred metal, soot, ashes, hot coals.

As quickly as she could, Star turned off the flow of images from her dog. Pumpkin was smelling the fire at Alien World in a historical flow of images even though all but a trace of what had once been there had been erased by the prairie wind and sand.

Even Star could smell the "old fire" scent of the place. She pictured where Papa Eagle Feather was driving, mentally adding back the buildings that should be there, past the Moon Glow Restaurant, the Greater Crater General Store on the other side of the center area from the museum and her astral readings room.

"Those giant fiberglass things, the statues are gone," he said. "Someone stole them."

"What would anybody want with *those*?"

The thirty-foot-tall figures were a part of the alien-themed layout of the miniature golf course. There'd been a lime green extraterrestrial with big black eyes and a spaceship — not the silver marbles that now hung in the sky all over the world, but the mythical, alien-invasion-movie version shaped like a saucer with a lump in the middle. There was an astronaut seeming to float in space and a fiberglass version of the wagon-wheel-shaped space station that had been occupied for more than a decade before both the United States and Russia abandoned it. Star had often wondered if it was still floating around in orbit out there. It must be. There would probably have been news about it if it had fallen back to earth. The thing was big enough to take out a lot of real estate wherever it hit.

"I think I saw the green alien one out on Interstate

40 near Albuquerque, sitting beside the highway with pieces missing, eyes poked out, broken-off limbs. Somebody's message about what humanity thought of aliens."

"Like they care."

They drove straight across the area that had once housed a petting zoo.

"What happened to the amusement park? The rides wouldn't have burned."

Star remembered hiding in the seat of the Ferris wheel when the men came with guns, shot up the place and killed Uncle Clyde.

"Still there. People have cannibalized the machinery to use for … who knows what. But the rides themselves are still there."

They drove all the way to the back of the property to the fence line and Papa Eagle Feather stopped the truck. On that horrible day and night Star had been in shock and had no real memories of where she and Papa Eagle Feather had laid Uncle Clyde to rest.

"After you … after they took you, I came back here, put up a cross."

Papa Eagle Feather took Star's arm and guided her, placed her hands on the top of the cross. It was about three feet tall.

Uncle Clyde was here.

Star dropped to her knees beside the cross. Dropped because her legs wouldn't hold her up anymore. Pumpkin came up next to her, leaned into her until she put her arm around him.

Tears streamed down her cheeks,

Papa Eagle Feather stood at the head of the cross, silent. Star could tell it was a simple cross, just two rough boards nailed together. Not painted. She was sure it didn't even have Uncle Clyde's name on it. She also knew it was temporary. Papa Eagle Feather had said that in one year, he would collect Uncle Clyde's bones and lay them with the bones of his ancestors.

"Thank you," she managed to get out. "For this, for the cross."

He said nothing. What was there to say?

Star got slowly to her feet.

"So, what happens now?"

"That's what *we* have to decide."

She felt a lump in her throat. Papa Eagle Feather had promised to look after her, to see that no harm came to her. He'd made the promise in the Taking Place and it was a sacred promise.

And then she knew.

"I ... I have to go," she said.

"Go where?"

"I have to go to Noah."

Chapter Twenty

THE SIGHT of the prison guard in the mouth of the alley hit Paco hard. The guards at Radcliffe Correctional Institute hadn't shown up after Astral Day. If they had, Paco and Tiberón and the other boys there that day as part of the Scared Straight Program would have been sent back to Los Angeles instead of becoming prey for a thousand animals. The rush of pure hatred Paco felt for the guard was so focused it felt like he could use it as a club to beat the man to death. He wanted to do that, to jump out and throttle the motherfucker.

Wait. Maybe he could.

Kill him, Santoro! Do it, now!

The footsteps stopped.

Paco realized that he was "shouting." Yelling in the man's mind and he instantly fell silent.

"What's the matter? You look funny."

"I … don't know."

The voice wasn't the cocky Santoro Paco had

heard only a few minutes before. The man sounded stunned, confused, maybe even frightened. His thoughts were a nonsensical jumble, reeling through his mind.

"It was like… I don't know. Seemed like somebody was talking, told me to …" His voice trailed off.

"Like who was talking?"

The one named Santoro approached the other man in the mouth of the alley and Paco was stunned to discover that he too, was wearing a guard uniform. And on closer inspection, he realized that the uniforms didn't make them guards. They had none of the guards' bearing, none of their swagger. The uniforms were dirty, not pressed. In fact, the one named Santoro only had on a guard's shirt. Instead of the gray pants that went with it, he was wearing jeans.

"It was the weirdest thing …" Santoro was saying.

"Somebody was talking? Who? What did they say?"

"I didn't say somebody was talking. I said it … *seemed like* somebody said something. Look, never mind, we got work to do and if we're late getting back, there'll be hell to pay."

I better tell Carver today. Santoro's getting squirrelly.

Paco understood that he couldn't shout into Santoro's mind, remembered how he'd felt when he first heard someone else's thoughts in his own head. He didn't want to sound like that, didn't want to sound like another person in Santoro's mind. He wanted Santoro to think what he was hearing was his own thoughts.

So he spoke softly, trying to sound like Santoro.

As soon as he sees Carver, he's going to rat me out.

Santoro looked disconcerted, but not as startled as he had before. He looked like a man who'd just had an idea, someone who'd just figured something out.

"You planning on having a little talk with Carver, are you? Soon as we get back, you gonna take him aside and tell him he's got a mutiny on his hands, that maybe old Santoro is sick of getting pushed around. That what you planning, Eduardo?"

"Why would you … what's wrong with you? Why would I tell Carver anything? That motherfucker beat the shit out of me once for showing up late. Why would I talk to him?"

How does he … it's like he knows, somehow!

"You don't look good, Eduardo," Santoro said, and began to advance slowly toward him.

What he looks is guilty, Paco whispered softly in Santoro's mind.

"Matter of fact, you look guilty, like maybe I caught you with your pants down."

Eduardo began to back away.

"What's the matter, Eduardo? What you scared of?"

"What's wrong with *you*, Santoro? You're acting all crazy-like."

"Only a guilty man gets scared when you figure out what he's planning. If you ain't planning on ratting me out, what are you afraid of?"

"I'm afraid of *you*, asshole. You're not acting right. You're nuts."

"Oh, that ain't what you're afraid of. You're afraid because you know that *I* know what you're gonna do as soon as you see Carver. You're going to spill your guts, tell him my whole plan, give him every little detail."

Eduardo turned to run then, but Santoro was quicker. Eduardo had made it only two or three steps when Santoro came up behind him and grabbed him around the throat in a chokehold.

"You think you was scared before. You don't know what scared is. I told you what I'd do if you ratted me out."

Eduardo tried to argue, struggled to free himself but Santoro held on.

"Let's you and me take us a little walk."

Santoro let go of Eduardo and he went down on one knee, gasping. Santoro grabbed his arm and shoved him roughly into the alley. He fell on his back in front of the dumpster. Paco had to move fast to keep from being seen, slipping between the dumpster and the buildings.

Eduardo looked up at Santoro, his hands out placating, his voice pleading.

"I don't know what's gotten into you. Santoro. I ain't done nothing. I ain't planning to do nothing. You *got* to believe me."

He's lying.

"No, actually, I don't got to believe you. You're lying, and *that's* what I believe."

Then Santoro pulled something out of his back pocket so quick Paco couldn't follow the action. There was a little clicking sound as the blade of the switch-blade slipped into place.

"Oh, Jesus, Santoro. Jesus God. You can't. I ain't gonna—"

Santoro plunged the knife into the other man's belly, then pulled the blade sideways, opening his gut all the way across.

Eduardo looked down in surprise and horror at the rip in his body where a river of blood gushed out, carrying with it most of his internal organs. Then his eyes closed slowly and he slumped back on the ground.

It seemed like Santoro sort of came back to himself then, maybe realized what he'd done, maybe questioned what it was that had led him to do it. He snapped the switchblade shut and stuck it back into his hip pocket. Then he grabbed Eduardo under the arms and began dragging him toward the dumpster.

"Need a hand?" Paco asked, stepping out into the light.

Santoro about wet himself.

"Who the fuck …?" He staggered back, fumbled in his pocket for his knife.

Paco wasn't armed, but neither was he afraid.

"I wasn't kidding. I'll help. You can't just leave him out here until somebody waltzes by on the street and sees him. Come on."

Paco leaned over and picked up the dead man's right arm. Santoro looked at him like he was a coiled cobra, but instead of going for the knife, he leaned over and grabbed Eduardo's other arm and the two of them dragged him toward the back of the dumpster.

"Put him inside," Paco said. And without waiting for Santoro's reply, he began to lift the dead man's body. His guts were streaming out the hole in his belly now and Paco had to fight the urge to vomit.

After a moment's hesitation, Santoro lifted the body up until the two of them could shove it into the dumpster. Paco dropped the lid down. It clanged with a finality that reminded Paco of the sound the doors in the prison made when they closed.

Now, I gotta kill him, too.

"Actually, you *don't* have to kill me, too," Paco said. "You can trust me. I helped you dispose of the body. I'm as guilty as you are."

"Who the fuck are you?"

What he didn't say was, "Who the fuck are you, *kid?*"

That tagline had been on the end of every sentence directed his way during his nightmare week in RCC. That it wasn't there now was enormously significant. Though Paco hadn't yet seen his own reflection in the mirror, he knew what he'd find when he did. He wasn't a kid anymore. Whether he'd been gone a month or a decade in Earth time didn't matter, he'd become a man in the bowels of an Astral mothership playing mind games with white giants. It wasn't just the beard that testified to that fact. So did his whole body structure. It might be that he'd just turned sixteen — finally old enough *now* to be sent to Scared Straight — but he no longer looked, felt or acted like the timid boy who'd been Spade's bitch. He was muscled like a man.

"My name's Paco," Paco said, but didn't hold out his hand to shake. "We got to get all this blood off. You know anywhere around here …?" Paco stopped. "There's an empty house down the block on the right. At least it was empty the last time I saw it. A washer and dryer there."

Santoro looked at him like he'd just grown a third head.

"Washer ain't gonna work without no electricity."

"There's water." Surely there was still running water. "We don't get this blood off, we might as well march" — he took a mental gulp — "up to Spade and say, 'Here we are, we done it, we killed Eduardo.'"

Santoro thought nothing then. His mind was blank. And Paco had to bite the inside of his cheek to keep from busting out laughing.

Then he came back to life.

"My place is only half a mile from here. We get there without being seen, I … I got clothes we can change into."

We. Good. Excellent.

"Out of your 'go bag'?"

The man's eyes looked like twin chocolate pies.

"Right now wouldn't be the best time to implement that exit strategy of yours, now would it? Soon as they figure out Eduardo's gone, aren't they going to come looking for you?"

"Yeah, I guess."

"The thing to do now is to act like nothing

happened. You just get cleaned up and go back to work. And when you get there, you ask Carver, 'Where's Eduardo?' like you got no idea in the world what could have happened to him."

Santoro stood like he was in a kind of trance.

It makes sense.

"Okay," he said. "I guess that makes sense. Come on."

He turned then and headed back down the alley to the street and Paco followed.

Chapter Twenty-One

THE NIGHT the men came and murdered Uncle Clyde, they had burned everything except the trailer. In the months since, the trailer had been ransacked. Teenagers maybe. Maybe just desperate people looking for food or supplies.

Someone had taken the chest of drawers out of her bedroom, but they dumped the contents on the floor before they walked off with it. So she was able to gather up some underwear and socks. She found shoes in the closet, all of them lone soldiers, no mates. Who takes one shoe and leaves the other?

She had never owned much, had few belongings and only a couple of things that really mattered to her. One was the Barbie Doll that had belonged to her grandmother. She searched through the debris, felt of every piece of flotsam and jetsam, and it wasn't there.

She had a charm bracelet that Uncle Clyde had given her two years ago for Christmas, and had added charms on birthdays ever since. A few days before the world came to an end, she'd knocked it off her desk and it had fallen between the desk and the wall. She kept meaning to get Uncle Clyde to get it out for her. Now, she pulled the desk out from the wall, felt around, and there it was. She squeezed it in her fist and willed herself not to cry. She put her meager belongings into a black garbage bag.

Sitting on the floor in her bedroom that no longer had a chest of drawers, with a bed frame but no mattress, Star waited for Papa Eagle Feather to return from "gathering up supplies" and tried to puzzle things out in her mind. There was much that her grandfather wasn't telling her. For starters, what had prompted his immediate agreement to go to Kentucky? Just leave everything he'd ever known behind and strike out on a dangerous thousand-mile trip to a place he'd never been.

He had not spoken for a time after she made her spontaneous pronouncement that she "had to go to Noah." She'd let it hang out there in the air between them, kept her mouth shut, did her best imitation of a cigar-store Indian. She hadn't begged or pleaded or tried to talk him into it. She just sat. If he refused to go, then … then Star would have to find some way to go by herself. She'd refused to intrude on his thoughts, respected his privacy. And she thought that somehow he knew she wasn't reading him, and he respected her for that, too. Finally, he had said simply,

"If it is where you should be, we will go there."

Road trip. The words popped into her mind. She liked the sound of those words. But it really felt more like a journey ... no, a *quest* ... than a mere road trip. Because it was not just across distance, across space. It was a journey back to where she was *supposed* to be though she'd never been there in her life. And back to *who* she was supposed to be, that she had never been until she and Noah had been together on the mothership.

Pumpkin stiffened. Images from his mind flooded into hers as she heard a truck pull up out front — bright, shining images. A horse. No, two horses. She got up and met Papa Eagle Feather at the door of the trailer.

"I am ready to leave if you are," he said.

"Tonight?" She had thought that they would strike out in the morning. Apparently, Papa Eagle Feather had other plans.

"Cooler. My truck has no air-conditioning."

Star didn't know there was such a thing as a vehicle that didn't have air conditioning. Traveling in it would be brutal in August when the daytime temperatures in New Mexico and Texas hung on three digits like a jacket on a nail. But comfort was not Papa Eagle Feather's only, and probably not even his primary, motivation for traveling under cover of darkness.

"Much has changed since you left, Star," he'd told her as they bumped along that afternoon. "The rule of law, it is no more. People have set up their own little kingdoms. Survival of the fittest. I know about the warlords west and north of here. Santa Fe has been taken over by Manuel Castilian and he has seized all the land around for hundreds of miles. In Colorado, a man named Nathan Andreas has established the "Andreas Nation." In the mountains, the Apache make their own law as they have always done."

The Mescalero Apache Indian Reservation was located in Ruidoso, New Mexico, a mountain tourist spot where the Indians operated casinos and luxury hotels.

"But east of here is … nothing, the Texas High Plains. I can't imagine anybody has claimed dominion over it. Who would want it?"

She pictured the flat, featureless miles of emptiness, probably deserted.

"I do not want to go farther south to Midland and Odessa, where the oil is. I am sure someone has staked their claim on that and I don't want to make their acquaintance."

Papa Eagle Feather's truck was so old he had to drive it himself, all the time. And it only got about fifty to sixty miles to a gallon of gas. But it did have a thirty-gallon tank and he'd gotten an additional tank somewhere with an additional fifteen. Without stopping for gas, they had enough to "make it all the way to Kentucky, change our minds, turn around and drive all the way back."

"Pumpkin smelled horses. Are we taking—?"

"They go where I go. Naki Kiiya and Chelee."

Star spoke very little Apache, had never been around those who spoke it for long enough to learn.

"In English?"

"Naki Kiiya means two-spot. He is a paint stallion,

brown, black and white all blended together. But on his face, there is a black spot around his right eye and a brown one around his left."

For some reason, that put her in mind of the skull, the tattoo on Paco's chest, the one made by scars his dying friend had carved into his chest.

"And Chelee … that one took me many moons. I smoked much peyote and had many dreams." He paused for a beat. "Chelee is Apache for horse." He patted her arm. "They get great gas mileage."

Star hadn't realized how tired she was until the hum of the tires on the asphalt and the gentle vibration as the truck headed up US 70 to Portales began to eat up the miles.

"It's a little over a thousand miles from Roswell to Jessup. Traveling on back roads at night, no big cities, stopping to hunt for game and feed the horses — five days, a week maybe. Depends on the river."

"What river?"

"The Mississippi. We have to cross it somewhere and bridges will likely be a problem."

She must have looked mystified.

"In a world with no laws, and you're the bad guy, wouldn't you look at a bridge over the biggest river in America and think, 'hmmmm, maybe me and the boys could take it over, charge people to cross, or maybe just not let them cross at all.'"

Nothing like that had ever crossed Star's mind.

"The last I heard — and news is sketchy and unreliable — the military out of Ft. Campbell had taken over the Caruthersville Bridge between

Missouri and Tennessee, keeping it open, but who knows."

As they drove north from Roswell to Portales, Papa Eagle Father had laid out the route for her in great detail, talking more than she'd ever heard him say at one time in her life. Explained why he intended to "puddle-hop" from one national forest or wildlife preserve to another, avoiding large population centers and providing game he could hunt.

"Why are you telling me all this?"

He didn't answer right away.

"You need to know where we are and how to get to where you're going."

He didn't say where *we're* going and she got it. He wanted her to be prepared to find her own way there if she had to, if something happened …

She let that go, listened to his monologue, the road hum and the sound of his voice soothing, hypnotic.

They hadn't even turned east from Portales toward Muleshoe, Texas, when sleep took her. She was leaned up against the front door of the truck cab with Pumpkin sprawled on the seat with his head in her lap, nudging his nose under her hand to get her to pet him.

Occasionally, a car passed, going in the opposite direction. And it was a product of half-sleep, or paranoia, but it seemed that the cars were hurrying by, scurrying through the emptiness from one dark place to another under cover of night, hiding. Frightened.

She awakened somewhere in the darkest ditch of the night, driving through emptiness. The dashboard lights, if there were any, were so dim they cast only a pallid glow into the black interior of the cab, too dim for her to see even a pale blob of illumination. She straightened up in the seat, shook her head to rid herself of the gauzy mantle of sleepiness and tried to think how she could start the conversation she wanted to have. She couldn't come up with any way except blurting it out.

"Why did you take me to the Taking Place?"

Chapter Twenty-Two

Noah had not expected he'd sleep well his first night back home in his own bed.

Back home in his own bed.

It was true and real, but every so often he found himself checking to see, was this just another simulation, maybe to see how he would react to going home and seeing his father again? Had the Astrals wanted to test that to find out—?

No, this was real. It had smells, and the stupid Astrals always left smells out of their simulations. And he needed to go to the bathroom. And he was hungry.

After he had shown up on the bank of the pond, his father wouldn't stop touching him, holding his hand, tousling his hair, a spontaneous hug. That's how he knew it was real because the Astrals wouldn't have known how to fake that. He wasn't sure how he knew that, but he did.

After supper, Dad made spaghetti and that special

sauce … not some secret recipe but just dumping two different store brands together in a pan, and after a bath and pajamas that smelled like sunshine, his father had sat on the edge of his bed for a long time, talking, telling him about going to visit Hillsdale College, his friendship with Garson, who Noah had met but barely knew, certainly didn't know the man was an expert on Ancient Aliens. When his father told him about the shuttle showing up at the college, he didn't ask … hoping … not wanting to say … and sure enough, it was only titans, the white giants with smiles that looked like they'd learned how from a manual. Which they probably had. No reptars. He would tell his father about reptars, about it all, but just not right now.

His father seemed to understand that, knew it was all too fresh and he felt too tentative yet to relive his experiences on the ship. So his father had done most of the talking.

And sometime during his father's talk, he'd fallen asleep. He didn't remember being sleepy, didn't even remember where his father had been telling him the story of moving Dr. Garczonski out to the academy and then he was just gone. Effortlessly.

His sleep was dreamless and he woke up feeling better than he had in … he didn't know how long. He felt good. And he felt unutterably lonely. He had somehow expected to see Star when he opened his eyes. He'd expected to feel her thoughts that seemed just as natural as hearing his own. But where she had been was a void, an empty spot, and it hurt to go there.

Not seeing Star ever again was just … he couldn't countenance it, he wouldn't consider it. Somehow, some way, he would get to Star. He just … would, that's all. He would.

He had awakened to the smell of bacon frying and wandered into the kitchen in his pajamas, barefoot, boasting an award-winning case of bed head to find his father making a breakfast that would have fed three boys his size.

"Hungry?" his father signed.

Noah looked at the still-growing stack of bacon.

"Not *that* hungry."

His father laughed merrily and Noah suspected he'd have been just as delighted if he'd said, could have said, Rumpelstiltskin or toe jam. He was as glad to see his father as his father was to see him. And so unutterably glad to be home where things were real, people were real, situations were real and … yes, even danger was real. He'd never have made it through all the unreality without Star.

"After breakfast, we'll go out to the academy."

Noah must have said with his face what his heart felt. Reluctance. Dread. Disappointment.

"I know that place has … that the last time you were there the memories were pretty ghastly, and …"

He stopped what he was doing, crossed to Noah, put his hands on his shoulders and got down on one knee in front of him. "Noah, if I could, I'd protect you from every bad thing in the whole world. I'd never have let you … what happened at the academy. And going up in that … a spaceship, for crying out loud. I'd protect you from all that. That's what fathers are supposed to do. That's my job. But I can't. I am so, so sorry, but I just can't."

Noah could hear unshed tears in his father's voice and the goodness — that's what it was, what it had to be — pulsed off him with every word. He thought he had never loved his father as much as he did right now and he threw his arms around his neck and squeezed so hard he knew he must be choking him. But his father didn't pull away. Just wrapped his arms around Noah and squeezed back.

Noah let go first. His father stood, wiped at his eyes where Noah saw tears that hadn't fallen.

"Zion Academy isn't the same place it was three months ago just like you're not the same person.

His father gestured to his hair and it was the first that Noah thought to consider how different he must look, hair down his back, and bigger, too. He didn't know how much bigger, but his pajamas were at least two inches too short and so tight they were almost uncomfortable.

"Now, Brother Sebastian is running Zion Academy."

Noah smiled at that. He loved Brother Sebastian. Everyone did.

"Why can't I stay here with you?" Noah signed, knowing the answer as he did so. Because there was nobody there to look after him after Mrs. Bailey, who shouted to make him hear her, left. And his father was working so many hours, he'd seldom be home. Still, he wanted to be—

"You can't stay here with me," his father said, then big dramatic pause, "because I won't be here."

He smiled at Noah's puzzlement.

"I have a room at the academy," he said. And Noah was so surprised he didn't know what to say.

"When you were … when they took you, I couldn't stay here by myself. I was …" He began to pace, ignoring the eggs he'd just made that were getting cold on the plate. "It was so empty here. So Brother Sebastian suggested I take a room at the academy. At the time he offered, he said it was because of fears there would be another attack on their supplies like the one the night before … and I believed him. Well, I wanted to. Now, I know he didn't want me there so I could help him, he wanted me there so he could help me cope with my worry about you."

"So you … we live there now?"

"Just about. I stay there more often than here, but … now that you're back, we'll move both of us out there, everything. Now, Zion Academy will be home."

On the drive out to the academy, Noah thought to ask how the sheriff could live outside of town and still be on call 24/7. His father shrugged.

"It's not ideal. But it is what it is. I live there. And if my response time to problems in Jessup is fifteen minutes instead of five … it is what it is."

"Whatever happens next … that sounds like some things have already happened. What …?"

He saw his father's face tighten and he let it go. His father was giving him time to process, wasn't pushing to know everything that'd happened to Noah immediately. Noah needed to show the same consideration to his father.

Chapter Twenty-Three

Santoro's "place" was a neat little frame house on the outskirts of Clarksburg. Well, it had once been a neat little frame house. The yard was overgrown with weeds, though you could tell that at one time it had been landscaped, strategically spaced bushes that now sprouted stems somebody should have clipped off months ago so they'd keep their shape. There was a fenced-off area that obviously had been a flower garden in the front yard, though it was just weeds now. And when they went around the house to the back door, Paco saw that there was a vegetable garden in the back yard, and it had been cared for and pruned. He saw ripe tomatoes, pole beans, a few stalks of corn, some cabbage or lettuce, and what were probably carrots or potatoes, he didn't know what a potato plant looked like on the top side.

"Nice garden," he said.

They were the first words he had spoken since they disposed of the body in the dumpster. They had passed a couple of people but the people had averted their eyes. If they saw the blood, they didn't let on, would never comment on it to anybody. Paco picked up thoughts from them, townspeople who were a combination of frightened, angry and resigned. Mostly resigned. They had memories, if he'd cared to delve into them, of watching their town be taken over by the escaped prisoners from RC, and the pictures were ugly. The cons had descended on the town like locusts, taking whatever — and whoever — they wanted, leaving the occupants to fend for themselves.

Clearly, many people had been killed, and the ones who hadn't had been "taken prisoner," forbidden to leave the town, forced to stay there and return the place to something approaching normal. The people who ran grocery stores had to open them, had to take customers, and the people who owned clothing stores, shoe stores, the electricians, plumbers, hairdressers ... they all had to go back to work, fill up the gaps where absent coworkers — ran off before the occupation or dead — had left vacant.

Paco learned a lot from skimming through the minds of the people they passed.

One woman had memories of gang rape. She was a small woman, eyes averted, walking like she was still suffering injuries. She might have been pretty once. It was impossible to tell that now.

The people he passed carried images of convicts tearing around town on souped-up motorcycles they'd stolen from the Honda dealership on the outskirts of the city. Images of them walking into homes all over town and taking whatever they wanted.

"Yeah, well I got to keep it nice," Santoro said.

Paco heard his thoughts about the "rules" for the convicts who now lived in the town, about how they had to help with the production of food by keeping up the gardens that were everywhere in the little burg. In Clarksburg, the countryside turned rural and many residents had kept up with their rural roots by planting gardens and the cons kept them going, watered and gathered the produce. If the original residents still lived in a house, they'd been ordered to plant a garden, to dig up their fine grass lawns and plant vegetables. And they were required to turn in their produce to the warehouse on the back side of the prison, which must have been converted into some kind of distribution point for food stuffs.

Paco had listened in amusement as Santoro walked along beside him, considering first one plan to kill Paco and then another. And other thoughts that were a little deeper, memories of the house when they approached it, the day he had shown up with two other cons and evicted a family with three kids. The ones who must have played on the kiddie seesaw, little tunnel, monkey bars, and ridden the bicycles and tricycles he saw discarded in a corner of the back yard.

The man had tried to stop Santoro from putting his family out and Santoro had shot him in front of his wife and children. He'd then given her half an hour to "get all your clothes and shit" out of the house so he could take it over.

He hadn't let her attend to her husband as he lay dying. But he didn't linger long. Santoro would have kept her on to service him, but she was fat and unattractive and there were younger women to be had … at least he'd thought so at the time. That was back when he'd still thought all the cons were going to be able to live like kings in the captured town. Before the "rules" were handed down, before he and the others watched a "ruling class" of cons emerge who made the rules, had a bunch of grunt cons to enforce them — not just on the citizens of Clarksburg but on the other ex-convicts as well.

At the top of the food chain was Spade. The image of him came into Santoro's mind at one point and Paco had reacted like he had stepped on something burning, had literally jumped back.

Which occasioned a new round of how-can-I-kill-him thoughts in Santoro's mind.

And he could kill Paco. Of course, Paco would get a little warning from his thoughts, but warning wasn't good enough if you didn't have any way to fight back. He needed to con this con. Get him to decide to keep Paco around and alive while Paco planned his next moves.

Clearly, this guy was not the sharpest knife in the drawer.

When they arrived at the house, they went around to the back door because he'd "had to nail the front door shut." He and the other cons had probably kicked it in when they first raided the house. By that time, Santoro had recovered from the "shock and awe" Paco had occasioned by appearing behind the dumpster and helping him dispose of the body. And had settled on how he planned to kill Paco and go on with his plans to leave the "employ" of the prison and the little town and strike out on his own in the "outlines," which apparently referred to any area beyond populated cities and towns.

The penalty for "deserters" when they were caught was death, but the manner of it could range from a bullet through the brain, to hanging, to being beaten to death. Depended on the mood of the higher-ups who happened to capture you.

They stepped into the kitchen and the stink was nauseating. Filthy. Food left to rot on the dirty dishes in the sink. Paco recoiled and Santoro muttered, "Cleaning lady comes Friday."

Paco caught himself before he laughed at the joke, which wasn't a joke. There was some poor townswoman who went from one filthy house to another, cleaning up the messes the escaped prison animals had made.

"It won't work, you know," Paco told him matter-of-factly as Santoro closed the door behind him and began easing his hand toward his back pocket for his switchblade. That caught him off guard.

"What won't work?"

"Your escape plan. You won't get halfway to Bridgeville before they set the dogs on you."

He'd pulled the thoughts from Santoro's mind

about the "dogs," the cons charged with keeping the peace in this brave new world.

Santoro was dumfounded.

"How do you know that?"

"Which? How do I know that you're planning on going to Bridgeville or how do I know you won't make it there?"

Santoro just looked at him.

"Let's just say I have friends in" — he paused and gestured toward the ceiling — "*high* places."

"Huh?"

"The Astrals, you stupid fuck. I was one of the people they abducted. And I came back … *a changed man.*"

Santoro just looked at him, curious, but unbelieving.

"The Astrals are how I know about the Jeep you've got hidden under the tarp in the garage."

Now Santoro was speechless.

"Ain't no crime … to have a car."

"No, but it is a violation to use that car to make a break for it, which is what you're planning to do."

Bullshit. This guy's crazy, insane.

"My *large white friends* have told me you also have three cans of gasoline stashed under the tarp with the Jeep and you think that'll be enough to get you to Bridgeville where you can get more. The dogs will get you before you get that far, and even if you did, you'd be shit out of luck. There's no gas in Bridgeville. Actually, there's not really a Bridgeville anymore."

Fear seized him, but before the panicked intent to

pull out the knife could completely form in Santoro's mind, Paco said, "Wouldn't try that, if I were you. You've seen what the Astrals can do when they're pissed." Half the inmates of the prison had been massacred by reptars when an idiot in a guard tower opened fire on a shuttle.

A jumble of tangled thoughts and emotions so filled Santoro's mind then, he was paralyzed. Paco saw more than the reptars killing inmates. He saw images of shuttles hanging above buildings, blinding lights, and the buildings disappeared. No rubble, just gone. Now *that* was impressive. Images of reptars tearing into a line of soldiers somewhere — jumbled images, clearly whoever was taking the video had been hauling ass at the time. Excellent.

Paco pushed his psychological advantage. He had to set himself up as the man in charge. Right here, right now, or Santoro would remain a constant threat to him. And he wouldn't be of any value, either.

"I know everything about you, Santoro. I know everything about everybody. I know you were the one who stuck the shiv in that guard's back, but you let Roselli take the fall for it. Roselli wouldn't be too happy to find that out, seeing as how he got fifteen years tacked on his sentence because of it. You raped Robertson's woman, slit her throat so she couldn't tell. You stole Hartnell's Vellum, broke it and stuffed the pieces into the hole in the kitchen wall."

He leaned close and whispered the rest. "You have very detailed fantasies about raping little girls — real little ones. Kindergarten. Or younger. You get turned on every time you see one that doesn't have breasts yet."

Santoro's face had turned deadly pale, his eyes huge.

"How could you possibly know …?"

"Like I said, my saber-toothed friends and I — we know everything about you."

Holy shit. It's real.

Paco pushed the thought into Santoro's mind. *This guy's dangerous. I better not fuck with him.*

"Okay, fine. I get it. What do you want from me?"

"Right now, I'd settle for a sandwich and a change of clothes. What's today?"

"Wednesday."

"What's the date?"

"Hell, I don't know. Middle of August sometime."

Either it had been about three months … or a year and three months. Or ten years … no. Things on Earth hadn't changed enough for that. Three months Earth time. Way more than that to Paco.

"You got running water, I'm gonna take a shower." Paco turned to go find the bathroom. "You need to do something about that blood on your shirt."

Little son of a bitch. I'll slit the motherfucker's—

"Touch a hair on my head and there'll be a reptar chewing through your door before my body hits the floor. You've seen those shuttles do their *not-there/there* number, right? Travel so fast you can't even see them." Paco walked away. Didn't even turn as he said, "Get cleaned up. We got a lot to talk about."

Chapter Twenty-Four

THERE IT WAS, the question Eagle Feather Yellowhorse had been waiting for, maybe even preparing for since he saw the little girl and her dog together on top of the mesa, the image he had seen in his mind a thousand, thousand times in his seventy-two years.

"Why did you take me to the Taking Place?"

"Because I knew they would come for you there."

"How?"

The word sounded haunted and frightened, but her body language showed only calm, the strange, otherworldly calm that pulsed off her like heat from a pot-bellied stove.

"I saw it in a vision before you were born."

She was visibly surprised by that, but her response was still muted, not the reaction of a typical eleven-year-old child. Of course, there was nothing "typical" about Falling Star Yellowhorse. Never had been, really, and certainly wasn't now.

Eagle Feather was still feeling his way around the

"difference" in the child, the change wrought by three months in an alien spaceship.

She was bigger, she'd grown, looked like a couple of inches, maybe, which was a helluva growth spurt for three months. But who knew about "three months"? Who knew how long she'd been gone in the time frame of creatures who could bend time, shape it — what was it that scientist had said on the juke — "make it stand on its hind legs and do tricks"?

Her hair was longer, too, he thought. And there was an indefinable physical difference in her face, a maturity that shouldn't have been there, but was.

It was the stillness, though, that struck him. The centeredness. The quiet, the way she seemed to make silence more than the absence of noise, make it a positive force, an aura wrapped tight around her. As he'd bounced across the desert with her from the Taking Place, grateful that she was blind so she couldn't see him studying her, he had the crazy notion that if he reached out his hand, he could touch the silence and it would feel like warm smoke.

"Before everybody's Astral apps broke out with measles, the things my grandfather told me that had been told to him by his grandfather and his before — were just folk tales, legends about 'white giants from the sky.'"

It wasn't only the Apache, or even just the Mescalero Apache — almost all native American tribes had legends, *oral history* about white gods. For the Choctaw, the stories were about a giant white race they called the Nahullo. The Comanche, who hunted buffalo on the plains stretching out beyond his pickup truck into the darkness told of a race of white men, ten feet tall, that the Great Spirit had wiped them and all the rest of the people in the world out when the giants taught men to forget justice and mercy. The Navajo called the regal race of white giants the Starnake, the Piute called them the Sitecah and they were cannibals.

"They were *gods*, not aliens, a shading of difference, but important."

Star sat silent and still. He watched the rush of cool air in the window set her hair not caught up in the ponytail to dancing around her face and he thought it must be tickling her nose. But she didn't move to brush it away.

"I grew up on the Mescalero Apache Reservation outside Ruidoso," he said. "My grandfather, Silver Moon, was a shaman."

"What's a shaman?"

"A holy man. Maybe in another culture it would be called priest, or perhaps witch doctor. What it meant to us and our tribe was that he was a man who knew things he couldn't possibly know that he'd learned when he went up into the mountains, smoked peyote and talked to the Great Spirit."

Eagle Feather described for Star the "tribal manhood ritual" that he had in later years come to believe might have been only the Yellowhorse family's tradition. The father and son would go alone into the mountains. The son would be given peyote to smoke, then sent out to speak to the spirits, who would give him his tribal name in a vision.

"My father was given the name Great Bear. I never knew him. He was a soldier who died somewhere on the other side of the planet. My mother, Little Dove, was pregnant with me, and my grandfather Silver Moon took us into his house and raised me to be a shaman. He taught me the old ways, told me all the old stories that only the shamans knew. One of them was the legend of the white giants from the sky who came to Earth and found mankind corrupted, so they wiped all trace of humanity from the earth, and started over with only a handful of people, our ancestors."

The road out in front of the old pickup truck was empty. Not another set of lights anywhere in the distance, and on this endless prairie, headlights could be seen for miles. There were no lights at all anywhere — clearly, whatever had provided electrical power to this portion of the Texas High Plains had gone down. It was almost possible to believe he was driving through the empty expanse of deep space.

Eagle Feather stole glances at Star as he spoke, but found no response of any kind readable on her face. Her blind stare was fixed somewhere out in front of them in the unknowable darkness and whatever effect his story was having on her was not evident on her face.

"On the night of my manhood ceremony, my grandfather took me to the top of the mesa, to a place I'd never been before, and told me for the first time about how he had gotten his name. He described how he had smoked peyote and gone out into the woods. And he had seen" — he paused, but only for a single heartbeat — "a great ball appear suddenly in the sky. It was late in the afternoon, with the sun on the horizon, and the ball was not like the moon."

Eagle Feather gathered himself.

"The ball hung low in the sky, above the mesa—"

Star finished for him.

"—above the Taking Place," she said, awe and wonder in her voice.

Keeping his voice level with effort, Eagle Feather continued.

"He said that the silver ball hung there in the sky, and then a golden light shined down on the mountain … *where a little girl stood with a dog.* And as he watched, the little girl and the dog vanished and the ball was gone in the blink of an eye."

Star appeared to stop breathing. Pumpkin sat up from where he'd seemed to be sound asleep with his head in her lap. He nuzzled close to her and she wrapped her arms around him and squeezed.

"There's more. Tell me the rest of it."

"My grandfather said that his grandfather, Two Moons, who had also been a shaman, had had the same vision. And his grandfather, Silver Light, before him. And his grandfather before him. On back into the dark of history. They all had the same dream on their manhood night — a silver ball hanging over the mountaintop. A golden beam of light. A little girl and her dog vanishing into the light."

Star said nothing for a time, just held tight to Pumpkin. When she did speak, her voice was so soft it was hard to hear above the wind whistling into the cab though the open windows.

"What did you see on your manhood night, Papa Eagle Feather?"

"Not the same as the others. There was a silver ball in the sky above the mesa. Only it wasn't sunset, it was sunrise. There was no little girl on the mountain-top. But then a golden light shone down from the silver ball, and a little girl and a dog *appeared in the light*."

When Eagle Feather had described his vision to his grandfather, the old man had said nothing, but instead of packing up and going back down the mountain to the village, he took the boy back to the tent and the next night, the two of them smoked peyote again.

"That night, I went out into the woods, sat down beside a tree and waited. It was cold and I was shivering, and then a great eagle descended out of the night sky and perched on a limb above me, looking down with eyes that seemed both wise and terrible. When Silver Moon found me, I told him about my vision. He stood staring at me, then he began looking around on the ground, searching … and he found an eagle feather."

"And did that *mean* something?"

"He said the feather proved I had seen a *real* eagle. And that meant the vision sent to me by the Great Spirit had been the one I'd had the night before. The Great Spirit had spoken to me then, and sent an eagle the next night to prove it. He said the spirit had shown my ancestors a little girl taken off the mesa, but had shown me that the little girl would return."

"Did you believe him?"

"At the time, yes. I was only thirteen. He said there were other … prophesies … about a little girl named Falling Star. He was absolutely convinced the little girl would be my child, his descendent, made me swear an oath, a sacred promise at the Taking Place, that I would name her Falling Star."

"Only that didn't happen."

"Nope. Silver Moon died when I was nineteen. I got married and when my first child was a boy, I decided that the stories of my grandfather were just stories, legends. They didn't mean anything."

He paused again.

"Your grandmother and I tried to have more children. Tried for years. But your father was the only one. Then he married and had a little girl. Of course, I didn't believe … and yet …"

Eagle Feather smiled a rueful smile Star couldn't see.

"When I told your father I wanted him to name you Falling Star, he laughed and said your mother already had a name picked out. Did you know you were supposed to be Elizabeth Nicole?"

"Why wasn't I?"

"Eventually, I changed his mind."

"How?"

"I told him if he didn't name you Falling Star, I would disown him. Legally. He would no longer be a

Mescalero Apache. Which would mean he would not be entitled to the government checks every month, his cut of the revenues from the Ruidoso casinos on tribal land."

Eagle Feather pictured the anger on his son's face, the young man who'd declared himself "John Henry" Yellowhorse, instead of Running Wolf, a name Eagle Feather had picked out of a hat because the boy laughed at participating in the manhood ritual.

They rode along in silence for a time.

"I still didn't believe it. Even though I made an enemy of my son for life just to make it happen, I didn't believe it. Then the spots appeared on the Astral apps. And when they said the ships were *round* … The message I got from your Uncle Clyde, it was almost like I'd been waiting for it, like I knew you would need to reconnect to your Apache heritage."

"Because of the … prophesies."

It hadn't been a question. He nodded, then remembered she was blind.

"Yes. My grandfather told me about them … and remember, for most of my life I thought they were just legends."

"About … *me?*"

The almost-a-wail incredulity in her voice — that was the first time since she'd come back that she actually sounded like a little girl. He told her that other shaman in their family line had for generations claimed that when they smoked peyote as a part of their religious ceremonies, they were given dreams, visions and predictions … from white giants.

"The white giants had blue eyes, and no hair. And there were many of them, as many as the stars in the sky, but they thought with one mind. They were the ones who came to the earth, saw 'what displeased them,' wiped humanity off the planet and started over."

"Did they see … others? Not white giants, but—"

He saw her shudder.

"Horror creatures, nightmares with needle teeth and eyes that changed colors, that made a purring sound and a sucking sound."

"They're called reptars. The white giants are titans."

"So they were there? You *saw* them?"

He'd seen news footage of them attacking soldiers at some army base somewhere, mowing them down. Still …

"I saw them."

He felt his breath catch in his throat. It was true, then, all of it. If what the shaman had been seeing for centuries was real — Star had *seen* them! — then there was no reason not to believe the rest of it.

"One of the prophesies is that a little girl 'named for the heavens' would go to the white giants and return with a gift that would save humanity from destruction."

Star's face snapped toward him as if she were looking at him in surprise.

"I didn't come back to Earth with anything I didn't leave here with."

But she was wrong. He could see that now.

"Oh, but you did. You came back a different you."

"A different me is a gift?"

"I went to the Taking Place every day for three months. Hoping every day you'd be there. I watched interviews on the juke, reporters asking the families of the other people who'd been abducted how they felt, what they thought, and they were all terrified. But I was never worried about you. If the visions of you leaving were real, so was the one about you coming back. You *did* come back, and so …"

"… so you think that means the prophesy about this gift is also true, this *something* I have that will save humanity?"

There'd been a time when Eagle Feather Yellowhorse put the Great Spirit right up there with Santa Claus and the Easter Bunny. Now he knew different. He didn't like it, of course, not even a little bit, but he did have to accept it — the Great Spirit had orchestrated events that were unfolding now, had "ordained" it to be. That was reality, and it pinched at his psyche like a new pair of boots pinched his toes until they were broken in. It was going to take a considerable amount of time before the reality of the Great Spirit's meddling in the affairs of humans was "broken in" enough so he didn't flinch every time he thought about it.

But it was useless to waste his time trying to force reality to fit inside his own belief system. It just flat-out didn't anymore. He might not want to believe in the Great Spirit, but the spirit existed whether one particular Apache warrior believed in him or not and liking or not liking that reality didn't change it.

He didn't have to think before he answered Star's question.

"Yes, I do. I believe the prophesy."

Chapter Twenty-Five

PACO SLEPT the sleep of the dead. He hadn't realized he was exhausted, until he took that shower. That hot shower. With real water in the real world. It had drained all the energy out of him. It was all he could do to remain strong, and seem normal, while he probed the man's mind. He spent the night at Santoro's, after he dug out some clean sheets from the closet that surely were left over from the previous occupants and put them on the filthy mattress the man had been sleeping on. He sent Santoro back to the prison to finish out his shift, and then with instructions to do some other little tasks that Paco needed done. After Santoro left, Paco dug around in the cabinets until he found a can of Presto Soup, popped the top to heat it up. It was tasteless, but the glorious hot liquid was a thousand times better than the perfectly flavored fare in the white boxes — had it even been real food?

Who'd have thought what he and Star and Noah had done on the mothership would be Paco's ticket to everything he'd ever wanted in life. And what he wanted in life was death — Spade's. That was number one on his agenda. Other things would fall into place along the way as he dedicated himself with a single-minded rage born of humiliation and pain to the total destruction of everything that was Spade.

He even knew how he would kill him. And what he would do to him before he killed him. But that was getting out past his headlights. He was a long way from accomplishing his goal. He could see a clearly lighted path to get there … shit, it was as broad, wide and obvious as that yellow brick road in that stupid vintage musical his grandma Rosa watched every—

Grandma Rosa. What had happened to her, when the shit hit the fan on Earth? He had technically been a runaway, and therefore a juvenile delinquent, for the six months of his life before the law busted him for selling a nickel bag and hauled his ass into court. He'd seen her that day, sitting in the back of the courtroom, a look of hurt and disappointment on her face that had made him want to run to her and beg for her forgiveness.

Where was his grandmother now? What had happened to her? They said there had been riots and fires and looting in every major city in the world. Los Angeles could turn out that kinda shit on every second Tuesday of the month, so how much worse must it have been when there was a real reason, and when the ranks of those doing the rioting, burning and rock-throwing had been swelled by John Q. Citizen and his wife, scared, desperate and stupid.

He felt a sudden stab of compassion for the old woman, and good little Catholic boy that he was, that was immediately followed by that most Christian of all responses — guilt. He should have been there, helped her.

But he'd been busy, okay. He'd been busy getting raped, and then getting abducted. Hadn't had a whole lot of free time after that.

He did now, though. Should he go looking for her, try to find her, find out what had happened to her? Rescue her?

Not a chance. Maybe the old Paco would have responded to the cry of compassion. But the new and improved, yes, definitely improved version of Paco just flat out didn't give a shit what had happened to the old crone. If she'd wanted him around to look after her when the shit hit the fan, she shouldn't have signed those papers that had him shipped off to hell.

His first order of business for the day was to take the temperature of the town and of the prison guards and cons who'd taken it over. He left the house early, wanted to watch the town wake up, and so he wandered. First through the residential neighborhoods, taking note of the condition of the houses. More than half of them looked either deserted, or like someone was living there who hadn't been the original residents. Only a few of the houses appeared to be in the condition they had been in on the day all the world looked at the Astral apps and saw the alien armada coming.

From the residential neighborhoods, he wandered

into town and walked up and down the streets. Most of the stores were closed. No fancy dress shops open here, or doodad places for the tourists, or barber shops, or beauty parlors. What was clearly still open were three bars along Main Street plus a fourth farther down that appeared to be new. He didn't know if there was law enforcement of any kind in the town except for the escaped cons and the guards. Even so, he was careful when he let himself in the back door of an already-looted clothing store and bagged up some things to wear.

Then he stayed in the shadows, not that anybody was paying any attention to him. The townies who were still there had downcast eyes and shoulders hunched. There wasn't a decent-looking woman anywhere on the street; either those that were had already been taken to the prison, or the females left in town made certain nobody thought they looked attractive.

During his walk, he listened to the thoughts of the people he passed. The townies, and a handful of cons. By noon he had learned everything he needed to know.

Spade had taken over the prison and the town right along with it. The place had had four thousand residents at one time. The ones that had remained, of their own free will or not, had been turned into Spade's servants and slaves, or forced to do whatever their normal job was to keep the wheels on the infrastructure that kept the town and the prison running.

But he wasn't just trying to gather information about what had happened in the town since the cons took over. He was trying to get a general feel for the townies. He hadn't realized he was doing it at first, but then it occurred to him that he had been seeking out those who felt like the man he had enslaved yesterday and the one he made Santoro kill. Paco was sensing *temperatures* from people. He knew what warm felt like. But Paco had discovered as he wandered around the town was that there were a lot of people as inclined toward a chill as he was, into whose minds he could reach. People he could influence as he had influenced Santoro. To help him kill Spade, and set himself up as king of the mountain he intended to push Spade off.

Chapter Twenty-Six

STAR AWOKE to the sun streaming straight into her face over the hood of the truck. She could feel the warmth of it, even squinted into the fierceness of the glow. They must have been traveling due east and it was sometime just after sunrise.

"Hungry?" Papa Eagle Feather asked, and the question released a wave of hunger and her stomach growled. When had she last eaten? She didn't know, but it was clearly a long time ago.

"I could eat a horse," she said. "Present company excluded. Where are we?"

"Coming up on 'Scenic Vernon' just on the Texas side of the Red River."

"Scenic?"

"That's what I said. Seen—*ick.* We'll find some-where to stop on the other side of town. Stretch our legs and eat a bite."

Leg-stretching wasn't high on her list of to-do items, but going to the bathroom was. It was daytime now, and there seemed to be a little more life around them than there had been at night. She heard a few cars passing, and in Vernon itself, she could see the featureless blobs of other vehicles. Even though she had never been here before, and knew the High Plains wasn't heavily populated, the sense of emptiness was everywhere around her. There had once been more people here than there were now. Where had they gone?

They continued to drive into the rising sun after everybody's legs were thoroughly stretched, and after a breakfast of jerky and cheese. She wished she could have had some input into the supplies Papa Eagle Feather selected but she was sure he knew what he was doing and that a box of Chocolate Wizards probably wouldn't have made the supply cut even if she'd been there to plead for it.

She would see Noah soon. The thought warmed her from the inside, the way the hot wind blowing in the window warmed her on the outside. Today was going to be a scorcher and she knew it wouldn't be long before Papa Eagle Feather found somewhere to hole up during the heat of the day. They'd passed the first day in a barn. The second day had been cooler and more pleasant. Papa Eagle Feather had found an orchard! They'd pulled the truck into the shade of the apple trees, and quickly realized that wasn't a good idea. Apparently, there'd been nobody to pick the apple crop and the fruit had fallen to the ground around the trees. The two horses smelled the fruit and Papa Eagle Feather realized he'd be fighting them all day to keep them from making themselves sick on the bounty of apples. So he'd found an abandoned house with a small corral where he put the horses. The two of them had lazed on the porch swing and rocking chairs, listening to the multi-toned buzzing of cicadas in the bushes.

After they crossed the Red River into Oklahoma, Papa Eagle Feather plotted a course that would take them well south of Oklahoma City, and well north of the Fort Worth/Dallas area. Traveling mostly at night, there would have been little for Star to see even if she hadn't been blind. There had never been a large population here, and after Astral Day, there was hardly anybody at all.

Whenever they stopped, the images from Pumpkin were thick, powerful and colorful. She wondered if she'd ever be able to catch more than a fragment of the information they provided, ever be able to reach through the pile of them to the necessary one and not attend to the others.

In just half a minute's attention, she'd learned that:

Jackrabbits had been here — two of them were sheltering in a hole a few feet from the back of the truck. There was a snake under the rock about fifteen feet away, and more to Star's horror, a tarantula in a shallow hole next to a yucca plant. An armadillo — she thought of Uncle Clyde's description of the creatures as "rats in body armor" and felt a sad ache that threatened to send tears down her cheeks.

They passed one day in the Ouachita National

Forest north of Hot Springs, Arkansas, went northeast from there and discovered, to Papa Eagle Feather's vast relief, that soldiers from Fort Campbell had, indeed, secured the Caruthersville Bridge across the Mississippi River. The river formed the border between Arkansas and Tennessee and they went north from there. When they passed a sign Star couldn't see, Papa Eagle Feather read it for her.

"Welcome to Kentucky."

Star wanted to cry for joy.

It wasn't particularly spectacular when it happened, though Star really had nothing to compare it to. She had never before been in a vehicle when it "blew an engine," which was the cause of death Papa Eagle Feather would record on the death certificate of the old truck that had served him faithfully for many more years than Star had been alive. There was a sudden clunking sound that grew louder and louder and she could smell an acrid smoke blowing in through the windows from under the hood.

Papa Eagle Feather said nothing as the engine stopped, died, and he guided the truck and horse trailer off the road onto the shoulder. Uncle Clyde would have issued a stream of creative and colorful obscenity over the circumstance, but her grandfather said nothing except a clipped, "Blew the engine," before getting out of the cab of the truck and unloading the paint horse named Naki Kiiya and the black stallion named Chelee out of the horse trailer behind.

Star bit her tongue to keep from peppering the

man with questions. She wanted to use her questioning right, such as it was, sparingly, save it for the things that mattered. So she merely commented,

"It was an old truck. How many thousand miles did it have on it?"

"Just over one point two million."

Star almost choked. She didn't know any vehicle got that kind of mileage.

"I kept it going long past when it would have been put out to pasture, nursed it along, performed rituals over it that granted it long life and excellent health."

One of the problems with being blind was you missed so many of the visual body-language clues people transmitted with every word they spoke. She was far better than any sighted person at reading the nonverbals she could hear or feel, but dry humor and sarcasm were hard to pick up when you couldn't see raised eyebrows, tightened facial muscles. Was he kidding? Star decided that was a question she didn't have to know the answer to, so she'd save her interrogation, her assigned lot of questions, to finding out information she did have to know.

Papa Eagle Feather got the tack out of the back of the truck and the front of the horse trailer and began to saddle up. As he was doing that, some kind of large vehicle showed down as he passed and a man called out "need any help," like he might or might not be willing to offer it personally but might be willing to see if he could find somebody who could.

"Engine's gone," Papa Eagle Feather said and then

the man stopped and reversed down the highway to where they were standing.

"Looks like you're not stranded," he said, apparently indicating the two horses.

"Would you be interested in making a little trade?" Papa Eagle Feather asked.

"Maybe." The skepticism on that one word was thick enough to spread on toast. "What kinda trade?"

"The tank on this truck is only about half empty, means there's still about fifteen gallons left. And I got cans with another fifteen in the back of the truck." Papa Eagle Feather must have gestured toward the horses. "Won't do me any good now. Might be willing to trade it to you for what you got by way of equipment."

The man was silent, considering. It occurred to Star that he didn't have to agree to give Papa Eagle Feather anything. All he had to do was wait until she and her grandfather rode away and then help himself to whatever they left behind that they couldn't carry on horseback.

But apparently they'd happened upon an honorable man.

"I got binoculars, the kind that see at night, the infrared kind," he said. He had ammunition, too, that he'd be willing to part with. Along with some Magna-Power bars, almost a whole box full.

"Deal," said Papa Eagle Feather, and while the two of them transferred items from the dead truck to the still-alive one, Star stood by the horses where her grandfather had led them out into some grass to let them graze.

When the man had driven away with his bounty, Papa Eagle Feather got ready to saddle up. He had turned Naki Kiiya into a pack horse, and distributed their supplies in bags on her back and strapped across her hind quarters. Then set Star in front of him on the saddle he'd put on Chelee. A saddle. There were probably Apache who would ride a horse with nothing but a blanket on its back, but Papa Eagle Feather wasn't one of them.

She wanted to ask him if they were going to try to find another vehicle. When she edged at the question, not asking it outright, he had said only that they couldn't afford to purchase another truck, and gasoline might not be available. What they needed to do was continue to travel forward, even if they had to walk every step, which he didn't think they would.

"Something else will come along. It always does."

Star knew her grandfather welcomed any chance to get out of his truck and into the world under the heavens and the wide skies. She knew that *about* him, not *from* him. She had purposefully not looked into her grandfather's thoughts, as she had done when she had read her grandfather's desire to know about the white giants. The once-clear thoughts she could hear in Papa Eagle Feather's mind had grown softer every day. She had to listen to hear them, the way you lean into someone who is speaking in a quiet voice. His thoughts were "speaking softly" and she wondered if her ability would fade out altogether with time. She hoped so. She didn't want to hear the thoughts of others talking in her mind. She only wanted to hear Noah.

Sometimes Papa Eagle Feather described what they were passing through as the two of them rode together on Chelee. But Star got most of her information from Pumpkin, who was trotting along happily beside the horses, stopping to sniff a pile of deer dung or a dead animal — details about the environment she didn't really want to know. This place was … well, if smell had been color, to Pumpkin this place was a kaleidoscope, every color in the rainbow and combinations of them, always changing and shifting. She didn't concentrate on understanding the sea of smells she dived into every time she attended to Pumpkin's mind. And she needed to do that. It was a mental discipline she needed to master. She had learned the mental discipline of not connecting to family members when she touched them and after a while it became second nature to her. She had applied it to images from Pumpkin's mind and it was easy to block it out and exclude it. But when she chose to attend to it, the flood was literally overwhelming.

Flowers, plants, rabbits, bugs, deer, antelope, mice, trees, running water, tree bark, gophers, skunks, foxes, birds … the list went on and on. It was all a jumble of smells from yesterday and the day before all tangled up with the ones from today, which she did think were a bit brighter than the others, their color more shiny. But she could have been mistaken.

She didn't want to tell her grandfather she was

hungry, didn't want to bother him. But the truth was, she was famished. Her mouth watered at the thought of a hamburger and French fries from Burger Nation.

By mid-afternoon, they stopped beside a stream to allow the horses to take water. "We'll make camp soon. I need daylight hours to find game."

He described the area where they had made a campsite, in the lee side of a rock face on a hillside, so their campsite was protected by the rocks from the wind and anything else out there on three sides. He built a fire and returned in less than an hour with two rabbits to cook over it. She hadn't heard any gunshots so he must have used his bow and arrows.

They traveled all the next day without incident. And the next. They had entered a place Papa Eagle Feather identified as Land Between the Lakes, a national recreation area between Kentucky Lake and Lake Barkley. Like Ouachita National Forest, here they would find campsites laid out for them, complete with grills and picnic tables. Several times the next day they stopped for Papa Eagle Feather to hunt and he'd bagged rabbits for supper. But there would be more than rabbits tonight, and it was getting dark when they crested a hill and he pulled the horses up short and described what he saw.

Star had known something was coming up that involved humans from the images she got from Pumpkin.

"There's a meadow and a creek and on the other side of it is a public campground. Not deserted like the other two we've passed. This one is inhabited.

Motor homes, campers. I didn't figure most people would be in the mood to go camping these days.

Star suspected she and her grandfather made quite a pair, two Indians on horseback, riding a black stallion and leading a paint horse no less.

"I would say, *we come in peace*' but that didn't work out too well the last time my people said that to yours," Papa Eagle Feather said, and she heard a gentle flutter of laughter. "So how about, 'I smell coffee and I'd sure like a cup if you can spare it.'"

Chapter Twenty-Seven

Noah had been home for more than a week and he was finally going to get a haircut! Most of the kids at the academy had amateur haircuts now that looked like somebody was learning to cut hair and they'd been the guinea pig. But Dad had asked old man Marcum, who'd been a barber in the Navy, to cut Noah's shoulder-length blond hair. As usual, his father had sensed without Noah having to tell him, that Noah was anxious to look "like he used to," wanted to return to *normal*, and a professional haircut — though it was surely the last one he'd ever get — would help.

On the way into town from the academy, Noah asked how Jessup's residents were faring and his father's jaw tightened. It was just about impossible to drive and sign at the same time, and equally hard to catch everything Noah was signing, so usually Noah didn't try to talk to his father then. But he'd been anxious for some alone time with his father to find out what had been going on in town, so he unfastened the seatbelt — which set the stupid buzzer to buzzing that was so loud even Noah could hear the vibration — then fastened the hook with the lift-up-the-tab part so it would shut up. Then he sat on the edge of the seat looking at his father, almost full on.

"Talk slow," he said. "I can understand you."

Looking at his father's face, he caught probably eighty-five percent of what he said by reading his lips. But that percentage was big enough — fifty percent would have been big enough — to know there was trouble in store for Jessup.

"The residents are … it's getting hard for them now. And they're scared. Some people have electricity, the ones who installed solar panels on their roofs — the school, hospital, everything that runs on solar power. But a lot of people, maybe most people, didn't install solar panels on their homes. Everybody's got water but there's only so much water in that tank, and when it's gone …"

Noah thought of the big white tower with Jessup printed on one side and Tigers on the other, for the Jessup High School football team. It was enormous, hard to imagine it running out.

His father must have followed his line of thought.

"The water company has big pumps that pump water from Ryerson Creek to refill the tank. We can't generate the volume of electricity you need to run those pumps, so when the tank's empty — and by my calculations, that'll be sometime this week, it's getting low now and I worry about whether it might be contaminated so I issued a boil water alert, but that only works if you can boil water, and some people don't have power to do it. Boiling water over a fire … that's just one more thing … one more thing."

He paused and Noah could see worry etched in the lines around his mouth.

"When the tank runs dry, there won't be water in people's houses in Jessup. Out in the county where there are no city water lines, people have wells or springs. They'll be fine. But in town — that doesn't mean they'll die of thirst. But they can't turn on the tap to get a drink of water, no showers, no flushing toilets, no washing machines, no dishwashers. They'll have to haul water from the pond in the park, or Damron Creek. We've got it all set up so people can come by and fill up containers. But life changes when you have to work — hard — just to have water to drink, figure a way to wash clothes, take baths. It'll be hard and folks have figured that out. They don't like it. Not one bit."

"What else?"

His father chewed on his bottom lip when he was upset and he was doing that now.

"I locked down the grocery stores and rationed, but all that ran out after a couple of weeks."

He read Noah's expression of confusion.

"Think about how food gets to a grocery store — say a can of beans. There is a complex system that makes it all happen and if any part of the system breaks down … farmers have to grow the beans, then there are people who pick them, take them to a processing plant where they're put into cans, then a truck that delivers them ... All that involves people going to work and doing their jobs. But after Astral Day ... people stopped going to work at their regular jobs. You're a garbage man — would you go pick up garbage same as usual when you think in a week the world will end? Why — because you get paid? In money ... little pieces of paper that don't mean anything anymore?"

Noah began to understand. Things he'd always taken for granted, things everybody took for granted, all depended on people all over the country doing their jobs. When that stopped happening, it all fell apart.

"We're a whole lot better off than most, a whole lot better! Every major city in the country — hungry, desperate people — they all became war zones, riots, hundreds of thousands of people have died. Lots of cities burned to the ground. When firemen quit going to work ...

"In Jessup, we'd have been hurtin' turkeys if it weren't for Best Bread Ever and Stephenson's Meat Packing. We've worked out a system — it still has a lot of kinks, but we have farmers bringing in their beef cattle for slaughter, and then we're freezing it in all the big freezers in town."

Best Bread Ever was a small bakery that employed fifty or sixty people, local people, made bread, rolls, doughnuts and—

"And Best Bread isn't making doughnuts anymore," his father said. "We've worked hard, pulled together — well, mostly pulled together. They had storehouses full of flour and they converted to making loaves of bread, different kinds. Distribution has been … no money, remember. We just give the loaves out, and bread was about all there was for a time early this summer, before the gardens started producing."

His father smiled broadly. "Wait'll you see the city park and the baseball and soccer fields, the football field at the high school and junior high — they're all gardens now. We plowed them up and planted this spring and tension eased considerably when there were fresh vegetables to eat. You won't see a yard with grass anywhere in town, either. Every family has their own garden, and they're storing away food for the winter, canning and freezing — those with solar power, that is."

His father got a faraway look, apprehensive, and stopped talking.

"You're worried about this winter, aren't you, Dad?"

"Did you learn how to read minds when you were up in that ship?"

As a matter of fact, he did, but now wasn't the time to talk about that. He had not read his father's mind, had willed himself not to, like Star said she did with her family.

Star.

His heart ached so bad from her absence, he felt like crying. But he kept it together and listened.

"Did you read the story of the grasshopper and the ant when you were little?"

Noah shook his head.

"As the story goes, the industrious ants worked hard all summer, storing away food for the winter. The grasshopper didn't work at all, just hopped around, doing his thing. When winter came, the ants had food. The grasshopper came begging to them because he had nothing to eat and was starving."

His father took a deep breath.

"There are both ants and grasshoppers in Jessup. And this winter, when the grasshoppers start getting hungry … And the only gasoline left in Jessup is under strict guard, for official use only — police cruisers, the ambulance and fire trucks. We have enough now to get by, but that won't last forever, and I can't imagine where we'll get any more when the supply is gone."

His father ran his fingers through his hair then and Noah noticed a healing scar on the back of his right upper arm. That hadn't been there three months ago.

"What happened?" he asked, indicating the scar.

"Oh, that." His father grimaced. "Garden clippers. I was breaking up a fight over a head of lettuce." He must have seen the look on Noah's face because he laughed. "It was one of those 'you kinda had to be there' moments."

Chapter Twenty-Eight

I DREAMED IT LAST NIGHT.

Just like that.

Star knew they would run into a group of people out here in the woods because she dreamed it. That was probably her ability to see the future on autopilot while she slept. Or it could be she had been given the dream by the Great Spirit.

Eagle Feather Yellowhorse had never really gotten used to Star's "special ability." That wasn't the reason he popped in and out of her life like a yoyo, but that the yo-yoing did make it possible for him to sidestep that particular little quirk in his only grandchild's personality. Well, he better get used to it. From now on, he was going to get a full-bore dosage of it. Star was his responsibility now. He was all she had. If he didn't look after her, take care of her ... a little blind girl alone in the world today wouldn't last long.

He had spent hours and hours during the months

she was gone thinking about that, about what it meant — to him and to Star.

That realization raised, in equal parts, fear and trepidation, and a sense of wonder and anticipation. He had a reason now, a purpose. He mattered, and he had not felt that in a very long time. He had spent a lifetime watching the old ways fade away, kept alive by an ever-dwindling group of desperately poor people who every year cared less and less about their heritage and more about finding a way to fit into a world not designed for them and was at best indifferent and condescending to them, and at worst hostile and aggressive.

After his wife died a slow, agonizing death from pancreatic cancer, her final days spent in a hospital where she was 'indigent" and treated accordingly, Eagle Feather had retreated to the desert wilderness. His son had gone off to college and then off the rails, married an Apache girl from Ruidoso one night when they both were drunk and left her for someone else — maybe even before he sobered up, but definitely *after* he'd gotten her pregnant. She'd been as shiftless as he was, died in the car accident that blinded Star when the child was three years old. Star had been put into foster care then because his worthless son couldn't be bothered with a child. Eagle Feather thought about it then, thought about stepping up, taking custody, raising the child himself.

He told himself at the time that the reason he didn't was that he had no way to support her. He had no "marketable skills," nothing he could parlay into a regular paycheck at the end of every month. He had clawed and scratched at life as a young man, scrambled to keep the wheels on, worked intermittently as a ranch hand and on an oil rig, trained horses, herded sheep, and *literally* "dug ditches" for a while until his only son "Johnny" — that's the name he picked for himself, and in truth his Indian name Running Wolf meant nothing anyway because he had refused to go out and "do that dumb Indian thing" on the mountainside when he turned twelve — moved off the reservation and out of their lives. Maybe that's what killed Morning Dove, not the cancer — losing her son.

So what he told himself about why he didn't claim his granddaughter after Johnny bailed on the child was that he had no way to support her, any better than he had supported his wife and son. And that was true, absolutely true. He knew the old ways, lived by the old ways, only worked at a job when he had to get money to purchase the few belongings he couldn't get from the land.

But there was an ever-truer truth than that. He was afraid. He was afraid he would fail the precious little girl he fell head over heels in love with the first time he saw her. That's probably what he held against Clyde Baker — he hadn't had a whole lot either, but he made a place in his life and his home and his heart for Star and for other little kids whose worthless parents abandoned them. Clyde did what Eagle Feather had been unwilling and unable to do.

All that was over now. And in a crazy way of the world and the Great Spirit, he had not only been given a second chance to matter in the life of his grandchild, his 'old way skills' that were totally unmarketable in the modern world with robots to make sandwiches in burger joints and cars that drove themselves, were infinitely valuable in the new order of things. Now, what Eagle Feather Yellowhorse knew mattered again, mattered more than stock portfolios or tech savvy or celebrity status.

And he mattered not just because he knew how to survive. Eagle Feather mattered because he knew *who* Star was, who she *really was*, and how important the small blind child might be to the lives of … who knew how many people.

He'd always said he believed the old Apache "oral history." Raised by his grandfather, he'd said he believed the story about the white giants from the sky and the Falling Star, the Apache to whom the Great Spirit would give a gift to save humanity. The white giants had been real. The taking had been real. They'd brought her back — just as the prophesy foretold, and he had no doubt that the Great Spirit had orchestrated that. She had brought something back from her time on the mothership — an alien spaceship, for crying out loud. But the aliens had not given her the gift. The Great Spirit had given her something that mattered, maybe used the alien giants and monsters to do the giving. But what Star possessed was a gift from the Great Spirit. A gift from … God …

that would save humanity. He couldn't have said what he thought the gift was. Sometimes he believed the gift was simply "who Star was," the person she had become during her time with the Astrals. Sometimes, he thought it was even more specific than that, but trying to figure that out was trying to figure out the ways of the Great Spirit and he knew better than to attempt that. What he did know was that he believed she was destined to save the world, in some literal sense he couldn't imagine, which meant that he had to protect her, make sure nothing kept her from using that gift.

The future of humanity depended on it.

Right … the future of humanity. No pressure.

After his lame attempt at humor had made the pair of them seem less menacing to these people, they were invited to join them "for dinner." Which consisted of a scrawny elk that hadn't been properly gutted and that they'd already cooked way too much for there to be any flavor … or food value left in it. But that black carcass might be all they had.

The first man to approach them was a man with curly black hair. He was broad-shouldered, with a full black beard.

"My name's Nick Wilson," he said, extending his hand. "This is my wife, Michelle." The woman had straight blond hair down to her waist and she was pregnant.

Eagle Feather introduced himself and Star — and Pumpkin, of course, who became the instant center of attention with his wagging tail and I-love-all-humans-great-and-small-so-let-me-lick-your-whooooole-face personality. It was good the dog drew the focus off himself and Star. Eagle Feather was used to it taking people awhile to realize he hadn't made the name up as a joke. He wasn't dressed in deer skins or anything like that — old jeans that were rapidly getting too big for him because he just kept getting skinnier and skinnier the older he got — a chambray shirt, a well-worn Stetson and equally well-worn boots. But he did have his hair in fat braids that lay on his shoulders, tied at the ends with small pieces of rawhide. Star was usually mistaken for Mexican or even Italian, but in his company people made the leap pretty quick.

He answered Nick's unasked question.

"Mescalero Apache from Roswell, New Mexico."

"We're from, well, most of us are from Nashville," Nick said. "The Schwartzes are," he smiled at an old couple sitting nearby in lawn chairs, "they're strays we picked up by the side of the road."

An old man rose, walked over and extended his hand. "Fred Schwartz," he said, "and that's my wife, Lottie. Actually, we were hitchhikers." He grinned with a mouthful of perfect teeth — implants or dentures — at Nick. "They only picked us up because Lottie was standing there looking sexy, showing a bit of leg."

"Fred," she cried. "Stop that."

"We ran out of fuel just outside Ashdown, north of Texarkana. We were taking the smaller roads to get around the city. We're from Shreveport and we were on our way to our son's. He has a little farm outside West Memphis, Arkansas. But Bessie didn't have much gas" — he pointed to a dilapidated motorhome parked nearby — "and we were dumb enough to think we'd just fill up the tank after we got on the road."

It began to feel a little like a wedding reception with him and Star in the receiving line. Eagle Feather was so uncomfortable he wanted to climb out of his skin. This was likely more humanity than he'd been in close proximity to in … who knew? He lived by himself in a tent on a mesa *for a reason.*

A black couple approached next, Ian and Jessica Maddocks — whose three children Rachel, Lamar and Latricia were on their knees scrambling to be the next one to pet Pumpkin. Two of the other gang of children gathered around the dog looked so identical Eagle Feather thought he must be seeing double. Their parents appeared next, Roberto and Carmen Lopez, whose twins were Lucy and Linda, and they had an eight-year-old, Bobby, running around some-where. Carmen noticed then that the boy was off somewhere and went looking for him.

There were other families, too — the Brentwoods, Bill and Selma and their two children, Art Whitlock and his wife Charlene, the Shepherds — he missed the man's name, but his wife was, no kidding, Tinkerbell. Her husband called her Tink. Harvey and Loretta Richardson, Bill and June Maxwell. And a handful of single men and women. They all came up to introduce themselves. In the end, there were probably forty or fifty people. And it seemed odd at first, until he noticed that they hadn't really come to meet and welcome him at all. They'd come to meet Star. They all gathered around her, chatting with her and with each other. It almost seemed like there was something about Star that *drew* the people to her.

Chapter Twenty-Nine

Paco stood at the back of the room, not making his presence obvious. Listening.

It was terrifying.

He *couldn't hear* the thoughts of the people as well as he had heard them just twenty-four hours ago. It was like the volume on a juke had been turned down. When he first got back, the volume was turned all the way up; shoot, it was so loud he could have rolled down the windows on the car and blasted his music out into the neighborhood.

It wasn't like that anymore.

Now what he heard from other people's minds was just voices. Not loud voices, in fact, some of them were so soft he had trouble hearing them at all and making out what they were saying. Clearly, the power that had been granted to him on the mothership was fading. And once it was gone, he would be helpless. It was *all he had,* his only weapon. Well, he would not lose it. He flat out would *not.* With every speck of his concentration, he focused on the thoughts of the men in the room, standing or sitting around tables talking. He felt a cool sheen of sweat coat his body from the effort.

Slowly, very gradually, the volume of the thoughts he could hear increased. He could hear them more clearly, they were not muffled didn't seem distant, like he was listening to someone calling out from the bottom of a well. He continued to concentrate, willing away every distraction, not knowing or caring if his presence had been noticed yet, focusing his every mental faculty and strength on hearing.

And finally, the volume was back to what it had been the day he arrived in the alley.

By force of will, he had required his mind not to lose the ability, and his mind had, however reluctantly, obeyed his command.

Fine, that was it, then. This wouldn't be easy; the mind-reading would not come automatically. But he could make it come. If he concentrated hard enough, willed with enough ferocity, he still had the skill he'd returned with. And he needed that skill right now, as Santoro chanced to look his way and notice him.

"Hey Paco," he cried out. "Got some folks wanna meet you."

Wanna rip your motherfucking little head off, you son of a bitch. Gonna silence you for good, cut your balls off and make you eat them.

Other thoughts shouted at him as he made his way to the front of the room and he welcomed them all, no matter how vile or threatening. He could hear their thoughts and he could speak into their minds.

Little fucker, who does he think he is?

I remember him. He looks like one of those Scared Straight kids, but older, the one that was Spade's bitch.

He stopped beside the table where the burly man who'd connected him to Spade sat. The man had tattoos on arms so hairy it was impossible to see the design.

"I'm not Spade's bitch," he said, managing to keep every speck of emotion out of the words, surprising given the rage and fear and humiliation just the mention of the name made him feel. "I'm *nobody's* bitch. But unless you stop dipping your dick in your sergeant's wife's honeypot, you're gonna end up his bitch."

The man literally choked. He'd been downing a small sip of some liquid that was probably supposed to be beer but what was clearly a poor substitute. He spewed the liquid out onto the table, onto the drinks of the other two men there and on the front of their shirts. They leaped to their feet, knocking their chairs back when they stood. At first shocked and then furious, they reached out for the man who still hadn't gotten his breath back. His name was Ivanov, Radek Ivanov.

Before the other two men could grab Ivanov by the throat and throttle him for spitting his drink on them, Paco, who had leaped back when the two men came at Ivanov, held up his hand.

"Leave him alone," he said, and managed a great imitation of forceful supressed violence, that was just enough to halt them in mid-attack. That was all the time he needed.

"Collier, the Astrals know all about that stash of dope you hid when Spade's men came around to collect it. Ribowski, you really need to stop daydreaming about fucking Spade. I've had some and it's not so hot."

The two men were so shocked by his revelations they stopped in mid-lurch, looked at each other and remained unmoving. They didn't sit down, though.

"I said sit down. If have to say it again, I might have to tell Joe Leggatt you're fucking his wife *and* his daughter.

Stan Collier flushed, and Paco inserted a thought into his mind, easy as sliding a needle into a vein.

This man got some stones.

The two men sat down and Collier said, "You got a pair alright. How you know all this shit?"

"Ask Four Fingers over there. He knows all about my balls. He squeezed 'em and put me in a world of hurt and I fully intend to return the favor."

Four Fingers was apoplectic. He'd been seated at the bar, watching along with the other men, but apparently Paco had changed so much, he hadn't recognized him.

"He and Harris *saw* what happened to me. Wish Harris could be here to testify, too, but Four Fingers slit his throat last Thursday, took his size-thirteen shoes, which I suppose are in short supply these days — and dumped his body in a garage on Pritchard street. Don't believe me, check for yourselves, but you won't have to get any closer than the driveway. In this hot weather that body is *ripe*."

Several voices spoke at once.

"You killed him? He was a friend of—"

"Wait'll Gonzales finds out. Harris was his number one—"

"Shut up and let him talk," Paco said. "Tell these gentlemen what you saw in that alley the day the reptars ate several hundred inmates."

Four Fingers's face wore a look of such disbelieving terror Paco almost laughed out loud.

"He ain't lying," Four Fingers said. "Me and ... I seen it. He was standing there and this shuttle appeared right over him, just popped out of nowhere. It shined this yellow light down on him. And then ..." He had to pause to draw a breath, like somebody'd kicked him in the belly. "He was gone. Vanished. They took him. The Astrals ... *took* him."

Paco had instructed Santoro, on pain of having his deepest secrets revealed to the world, to gather up the men with whom he'd planned his grand escape plan — Paco had listed them by name. And for them to bring along anyone else they thought might be interested in making five times what they were making now, turning the tables on the former cons who now stood with their heels as thoroughly on their necks as the real guards ever had.

He'd expected that all the men whose names were on the list would show. He had not expected that they'd bring at least as many more malcontents. Paco had searched the thoughts of every townie he could find for most of the afternoon before he found a man who had stashed a case of real beer in his basement.

As he talked, as he saw the effect he was having, and heard the thoughts that reinforced his assessment, Paco's confidence grew. He was in charge.

Chapter Thirty

Papa Eagle Feather never did figure out how it was decided that the whole band of stranded people were going to join them and travel to Zion Academy. Oh, he heard the discussions, as Star talked about the monastery and the academy, information that she'd picked out of Noah's head, and it didn't take a Rhodes Scholar to figure out they couldn't stay where they were for much longer. They had no food and nobody any good at getting them any. He had gone out early to hunt the first morning after they arrived in the camp of those he called The Stranded. He bagged a deer and an antelope, hauled the first back to camp before noon and the second one later in the afternoon. By the time he had finished field dressing them both and preparing them to be cooked over the spit that night, the group was already talking about going with him and Star to Zion.

It was Nick Wilson, the curly-haired man, who actually asked Eagle Feather if he minded if "we tag along with you" and Eagle Feather had been so surprised he probably didn't seem very hospitable. But it was one thing to make your way across the country, staying out of sight, living off the land, traveling on horseback through the byways to Kentucky — just two people. It was another thing altogether to haul thirty or forty — how many were there? — people along with you, people who would have to travel on roads, not across country as he had planned and who would very shortly be on foot, as one after another of the big vehicles ran out of gas.

"Why do you want to go with us?"

"Because we can't stay here. We came here because we had to get out of Nashville ... anywhere was better than in a city. We'd all come here before, well, except for Fred and Lottie, and we knew the area. We didn't actually come *to* the Land Between the Lakes. We ran *away* from Nashville. Now ... we're stuck."

"Do you know what you're asking? We're talking ... a caravan here. Do you know how unwieldy ...?

"We won't make it through the winter if we stay here," Nick said. He'd served in the military, Papa Eagle Feather was certain. "That simple. Star says there would be enough supplies to accommodate us in this place in Kentucky. And ... you're going to think this is weird ...

"Try me."

"Star is ... we feel like ... we don't want her to leave. We want to be ... oh, it's going to sound crazy."

"Keep chipping away at it and you'll get to it eventually."

"Star is … do you know, do you realize how … *special* she is?"

"I know way more about how special she is than you do."

"Oh, not just because she went up into one of those spaceships and came back down."

"I don't mean that part either. I'm talking about the fact that it was foretold that she would do that back in the days of my grandfather's grandfather."

That was a conversation stopper. Ian Maddocks had joined the conversation, standing quiet as Lamar and Latricia played chase and basically made nuisances of themselves. Roberto Lopez heard that last part and put in.

"I'm not surprised. Is anyone here surprised? She's … different."

"And because you get a warm, fuzzy feeling from this little girl, you're willing to uproot yourselves and travel — do you have any idea how dangerous travel is? — travel a hundred miles with her to a place you've only heard of but never seen. That seem reasonable to you?"

They almost answered in unison.

"No, but it is … it is what it is," Ian said. "Nothing much seems reasonable these days. If you don't want us to travel with you, and we can certainly understand why you might rather go it alone. But … but I think we will probably come along behind you."

"Star has *something*," Nick said. "I don't know what

it is, but it's the first time I've felt any real hope since they spotted those damn little spots on the other side of Jupiter."

"How do you plan—?" Papa Eagle Feather didn't get to finish. They'd already talked about it, how they would use only some of their vehicles, consolidate and ride in those, siphon the gasoline out of the others.

"You know you can't make it, with the gas mileage those guzzlers get, you won't—"

"We know, and then we'll have to walk," Ian Maddocks said.

"But it's either that, walk with some destination in mind that's better than where we are right now, or sit here and starve this winter," Nick said. "Plan B is not an option."

What was he supposed to do? Eagle Feather absolutely one hundred percent did not want to team up with a caravan of palefaces, total greenhorns, who had no weaponry to speak of and no ability to use any if they'd had any. But he could keep them all in meat. This forest was full of it. After that, though, when they got past the forest, how would …?

"I can't guarantee I can provide …"

"We're not asking for guarantees of anything," Nick said. "The only guarantee we have right now is that if we stay here we won't live to see another spring. Whatever it's like traveling with you, it's better than staying here."

And just like that it was decided. Eagle Feather had been negotiating his way through the forest using Forest Service maps, riding down the hiking trails.

Those vehicles couldn't transverse the trails, so he'd have to plot a new course that used roads. That was more out in the open, less hidden. These behemoths weren't going to slip through unnoticed. The roads weren't thoroughfares, by any means. Most were gravel maintenance roads for the National Forest Service. But they were more well-traveled than the hiking trails.

It was what it was, and they would just have to manage. For lots of reasons, some humanitarian, some … Bottom line was Eagle Feather couldn't get around the knowledge that these people were right — there *was* something about Star, there was some … he didn't know what to call it. But whatever it was, it had called out to these people.

And it occurred to him, not to his delight, that she probably "called out" to other people too. He sincerely hoped they didn't run across any more stragglers along their route. The last thing he wanted was to accumulate a following.

Chapter Thirty-One

NOAH HEARD it in his mind, the thought shouted so loud he would have sworn he'd heard it with the ears that hadn't heard a real sound in four years. His father's face spoke, his mouth opened, but Noah didn't know if he had shouted a word or if he had just screamed, some inarticulate sound that didn't need a word to accompany it.

Noah's ability to read the minds of others had been fading away since he got home — which suited Noah just fine. He had no desire to be inside anybody else's mind except Star's.

But this "sound" was so loud in his head, he thought maybe anybody could have heard it. Noah knew what it was before he even looked up, saw the image clearly in his father's mind.

A shuttle.

The shuttle was descending from the sky rapidly, erratically, seemed to be heading right for them. Instinctively, his father yanked the wheel of his cruiser hard right and hit the brake. The violent motion knocked the plate of Lucy's cookies they were taking to Dad's office to share with his deputies out of Noah's lap and the cookies dumped onto the floorboard. But the shuttle would have missed them even if his father hadn't swerved to dodge it. It was coming in low, like an airplane landing, which didn't make sense because the shuttles didn't glide in any way that would translate to the aerodynamics of an Earth aircraft. They moved up and down, side to side, with total precision, without making a sound, without any evidence of thrust, like the wind from a helicopter's rotors or the wash of a jet trail.

This one came right over their car about a hundred feet in the air. And when it was closer, Noah could tell it was spinning, going around on its own axis and he'd never seen one do that either.

It passed over the car, clipped the top of a huge live oak tree and snapped it like a twig. As it lowered, it plowed through the tops of other trees, which slowed it down, though if the impacts harmed the hull of the craft in any way it wasn't apparent from where Noah and his father sat, gaping out the back window of the cruiser.

Then the craft hit a utility pole, didn't exactly bounce off, but it didn't clip the top off as it had the trees. The pole deflected it to the left and down, and the craft hit the ground in a field, dug a crater in the ground when it connected with the earth, pushing a pile of dirt up before it as it slowed. Then it rolled, looked like a golf ball rolling across a green until it came to rest against the trunk of a sycamore tree at the edge of the woods.

Noah and his father sat slack-jawed with shock for a full two or three seconds. Then his father keyed his radio, with the command, "Dispatch to all units, I repeat, all units, an Astral shuttle has crashed in a field half a mile off Perryton Road about two miles south of Ben Johnson's dairy. Report to the scene using disaster protocol. I repeat, *use disaster protocol.*"

Noah read his father's lips and he knew what disaster protocol meant because his father sometimes took him along when he was conducting training exercises. Though he didn't know exactly how it was set up, its purpose was to prevent all officers from rushing to the site of a disaster at once. His father said it was the "lesson of 9-11," which had been some terrorist attack on New York City decades ago, where hundreds of firemen and policemen had been killed when they all dashed at once to the scene of the disaster. A building fell on them or something. Disaster protocol was designed to prevent that, to ensure that all hands on deck were *not* put in harm's way at the same time. It required that the first two officers on the scene would assess the need for other officers, who would then pull up short of the fire or explosion site or whatever it was and stop traffic, keep spectators away and await further instructions.

His father and whichever officer showed up next would advise other deputies when they might be needed.

The dispatcher, Betty Hawthorne, acknowledged

his father's message had gone out, her voice strained and airless. His was the only unit that could bypass her and speak to all the other units. Though Noah could tell she was shocked and terrified, she managed to remain professional. Then the radio was silent.

"Stay here," his father said as he opened his car door and stepped outside. The first cry of a siren could already be heard in the distance. "No matter what happens, you stay in this car."

Other siren wails joined the first almost instantly.

Before his father had a chance to take two steps, the side of the shuttle melted away — the motion that passed for a door opening on the Astral ships — and a titan stumbled out. He was missing most of his left arm, and was looking at the stump stupidly, like it couldn't figure out what had happened. It took a couple of steps, then settled down to its knees in the dirt.

It was such a small shuttle that it was possible to see into it through the open doorway. Another titan lay unmoving on the floor. A third was seated on the floor, might or might not have been injured.

"Dad, those are titans, they don't hurt people. It's the others, the reptars, that are dangerous."

"I know," his father said, and it occurred to Noah that in the three months since he was last on Earth, there had surely been lots of news coverage that showed the creatures, both kinds. His father began to advance slowly toward the ship, had his hands at his sides — inches away from the pistol in his holster, but clearly not threatening.

Noah didn't stay in the car. He leapt out the door his father had left open and took several steps toward the crashed shuttle fifty yards away.

He didn't know shuttles could crash, but he wasn't surprised. The Astrals might be an incredibly advanced species, but they weren't perfect. He and the others had figured that out when they were in the mothership, how ignorant the Astrals were about commonplace things, how little they understood about how humanity really functioned. If they could be wrong about so many ordinary things, they could screw up a shuttle, too, he supposed. And clearly the crash had to have been some kind of mechanical failure. There was not a mark of any kind on the clean, white skin of the craft, not even any marks where it had collided with the trees as it crashed. It hadn't been knocked out of the sky with some weapon. Everybody knew *that* was impossible. Mechanical malfunction was the only explanation.

His father advanced slowly toward the injured titan, then glanced over his shoulder at the cruiser.

"Get back in the car!" He hadn't signed the words, and couldn't reasonably have assumed Noah could read his lips at this distance. But Noah "heard" the words in his head, and they carried with them the severe "or-else" tone that moved Noah back toward the vehicle. Still, he didn't get inside.

Just then, the first of the summoned deputies' cruisers careened around the corner, coming from the opposite direction. It screeched to a dirt-throwing halt on the side of the road fifty feet or so from his father's cruiser. Billy Ray Tyler had the door of the cruiser open before it even came to a complete stop, and leapt out instantly, his service rifle to his shoulder. His partner, Roger Hawkins, was a heartbeat behind him.

"Stay back," his father called out. "I don't want anybody doing anything aggressive. It crashed. They're injured. I'm not here to start a fight."

They had heard the instant wail of sirens after the dispatcher confirmed his father's alert. They were only a couple of miles from town so it would take only minutes to get to the scene.

In seconds, two more cruisers came into view, one from the direction they'd been traveling, one from the other. They slid to a stop as well and two officers leapt out of each one. They were *not* following orders. Disaster protocol required them to hang back until they were needed, but they'd all come charging up at once.

"Hold your position," he told the officers who'd just leapt out of their cars. *"Do not approach the ship."*

Noah tried to tap into the minds of the aliens, but he couldn't. He and the others had tried to do that a couple of times when they were on the mothership, hoping maybe they could learn something that would help them get out of whatever "circumstance" they'd been put into. It never worked, though. The aliens' minds were not individual. They were each part of an incredibly gigantic hive mind that was so full, the thoughts going by so fast, it was like trying to hold out a thimble into Niagara Falls to get a drink.

Noah didn't know what his father intended to do,

how he intended to handle contact with the injured titans, and he never found out his father's plan because he never had a chance to implement it. An old pickup truck with two men in the cab and maybe half a dozen in the back came roaring toward the downed shuttle from the other side of the field where it'd crashed. Apparently, they'd seen the ship go down and came rushing to the scene to … to what? They probably didn't know what they intended to do either. You see something crash, you go. And if it's a *spaceship* …!

The pickup slid to a halt and all seven of the men leapt out and went running toward the ship. They all were armed with rifles or shotguns.

"Get back in your truck and get out of here," his father yelled at the men.

His father's words only slowed the men down, didn't stop them. They stopped running but continued walking. The titan who'd been sitting on the floor inside the shuttle got to his feet and stepped to the doorway, looking at the titan on his knees in the dirt. His father again ordered the men approaching the shuttle to leave, and they continued to ignore him.

Noah didn't see which one of them fired. They all had guns and raised them when the titan inside the shuttle stepped into the doorway. A single gunship ripped open the air and the titan yanked sideways and grabbed his right shoulder. Blood squirted out between his fingers.

"Stop firing," his father screamed. "Stop! These are peaceful—"

What happened next took Noah's breath away.

The injured titan bent at the waist and began to … change. Its pasty white skin turned dark. The bottom part of its body grew, elongated, and legs appeared, *too many legs*. Black scales popped out on white flesh.

It happened so fast. There were three titans, white giants, bald and blue-eyed and, as far as he had ever seen, harmless. And then they were gone. In place of the two live titans were reptars. He heard the horrible purring sound and tried to scream, but couldn't. He found himself running long before he willed his feet to take him anywhere. Not back to the car, but into the woods. He could hide there. It wouldn't be the first time he'd hidden from reptars. He glanced over his shoulder at his father, willing him to run, to get out of there, but he stood his ground as the reptars turned into killing machines. Then Noah was running and didn't stop until he made it into the woods, dived into the undergrowth, crawled under a crepe myrtle bush that had blossoms hanging all the way to the ground. He peeked out between the blossoms and watched the bloodbath.

Chapter Thirty-Two

ELLIE FIDGETED IN THE CHAIR, couldn't seem to sit still. She picked up a dog-eared magazine off the table between the two rows of chairs in the waiting room. *A World of Homes* magazine, the Christmas edition from four years ago. The tree on the front was the kind her father had gotten for Gretchen's bedroom in their New York apartment when she was only two years old. With a tiny remote, you could change the kind of tree — from a pine to a blue spruce to a weeping willow, and the tree itself glowed without benefit of lighting, little sparkles of light appeared on the limbs and you could pick the colors, the size, and make them blink or twinkle.

Baby Diana would have giggled at those lights. She giggled at everything, and the child's face bloomed bright in Ellie's mind. She was … what was it the Bible called it? A pearl of great price. Ellie had paid dearly for that baby girl — the baby's mother had paid with her life — and Diana was the light of Ellie's existence ... even though her own daughter, Gretchen, was still jealous of the child. Gretchen would get over it.

Ellie felt in her belly now the same desperation that had sent her running off to Ft. Knox when she found out there was a still-functioning hospital there with surgeons she might be able to convince to remove the lump she'd found in her right breast on Astral Day.

She was here today to try to persuade yet another doctor to do something about it.

The little girl seated next to her sneezed noisily, without covering her mouth, confirming Ellie's long-held belief that a doctor's waiting room was a Petri dish for infection — that's why her doctors always came to her. But the days of doctors showing up at her beck and call were long over now.

She had made an appointment with Dr. Sedgwick, the Jessup doctor she'd tried to see the day after Astral Day — and his absence had occasioned her night-mare trip to Louisville to see a doctor there, and an equally nightmarish flight to Ft. Knox. Dr. Sedgwick and his family had returned from their cabin in the woods after about a month and his practice was now flooded with patients, the waiting room was jammed and Ellie had been waiting for more than an hour. Being the only act in town took on greater signifi-cance when patients had no access to doctors anywhere else ... well, anywhere you could get to from here.

A nurse stepped into the room and Ellie jumped

when she called out her name. The old woman sitting on the other side of her patted her knee reassuringly.

"Been coming here ever since Dr. Sedgwick opened up his practice and he ain't bit me a single time."

Ellie made an effort to smile but couldn't pull it off.

There was no clean sheet of paper covering the examining room table. Must have run out. But she climbed up obediently onto it regardless and sat for another half hour, staring at the doctor's diploma from the University of Kentucky School of Medicine, hanging on the wall: Dr. Gregory Herbert — had to be a family name — Sedgwick, M.D. General Practice.

Ellie needed a specialist, but supposed she should be grateful she'd found a doctor of any kind. The only other "game in town" was a chiropractor.

When the doctor finally arrived, he was much younger than she'd thought he'd be — late 30s maybe — with a nose that totally dominated his face, and a high, wide forehead that made his too-small eyes look like brown M&Ms. He looked exhausted, like maybe he used to be a lot bigger and had lost weight, but he had a kind smile that drained a little tension out of Ellie.

He looked at the information sheet she'd filled out.

"A lump in your breast, huh? Let's have a look at it." She hadn't been offered the standard paper coverup that followed the "strip to the waist." They must have been out of those, too. She'd just been told to take off her bra and leave her shirt unbuttoned. As he examined her, she told him the condensed versions of her various attempts to get medical attention … and what had happened after.

Then he stepped back and told her she could button her blouse — which she really couldn't because she had to put her bra back on.

"There are any number of things that can cause—"

"You can skip that part. I've read everything there is to know about breast lumps, up to and including medical textbooks. I know what the bottom line is. There's no way to be a hundred percent sure whether or not it's malignant without a biopsy."

"Correct, and I'm afraid there's no way—"

"I've already been down that rabbit hole, too. I know there's no way to get a biopsy now."

She took a deep breath.

"So if you did surgery and removed the lump, could you tell by looking at it whether or not it was malignant?"

"*I* couldn't," he said. "An oncologist surgeon might be able to give you an educated guess just because he'd seen so many different kinds of tumors. But even then it would still be just a guess. All I've ever seen is pictures in textbooks and the pictures in medical text-books never look like the real thing."

He paused, clearly not wanting to say what he was about to say.

"You said this lump is growing. If it is malignant, there's a high likelihood that it has spread. Depending on the kind — some breast cancers are very aggressive, others not so much — it could have spread throughout the breast and into the lymph nodes under your arm."

That wasn't news to Ellie. But hearing him say it took her breath away.

"Could you remove the lump?"

He'd been expecting the question.

"Under normal circumstances, I'd have said absolutely not and referred you to a surgeon." He didn't bother to continue. "Given the size and the location, though, I could remove it in an outpatient procedure."

When he looked at her now, there was kindness in his little M&M eyes.

"There really isn't any reason to do that, though. If it's malignant, the whole breast is likely already … If it's not, you can live the rest of your life with it."

Ellie found she couldn't make her mouth say the words. She'd practiced them, had said them aloud.

"Would you do a mastectomy?"

He hadn't been expecting that question. He sputtered.

"I'm not a surgeon. I'm a G.P. That's a complicated, difficult, dangerous surgery. There's no way—"

"*Please!*"

"I'm sorry, Mrs. Hampton, I couldn't possibly—

"It's not like you're going to get sued if I die on the table! And I am going to die if this is cancer and I just leave it there to eat me alive."

"You don't understand, it isn't just that I won't. I

can't. I'm not qualified." He finally lost a bit of his composure. "I don't know how!"

"But you could learn. You could study and figure it out. I know you could."

She bulldozed by him before he could protest.

"Will you at least think about it? Please, please just think about it. That's all I ask. I'm begging for my life here. Will you at least consider it?"

He came within a hair's breadth of saying no, but didn't. Just studied her face.

"You probably don't even need a mastectomy, you know. This is likely just a cyst and …" He took a breath. "I will *think* about it. That's all, just think about it. Don't get your hopes up. Right now I'm ninety-five percent certain I can't do it. I'm only holding out for the other five percent."

Ellie couldn't breathe. A little ray of hope.

"I'll give you a call in a few days and——"

"No, I'll come back into the office … say, Friday. I want you to tell me to my face."

That made him uncomfortable, which told Ellie he'd pretty much made up his mind already to refuse. But he nodded.

"I'll see you Friday, then."

Ellie walked out to her car through sweltering heat and the grating cry of cicadas, lifted her key to punch the unlock button and saw a silver shuttle hanging above the building across the street.

Chapter Thirty-Three

It all went south so incredibly fast. Tyler and Hawkins had been the first officers on the scene, the team he'd sent to shut down Foodtown on Astral Day a lifetime ago. That should have been the only two-man unit. The others were *supposed to*— They'd ignored disaster protocol, all leapt into their cruisers and came barreling out here hellbent for leather *because it was aliens. Three units, six officers.* They ignored all their training because it was aliens. *Dammit!*

Sawyer'd intended, if he had any plan at all, to offer assistance to the aliens. One clearly was dead and unless they had healing powers of which he was unaware, the one missing an arm wouldn't last long. What possible assistance he could—

Then he'd heard the whooping, looked up and saw the pickup truck bouncing across the field behind where the ship had crashed, barreling toward it. There were men in the back of the truck, half a dozen maybe and two men up front, and they were all hollering like they were on their way to a rodeo.

The pickup pulled up short in a cloud of dirt and the men were out of it running toward the ship before Sawyer could do anything to stop them.

"Get back in your truck and get out of here," he called out to the men, who totally ignored his words. The one in front, the driver, yelled out, "Like hell I'll get back in my truck!"

Then Sawyer knew who it was. Arliss Jenkins. It wasn't even noon yet, and back in the day, Arliss would already have consumed a six-pack before nine o'clock. Whether he still drank now like he once did was questionable, but he was probably meaner sober than he was drunk. Sawyer suspected he had been among the men who attacked Zion Academy the night the aliens landed.

"I said get back in your truck, Arliss," he called. "I'm ordering you to leave right now.

"Them's aliens," one of the other men cried. "You just gonna let them land here and not do nothing about it?"

"I'm gonna get me a piece of alien meat, I am," Arliss cried. The men had stopped running when Sawyer first called out to them, but they were still advancing on the craft, weapons drawn.

"They didn't land, they crashed, and—"

Somebody fired.

The bullet caught the uninjured titan in the shoulder, knocked him backward. He looked down and saw blood begin to pour out of a hole in his massive shoulder.

Then both the injured titan and the one who'd just gotten shot bent double at the waist. It took less than thirty seconds, the transformation complete before their very eyes.

The two titans had transformed into reptars. One of them was missing several of its many feet on the front. Blood slipped out of the shoulder of the other, but they were reptars, and they were pissed. The one missing limbs charged at the deputies who were standing in front of their cars. The one bleeding from the shoulder took off after the men in the field.

There was a rattle of gunfire. The deputies and all the men in the field opened fire and riddled the two reptars with bullets that bounced off the shell-like armor as if it were iron. It took both the men in the field and the deputies a second or two to realize that the reptars were impervious to their weapons … to realize that they were standing in front of killing machines with useless weapons.

By then the reptar had reached the men in the field; they moved so fast, scuttling along the ground like cockroaches. It tore into them like a woodchopper, its teeth a buzz saw. Tearing off limbs with its claws, biting off heads with its razor teeth. The men were retreating but the reptar picked them off one by one as they ran, ripping them apart. Only two made it all the way back to the truck and Arliss Jenkins jumped in the front seat behind the wheel, a huge man Sawyer knew only as "Big-un" Blocker leapt into the back.

Then the big man leaned over in the bed of the pickup, picked up an ammo bag, reached into it and brought out something. It looked like …

Holy … where did Big-un Blocker get a hand grenade? But that's clearly what it was. He was a gun nut and former military … but a *hand grenade*? He had pulled the pin and raised his arm to throw when the reptar leapt at him. It bit him completely in two at the waist. The whole upper part of his body disappeared in a spray of blood and bone and guts and then there was a mighty explosion.

That's when it slowed down into slow motion for Sawyer. Just like it had when he had seen the shuttle hovering over the pond and knew it meant to take away his son. The world had slowed down, every motion taking ten times normal time. Sawyer watched the reptar explode into blood, guts and gore that flew out over the whole field, pieces of the creature mixed with Big-un's body parts flung out in every direction.

The other reptar was taking out Sawyer's deputies, who were firing at it from point-blank range.

He watched the creature rip Billy Ray Tyler in two and tear Roger Hawkins's head off with his claws. Pee Wee Watson was getting into his cruiser when the creature bit into his back side, cutting him in half. Then it was on the other side of the cruiser, so outrageously fast, taking out Joe Thurman, Watson's partner, who emptied his pistol at the creature as it advanced on him. Ralph Morrison tried to dive under the cruiser for protection but the reptar grabbed him with its teeth, yanked him backward, then chewed off both legs. Of his six deputies, five were dead in less than a minute, and the creature was bearing down on Sam Henderson, who had stood his ground with his service rifle, firing at the creature as it came at him. Sawyer was firing, too, emptied his pistol and watched the bullets ping off the plating that covered the creature's body.

And then pieces of Sam came flying at Sawyer. Some piece of the deputy's body, his arm maybe, hit him in the face, temporarily blinding him. Sawyer looked toward the car and couldn't see Noah anywhere. Thank God. The boy had run away, or was hiding in the car, but either way he was not in plain sight. Sawyer was seconds from death, but found nothing but gratitude that his son would live.

Arliss Jenkins was the only one of the men in the field who had survived. He'd dived into the cab when Big-un leapt into the back and pulled out his hand grenade. Arliss might have lived to see sunset if he'd just stayed out of sight. He didn't. With the back window of the pickup blown out and part of the cab roof sitting at an odd angle, he suddenly sat up behind the wheel and started the engine. He put the big double-wide cab truck into gear and roared forward. The vehicle crossed the space between it and the downed spacecraft in seconds, roaring toward the reptar that was advancing on Sawyer. Clearly, Arliss meant to mow the creature down.

The reptar turned toward the truck and that's all the time Sawyer needed. He turned, too, and bolted back to his cruiser, yanked open the door and took his rifle off the rack. This was not a service rifle or a shotgun. It was a deer rifle, a .30-06 XXX Springfield, the most versatile rifle on the market, and the scope was so accurate he'd once dropped a buck at more than five hundred yards. Typically, he fired small, fast shells that did less damage on impact. If you're hunting for meat, you don't want to blow away the whole side of a deer or elk. But by the grace of God, the rifle was loaded now with .308-inch cartridges weighing a whopping five hundred grains. You could stop a charging rhino with a round like that.

Now, he used the scope to zero in on the reptar that had easily dodged the charging truck. When Arliss missed the reptar, he pointed the vehicle toward the road to escape, but the two cruisers that had arrived last were parked too close together and when he tried to drive between them, he got sandwiched, sideswiping them both, and the truck stalled. He couldn't open either door of the truck, turned to leap out the broken back window and run. The reptar was in the bed of the truck, waiting for him, and when Arliss didn't come out — cringed in the truck cab, screaming — the reptar went through the broken windshield after him.

Sawyer had kept the reptar in his sights, waiting for his shot to open up. He was aiming for the small space of skin he had seen where the reptar's shelled armor connected with its neck. It appeared to be unprotected. He squeezed the trigger and absorbed the big gun's kick. The bullet hit where Sawyer'd aimed, but the exposed area wasn't unprotected. What looked like skin was some kind of flexible shell as tough as the plates of armor on its sides.

The creature felt the bullet, though, turned, pieces of Arliss's guts still in its razor teeth, and scuttled out of the truck bed toward Sawyer. Sawyer laid the rifle on the roof of Tyler and Hawkins's cruiser, ignoring the gore of their dismembered bodies strewn about like chicken guts. He put his eye to the scope sight, drew in a breath, held it. Let the creature get closer. Closer. When it was barely twenty feet away, it opened its razor-toothed maw in anticipation of devouring, and Sawyer placed a bullet right in the creature's mouth. The bullet broke off several teeth as it entered the reptar's mouth and blew out the whole back of the creature's head when it exited. The creature was running so fast that its momentum crashed it into the side of the cruiser, smashing in the driver's side door, knocking Sawyer backward a step.

And the horn began to honk.

Then everything went still.

The sound of the car horn was the only sound. Sawyer had been in the military, had seen action, had heard the keening cries of the wounded on a battle-field. But there were no wounded. Every man the reptars attacked had died in their teeth and jaws. The only man left standing was Sheriff Sawyer Matheson.

Sawyer laid the rifle on the roof of the cruiser, and stepped back, staring at the kind of blood and gore you'd see if a mortar shell had gone off in the middle of half a dozen soldiers, blowing them apart. There wasn't a single intact body in sight.

The horn wailed into the silence.

"Dad, Dad!" a voice cried out. Noah!

Sawyer knew Noah had no idea how loud he was calling, couldn't hear his own voice. The sound came from just inside the woods, from a crepe myrtle bush. Sawyer ran to the bush, got down on his hands and knees.

Suddenly, Noah grabbed hold of him and yanked him forward into the flowering bush's tangle of stems.

"Noah, what—"

Noah pointed. Another shuttle hung in the sky fifty feet above the one that had crashed.

Chapter Thirty-Four

From the tangle of crepe myrtle branches, Sawyer and Noah peeked out at the craft dangling in the sky above the downed shuttle. It didn't land. It just hung there suspended for a time, thirty seconds maybe. Not a minute, surely. Neither Sawyer nor Noah spoke. They just huddled, *cowered* in the limbs of the crepe myrtle bush, staring at the shuttle that hung above the shuttle that'd crashed. Hung over the carnage, the blood, the mutilated bodies.

Billy Ray Tyler.

Roger Hawkins, Pee Wee Watson, Joe Thurman, Ralph Morrison and Sam Henderson.

They were … How had it happened so fast?

They'd come out here, disobeyed orders, because just like everybody else they wanted to see a real, no kidding, flesh-and-blood alien, and they'd gotten their wish. And it'd killed them.

Sawyer was trembling, staring at the monstrous silver orb that hung there, impossibly just *hung in the sky,* and he was unutterably terrified. Not for himself. He'd left fear of dying behind on some battlefield in some war years ago. He was sometimes concerned on the job, but … then he'd seen the monstrosities with the needle teeth and the claws.

He'd heard, he could swear he'd heard a sucking sound, when they were tearing his men apart, and the purr almost like a cat, but more grating. He had never been a kid who had nightmares, saw boogie men in the closet. He didn't indulge in horror movies, either. They just didn't interest him. These creatures were so far out on the other side of anything Sawyer Matheson could have conjured up in his wildest imaginings that he had no place to put them in his head. He didn't know how to think about them.

The white giants were horrifying in their otherness, but they were not terrifying, until they became the bug monsters with the bright blue eyes.

He would see the blue of those eyes — and they changed colors, he would swear they changed colors — in his nightmares for the rest of his life.

And so he cowered, praying the monsters wouldn't see. *Could* they see out of that silver thing? Who knew? He prayed they wouldn't see him and Noah. He wasn't afraid to die, but he couldn't protect Noah by dying. Couldn't sacrifice himself, my life for yours, for his son. He would, but the monsters didn't play by those rules. The boy had a right to grow up. He was just twelve years old and they'd already taken him away, studied him, poked and prodded and God knew what else to him — he would ask one day, but not now. Hadn't they gotten their money's worth from Noah Matheson? Surely, he got a pass here. He got credit for time served.

Leave him alone. He might have ground the words out through his teeth, but if he did he hadn't meant to. He had only thought them.

Go away, and leave my son alone.

The orb hanging in the sky lifted up and scooted away. Not vanishing away. Just fast, still right above the treetops.

Had it left because …?

No, it couldn't.

Then it penetrated his sluggish mind the direction the shuttle had been traveling. It was going toward Jessup, sped away, like the shuttle that had taken Noah. Sawyer had stood watching it, moving impossibly fast, until it was out of sight. During the horrible time when hostages had been taken and were being returned there had been much scientific hoopla about the speed of the spacecrafts in relation to the welfare of the hostages. The scientists pointed out that the crafts could not possibly move as fast as they were capable of with humans aboard or the people would be nothing but a pile of goo at the other end of the trip.

This shuttle had no hostages aboard, but it didn't just vanish. It *left*.

And then it was quiet again, except for the insistent honk of the car horn.

"Come on, son, we need to get out of here."

Sawyer understood that he was in shock, recognized all the symptoms and bowed to every one.

His deputies …

Billy Ray Tyler's wife was expecting a baby any time now. How could he tell her …

Joe Thurman … Sawyer'd sent him to shut down Castor's Supermarket on Astral Day. Howard Castor had threatened to sue the sheriff's department.

Sam Henderson had refused to move his family into town, stayed on his small farm out by the monastery, said he'd make his last stand there, if he had to, die protecting his home and family.

They'd all been alive five minutes ago. Now all of them were dead. Four of them because they'd disobeyed orders. If they'd obeyed disaster protocol, only he, Tyler and Hawkins would have been killed. And the yahoos in the field.

Now his entire department had been wiped out.

There was the sheriff and the dispatcher in the sheriff's office in the courthouse. Not another officer remained.

Sawyer took Noah's hand and led him out from under the crepe myrtle bush.

"I want you to look at the ground, Noah, until we get in the car. Then you get in the backseat floorboard, like you did when we went to Louisville to get Ellie. Can you do that for me?"

It was senseless, he knew. The boy surely had watched the men get killed. What good did it do to protect him from the sight of the dismembered bodies? Maybe no good at all, but he wouldn't let his boy see that.

They went to the car and Noah got into the back seat. Sawyer stepped over a body part, someone's leg from the knee down, and picked up the deer rifle he had left on the roof of Tyler's cruiser, put it in the gun rack, got into the cruiser and reached for the keys to start the car.

His hands were shaking so violently he couldn't grasp them. They were dangling there in the ignition, but he couldn't keep his hand on them firmly enough to turn the key and start the car.

He bit down as hard as he could, clenched his jaws, felt tears squirt down his cheeks, and willed his hands to calm. It did no good. And then he felt Noah's hands close around his, help him turn the key and the motor roared to life. Sawyer looked up at his son, who had climbed over the seat to the front to help him.

He wanted to thank him, but all he could do was look into his eyes. Noah was crying. So was Sawyer.

Chapter Thirty-Five

Harmony Hollis pushed Chloe's stroller down the street toward Dr. Sedgwick's office, the heat beating down on her and no air conditioning to look forward to. It had been cloudy the past two days. The solar panels on the roof of the house had barely generated enough electricity to keep the lights on. She should have used the power to boil the tap water. That's what made Chloe sick, she was sure of it, up all night throwing up and diarrhea. And Harmony'd run out of paper diapers months ago, only had cloth tea towels she had to wash—

She looked up and saw a woman standing by her car in the doctor's office parking lot. She was staring at something. Harmony looked back over her shoulder. A silver ball, *oh dear God in heaven one of those alien things,* was floating in the sky above the courthouse. Harmony screamed.

~

JEB BISHOP CAME out of the shoe store at the corner of Main and Elm streets, carrying the box that contained his new work boots. These better last because no telling when or where he'd ever get another pair. Bob Grayson had told him at church on Sunday that he thought he might have a pair left that'd fit Jeb and he'd opened up this morning so Jeb could take a look. There were still shoes on the shelves — boxes of high-heeled and fancy shoes nobody cared about anymore. But sturdy work boots, children's shoes, running shoes — those shelves were bare. He'd traded fifteen pounds of ground hamburger, which he wouldn't have until he slaughtered one of his heifers, for the boots and thought he got the best—

A woman screamed, a shrieking cry. It was Harmony Hollis, on the other side of the street, looking his way. He followed her line of sight.

There was a silver ball hanging in the sky above the courthouse two doors down. One of them Astral shuttles, looked like. Then he felt a hum in the air, a tingling like static electricity.

MABEL DONAVAN and Clara Swartz came slowly down Elm Street toward Main. Clara's walker was decorated with colorful stickers and silk flowers, smiley faces and the arrougah horn her grandchildren had given her last Christmas. As a joke, but she didn't take them off. She didn't even clean the front of the refrigerator for like six months because it had Bethy's tiny smudged handprints on it.

One call had come through from her daughter and son-in-law since two days after Astral Day, before they were cut off. Sarah said they were getting out of the city. Nothing since then. And Seattle had burned to the ground.

Mabel suddenly stopped.

"Do you hear that?"

Clara had heard almost nothing since she ran out of hearing aid batteries.

"Hear what?"

"Somebody's screaming."

"Screaming what?"

"Just scream—" She sucked in a gasp. "Oh Clara—"

Clara looked where Mabel was looking. Her vision wasn't terrific but you didn't need 20-20 to see the shiny silver ball in the air above the courthouse. One of those alien things, a shuttle.

Clara was suddenly filled with an inexplicable rage, an anger the likes of which she had never known in all her eighty-one years.

"Come on down here, you bastards," she screamed and Mable turned to look at her, dumfounded. Clara'd overheard her oldest son tell a friend once that "Mom wouldn't say shit if her mouth was full of it." Her oldest son had lived in Houston, which was mostly gone. She hadn't heard from him and the refinery fires had burned for weeks. "I'll kick the holy living shit out—"

Then her skin began to tingle and she could feel her hair standing up, full of static electricity. The bottom of the silver marble in the sky began to glow.

~

HERB WILCOX FLIPPED THE HASP, hooked up the lock and snapped it shut. Then he shook it. Wouldn't stop anybody determined to get in. A hacksaw'd make short work of that lock. But it was all he could do and he was just going home to fix himself a quick lunch — spaghetti, if he had enough power to boil the water.

Deputy Pee Wee Watson was nowhere in sight, hadn't said nothing, just leapt into his cruiser and went roaring out of town like his hair was on fire. Whatever the emergency was, it couldn't be more important than guarding the town's food supply. Locked up in the huge warehouse, behind nothing but a padlock, were Jessup's winter stores. Sheriff Matheson had loaded up all the stored supplies of food from every place in town two days after Astral Day. The back storage rooms at the three supermarkets, the pantries in the three elementary schools, the junior high and the high school, any place that had a stockpile, however small, of non-perishable food. Wouldn't let anybody touch it even when food got so short early in the summer that folks was just eating bread from the Best Bread Ever Company.

Folks who could was laying back their own stores for the winter. As farmers slaughtered their herds, the sheriff hauled off meat from Stephenson's Meat

Packing to freeze in the big grocery store freezers, and kept all the supplies of flour and such from Best Bread stored here, too. It being his warehouse and all, Herb had been put in charge of the storage, ran the fork lifts and such. The place was sixty to seventy percent full, stacked floor to ceiling with goods. He didn't have no idea if that was enough to feed a town full of people through the winter. Nobody knew.

When he turned toward his truck, he saw a silver ball hanging in the sky over Main Street, six blocks south. He stood, transfixed. But when the bottom of the ball began to glow, he leapt into his truck and went screaming out of the parking lot and down the street. Out of town. *Away!*

HARRY SANDERS, who'd worked in the property valuation administrator's office back when there'd been a property valuation administrator, carried the fancy leather briefcase he'd always kept beneath his desk. He'd gotten it for Christmas and thought he could use it now for the sandwich bags of seeds he was collecting and swapping with his neighbors. As he stepped out the door of the courthouse, he heard somebody screaming, and static electricity enveloped him, and a hum, a buzz, like wasps were boring into his skull.

An impossibly bright white light suddenly shone down from above. He looked up into it, dropped his briefcase and his eyes were burned to cinders in their sockets a millisecond before his whole body turned into black powder.

~

ELLIE STOOD ROOTED to the spot, gawking. Somewhere down the street, someone was screaming. The bottom of the silver orb began to glow. A man carrying a briefcase on the steps of the courthouse looked up at it. Static electricity lifted Ellie's hair off her neck, the glow turned white and she squinted into it.

Then there was a "whump" sound and the white became Niagara Falls, cascading down in a million glittering points of light, too bright to look at. It filled her whole vision and remained even when she squeezed her eyes tight shut. Heat hit her in a wave with a force that almost knocked her backward a step, the next breath seared her throat, burned her lungs.

When she opened her eyes — couldn't have been more than one, two seconds later, *couldn't have been* — the courthouse, the building that'd been under the shuttle, was gone.

Not destroyed. Or in ruins. Or a pile of rubble. Completely *gone.*

Where it had stood was a blackened crater in the earth and the air rained down ash, black baby powder on the street, the cars, into Ellie's hair. There were little sparkles of glowing something, like a tissue paper dropped in a fire dances and writhes, glowing fire eating around the edges as it crinkles and then turns to smoke.

The screaming continued. Ellie turned to look, her vision distorted, false haloes of glare circling like shiny butterflies in the air, and saw a young blond woman with a stroller, staring at the shuttle, shrieking as the shuttle moved to hang above the building that'd been beside the courthouse. A furniture store.

It was one building closer now to the young woman and her baby.

Stop screaming, you idiot, and run!

The woman made no effort to move.

The bottom of the craft began to glow again. Ellie felt the wasps return to dig holes in her skull and her hair tickled her nose as it floated in the air.

This time, she looked away, braced herself for the blow of heat.

Whump!

A scorched scent burned her nose.

The furniture store had vanished. Its black crater joined the one next to it and the new ash joined the old ash that had not yet settled out of the air. There was a film of it on the top of Ellie's car. Her hands were sooty; how had that happened?

Again the shuttle moved to hang above the next building, making its way farther and farther down the street from Ellie. Now it was just one building away from where the woman stood nailed to the sidewalk shrieking. Out of the corner of her eye, Ellie saw a man who'd just come out of a shoe store, drop his box and race across the street toward the frozen woman, shouting something. Ellie's ears were ringing and she couldn't hear what it was.

There was a sudden blast of light. Like the light that came from the glowing bottom of the ship, but not as large, more like a laser. The running man vaporized. Literally vanished in a puff of smoke and ash.

The hat he'd been wearing, a green John Deere Implement Company hat, escaped the destruction, fluttered in the air where the man no longer stood and plopped down on the street.

The woman stopped screaming as abruptly as flipping off a switch. She began to back away slowly then, inching backward, never taking her eyes off the silver sphere, like a mouse hypnotized by a cobra. She'd never make it, would still be too close when the shuttle arrived at the building beside her after it dispatched the laundromat to ash.

The bottom of the sphere began to glow. Suddenly an elderly woman came out of the side street, running, a bent-over, limping run but moving remarkably fast. She grabbed the young woman's arm and pulled, but the woman remained transfixed as the light became too bright to look at.

Whump!

Ellie squeezed her eyes shut through the flash. The wave of heat struck her that stank of scorched fabric and burnt wood, and it seemed she could taste it as well as smell it. Though she hadn't had her mouth open, the charred, blackened ash on her tongue made her gag. Through glaring haloes, she watched the old woman yank again on the young mother's arm, but she stood transfixed. Then the bent old lady snatched the stroller out of the woman's hands and limped/ran off with it down the side street the way she'd come.

The shuttle moved to the building next to the young woman. She looked up at it. Ellie turned away, couldn't watch.

When she looked back, after the light, the heat and the whump, at the black crater and the … nothing, absolutely *nothing* … on the sidewalk in front of the building, the silver sphere was no longer hanging in the sky.

It was g—

A shadow blotted out the harsh sun.

No, it wasn't gone!

The shuttle hung in the sky above the doctor's office building not fifty feet away. A laser light fired out of the bottom and hit something, no some*body* on the other side of the street, but Ellie didn't look to see who. Ellie didn't wait for the glow, the light or the whump. She turned and bent low, dashed around the front of the car parked next to hers, leapt over the small concrete abutment and raced into the woods. She heard the destruction behind her, but she didn't turn to look. She just ran.

Chapter Thirty-Six

Sawyer could see the orb hanging above the town as soon as he crested the last hill and he couldn't push the cruiser to go any faster, couldn't make the curves in the road if he drove any faster, but he could see it and he couldn't imagine what it was doing.

When he was about half a mile away, he realized he couldn't see the cupola of the courthouse. Noah must have noticed the same thing because he signed something Sawyer didn't catch. They should have been able to see it from here. Sawyer had seen it from here his whole life, and now it was gone.

When he roared into town down Main Street, Sawyer literally couldn't believe what his eyes were telling him. This couldn't have happened. All this, it couldn't have happened in the — what, fifteen minutes? No, not that long, maybe ten — since the shuttle left its position above the downed crashed shuttle and zipped away.

To Jessup. For payback.

He could see the shuttle on the far side of town as he drove down the street. Watched the bottom of the orb glow a bright golden, then an impossibly bright light came out of the bottom, shot down from it.

It looked like the light that'd come from the mothership that was over Moscow.

After the light went out, the ship rose up into the air and … was gone. This time, *vanished* gone. There. Not there. Moving too fast for the human eye to see. There wasn't a soul on the street. Not surprising. Downtown Jessup hadn't been a hub of commerce even before Astral Day, when all the stores were open and doing business. This was a small town, after all. People didn't live downtown in high-rise apartment buildings. They lived in single family homes that lined the streets around downtown. And After the little spots broke out on the black sky, the town center died. Businesses closed up. Folks didn't want party supplies, or new kitchen cabinets, or a new lawn mower now. The whole value system of humanity had completely changed between one heartbeat and another.

Since Astral Day the downtown area had been mostly deserted except for people going to the courthouse …

He stopped his cruiser and signed for Noah to stay in the car. And this time, the boy obeyed. He didn't want to see. Or maybe he already had seen, something like this might be familiar to a boy who'd spent three months aboard an alien mothership.

Sawyer got out of the car slowly and stood with

the door open, leaning on the door, to hold him up. He surveyed his world, the world he had known just about every day of his life. And much of it was gone.

There was nothing but black craters all down the north side of Main Street. The courthouse and every building between it and the corner were gone. A thick, sticky black ash covered everything, like snow, black snow, half an inch deep on everything. Powdery, like baby powder, only black.

On the other side of the street, the doctor's office was gone, Sweet Swishes Dress Store and Gillespie's Pool Hall were gone. The McClintock County Water and Sewer District Building, Archibald Dennis Insurance Agency, and the Hair and Hound Beauty Parlor — gone. There was literally nothing to see. Burton's Shoe Store. Gone. There were no smoldering remains, no shattered foundation stones sticking up like blackened broken teeth. Like all that had been left of his house when it burned to the ground. These structures didn't burn. They disintegrated. They were vaporized. He didn't think fire in any traditional sense had anything to do with this destruction.

Sawyer!

He saw Ellie Hampton running out of the woods behind the doctor's office. She ran full tilt down the length of Main Street and threw herself into his arms. She didn't cry, though. She wasn't hysterical as she had been the last time he'd come upon her in a war zone. But she was shaking violently. Without releasing her hold around his neck, she spoke in something like a monotone.

"It zapped the courthouse first. This white light and a buzzing sound, then a whoosh and it was gone. Completely gone. Nothing but the ash, this black stuff that I can taste, I swear I can taste it on my tongue. It's gross!"

She took a breath.

"Then one after another. Bam. Bam. Bam. There was a woman … she had a stroller and she was just staring up at it. And a man tried to help her." She pulled back out of his arms then, her eyes searching the street.

"There. That's his cap. That's all that's left …" She turned toward the scorched earth that had been the offices of Dr. Sedgwick. "The little girl with a cold, and the old woman who said the doctor had never bitten her … they're gone."

Some sort or new horrible realization struck her.

"So is the doctor who said he'd remove the lump and promised to think about … *He's* gone."

Then she sagged, her knees gave way and she would have collapsed if Sawyer hadn't held her upright.

"Here, sit down." He guided her to his car and sat her in the front seat with her feet on the street.

She put her head in her hands and her elbows on her knees and her whole body shook as she sobbed.

Sawyer turned away from her then and surveyed the devastation, feeling like a survivor of Hiroshima or Nagasaki, but even those had ruins left. Debris. Something. Not just black ash.

A car drove down the street slowly, stirring up

swirling black ash in its wake, its driver gawking at the destruction. The driver was Herb Jacobs, who owned the warehouse where … oh no.

He rolled down his window and leaned out. Didn't even get out of his car.

"It's gone, Sawyer. Just like this. Nothing left but a black dust."

Sawyer felt again like he'd been kicked in the stomach. The food supply for the whole town for the winter gone.

"It gets worse."

How could it get worse?

"They zapped the elementary school but nobody was in it. Got that whole row of businesses at the edge of town, just seemed to be random destruction. Mostly houses, though. I bet half the houses are … no, more like three quarters of them are just gone, along with the people who lived in them." He paused, took a breath. "And in that random destruction, they zapped Stephenson's Meat Packing. Just a crater and black dust."

Sawyer's knees felt like bags of water and he had to lean back against his car to stay upright.

"What happened? Why——?" Ellie began.

"There was a shuttle. It crashed out Perryton Road, by Ben Johnson's dairy. Something was wrong with it, came zooming in out of the sky and crashed into a field."

"That's why? Because a shuttle crashed?"

"They were alive, a couple of them survived, and then Arliss and his buddies …

Suddenly, Sawyer was so outrageously angry his breath caught in his throat and he couldn't even talk. Arliss and his redneck friends had caused this. His stupid, trigger-happy buddies had destroyed the whole town. Had gotten all his deputies …

It hit him then like a wrecking ball. His deputies were … all of them were dead. The magnitude of the destruction hit him then and he had to bend over and put his hands on his knees to get his breath.

The town's whole police force had been wiped out. The town's winter food supply was gone.

Only Best Bread Ever had survived to make bread for the town. Out of what? The flour had been stored in the warehouse. People had their gardens, and there were the town gardens. Could the townspeople survive on that through the whole winter? He didn't think so.

Sawyer would have cursed, but he couldn't think of obscenities foul enough — they'd killed the town. Arliss and his asshole friends had killed the whole town. Some part of him knew it wasn't their fault. It was the Astrals' fault, in their starships that had invaded Earth … as Garson said, to judge mankind.

Well, who got to judge them, huh? Wanna tell me what moral high ground they're standing on when they devastate …

But they didn't care. Humanity didn't matter at all to them. If Garson was right, they intended to kill the rest of the 3.7 billion people on the planet, just like they'd zapped the innocent residents of a little town in Kentucky.

Then he cried. Well, he shook anyway. He didn't

make a sound, but tears were streaming down his cheeks and Ellie got out of the car and put her arm around him. He wasn't sure of much of anything that happened after that. After he realized his job protecting the town was over. The town was doomed.

Chapter Thirty-Seven

Paco lay in the dark, in the quiet, just taking little sips of air because the movement of breathing, the movement of anything was excruciating. It had begun to come on him about halfway through last night's meeting. He'd felt it, like there was a pair of vice grips on his temples, and as the night wore on the grips were pulled tighter and tighter and tighter.

The effort, the incredible effort it took now to see into all those minds at once. Maybe it would have been the same if he'd tried to do the same thing when his feet first touched down in the alley where he'd been taken away three months ago. But Paco didn't think so — well, as much as he was able to think, he didn't think so. The ability to see into the minds of others had started to fade almost immediately when he got back. The ability to have full conversations without ever saying a word had been commonplace, no more than that, had simply been the way of the world when he and the others had been on the ship. And when he got back, he heard Santoro right away.

But every day, every hour of every day, it slipped a little. The ability, skill, whatever it was, it began to fade away. He couldn't hear the voices as loud as before. Then he could only hear something like whispers.

But he'd grabbed hold of it, had seized it with the power of his will, had *willed* his mind not to lose the ability, had willed himself into the minds of others, squirmed into their heads to hear what they were thinking, what they were planning.

It had taken enormous effort and the tension, the effort, became pain in his skull.

He'd been standing in front of the room of about eighteen people when he felt the first twinges of pain and realized he'd been feeling it all along, the tightness in his skull, the throbbing in his temples. But the pain of it didn't register, didn't reach the higher centers of his consciousness right away.

"So here's how it's going to go down, gentlemen. We are going to overturn the order of things, we're going to stage a revolution."

He'd heard the rumble in their thoughts as well as in their voices. The negativity. The fear. The uncertainty. The ones who weren't the slightest bit convinced the kid could pull it off. And the traitor.

He'd heard the traitor's voice, his mind just whispering at first. He'd tried to attend to it but the thoughts of the others were rumbling so loud it had been blotted out. But once he began to talk and the others merely listened, he could hear it more clearly.

There was a man in the crowd who not only didn't believe this would work, not only didn't think Paco could pull it off, but who was actually planning to see to it that it didn't work. There were a handful of others who were still on the fence, wanting what he promised, fearing what he threatened, but still not one hundred percent in his camp. But this dude never gave it any consideration. He wasn't interested in Paco's offers or threats because he intended to rat them out, every one of them, just as soon as he got back to the prison barracks. He was going to seek out the mythical Carver, the one to whom Eduardo intended to rat out Santoro, and tell him the whole plan, chapter and verse.

Paco realized that one reason he had had such difficulty hearing the man's thoughts was that he was hiding them from Paco. How had he learned to do a thing like that — hide his thoughts — and why had he ever needed to employ the skill? The others on the ship with him had learned it. All of them figured it out pretty fast. It was a thing like discovering that when you lowered your voice, people not standing close to you couldn't hear you speak. It was sort of reverse whispering. And they all figured out how to do it, how to lower the volume of their thoughts, and put up a kind of barrier of ... of static, for lack of a better word, on the outside of their thoughts to keep others from listening in. They'd all learned how and used the technique with each other from time to time — guarded their thoughts, kept them private, didn't want others peeking at them, finding out what you were really like, deep down in your deepest self.

He was probably the first one of them who figured it out, because he had a whole lot more to hide than the others did. Star was almost an open book. She was full of the pain of grief that screamed out of her mind when she first got on the ship, drowning out all other thoughts. But as that eased and the rest of her mind surfaced, there was little there a person would mind others knowing. Noah had been quite different. If he could have held up a black sheet in front of his every thought, he would have, but he couldn't at first and his horrible secret came out before he knew how to keep the others from hearing it. How he had caused the house fire that had killed his mother and sister. The pain of that washed off him in waves, and it drowned out most every other thing there was in the kid. But when you could get below it, you found … not much of anything, really. He was … a good kid.

Paco had walled off what he'd done … until the other two ambushed him and saw it all!

He wouldn't go there, couldn't. He did allow his mind to go to the traitor, though. Hakeem Zahair. Even in the pain, the thought of the look on his face when Paco outed him brought a thin smile to Paco's face.

"Just one more thing before we call it a day here," he'd said, his eyes surveying the group of burly men, all of whom would cheerfully have strangled him on the spot … if they'd dared. "We have someone special among us and I'd like to introduce him to you."

They all looked around, both curious and suspicious. They all knew each other. There were no strangers in the crowd.

"He's a man you will all want to get to know very well, because he intends to kill us all."

That stopped the murmuring. The silence in the room, at least what they could hear, was deafening. But it wasn't silent in Paco's head. The thoughts throbbed there. The level of pain he'd been feeling from the effort to hear ratcheted up one level, two. The throbbing pulsed in his eyes. They were all yelling thoughts, all except Hakeem Zahair. He was thinking nothing. Nothing at all. His mind was totally blank, as if he were meditating. And maybe he was, maybe that was how he kept his thoughts to himself, but it wouldn't work with Paco.

Bong. Bong. Bong.

His head throbbed with the effort to penetrate Hakeem, and he quickly gave up, couldn't stand the pain. If only there were no one else present, if he weren't distracted by all the yelling in everybody's head.

But here, now, he couldn't manage to break through. And he was losing his grip on it all. The pain in his skull must surely show on his face and he could not, he absolutely could *not* show a sign of weakness. With a huge force of will, he kept his voice level, must get this over with, done, dismiss these men, get somewhere quiet and silent and dark. If he couldn't do that soon … he would … his brain would bleed.

The thought was horrifying, but he couldn't deny

its reality. If he couldn't get away by himself in the next few minutes, he would have a stroke.

"Our guest here tonight is …" He said the words quietly, not for emphasis but because he no longer had the air to say them loud. If he shouted, his head would split apart. "… Mr. Hakeem Dubali Zahair." He turned to look at the man, whose only reaction was a widening of his eyes. He was good. He was very good. He must be one of Spade's right-hand men. "Mr. Zahair plans to tell Carver the names, addresses, phone numbers, blood types and nose hair numbers of every man here tonight, is already picking out the house he plans to take over when he gets the promotion revealing our little plot is going to earn him."

"I don't know what you're talking about," Zahair said, and managed a pretty good imitation of shock and contempt. "You know me," he said to the others. "You know I wouldn't rat you out."

"Just like he didn't rat out Martinelli. Why do you think Spade blamed Martinelli for stealing that last jar of Chocolate Thunder?" Spade craved the chocolate spread that had pieces of fresh bananas in it that stayed soft and yellow. He'd torn the town apart looking for every jar. When the last jar went missing, he'd blamed Martinelli, slit his throat, and then put the whole lot of them on a nothing-but-a-cup-of-rice-a-day diet for a week. "Might want to check under the loose board in the floor of the pantry of that little house where Zahair's been living. There's still a little Thunder left in the bottom of the jar."

A rumble of sound washed across the room, a mixture of surprise, suspicion and anger.

"And he is the man who tells Spade about slackers on work details. The *only* snitch. He's gotten every man in this room in trouble at one time or another." The penalty for not getting a job done ranged from a beating to strangulation with a piano wire. The cons always assumed other cons on the work details had ratted them out and payback for snitching started most of the fights among the cons.

Paco paused to get his breath and realized the revelations had so shaken Zahair that his defenses were lowered and he saw the secret he kept waaaay down deep in his psyche.

"By the way, he's the man who was *really* banging Spade's redhead, got Gillespie blamed by planting a pair of her panties under his pillow." Gillespie was a nice guy in a world where those were scarce. The cons were secretly outraged when Spade beat him to death with a claw hammer.

The crowd roared, and the con sitting next to Zahair grabbed him, dragged him out of his chair and slammed him up against the wall.

"That was you?"

"But, I didn't … I wouldn't—"

"But he *did*, gentlemen, and he *would*. He'll tell everything he has seen and heard here tonight. Well, unless you silence him. Maybe … rip out his tongue. Or … perhaps …"

Paco felt sorry for Zahair. He probably could have been converted into one of Paco's strongest allies.

Those willing to separate themselves from the herd and go their own way were the kind of men Paco needed. Paco stood for agonizing seconds, feeling the emotional pain of the horror he was about to perpetrate on this man. Zahair didn't deserve what was about to happen to him just for refusing to be a sheep, but Paco hadn't deserved rape either. Shit happens.

"This room is where the church stores its summer sports equipment," Paco said. "There are baseball bats in that closet. I suggest you gentlemen get some …" He looked at Zahair's pleading eyes. And he didn't care. "… and smash every bone in Mr. Zahair's body. Do start at the bottom, though, so he'll be able to appreciate the process."

It was really ugly then. Zahair died a grizzly death. But his sacrificial death cemented the loyalties of the others. They still didn't quite trust Paco and sure as Jackson didn't like the little shit, but they feared, respected and believed him. That was all he needed.

He'd intended to outline a plan to the group last night, but he had been lucky to get out of there alive. He had never had to exert more strength than he'd expended to appear normal after Zahair's death, to dismiss the men and tell them there'd be more coming down the road, to wait for his call.

Then he had stumbled out the back door and up the stairs of the church basement. No one had seen him let himself into the sanctuary by a side door and lie carefully down on the front pew. Carefully. His head was fragile, made of blown glass, the slightest disturbance …

If there had been a fire, and a siren had wailed, back when there were sirens and fire trucks and such, if someone had even turned on loud music nearby, Paco would have died there on that pew. As it was he lay there trembling in pain, every heartbeat a separate agony, literally feeling the massively swollen blood vessels in his brain, the engorged blood vessels slowly begin to discharge their blood, letting it ooze back out, releasing the pressure. It took all night. He saw the sun begin to send purple, blue and gold light down through the remaining intact window, the stained glass one high in the wall above the cross, before he was able to breathe normally, before he no longer feared the walls of his blood vessels would burst from the internal pressure.

As the pain eased away, he fell into an uneasy sleep. When he awoke, he felt ... *different* and he lay very still trying to figure out what had changed. Understanding settled over him slowly and he began to smile. Oh, maybe he was wrong, there was really no way to tell such a thing without trying it out. He'd know then, when he tried he would know if he really had stretched the blood vessels in his brain, made them able to carry much more blood without the pressure rupturing them. He had an image of ... of *panty-hose*. His aunt in West Virginia wore them sometimes and he'd noticed that when she took them off, the part that covered her knee had stretched out so that it retained the shape of her knee even when she wasn't wearing them. Could it be that the effort he had expended last night would make it possible to do something similar again without the threat of a stroke? Or, maybe attempt something even more ambitious? The more he thought about it the more he settled into the belief that he had actually strengthened the walls of his blood vessels by stretching them — a painful, *dangerous* process to be sure, but if it were true, just think of the possibilities!

He was *determined* to hold onto the skill he had, his secret weapon, his mind-reading ability. But he would use it sparingly while he tried to … he thought, *hoped* he could … exercise the skill to build up stamina. He would kill Spade. And he'd already planned how the man would die. That brought a smile, a genuine smile to his lips. He'd seen the machine the first day he'd been scouting the town. Later today, he'd dispatch Santoro to fetch it.

Chapter Thirty-Eight

STAR RODE IN THE WILSONS' Winnebago the next morning, playing with the three-year-old, Jody, while Jarrel poked at Pumpkin's eyes and pulled his ears. Fred and Lottie Schwartz rode with them. The Maddocks and Lopez families had doubled up, too, as had the others. Star didn't know how many people there were, but from the "crowd sound" she could hear — and she was pretty good at judging such things — she knew there were a couple of dozen, maybe more. Many of them walked along behind the horses and in front of the first motorhome.

It was crowded inside the motorhomes, so the group took shifts walking and riding. Papa Eagle Feather probably felt terribly foolish, leading the parade on horseback at a crawl down the winding maintenance roads that crossed the mountains. They started early, stopped in the shade by a stream during the heat of the day, and traveled again late in the evening into the night. It was cooler, used less gasoline, and — though nobody said this part — it kept them off the beaten path as much as possible.

Lunch the second day consisted of their own dwindling supplies, supplemented now by what Papa Eagle Feather had bagged. They stopped by a stream that had a pool deep enough that the little kids could play in it like it was a swimming pool. Everyone spread out in lawn chairs after lunch, watching the children. Star couldn't stop smiling; being with a family again felt so good. Oh, her time with her grandfather had been good, and he'd looked after her, but the laughter of children and the hum of conversation fed her soul, eased the ache there where she missed her Uncle Clyde. Nothing could fill up the hole where Noah should be, though, but she was going to be with him soon.

Star sensed the *warmth* around her that was entirely different from the heat of the sultry day, that grew more and more stifling as the temperature climbed toward mid-afternoon when it seemed that even the drone of the cicadas in the bushes was relenting in its intensity in tribute to the heat.

She might have dozed off, sitting on the creek bank leaned against a tree, with her feet dangling in the water and the sweet gaggle of playing children noises behind her. Maybe that's when it began to come to her. It was certainly there full-blown as soon as she woke up. *Something was wrong.* The foreboding, the sense of impending disaster was as strong as it had been the day the men came to kill Uncle Clyde. She had felt it in a general sense as soon as they'd entered the forest, that it wasn't a good place and that maybe bad things happened here. But she'd shrugged it off. Now, it was like a heartbeat thudding in her veins.

This time, she told her grandfather.

She directed Pumpkin, without speech, to "find Papa Eagle Feather." Her connection to the dog's mind was as crisp and clear as it had been the first time she felt it as the two of them sat alone on the mesa after she was returned from the mothership. But her connection to the minds of other people was fading fast. She had heard Papa Eagle Feather's thoughts clearly that first day. She had studiously avoided hearing them after that, but when they met the stranded people, she could hear the collective of their thoughts as whispers, not voices. If she concentrated and attended, she might be able to tell what they were thinking, but she didn't do that. She didn't want to know what they were thinking. She wanted to communicate with Noah without the necessity of speech, but had never wanted the intrusiveness of others' thoughts. She could still get images from people as she had long before the universe broke out in little dots and that was as strong as ever — no, in a way, stronger, more crisp and clear. Still random, though — she couldn't decide what she wanted to see, but still very much there.

Lottie had clasped her hand to help her down the steps of the Winnebago and she'd gotten the image of a tall young man with sandy blond hair, wearing a Western shirt and boots. It was her son, the one in Houston. That brief image was it, though she could have seen more if she'd tried. But she didn't want to know, didn't want the burden of knowing that the old woman was never going to see the smiling man again, the way she had watched in horror as Darlene Littlewood left pink footprints in the snow. She'd thought this morning that she should try to see what was out there in store for them, but now ... now she didn't want to. She didn't think what she would see was a good thing, and she still felt too fragile.

"Something's wrong," she told Papa Eagle Feather after Pumpkin brought him to her. He'd been cleaning his knife on a rock.

"What?"

"I don't know, but something isn't right. I ... the night the men came and burned down Alien World and ... I knew something bad was going to happen. I feel the same way now."

"Did you tell your Uncle Clyde about it?"

"Uh huh."

"What did he do?"

"Nothing. What could he do?"

"Exactly."

Star understood. Vague warnings of gloom and doom really didn't help anybody.

"When you know more, tell me. Meanwhile, I will be extra careful."

The caravan set back out again at four o'clock. Nick Wilson was riding along beside Papa Eagle Feather on Naki Kiiya, unburdened by supplies, and Star was certain that was because of what she had said. Both men were armed. They would travel until just about dark before they made camp again. The windows were open on the RV, couldn't run the AC because it used too much gas, and she was sitting in the front passenger seat while Fred drove the Wilsons' vehicle. Everyone drove their vehicles manually to save gas. Pumpkin was seated beside her on the floor with his head in her lap while she rubbed behind his ears as she listened to the story of when his ancestors had come to America "from the old country." What country that was, exactly, he wasn't sure, and perhaps the whole story was just a tale he'd made up, but he was a gregarious old man, with a musical laugh and a gift for storytelling and she was thoroughly enjoying it.

Suddenly, Pumpkin tensed. Went from relaxed to rigid, hackles up, growling low in his throat. His mind shouted an image that made no sense. A male animal, black … she couldn't tell what it was because it was moving through the woods so fast, stirring up all sorts of scents as he barreled toward them. Coming. Dangerous. Aggressive. She grabbed Pumpkin's collar, opened her mouth to call out the window that—

But somebody up front was already screaming.

Chapter Thirty-Nine

Naki Kiiya caught a scent. He stopped in his tracks, reared back. Chelee bleated a frightened whinny. That was all the warning Eagle Feather got before something black streaked across his vision and launched itself at the tall man in a black-and-red plaid shirt who'd been walking along on the outside of the group of people in front of the first motorhome. The man went down in a heap, shrieking, trying to fight the animal off. Eagle Feather leapt off the black stallion, pulling his pistol from its holster as he did so, but before he could take two steps, there was a strangled, gurgling sound and the screaming cut off instantly and the animal turned on the woman who'd been next to the downed man. She tried to run, but the animal launched itself at her back, knocked her to the ground and was mauling her. She was shrieking, as was everyone else. Instant panic, everyone was running for the motorhomes, trying to get inside, away from the — what the hell was the thing?

Eagle Feather couldn't shoot it for fear of hitting the woman, so he pulled his knife and ran at the beast, who was so intent on his victim that he didn't see Eagle Feather until it was too late. It let go of the woman and tried to turn on him, but Eagle Feather plunged the knife into the animal, aiming for his back but getting him in the side instead. The animal rolled to the side and started to leap at Eagle Feather. The Indian shot him in the face with his pistol and he collapsed in a heap at his feet.

The whole incident had taken less than a minute. The crowd was hysterical. A screaming woman was leaning over the form of the man who lay in a puddle of blood on his back in the dirt, his throat ripped out. The mauled woman lay on her face on the ground, bleeding from the back of her neck, where a flap of flesh hung loose.

While the others tried to help the bleeding woman or comfort the screaming woman, or stood around with weapons drawn, peering fearfully into the gloom, Eagle Feather knelt beside the beast and turned it over.

"What is *that*?" Nick Wilson asked, stooping to get a better look at the creature. "It never made a sound, like a ghost——"

"Rottweiler," Eagle Feather said.

"A *dog*? It never barked, never … holy shit, if the thing's rabid, what——?"

"Not rabid." Eagle Feather turned its head to the side and pointed to the white scar that stretched all the way across the bottom of its neck. "It didn't bark because it couldn't. Larynx has been cut."

"What? Why would …?"

"To keep it from barking so it can attack without warning. This dog's a trained killer."

"What is it doing out here?"

Eagle Feather got slowly to his feet and looked out into the growing gloom.

"I don't know," he said slowly, his eyes surveying the shadows around them, searching for sharp edges where there should be rounded ones, puddles of dark too deep. "But I'm not anxious to meet the person who trained him."

As if on cue, a sudden roaring ignited like a bomb in the woods, like bees or angry wasps. It came from all around them. Lights appeared everywhere, single headlights, bouncing as they came closer and closer. There was a deeper engine rumble, too, on the road in front and behind them, and headlights appeared there, coming fast.

Star!

There was nothing Papa Eagle Feather could do for her, though. The force of men on dirt bikes was on them in a heartbeat, roaring out of the woods and skidding to a halt all around them. Surrounding them. The cloud of dust their approach kicked up into the air obscured them, hung there, then settled slowly, revealing their forms as trucks came roaring down the road from both directions to join them.

There must have been at least twenty men — maybe

more, it was hard to tell — on dirt bikes, all kinds, some of them pieces of junk held together with duct tape, some elaborately customized, with fat front tires, tall handlebars, and custom-painted tanks. The men aboard them were in no better shape than their rides.

The bike and rider revealed out of the clearing dust nearest Eagle Feather was a custom horror, the tank and both fenders of the bike made of thick, heavy iron plate flattened by hand. The man riding it had his head shaved except for a mohawk strip on top died bright red and his entire face was covered in tattoos. Rings in his nose and ears, and a big one in his bottom lip. He wore something that looked like football shoulder pads, but he had fashioned an elaborate cape of black feathers that flowed down the back. His pants were leather, hard knee pads, high black motorcycle boots, but there were darts affixed to both pant legs, that could be fired from the dart gun bow strung across the handlebars. He was revving his engine again and again, a maniacal smile on his toothless mouth.

The bike beside that one held a rider decked out in hockey gear, pads and gloves. Painted on the helmet was a vicious monster face and there were fake horns attached to the top.

The man on the other side rode a bike with a cow skull mounted on the handlebars, the tips of the horns painted blood red. He had long blond hair that hung in a tangled mass around his head, and wore something that looked like a dog muzzle across the bottom portion of his face.

The man next to him didn't have an inch of un-tattooed flesh anywhere that Eagle Feather could see. His shaved head and face were covered — even on his eyelids, where tattoos of eyeballs gave him a fiendish look when he blinked. He was bare-chested, and the designs on his chest were not only tattoos but scars, still-healing cuts, skulls and gargoyle figures, more than one of the raised welts appearing infected.

All the men were in tattered rags, their faces filthy, beards died bright colors or cut into odd shapes. Here there was clearly an effort to intimidate, a concentrated determination to look like the meanest dogs in the junkyard, like they'd walked off the set of *Mad Max* to have a latte at Starbucks.

They all were wild-eyed, either purposefully so, mentally unstable or on drugs, or all of the above.

The woman whose husband had been killed by the dog was still kneeling at his side, sobbing. The woman who had survived the dog bite was hysterical, losing blood fast, shrieking, though another woman was trying to hold a towel to the wound as a pressure bandage.

"We are in deep shit," Eagle Feather whispered to Nick Wilson.

Wilson's face was set in a grim line. In the glow of dozens of headlights, his black hair and beard made him look like an over-exposed photograph.

Eagle Feather edged behind him and went to the door of his motorhome. Star and Pumpkin and Wilson's wife and kids were inside, as were Fred and Lottie Schwartz. The Indian didn't want to call undue attention to the vehicle by opening the door, just stood beside it, waiting.

He was armed. Had a knife in a scabbard and a pistol in a holster. He could take out a considerable number before they got him, but he was carrying a revolver and they'd cut him down when he ran out of ammo, before he had a chance to reload. There was nothing to be done, so Eagle Feather did nothing.

The man with the feathered cape put down his kickstand, leaned the bike on it and dismounted.

"Who owns this piece of shit?" he asked, gesturing toward Ian Maddocks's Winnebago, which was out front. No one spoke. "I have to ask one more time, I'm going to kick in the skull of the owner. Now whose is this?"

"It's mine," Ian said from the back of the crowd. He had left the vehicle to join the crowd and apparently had been trying to inch his way back to the vehicle, maybe to lock himself and his family inside.

"Not anymore it isn't, motherfucker. Gimme the keys."

"They're in it." Ian gestured back toward the RV, clearly so frightened he was having trouble talking.

"Then get them for me, son of a bitch, before I rip you open," he made a languid motion of pulling a homemade sword/machete out of a scabbard at his waist, "and leave you with your guts in your lap."

Ian's wife, Jessica, let out a little squeak of a scream at that and the man searched the crowd for the source of the sound as Ian ran to the vehicle and retrieved the keys. A big truck that had been lumbering toward them arrived at that time, and the man contented himself with grabbing the keys from Ian and dropping them into his pocket.

The truck was an army transport kind of truck, high clearance, big tires with deep treads and space for twenty or thirty soldiers in the back. Only about half that many got out, but added to the bikers already here, there was a force of at least two dozen armed, dangerous men.

Two other trucks bumped to a stop behind the first, but no one got out of the back of either of them.

The man who stepped out of the first truck was clearly their leader. He was not dressed in a bizarre fashion, just jeans and a tee shirt and a denim jacket. His head was shaved, his beard full and the color of rust. His eyes were heavy-lidded, and his fair complexion made the rest of him look almost hairless. He didn't appear to have either eyebrows or eyelashes. A single tattoo adorned his face, a spider, crawling out the corner of his right eye.

When he smiled, his lips stretched out so thin they almost vanished. His teeth were over-large, and made Eagle Feather think of a horse's teeth.

He held an oversized pistol of some kind and waved the barrel around for emphasis when he spoke.

"Well hello, hello, hello, what do we have here?" he said, approaching the group of people. He called out above the crowd. "Everybody get out here, empty those vehicles. I want to see your pretty faces all right here in a row in front of me, a single line. Drop your weapons on the ground."

Eagle Feather opened the door to the Wilsons' motorhome and gestured for those inside to get out. They had the windows open and had heard the command. He could see Michelle Wilson speaking into Star's ear and knew she was explaining what Star couldn't see. The Schwartzes exited first, Michelle was next. Star was at the end holding Pumpkin's collar. The dog was growling the low growl of an animal that would need almost no provocation at all to attack. As she stepped to the ground, Eagle Feather leaned in and whispered, "Send Pumpkin away, tell him to hide." Star didn't question, just reached down and unhooked his halter, leaned in and whispered in his ear and the dog slipped along the side of the motorhome and was gone.

The group did as they were ordered. The mothers held onto terrified children, who were whimpering but actually too frightened to cry. They just stared at the intruders with wide, horrified eyes. The man's "soldiers" darted into the crowd and collected the dropped weapons.

"This here's the head dick," said the man who'd relieved Ian of the keys to his vehicle, pointing to Ian. "Drives the lead dog."

"I'm not—" Ian started to speak.

The feather cape man punched him hard in the belly and he doubled over, and this time Jessica did cry out, rushing to him as he collapsed to his knees.

"I want you to talk, I'll tell you to talk. I don't tell you to talk, you keep your motherfucking mouths shut," said the bald man from the truck. "That clear?"

No one spoke.

"I said *is that clear*?" he roared, and everyone in the crowd nodded their heads and said it was clear. But the woman whose husband had been killed and the wounded woman still continued to cry and wail.

The man walked over to the sobbing woman, grabbed her by the hair and pulled her upright. He cocked his pistol and stuck the barrel an inch from her nose.

"I said, shut the fuck up," he said. She gasped, gulped and was silent.

He stepped to the injured woman, kicked her with his big black boot and rolled her over. "Did you hear me?" She was too far gone to care and continued to cry. He put the gun to her forehead and pulled the trigger. The crowd went off like a bomb, women and children crying, horrified. The man pointed his gun in the air and fired again and the crowd fell silent.

"She'd a been dead by morning anyway," he said. "He walked back to his position at the front of the crowd and said, "My name's Bubba Blacksnake. Just Bubba is all you need to know." He paused and Eagle Feather wondered if he'd just made up the "Black-snake" part — that it sounded meaner/sexier that Bubba Snodmotz or Bubba Pickledorph. The man looked the crowd over, sizing them up. "And I wanna know who killed my dog."

Oh *shit.*

Papa Eagle Feather stood up tall, proud that his voice didn't quaver. "I did," he said.

Chapter Forty

Sawyer Matheson was drunk. Oh my, yes, he was drunk. Very drunk indeed. But not as drunk as he planned to be. Nope, he had not gotten to that place in drunkenness where nothing matters and it doesn't hurt anymore. That's the place he was seeking.

He lifted the bottle of Maker's Mark whiskey to his lips and took a big gulp. His eyes watered and he gasped. Though there had been a time in Sawyer's life when he drank a considerable amount, he hadn't tied one on in years. Not since ... Nope, not going there!

He had planned this drunk strategically. He'd come back to the house from the academy where he left Noah in the loving care of the monks. And of Garson, too, of course. Garson had always been fond of Noah. Now, he almost followed the boy around like a puppy dog. Noah had done what Garson had only dreamed of doing, but had dreamed of it every night for his whole life. Noah had gone up in an alien spaceship. Ahh, what Garson would give to do the same thing. He had bemoaned that fact just the other day at breakfast.

"I can't see any rhyme or reason to the selection of people the Astrals abducted," he said. "Why wouldn't they take someone with whom they could have an intelligent conversation?"

He realized he had stepped in it and tried to back-track as Garson always did when he got into interpersonal relationship deep shit, which was mostly every time he tried to interact with another human being.

"Oh, I didn't mean by that to say Noah is not an intelligent human being. He's a very smart little boy, you know, for a little boy. No telling what he could have done with his life if the world hadn't turned wrong side out. Now, he'll probably wind up just like his father, in some small town not doing anything that matters."

He blew right by that one and continued.

"And he tells me they never asked him about anything. That's what was so astonishing to me in the beginning. I'd have thought they would have peppered him with questions, given his station as a prodigy. But I'm not sure they took him because he was a prodigy. I'm not sure at all why they took him."

"I don't really care why they took him," Sawyer said. "I'm just glad they brought him back — unharmed."

"Unharmed, yes, unchanged … not so much."

"Meaning?"

"Oh, don't be dense, Sawyer. You can see how different he is. You have to see it."

He did, of course, see the change that had been wrought on his only child. And he had nowhere to put it in his mind. Nowhere with a convenient file labeled: "How to feel about your son who's been changed by aliens."

"You tell me, then, how is Noah different?"

"He doesn't look so desperate anymore, for one thing."

That hit home, hard. It was true. Since he had been back home from his three-month stay in the Astral mothership, he had seemed much more like his old self. More outgoing, smiled more, didn't seem to always be carrying the weight of the world on his shoulders. Sawyer had attributed his withdrawal, his sadness, his listless disinterest in the world around him to grief over the deaths of his mother and little sister. And Sawyer still believed that had been the problem. So what had happened to him on the mothership that helped him get over his grief? And why wouldn't he talk about it?

"Has he talked to you much about it, about what happened to him there?"

"I peppered him with questions, most of which he couldn't answer, about the ship and the occupants, both the Astrals and the other abductees. When he talked about the reptars — I think that's the word they're using for those beasts — I thought I would shit my pants right then and there."

Noah had described the insectile beasts with too many legs, blue eyes and needle teeth, but didn't seem to want to talk about them, so Sawyer hadn't pushed.

Now, sitting here on the kitchen floor clutching a bottle of Maker's Mark like a kid holding his teddy bear, he wondered if he should have pressed harder to find out what had happened to the boy. Now that he'd made the personal acquaintance of a pair of reptars, and could imagine the horror Noah had been exposed to.

Why was he sitting on the kitchen floor? There were chairs at the table. But he didn't get up and sit in one, just remained where he was. Maybe he fell there. Whatever.

He lifted the bottle to his lips and swallowed two big gulps. It burned going down, his eyes swam with tears and his throat felt like he'd seared it with an acetylene torch. Why wouldn't this damn stuff work — take him away, wipe his mind of images …

Deputy Tyler and his wife Sarah Jo were expecting their first baby. They had been trying for years and finally gave up and began adoption proceedings. As soon as they did, Sarah Jo got pregnant, something about relaxing and just letting it happen. Sarah Jo had come into the office just Tuesday, strutting that baby bump. So proud of it.

Roger Hawkins was the first of his deputies the reptar tore apart. Or was it Billy Ray? It all happened so fast, so incredibly fast. From where Sawyer was standing, it looked like the beast … like it tore Roger's head right off at the shoulders.

He shuddered and took another gulp of whiskey. It was beginning to go down smoother now, and Sawyer's lips felt numb.

But he could still feel, dammit. Impotent rage sliced through him like a scythe through wheat, ripping him open. His hands clenched into fists and he wanted to punch somebody, anybody. No, he wanted to punch one of those monsters.

Who would then have relieved him of his arm, probably both legs before it ripped out his throat. And Noah needed him. He had to pull it together for the boy who needed a father worse now than he ever had before.

Sawyer sighed. Well, he'd be getting huge doses of Sawyer from now on, given that he no longer had a job as the McClintock County Sheriff.

After the debacle with the shuttle, he'd have gone into the office of the mayor and ceremoniously laid his shield down on Jack Rupert's desk … if there'd been a desk or a mayor, or even a building to walk into. Black dust, that was all that was left. Powdery black baby powder that seemed to clog up his nose and get into his throat somehow like it was choking him.

They were dead, all of them. The entire county police force — six deputies wiped out by the reptars — and the dispatcher, Betty Hawthorne, along with part-time deputy Jake Purvis had died when the shuttle wiped out the courthouse … he bet it hadn't taken five minutes, not three even.

And with no deputies, what good was a sheriff?

The answer to that question, ladies and gentlemen, was no good. No damned good for anything, well, except to sit on the floor in his kitchen — why was he sitting on the floor again? — getting snockered.

And after he got snockered … what then? Hell, he didn't know, and didn't care. Well, didn't want to care. And if he kept drinking long enough, maybe he wouldn't care. So he took another belt, wiped his mouth on the back of his hand and belched loudly.

"Now, that's a lovely sound," said a voice from the kitchen door and Sawyer almost crapped his pants. He dropped the bottle of Maker's on the floor and it rolled across it until it was stopped by a shoe. Okay, a foot in a shoe. He followed the progression upward until he was looking at Ellie Hampton. Elliot Thurgood Hampton, to be precise. The day she'd dropped that name on him you could tell she was waiting for him to be impressed by it. He'd never heard of Hampton Construction Company, and by that time it probably didn't exist anymore anyway.

"Hi, Ellie," he said. Feeling stupid.

"I thought I'd find you here. And I suspected this would be what you'd be doing when I found you." She looked down at him, genuine compassion, profound compassion in her dark blue eyes. "And I don't blame you."

"Good, then roll that bottle back over here. No, pick it up. It's spilling."

"I suspect you've had enough out of this bottle for the night," she said and bent to pick it up.

"Give it back to me," he said, and was even surprised himself by how stern and authoritative his voice sounded. "I mean it. Give me that bottle."

She took two steps and wordlessly handed it to him.

"Unless you intend to join me, I hope you won't think me rude to ask you to leave."

Crap, he sounded like the butler in an old English drama.

"Those are my choices, then. Leave or drink with you?"

He nodded.

"Okay," she said, slipped the strap of her purse off her shoulder and hung it over the post on the back of a chair. "The monks are looking after the girls. I'm good." Then she crossed the room and slid down the wall until she was sitting beside him.

"If the object of this little endeavor is to get roaring drunk, then let's get after it." She turned up the bottle, took a drink, choked and spewed most of it back out onto his shirt and in his face.

"What is *that*?" she gasped.

"Rocket fuel," he said, and took the bottle back from her. "Put enough of it in your tank and you can go jetting out across the universe."

After that, the night began to gray out.

Chapter Forty-One

THE MAN APPROACHED EAGLE FEATHER, looked him up and down.

"You a real Indian?" Before he had a chance to respond, the man continued, "Yeah, you are, ain't you. A *real* Indian." He leaned close to Eagle Feather and his breath smelled of rotted teeth. "That was *my* dog you killed, motherfucker."

Papa Eagle Feather said nothing. What was there to say?

The man addressed the rest of the crowd as he spoke next, but he kept his focus on Eagle Feather.

"I don't want to kill all you people ... but I will. Oh, yes, I surely will indeed. If you make me, if you cross me, you will die and it won't be pretty."

Eagle Feather figured the number of breaths he still had to breathe was probably in the single digits. And he was glad to see that he wasn't terrified. He was scared, shit yeah, every man was scared when he faced the end of his days. But he stood up straight and tall, his hands didn't shake. He was an Apache warrior and he would die like one.

But Star.

His heart broke for her but he continued to stand ramrod straight, staring out in front of him, awaiting his fate. The man didn't shoot him, though, or hack him up with the machete he carried at his side. Instead, he turned toward the whole group and started preaching.

"Guess I don't have to tell you the whole world has changed, and in this new world order a man has got to carve out his own place in the world, survive as best he can, only now that's without benefit of the enforcement of laws and morality and such.

"If you don't never remember another thing about meeting Bubba Blacksnake, you got to remember this. Listen up. This here is the new world order. *Fight or die.*

"And that's good. Real good. 'Cause I been operating outside the laws of man for most of my born days, just like my daddy before me and his daddy before him."

He turned back and faced the group.

"You're the kind of folks who do what you're told and obey the laws, cross on the green arrow, shit like that, am I right? Well, me and mine ain't never been that kind. My great granddaddy was a moonshiner. You know what that is?"

He turned to Fred Schwartz.

"You, old man, you know what that is?"

"It's somebody who ... illegally makes alcohol, whiskey."

"Close, but no cigar. Nothing illegal about making whiskey. The illegal part's where there's a tax on it and you don't pay. See, that there's the thing. The government decided it'd ought to tax booze and up in the Kentucky mountains, we decided we wasn't paying no fucking government tax."

Clearly, this man liked the sound of his own voice.

"Then my granddaddy went off to shoot gooks in the jungles of Vietnam and come home with tales of how folks was paying good money to smoke the stuff that grew wild out behind Grandma's barn. See, Kentucky farmers used to grow hemp for rope, and hemp and marijuana is kissing cousins.

"If you can grow tobacco, you can grow dope. Requires the same machinery, the same expertise, the same labor, the same barns. And my great granddaddy become a millionaire, used to carry a black garbage bag stuffed full of money in the trunk of his car ... he got caught with a piddly two joints in his pocket and got his self sent up on a mandatory twenty-year sentence.

"Dope started out illegal and then the government legalized it and taxed the shit out of it and I ain't gonna pay them motherfuckers a dime. So I grow tax-free dope. You got any idea what the profit margin is when you don't got to give Uncle Sam a cut? Whew doggies!

"Then the aliens come. No more hiding sinsemilla from the revenuers between the plants in a cornfield. The day after Astral Day I was out planting three times the regular crops of dope and tobacco. I figure the man who's got dope, tobacco and hooch's gonna be a rich man even when a dollar ain't good for nothing but to wipe your ass with.

"But here's my problem."

He'd been pacing back and forth in front of the group and now he stopped.

"Labor. Cutting tobacco and curing dope is a labor-intensive process. I'm telling you. Middle of August is harvest time. And I ain't got no workers. Folks supposed to show up, didn't show up. I got crops and I got work to do so … I'm looking for laborers. And you fine folks just volunteered.

"Can I get an *amen, brother* to that?"

There was a pause,

"I said, could I get—?"

And the crowd parroted. "Amen, brother."

"Fine. Good. *Excellent*. So I just became the boss and you just became em-ploy-ees. Gonna pack you up and ship you off to my farm, get you tucked in bed early tonight because tomorrow's gonna be a busy day. We all good with this?"

Most shook their heads, a couple said yes and then the rest said yes, too.

"There's just a couple of little matters we need to clear up before we go on our merry way. There's the matter," he paused and turned to Eagle Feather, "of my dog."

He addressed the crowd as he walked back to where Eagle Feather stood. "Dogs like Sarge that don't bark — silent killers to guard my dope — is hard to come by. Slit the throats of a whole litter of

Rottweilers and usually don't but one or two survive. That there was a valuable animal."

Eagle Feather wished he'd just get to it. It was hard for any man to hold his composure in the face of certain death. The longer Bubba delayed, the more Eagle Feather's thoughts went to Star. Knowing he'd failed her, that he was abandoning her to make her way in this crazy world by herself hurt far worse than knowing he was about to die.

"And by all the laws of God and man somebody needs to pay for killing it." He lifted his pistol and pressed the end of the barrel to Eagle Feather's forehead and the old man was glad Star was blind so she wouldn't have to watch him die.

Chapter Forty-Two

Bubba stood with the barrel of his pistol shoved up against Eagle Feather's forehead.

"Yes, sir, somebody's got to pay for my dog."

He cocked the pistol. Paused. Everyone held their breath, cringing away from what they knew was coming.

"It ain't gonna be this old Indian, though." He uncocked the pistol and lowered it. "And when you pay me, you don't get to pay with a bullet in the brain. Pay me, you got to die slow."

He stepped back and looked at the line of people in front of him.

"See, it's like this. Ole Bubba found out a long time ago that scared people are obedient people. And it's easier to scare a man if he don't know what's coming next. If life and death's just random. You cross me, you disobey me, you displease me, you can lean over and kiss your ass goodbye — you can count on that part. But even if you don't cross me, ain't no guarantee you're gonna see another sunrise. Disobedience is a guaranteed death. But obedience ... be a good little soldier, work hard, suck up harder ... and maybe you get to live. Maybe."

He paused for effect. "But maybe not."

He put his pistol back in his holster and gestured to the man with the red mohawk and the cape of black feathers. The man pulled out the handmade machete/sword and gave it to Bubba. The machete blade was stained brown.

"One of you" — he pointed the machete from one person to another and they all cringed away — "has got to die here tonight to pay for my dog. Eye for an eye. Sooooo ..." He began to walk slowly down the line of people. "Who's it gonna be?"

Eagle Feather was sick. They'd stumbled into the hands of the devil himself, walking around the earth in a human being suit. Bubba got to Star, and Eagle Feather's heart was pounding so hard he could feel his vision pulsing with each beat.

"You're with him, ain't ya?" he said to her, nodding back toward Eagle Feather. Star didn't know he was talking to her. "Shit, you're blind." He turned back to his crew of soldiers and the bikers encircling their camp. "Would you look at this, the little Injun kid's blind." He gripped the machete in both hands and lifted it high over her head as if he meant to cleave her in two with it. The crowd gasped and produced an uneasy grumbling sound, but Star had no response at all. "See, she really is blind, no shit." He laughed, acted like he was going to slice her head off and still she didn't respond. "Boys, we got ourselves a little blind mascot. Gonna call you … Stumbles." He laughed uproariously at his own wit and his men joined in. "Yeah, you gonna be Stumbles and you gonna work just like everybody else 'cause you don't need eyes for what you're gonna be doing, sweet thing."

He walked on past her and Eagle Feather let out the breath he'd been holding. He was glad she'd sent Pumpkin away. This lunatic would surely have killed the dog, an eye for an eye.

Bubba got to the end of the line, turned and began to walk slowly back down it, waggling the machete in front of each person's face in turn.

"Is it … you, old woman?" He held the machete in front of Lottie Schwartz. She was crying softly and when Fred went to put his arm around her shoulders to comfort her, Bubba snapped, "You wanna die, old man, that's a surefire way to git 'er done."

Fred let go of his wife and drooped his hands down to his sides.

"Is it you?" He wiggled the machete in Nick Wilson's face, then moved on to Michelle. "Or maybe you?" He pointed to her belly. "Kill two birds with one stone."

"How about one of the kids?" He stepped back and surveyed the crowd. "We got lots of kids here and they're useless as tits on a boar hog. You don't get no extra food for them, by the way. They eat what you get and it ain't much. You sure you wouldn't rather just get rid of them right now?" He laughed again and so did his men. Bubba was definitely enjoying himself, and his men seemed as unhinged as he was.

All the parents held their children crushed up against them.

Bubba walked on.

"Maybe it's you." He held the machete in front of Ian Maddocks. His and Jessica's three children were clinging to Jessica, their faces buried in her skirt.

Bubba walked on a step, then turned on Ian Maddocks with the speed of a striking rattlesnake.

"Yeah, it's *you!*" he cried and sliced Ian's belly with the machete, opening it up all the way across.

Jessica shrieked and grabbed Ian as he dropped to his knees, a look of surprise, not pain, on his face. He looked down at his internal organs and they began to ooze out the slice in his belly. The children screamed, "Daddy, Daddy."

Bubba stood for a moment staring at the man on his knees, his guts spilling out onto the ground. He smiled, then turned and strode away.

"Alright, we done here," he called out. "Get everybody loaded up. Need to get these good folks settled in their bunks for the night."

Without looking back he strode toward the troop truck, tossing the machete to its owner, who caught it deftly with one hand.

And that was that.

Jessica was shrieking, the children crying, most of the other women crying right along with her, as Ian collapsed on his side on the ground.

"Help me, somebody, help me," Jessica cried, looking from one helpless person to another.

"Kill him," Bubba tossed over his shoulder. "We need to book."

The man with tangled blond hair took two steps toward Ian, pointed his pistol and shot him in the head. He went limp and Jessica screeched.

The man turned to the others around Jessica.

"Get her out of here and loaded up with the rest of you or I'll put a bullet in her head, too." The other women took Jessica's arms and dragged her away from her husband's body. The children still clung to her, crying.

Bubba paused and looked at Eagle Feather's two horses. Naki Kiiya and Chelee had remained steadfastly where Eagle Feather had left them, even though they'd obviously been terrified. Bubba called out to his men. "Anybody know how to ride a horse?" and several of them men did. "Bring them along. I want me some Indian ponies!"

One of the men from the troop truck shoved Jessica and her children into the motorhome belonging to the Wilsons and her cries cut off abruptly when they slammed the door shut behind her. Then they began loading people into the back of the troop trucks, while the men who'd been riding in the first one dispersed to guard the other two, with others climbing into the motorhomes.

The bikers began to crank their bikes and the air was split with the squall of the engines as they revved them up and then took off down the road.

Eagle Feather made his way to Star, standing in a group of the "stranded," who had gathered around her, and took her by the arm.

"What happened?" she asked. "What—?"

"These men are monsters. They killed Ian Maddocks for no reason." He pulled her along beside him as he spoke softly to her. "You stick by my side like you're attached with Velcro, you understand?"

She merely nodded. He got to the truck and several people reached out to Star to help pull her up but she couldn't see their hands so Eagle Feather lifted her up until they could reach her. Then the group ... closed ranks around Star. There wasn't any other way to describe it and Eagle Feather was sure they weren't aware they were doing it. But they ... *instinctively* moved her to the back of the truck and stood in front of her, between her and Bubba's men. He made his way to her side and took her hand. Somebody slammed the tailgate shut and with a grinding of gears, the truck lurched down the road into the night.

Eagle Feather described to Star the camp as they drove into it.

"It's a Boy Scout camp," he said, as the truck passed beneath the archway where it was printed "Boy Scouts of America." The truck pulled to a stop in the center area between what looked like barracks and the parade of RV's being pulled up behind it. The men who'd been guarding them let down the tailgates and ordered everybody out.

When they opened the door to the Wilsons' RV, the people in it carried out Jessica Maddocks and laid her on the ground. Her children gathered round her like chicks around a mother hen, wide-eyed and shocked.

Bubba climbed down out of the cab of the truck and casually looked over.

"She wouldn't stop that caterwauling," said the man who'd been riding in the RV. "Had to shut her up."

"You kill her?"

"Na, just punched her in the face. She's likely got a broke nose, but when she comes to, she'll be able to work tomorrow."

"Men's dorms is over there," Bubba called out and pointed to a barracks-looking building on the north side of the open area in the middle, where the truck had bulldozed down a sign that said the area was for campfires. "Women's is over there. Children go with their mamas ... and you mamas listen up. Them brats cause me the least little bit of trouble, they're gone. You understand what I'm telling you? I'd just as soon shoot a kid as not. Get to bed now. We get up before the sun around here. Big day. Big day."

Eagle Feather leaned over to Star. "I guess I won't see you until the morning."

"Don't worry about me. I'll be fine." She leaned close and whispered, "Pumpkin followed us. He's out there in the woods. I've put him on down stay so he'll be waiting in the morning. But I don't know what he's going to eat. And water ..."

"He's a smart dog. He'll figure it out.'

Then several women came to Star and they

shooed her away in front of them. Eagle Feather supposed they'd take good care of her.

If the barracks were identical, and Eagle Feather supposed they were, they both were sparse but clean, a place you'd like to send your son for a week of fun camping in the woods. The buildings were sweltering, though, and Eagle Feather soon discovered why. All the windows were closed and nailed shut. Each of the barracks had a porch on the front and there were still rocking chairs on them. Bunk beds stretched on both sides of a center aisle. No way out but the front door, and there were two guards stationed there, sitting in the rockers. But they did at least leave the door open, though with the windows nailed shut there was no air flow to cool the building. The heat would be staggering in the daytime.

The men didn't mingle and talk. They were all too angry/scared/traumatized. Eagle Feather had just gotten comfortable on one of the low bunks and dozed off when a big bell began to ring, *clang, clang, clang.*

Chapter Forty-Three

HARRY WINDOM STEPPED CAREFULLY around the watering can on the front porch and then rang the doorbell. He heard movement inside and figured somebody was peeking out through the drapes to see who it was before they opened the door.

While they inspected him, he inspected the garden-that-used-to-be-a-yard that stretched from the edge of the porch to the street and from the driveway all the way to the neighbor's fence — where the neighbor's garden stretched out across his not-yard-anymore-either from there.

Tomato plants, green beans, corn, and carrots. Potatoes or sweet potatoes, too, it was hard to tell which until you dug them up. They looked about the same on the top side. There were—

The door opened a crack.

"What do you want?" a man asked, in a tone that was somewhere south of accommodating on the pleasant-to-rude scale.

"This here your dog?" Harry asked, indicating the animal at the end of his leash.

He knew it wasn't, of course. He'd found the dog on the other side of town as he was driving into Jessup, just lying there by the road in the weeds. Harry had put on the brakes and screeched to a stop and backed up to get him. The dog likely would have run away from Harry if he'd had the strength. Instead, he just looked up at Harry pathetically, expecting a blow.

The dog was dragging a frayed rope he must have chewed through. Obviously, his owners had moved away when the Astral app showed the ships and hadn't bothered to take old "Hungry" — that's what Harry called him — along with them, left him tied up, starving. By the time Harry found him on the roadside he was nothing but bones, ribs poking through his skin, his face a skeletal mask. He looked horrifying, which was why Harry'd stopped and loaded the dog into the back of his truck.

This was his first "sell job" using Hungry and Harry was anxious to see how it would go.

"No, that's not my dog!" the man cried. "What happened to the poor thing?" The man opened the door and got down on one knee in front of Hungry, while his wife and a couple of children crowded around behind him, all of them astonished and horrified — pretty much the reaction Harry'd been hoping for.

"I don't know what happened to him, just found him right down there" — Harry pointed toward the end of their street — "figured he must live around here somewhere. I couldn't just leave him there, had to try to find his owner."

"His owner!" The woman's voice was filled with indignation. "You can't give him back to somebody'd let a defenseless dog like this starve. What kind of person'd do such a thing?"

"I couldn't tell you that, ma'am, but — now, mind, I ain't defending this dog's owner, but might be he didn't have no choice in the matter. I mean …" He let the rest dangle and the woman took the bait.

"What are you talking about?"

"Well, if there ain't no food to eat, this here's what you get." He let that soak in for a beat, then went on. "And since them Astrals come and destroyed the town's food supplies for the winter, might be there'll be *people* in Jessup looking like this come spring." He glanced knowingly at the two small children.

The man and woman shared a horrified glance, then the man stuttered on for a minute or two about how that wasn't gonna happen because he wasn't gonna let it happen and they had a garden and he'd go hunting in the woods and … and …

Harry let him talk until he wound down.

"Oh, I'm sure you want to take care of you and yours best as you can. I do, too, but I ain't betting the lives of my kids on a garden and a prayer."

The man looked interested, so Harry reeled him in.

"I know where there's plenty of stores for the winter and I plan to go get me my fair share for my family."

"Where?"

"That rich-kid academy out there's got barns full of supplies, way more'n they need. I'm getting me some …" Then he seemed to consider. "If you're interested in getting some for your family, too, me and some other folks is gonna get together in the Senior Citizens' Center about six o'clock tonight." The center was vacant, hadn't served up "a hot lunch and conversation" since Astral Day. "You might want to hear what the rest of your neighbors got to say about it."

The man said he might do that. Yes sir, he might just do that.

"Name's Harry Windom." Harry stuck out his hand and the man shook it. "Me and the missus, Betty Ann, got a pig farm on Trundle Road, just this side of Danbury." Harry didn't have a missus or a pig farm. "See you this evening. Now, I got to see can I find this poor thing's owners. It was good talking to you."

Harry stepped off the porch and made his way on the sidewalk between the corn plants to the driveway and down the street to the next house and thought about the destruction the alien spacecraft had visited on Jessup.

It wasn't what he'd seen in pictures where bombers in World War II dropped their payloads on cities and leveled some buildings, damaged others, tore the shit out of things. That was not this. There were no ruins here. No rubble. Whatever the green sons of bitches trained their laser ray on just vanished. *Poof.* Like it'd never been there at all except for the black dust, fine as black baby powder. He'd stirred up little whirlwinds of the stuff as he'd walked up and down the streets where buildings used to be.

Harry was a practical man. And orderly, a man who made lists of his lists, though not so — what did they call it? OCD — that he organized his soup cans in alphabetical order. But he did make sure the toes of all his shoes were pointed in the same direction in his closet, and a picture hanging crooked on a wall would literally make him crazy.

He'd come into town from his farm out in Burnett Hollow, stopped and surveyed the damage to the rest of the town as he drove in. He'd known then he could pick up some supporters from among them that was left. Where there'd been homes, now there was just powder. He didn't know if anybody'd been inside when the houses got zapped. Wasn't no way to tell. Wasn't like there was charred bodies or anything like that left behind. Just that black dust — car-dust and person-dust all looked the same.

The elementary school wasn't there anymore where his kids, Katie and Mark, had gone to school before Betty Ann used Astral Day as an excuse to cut and run, take the kids to live with her mother on a farm on the other side of Cincinnati. Oh, he knocked her around some, but wasn't no call for her to leave like she done, with him in the house in the woods all by himself, liked to lost his mind until he got used to the silence. She'd pay for that, one day she'd pay dear. He hadn't never fancied kids much, having them was all Betty Ann's idea, but he'd got where he kinda liked having 'em around 'fore she took 'em. Yes, sir, she was gonna be sorry she done such a thing. Real sorry.

Not somebody you'd pick out of a crowd as a "a natural-born leader," Harry was equipped for the job in ways you didn't notice at first.

He listened. He kept his mouth shut unless he had something to say, and consequently whenever he did talk, folks were apt to shut up and hear him out. He was not particularly intelligent, but he was clever, and he knew enough to surround himself with people smarter than he was, who would make him look smart.

And the man who'd attacked Zion Academy three months ago, Oscar Higgins, had definitely *not* numbered in that group. Oscar had been as dumb as a sack of doorknobs and his "attack" on Zion Academy had been so poorly planned and executed, it was a good thing he died in the encounter or his own men would likely have strung him up afterwards.

Harry passed by an empty house where trash was strewn across the porch. The yard out front had been appropriated by the guy's neighbor and added to his own garden plot that was now knee-high in vegetables. The garage door windows were still intact — the ones in the house'd all been broken out — and Harry caught sight of his own reflection. Tall and slender, he had sharp features, lots of angles with a single black unibrow over his dark eyes. All he'd had to do was lower that brow at the kids and they'd stop doing whatever it was he wanted them to stop doing.

He missed 'em. More than he let on. He wasn't

gonna just go on like he'd been doing and suddenly it was Christmas and he was still sitting in that house back in the hills all by himself with nobody to buy Christmas presents for and no kids to put up a tree. No sir! He'd have Betty Ann back where she belonged, and he wouldn't go so easy on her like he done before. She'd learn her place!

He had gotten involved with Oscar Higgins's stupid plan to attack Zion Academy because he understood, probably a whole lot better than Oscar did, that it was indeed a strategic location and that its supplies and facilities were definitely of great value in the new world order.

But he'd never have run off half-cocked as Oscar had done with only a handful of men and no real plans other than to climb over the wall — which, oh by the way, had been topped with broken glass. Harry rubbed the scar on the palm of his hand he'd gotten thanks to obeying that idiot's orders, had sliced open the palm climbing over the rock wall fence. Oscar'd thought he'd just surprise everyone inside. When that didn't work, the man was so stupid all he could think to do was go waltzing in the front door, point his gun at anyone he came across and assume he could simply take over the place because he was mean-looking.

Harry was far more clever than that.

Chapter Forty-Four

EAGLE FEATHER barely had time to figure out where he was — A bunkbed? Where? — when a voice over a megaphone followed the clanging of the bell. "Breakfast is in fifteen minutes in the mess hall. You're late, there won't be any food left."

The mess hall had a standard school-cafeteria feel to it, but the Boy Scouts had made an effort to make the place look rustic with exposed beams and faux log walls. The guards escorted the group to the building and then stood guard at the door, so the people inside were free to mingle with each other. Eagle Feather quickly found Star. Her hair was clean, her hair neatly braided. They were taking care of her.

As they passed down the cafeteria line with their trays and bowls, Eagle Feather told Star, "I'd tell you what this is we're eating, but I have no idea. Oatmeal, I suppose. But it could be cornmeal mush, or tile grout."

The cafeteria workers he could see, and likely the

kitchen crew he couldn't see, were obviously captives, just like him and the rest of the stranded. They dolloped out a glob of goo into every bowl as the people passed down the line. But Eagle Feather could swear they put extra food in Star's bowl. Maybe he was imagining it.

With everyone together in the mess hall, Eagle Feather got his first view of the whole population of captives and he was surprised at the number. There must have been 150 people at least, maybe two hundred counting the children. All of them captured at gunpoint, he was sure, as he and the others had been.

After breakfast, they were loaded back into the trucks for a short ride to the fields that were surrounded by huge barns, all painted jet black. The sun was coming up as they arrived, and the crew bosses put everybody to work. The men were given vicious-looking machetes and told as they were handed out, "Know you're already thinking about using this as a weapon. Forget it." The man pointed to the trees. We got snipers in the woods with rifles trained on you people every minute." He picked up a shovel and held the business end high in the air. A bullet twanged off the metal and everybody jumped. The guard was grinning. "You take out a guard with one of these, the snipers got ordered to kill *five* of you. So keep your buddies in line because you'll buy the farm, too, if anybody gets antsy."

Eagle Feather thought that was a bluff. They

wouldn't waste manpower like that. But even the bluff seemed sufficient to get the people in line.

The men were put to work cutting tobacco, slicing the bright yellow leaves off at the base of the plant with the big tobacco knives and then placing the leaves on "tobacco sticks" — stakes in the ground with pointed ends — like you'd stick a piece of paper on one of those pointed things on a desk. It was back-breaking labor. Eagle Feather hadn't been at it long before his back was numbing with pain, his arms ached and his legs felt like they would collapse under him.

The women were taken to the barns. The children were herded together in a pen and one woman was allowed to look after all of them, at least two dozen children ranging in age from eighteen months to eight or nine years old. Children older than that were forced to work alongside their mothers.

The sun rose in the sky, beating down on the workers, whose shirts were now soaked through with sweat. Once a tobacco stick was full, it was loaded on a truck and hauled off to one of the barns, where tobacco and marijuana appeared to be in various stages of curing. Eagle Feather could see in the door of one of the barns and watched men climb high up on rails, just balancing there, hanging the leaves to dangle down in the air to dry.

The tobacco in another barn had apparently been hanging for a while. The leaves were brown, looked like tobacco, and men were on rails there taking the tobacco *down,* handing the sticks from the man on the top rail to the man on the rail below, hand over hand until the sticks reached the floor, where the women worked at tables. Eagle Feather couldn't tell exactly what they were doing, but it appeared they were stripping the leaves off the stems and bundling them up in some way. The women working in the barn filled with marijuana were pulling the seed pods that looked to be three or four feet long off the plants and doing something with them, probably bagging them in sandwich bags for sale.

Lunchtime came at high noon. Eagle Feather collapsed in a heap, as did the other men, and didn't feel like eating the piles of hastily made sandwiches they were offered. The lunch break was only half an hour. Even then, the guards were pacing back and forth, anxious to put the crews back to work.

"That guy acts like his pants are on fire," one of the captives Eagle Feather didn't know asked. "What's the hurry?"

"Rain," said a man leaned against the truck tire in what little bit of shade he could find. He looked up into the blue sky. "They're in a race to get the crop in the barn, 'cause if those leaves get wet, you can't cut 'em. You gotta wait until they dry out."

Bill Brentwood leaned toward Eagle Feather.

"Don't suppose you know any rain dances?"

Eagle Feather shook his head. "Best I can do is think wet thoughts."

Chapter Forty-Five

PACO HAD SUMMONED ONLY five of the men who'd been at the previous meeting. He needed to work with smaller numbers of people. It would be easier on him to get inside their heads if there wasn't a room full of them.

Santoro, of course, who Paco could see was actually coming around to developing a genuine loyalty to Paco, was a man who could tell which way the wind was about to blow and wanted to be in the right boat when it hit the sails.

Greg Cox, Bill Lewis, Aasen Ivanov and Angelo Russo.

They met again in the church basement. Paco had spent the time in between meetings scouting out the opposition, getting close enough to drunk guards in bars to hear the whispers of their thoughts, pushing just a little to direct the head guard to start talking about how the whole operation was set up.

"We're here to talk about—"

Paco got no further before Aasen Ivanov said, "I want to know how you got them aliens up there in them little silver balls on a leash. You say they's always looking out for you. Why is that?"

"You don't need to know why."

"What's in it for them?"

Paco leaned back in the chair. "You heard what Four Fingers said. He saw the Astrals take me, saw the white light and the shuttle."

"I ain't sayin' you didn't go up there. I just wanna know why that entitles you to tell us all what to do? Why do the Astrals care if one of us slits your throat? What's it to them?"

"Because I am one of them now."

That was a conversation stopper. Paco hadn't planned the response, but it'd been a pretty good one off the top of his head.

"One of … *them*?" Ivanov literally glanced up at the ceiling.

"There are tens of thousands of them up there, but there are not thousands of minds. There is one mind, *a hive mind*, and they are all a part of it." He let that soak in for a beat. "The Astrals know everything. Their hive mind is so much more powerful than your pitiful little brain … they know your thoughts, can see you no matter where you are. They know everything you've ever done." He paused for effect. "I am part of that hive mind."

The silence in the room was so thick you could have spread it on a muffin.

"What's in it for them?" Paco let out a bark of

laughter. "You have nothing they want. If you did, they'd just take it. This isn't about what's in it for them. It's about what's in it for *me*. I am one of them now, and if I want it, they want it."

"What do you need us for? If them Astrals can just swoop in here——?"

"They have bigger fish to fry than what's going on in this little hellhole. Just know that as part of the hive mind, I know what they know. And if you dare to touch a hair on my head … I don't have to tell you guys what a reptar can do." They'd been in that prison yard the day the con on the guard tower took a shot at a shuttle. They'd somehow survived the reptar attack, and they were scared shitless of them. It made Paco want to laugh. He didn't, just kept his face straight and stern.

Though he didn't dig deeply into the minds of the men sitting there, he scratched along the surface enough to know that there were no doubters in this crowd. They would never have been willing to follow the lead of the sixteen-year-old boy who'd been Spade's bitch. But he was no longer that boy. He was a tall, bearded man, black hair to his shoulders and eyes so dark brown you couldn't see the centers. He was formidable, and he had them convinced he had friends in high places.

Someday, Paco was going to have to transfer that fear/loyalty of the Astrals to himself, so they followed him because he was the leader as much as because he was chummy with the dudes in the silver balls. He didn't really think it would be all that hard;

give him enough time and he would turn these men and others like them into minions who willingly did whatever he said. Of course, he'd have to step up and be as big a badass as they were. And he was fully prepared to do that. His first big display of ruthlessness would come when he killed Spade and it would be a lesson none of these men would ever forget.

The group seated in the church basement got down to business quickly. Paco had a plan, but he wanted to get input from these guys because in reality he had sixteen years of limited life experiences and these guys had been fighting and scratching and clawing for dominance among their fellows their whole lives. They knew a whole lot more about this than he did.

Angelo Russo was one of the men who stood personal guard duty around Spade's house. What he said was encouraging.

"Shit, he don't think about real security. When you're the meanest dog in the junkyard and you have made sure all the other dogs know it, you don't have to be afraid somebody's going to come rattle your cage. Oh, he keeps guards, but not the kind of guards we're used to. I figure several of them could be bought off."

"Bought off with what?" asked Bill Lewis.

All heads turned to Paco and he swallowed hard before he spoke.

"For starters, we're not going to buy what we can take without paying for it. We don't need to bribe some lard-ass to roll over on Spade. We'll be in charge and we'll be the ones rolling over everyone who gets in our way."

"So … it's clear what your stake is in all this, but what's in this for us?" said Ivanov. He saw the stern look on Paco's face and backed up so fast he almost tripped over his own feet. "I don't mean nothing bad by that, Paco. Just not having to kiss Spade's ass is reward enough. But what's it going to get us, you know, long term, when we're running the place."

Paco listened to the man's thoughts. This guy figured what was going to go down was exchanging one mean-as-a-snake leader for another one. Swap Spade for Paco, same, same. And the guy was closer to the truth than he knew, only they weren't exchanging one badass leader for a different badass leader. They were exchanging one badass leader for a tyrant who would make them toe the line in ways they never dreamed. That was for later, though. Right now he needed to dangle a carrot.

"What you get by throwing your lot in with me and the Astrals is your share of what we take for ourselves when we blow this pop stand and find greener pastures."

"What the fuck does that mean?" asked Greg Cox.

"It means, that this little prison and this little town are not big enough or grand enough for the plans I have. This place is where we launch our," he paused for effect, made sure his face had no expression whatsoever, before he continued, "our *army* out to conquer the badlands."

He paused again, leaned close, and spoke softly.

"We are going to live like kings with the best-looking women, the best booze, the best drugs and the best whatever else we want out there anywhere. We will own what we take over. And I want to *own it all.*"

Again, the silence was thick enough to cut with a butter knife. Paco looked from one man to the next, deep into their eyes, listened to the whispers of their minds. They were interested, intrigued, but nowhere near sold on what he had in mind. But that was okay. They'd be a whole lot more sold after he kicked Spade's ass. And after he weeded out the dissenters in the group. Ivanov was one of them. He hadn't liked much of anything that Paco said. Had believed him, wasn't exactly considering going over to the other side, but certainly wasn't happy with this side. He needed some … training. Some coaching. That, and a good ass-kicking.

If he needed to, Paco would kill him. And if he did, he would kill him in the most gruesome way possible. He hadn't made that decision yet, right now he needed Ivanov. But he was totally expendable. They all were. He would kill any one of them at the drop of a hat. And he needed them to know that.

"So are we good?" Paco asked. "Everybody know what you're supposed to do, where you're supposed to be, to pull this thing off?"

Heads all around the table nodded.

Then Paco slapped his hands down on the table and stood. Sensed more dread, more confusion and more fear from the men than they had when they walked in the door. That was good. That was very good.

He turned to Santoro.

"You get that machine I told you about?"

Santoro nodded. "I got it hooked up to my Jeep right now, parked in my garage." It was the Jeep Paco had mentioned that first day to convince Santoro he knew all about him, and he heard Santoro recall that memory.

"So there won't be any problem driving it right into the gymnasium, right there on the floor. You're sure?"

"I'm sure."

"That's good. That's very good," Paco said.

"You mind me asking what—"

"Yes, I do mind," Paco told him. "You'll find out what I'm going to do with it the same time everybody else does. Now, let's get busy. We got work to do to pull this off. I'll see you guys tonight, outside Spade's front gate."

They all nodded, got up from their seats and walked wordlessly out the door. Paco didn't bother straining to hear what they were thinking or what they were saying after they left. It was more energy than he was willing to expend. And besides, he didn't need to. He had won them over, at least for now. And that was all he needed.

Paco suddenly smiled, thinking about the look that would be on Spade's face when he saw the machine, and figured out what Paco intended to do with it.

Chapter Forty-Six

AFTER LUNCH, Eagle Feather's crew worked in the barn, hanging the tobacco up on the high bars. That, too, was back-breaking work, with the additional thrill of balancing fifteen, twenty, thirty feet up in the air. Papa Eagle Feather tried to keep his mind off the agony in his back by studying the other workers. Some of them appeared to perhaps be the men Bubba'd actually hired to do the job. It was clear that a good portion of them knew what they were doing. Locals, maybe, pressed into service. They would have been indistinguishable from Bubba's forces were they not the captives instead of the captors — farmers, men who worked the land and knew their way around equipment and likely firearms, too. They were as rugged and tough as Bubba's Mad Max wannabes, strutting around in their Halloween costumes, must have watched waaaay too many Thunder Dome movies.

Suddenly, one of the workers got violently sick,

began throwing up and looked like he was having seizures.

"Hose him down," said one of the guards. "That's nicotine poisoning, from them leaves. That's why we tell you assholes to wear shirts so it don't touch your skin. You're too stupid to listen, this is what you get." They washed the man off and hauled him off and laid him in the back of the truck.

There were lights in the barn and the work continued long after sunset. When the crews were finally loaded into the trucks and taken back to the camp, they all looked ready to drop from exhaustion.

They ate dinner together, which consisted of gruel that could either have been grits or cornmeal mush or toenail fungus. Eagle Feather found Star, her hands chapped from working with the tobacco. He had to get her out of here, had to get himself out of here, too. He was seventy-one years old and this was work for a teenager. He wouldn't last long, and he wasn't the only older person there. They'd let Fred Schwartz work with Lottie in the barn, but the two of them looked like death on a cracker. He saw Jessica Maddocks. The woman was a zombie, with three little kids clinging to her, the only thing keeping her alive.

Eagle Feather sat down beside Star, and it wasn't his imagination this time. He watched. Other people came to sit down close to them. They might not even have been aware they were doing it. He doubted it was his sparkling personality. It was Star, of course. She was like a magnet, drew others to her.

Nick Wilson sat down beside Eagle Feather on the other side and leaned close.

"We gotta get out of here."

Eagle Feather merely nodded.

"The crew I was working with, two of them grew up five miles from here and know those woods," said one of the other stranded, a short, stocky black man. Eagle Feather thought his name was Whitlock, Ben or Ken Whitlock. "They say there are places we could hide where nobody'd ever find us."

"You can't hide forever," Nick said, steel in his voice. "We need to get our hands on some guns."

"Bubba has a big armory," Star said.

Everyone at the table turned to look at her in surprise, but she didn't see.

"How could you possibly know that?" Nick asked.

"Oh, I ..." She turned toward Eagle Feather. "Pumpkin was at the camp last night. He was smelling around and ..." Her voice trailed off. "And he could smell the guns. Uncle Clyde used to take us with him when he went hunting. He pictured guns, a lot of them."

"Pumpkin ... your *dog*?" Nick was incredulous.

Star nodded and the table fell silent.

Eagle Feather had to offer some kind of explanation.

"Star ... sees things. She always has. And" — he took a deep breath— "she's one of those people the Astrals kidnapped. She was up in one of the mother-ships for three months, and when she got back she could ... *connect* with people. And with Pumpkin."

"You mean she can hear what they're thinking?" Roberto Lopez asked. "That's im—"

"*Possible*, absolutely *possible*."

Everybody turned to look at the man on the end. Eagle Feather finally placed him as Bill Brentwood. "Any of you people seen them rocks the Astrals dropped all over the place?"

"Yeah, there's a stone circle right outside Nashville," said Ben/Ken Whitlock and took up the story. "A line of rocks in two rows leads up to it." He paused. "You ever get near rocks like those?" Nobody answered. "Well, I have. And … I'd say this sounds preposterous, but we got aliens from another planet living among us so don't nothing that used to sound preposterous sound so strange anymore." Eagle Feather remembered now. It was *Ken* Whitlock and he was a farmer from northern Tennessee. "My buddy and I was out in the field and we seen them rocks. And when we got close to them. We could … I could hear what he was thinking! And what the people on the other side of the field were thinking. He could hear my thoughts, too, I swear to God he could. Then after a while, it faded away and we couldn't do it anymore."

"Can you hear the thoughts of Bubba and his men?" Nick asked Star.

"If I concentrate very hard, I can hear it like whispers, but very soft. Thinking with a hive mind—"

"Hive mind?" Roberto Lopez asked, clearly struggling with the whole thing.

"The Astrals don't *talk* to each other. They don't

have to because they are all connected to each other through a hive mind."

"They are many, but they think as one," Eagle Feather said. When the others looked questioningly at him, he said it was part of ancient Indian legends about white giants who came to Earth and seeded humanity.

"Everybody laughed at the people who claimed crop circles and Stonehenge and Machu Picchu were evidence of alien visitations. Nobody's laughing now."

"It didn't fade with Pumpkin," Star said. "We're as connected as we were on the ship."

"… and the dog says there are guns, a bunch of guns …?" Whitlock asked.

"He smelled guns."

"We outnumber the guards," Nick said. "Give me ten armed men and I could take them all out."

"Where is the armory?" asked Roberto Lopez.

"I can only tell you what Pumpkin smells … and around the armory he smells rubber and gasoline … but trees, too, the forest smells of dirt and leaves and lots of small animals."

"It's gotta be that building over in the corner beside where they park the trucks," Nick said. "Pumpkin smells the garage, but the forest, too, and that building is right up against the fence. Has to be that one. None of the other buildings are next to both the garage *and* the fence."

Then they put their heads together and came up with a plan.

Chapter Forty-Seven

SAWYER OPENED IN HIS EYES. Bad idea. He closed them again immediately. But just the tiny ray of light that sliced in through his retina had drilled into a crack in his forehead roughly the size of the San Andreas Fault.

There was a throbbing sound — thud, thud, thud in his temples.

"Oh, so I see you're awake now," said a voice that he almost recognized but not quite. He would have opened his eyes to see who it was, but he remembered that bright light and decided that was still a bad idea. Maybe whoever was speaking to him would think he was asleep and go away.

"Don't play possum with me, Sawyer. I am not your mother tiptoeing into your room after I put you to bed to make sure you really did go to sleep."

Sawyer finally made a connection in his mind, which at the moment seem to be filled with a substance as thick as pudding. It was Brother Sebastian's voice. Where was he? What had—?

Then he remembered. Sitting on the floor in his kitchen. Why had he been sitting on the floor? He never did figure that part out. He remembered sitting there, though, with the bottle of Maker's Mark, chugging it. He remembered Ellie coming into the room, sitting beside him and drinking with him. He didn't remember much else after that, but it was clear he had passed out. And since it was Brother Sebastian who was talking to him, he must be at the monastery. He wondered how he got there. He wished Brother Sebastian would go away and leave him alone.

"Here," the voice said. "Drink this. It'll make you feel better."

"Nothing short of death would make me feel better," he said and speaking set a Chinese gong in between his temples banging, *gong, gong, gong.*

"Sorry, I don't do the death thing here. Though we do specialize in the hereafter. You'll have to settle for continuing to live, but not in your current state of discomfort. Drink this."

Sawyer opened one eye, saw the old monk sitting beside his bed in a straight-backed chair, holding out a glass. Even the movement of his eyelid enough to allow him to see caused the crashing pain in his skull again and he closed his eyes.

"What is it?"

"Well, you take a teaspoon of salt and eight teaspoons of sugar and stir them up in five cups of distilled water." He sounded like he was sharing his best chicken soup recipe over the fence in the back yard. "Then you whisk in half a cup of orange juice and a quarter cup of mashed banana. Then—"

"That sounds heinous."

"It's really quite good. But more to the point, it really will make you feel better, restores the electrolyte balance in your bloodstream, whatever that is. I could give you the science behind it, but Garson swears it works."

"Garson came up with the concoction?"

"Oh my, yes. There's not a whole lot of need for a hangover remedy at a monastery, though a few of the monks have been known to tie one on from time to time."

Sawyer opened both of his eyes and forced himself to keep them open, plowing through the pain.

"I'll pass on Garson's elixir."

"Oh no, you must drink it. Seriously. He says it will work wonders on someone in your condition." He paused. "You do want to feel better, don't you?"

Sawyer slowly raised himself up on one elbow. The movement made him dizzy and nauseous, but he took the glass from the brown-robed monk and put it to his lips. The monk steadied his hand as he took one swallow … then two. It tasted bad, but anything would have tasted bad right now.

Then he eased his head back down on the pillow.

"You want to tell me how I got here? I remember drinking in my kitchen. I remember Ellie. Nothing else registered, or if it registered at the time, booze erased it."

"Ellie managed to get you into the back seat of her car while you were still … ambulatory. You passed out there and she brought you here." He paused, and said softly, "We told Noah that you were just very tired and had fallen asleep, but frankly he's too sharp to buy a line like that."

Sawyer looked around. The room swam in dizzying circles, then settled. It was his room at the monastery.

He suddenly realized he was out of uniform, wearing only a tee shirt and his skivvies.

"How did I get undressed, who——? It wasn't Ellie, was——?"

"Oh no, my son, we took care of your … attire."

As awareness began to settle around him, the memories of what had driven him to sit in his kitchen chugging a bottle of whiskey returned as well. The reptars ripping apart his men. All his men. The devastation of the town. Everything. Gone.

"You should have left me on the floor of my kitchen," he said, the pain of speech not even beginning to ease. "I'm pretty useless now."

"Oh my, if you'd told me you were going to throw a pity party I would have dressed for the occasion."

"Not pity, reality. I can't 'defend and protect' — that's what's written on my shield and the door of my car — when there's no town left … and without any deputies. They're all … gone."

"Indeed, they are, and I'm sorry about that, Sawyer, I really am. They were your … friends."

The pain of loss hit him in the chest with a

hammer blow of despair and he had to struggle to keep his composure.

"Billy Ray's wife is pregnant, did you now that? They've been trying to …" He let the words go. Billy Ray was gone. As was Roger Hawkins, Pee Wee Watson, Joe Thurman, Ralph Morrison and Sam Henderson. They were all dead. Killed by aliens.

The beginnings of rage welled up in his belly. But he didn't have the emotional bandwidth in his current physical condition to sustain both rage and grief at the same time. Grief won. Anger, rage, could wait.

"You'd don't actually think you're useless, do you, Sawyer? Seriously?"

"Well, duh, why wouldn't I? What good is a sheriff without—"

"Oh, maybe your job as sheriff might be officially over. But you're certainly not useless."

"So what is it I'm supposed to do now?"

"Why, protect *us*, for heaven's sake. And teach us how to protect ourselves."

Sawyer stared at him, not quite getting his train of thought.

"Surely, it has occurred to you … well, perhaps it hasn't occurred to you. In your present state, I don't imagine much has occurred to you. But it needs to now. The town … Jessup has been almost completely obliterated. I don't know how many people were killed in the attack. There is no way to tell because there aren't any … bodies. No way to know who just left and who was …"

"Hard to count clouds of black dust."

"And that warehouse full of supplies for the winter. What are the people who remain going to do to eat when it gets cold?"

Sawyer had thought about it, but not by way of solving the problem. Not answering the question *what will they do?* but bemoaning the reality that there wasn't anything they *could* do. The residents all had gardens. That would provide food … but was it enough to keep them alive through the winter? Depended on how many … survivors there were, and he didn't know.

"That man, that Oscar Higgins who came out here, the one Dr. Weiss killed, he is not the only person in this county who has figured out that we have stores of supplies here. People need what we have. We are doing everything we can to provide enough supplies to be able to support more people … but there are those who aren't going to want to take a reasonable share. People who are going to want it all."

The monk was right, of course. It was now a battle for survival. Those who had stores would live. Those who didn't, wouldn't. The academy and the monastery had become the bank now, where all the "money" was kept — where what mattered to sustain life was kept. And as God made little green apples, there would be somebody out there, probably a lot of somebodies, willing to take that resource by force.

"So you want me to be what? The *head of security*?"

"Don't be ridiculous. You're still the sheriff. But your jurisdiction will be the monastery and the academy. And you're going to have to replace the deputies you lost from among the ranks of the people here."

"The monks?"

"There are other adults here besides monks. We are well armed. We just have to learn *how* to defend ourselves. And that's where you come in."

Sawyer said nothing. It was too much. His head hurt, he was still not at all certain he was going to be able to keep down the glass of whatever it was that Brother Sebastian had given him. He wasn't in a position to analyze, make a decision, was in no condition even to think …

He closed his eyes.

"The children …" the monk said, his voice quiet.

Zion Academy had, after all, been a boarding school … for *deaf* children.

"If someone comes here armed, they might … or if we let somebody waltz in here and take whatever they like … We have to think of the children." He paused. "Of Noah and his friends."

They all were helpless … unless Sawyer trained somebody to fight for them.

"I know you're … not well, Sawyer." He heard the straight-backed chair's legs scrape across the hardwood floor when the monk got to his feet. "I will come back later, when you're feeling better."

He started for the door.

"Brother Sebastian," Sawyer said. "I need to know … what kind of firearms you have here. And how much ammunition."

He opened his eyes then to see a smile on the monk's face, relief and gratitude.

<h1 style="text-align:center">Chapter Forty-Eight</h1>

HARRY WINDOM LED Hungry up the driveway to the porch of a small, neat house with lace curtains on the window and the obligatory garden in the front yard. He knocked, waited patiently for whoever was inside to decide he didn't look too menacing to open the door.

As he did, he thought about all the buildings that had been vaporized on Main Street. One of them had been Baxter's Shoe Store.

Harry hated it about the shoe store in particular. He remembered the only pair of shoes his father ever bought for him when he was a kid. He and his family didn't have nothing, lived so far up in a hollow sun only showed up about three days a week. He and his brothers and sisters went to school barefoot until the do-gooders from the state Department of Human Resources swooped down and bought them all shoes and coats for the winter.

His parents had been mortified. His father was

poor but proud, a coal miner who had gone down under the earth to dig out black sunshine his whole life. And there at the end he sat in a rocker in front of the fireplace coughing black phlegm and spitting it to go sizzle sizzle in the flames. It had humiliated him that the fancy-pants do-gooders from the city were able to buy shoes he couldn't afford to buy for his family. He had refused to go with them when they went shopping, refused to look at their purchases when they got back home. And when Harry managed to lose his shoes in the mud after a flood washed out the footbridge, he had supposed he'd be barefoot again until the next time the do-gooders came. But his father had marched him down to Baxter's Shoe Store, walked in with him proud as he could be and told the man he wanted shoes for his son. He let Mr. Baxter try half a dozen pairs on Harry before Harry found one he really liked and that fit well. Then he reached into the pocket of his coveralls and took out cash to pay for the shoes. It was years before Harry found out his father had sold his shotgun to get the money to buy his shoes.

The shoe store wasn't there anymore. Neither was the big warehouse where the whole town had been socking away supplies for winter. Gone. Black dust.

Which meant a whole lot of these good people was gonna go hungry. Harry hoped they'd already started thinking about that. If they hadn't, he intended to remind them of it.

He knocked again, fairly certain someone was home, just too afraid to open the door to a stranger.

Fear had become a fact of daily life for three months now but it never felt normal, never felt right. And the more folks thought about their prospects for survival this winter, the more scared they'd get. Harry had to capitalize on that. He intended to do *successfully* what Oscar Higgins had so terribly botched — take over Zion Academy. And he had bigger plans than that but had the good judgment to go one step at a time. And the first step was *not* marching out to Zion Academy half-cocked. The first step was finding a bunch of scared people, put guns in their hands, and make them fully understand that if they didn't accomplish the task at hand, if they didn't manage to take over the place and all its food stores, their children would starve and freeze this winter.

The academy hadn't called the sheriff when Oscar and his idiots had come calling. They'd decided to defend themselves, with a right remarkable display of marksmanship and an even more remarkable display of bluffing. If all the other men hadn't cut and run as soon as Oscar hit the dirt, they could have taken out the one man actually willing to shoot somebody, disarmed a few namby-pamby civilians, and a hundred deaf kids, and marched off with what they had come for.

Harry wouldn't make any of those mistakes. When he and his men showed up — the ones he'd been recruiting and training in the hills for the past three months, their ranks augmented by the scared citizens of Jessup — they would be well-armed and well-trained and they would mow down any opposition the school might offer.

Harry had one other characteristic Oscar lacked — Harry was utterly ruthless. He had killed before, more often than anyone in the county would ever believe. As a young man, he had been a hitman for a drug-running operation working out of Arkansas. He'd sliced enough throats, smashed enough heads and gutted enough men to know that such a show of brutal force would end a battle quick. Do something utterly nasty, and folks would drop their guns and head for cover.

When the unsuccessful Oscar Higgins had attacked, the academy's crazy director had elected not to call Sawyer Matheson, so the sheriff and his deputies didn't swoop down to save the day. Now, the sheriff *couldn't* save the day, had no deputies to swoop with. The academy could set off a klaxon, ring an emergency bell, call over walkie-talkies or still-functioning landlines or send carrier pigeons or smoke signals. Sawyer didn't have any deputies to bring to the fight. The aliens had killed them all. From what Harry could gather, killed them by ripping them into little pieces and eating them!

Harry was exceedingly grateful to the little green men for getting rid of the opposition. With them gone, Harry could execute his two-part plan with ease, and with as little bloodshed as possible.

Part A of the plan was simple. He would lay siege to the facility. Surround them, and with a huge show of force, convince them to lay down their arms peacefully. That huge show of force might involve killing a few of them — some of the deaf kids — to convince them resistance was futile.

In Part B, he would waltz into the facility and evict them all — every man jack of them. He could kill all of them, but he suspected he might meet some resistance from his own troops at that kind of carnage. So he'd just march them out the front door to the gate and kick their asses out. Let them figure out where their next meal was coming from.

Then he would move his already hand-picked crew into the facility and make it the headquarters of his organization. He'd already named it: Javelin. He wasn't entirely sure what a javelin was, some kind of spear maybe. He didn't care what it was, just liked the sound of the name, of being the leader of Javelin. And Javelin would become a force to reckon with in the months and years to come.

First thing he'd do was go get Betty Ann and drag her sorry ass back home where she b'longed. Wouldn't be hard to put her in her place once she seen that Javelin controlled everything from the Kentucky River to the Tennessee border. He'd feed his troops and their families from the stores the academy had accumulated and turn the monks into minions, working the fields to make sure those stores were always replenished.

Harry tried one more time, one more knock. When no one answered, he turned around and started toward the house next door.

Suddenly, the door behind him opened just wide enough for a young woman to peek through the crack.

"If you want to talk to John, he's out chopping firewood right now and will have another load available to buy tonight. You'll have to come back then."

She started to shut the door but Harry stopped her.

"This your dog?" he asked.

And then started doing his dance.

Chapter Forty-Nine

THE NEXT MORNING in the breakfast line, Nick Wilson edged up to Eagle Feather, leaned in close and whispered in his ear.

"We're on our own with this one. Just those of us who were talking about it earlier. I've taken the pulse of everybody else and nobody wants any part of it. Bubba scares the shit out of these people and they have no desire to go up against him. So technically we don't outnumber them five to one. It's the five of us — you, me, Roberto Lopez, Bill Brentwood and Ken Whitlock against ... what? Maybe thirty, thirty-five of Bubba's men. Bill was in the army, fought in Afghanistan back in the day. That's it. Everybody else plans to be a spectator.

"I'm not surprised," said Eagle Feather. "It's a hard thing to think about fighting men as mean and dangerous-looking as these are."

"Copy that. But it won't get any better as time goes on. These folks aren't thinking long-term. He will plow through workers like Sherman marching through Atlanta. I would not want to have to run the actuarial tables on this camp, But I bet the life expectancy here is less than six months."

"I give it three."

Then the two of them spread apart, not wanting to call attention to themselves. Star wanted to know what was about to happen. Either she had heard the whisperings of people's minds around her, or she just figured out their plan to make a break for it. But he couldn't tell her about it right now, some guard might overhear. So he just put his hand on her shoulder and squeezed.

"Everything's gonna be all right," he said.

"That's what Uncle Clyde used to say to me." He could see tears in her blind eyes. He just hoped he would be able to come through with what he promised her.

The guards stood back and allowed the prisoners to mingle freely in the cafeteria. And again Eagle Feather saw it. People drifted over to Star, seemed to want to be near her, maybe talk to her, though few attempted conversation. They just ate their breakfast yuk, whatever it was, and looked at her.

The phenomenon was limited, of course. Not everybody on the whole crew was huddled up around Star. The tougher ones, perhaps men Bubba had hired and for one reason or another decided to enslave instead, were mean, cut-your-throat-in-a-minute men who actually seemed to move away from where Star was sitting.

Eagle Feather shook his head. The imaginings of an old man who ought to be sitting comfortably in front of his teepee with grandchildren running around his feet instead of out here in the wilds fighting for his life. But he supposed most everybody in the world was in the same spot. They all felt disoriented. How could you not when your planet had just been invaded by aliens?

He kept making eye contact with Nick Wilson at breakfast's end and the guards started through the cafeteria, dividing the slaves up into work crews. It was still dark outside. There'd be four bus loads, once the crews had decided who was going to work where, and Nick casually maneuvered people into place so that all the people who'd wanted to break out of the camp would be on the last bus.

They hadn't even started to load the busses when the rain hit.

The sky was overcast — no stars or moon — but there'd been no way to tell there was a storm coming until it hit. The rain fell in torrents. It was amazing to Eagle Feather, who had spent his life in the desert, that rain could come up so suddenly, a storm so violent and you had no warning at all. He supposed that was part of the gift that keeps on giving, that had been the alien invasion and all the satellites that predicted the weather and all the technology that controlled storms and such now no longer functioned. There was not so much as a weatherman on the television predicting rain tomorrow, or an app on your phone telling you the sun would shine. Humanity was back to playing life by the seat of their pants and today the seat of their pants would be getting very wet.

The guards had nothing to do with no workers in the fields, just sat around and played cards and smoked dope and told lies. Though they tried to put a grim face on it, it was clear the guards were almost as tickled as the prisoners that the rain had stopped their marijuana and tobacco harvest dead in its tracks. Bubba was not happy about it, though. He had shown up to talk to the work-crew bosses and was there at the Boy Scout camp when the rain started. The captives could hear him screaming obscenities even with all the doors closed.

Nick was sitting beside Eagle Feather, drinking a cup of hot water because there was no coffee or tea and he at least needed the hot water to clear the crud out of his throat. He leaned over to a middle-aged man with a paunch, a gray stubble of beard, and a leather face.

"You're local, aren't you, Chesley?" Nick asked.

"Yep. Lived here my whole life."

"So after a rain like this, how long will it be before the fields are dry enough to work in?"

"Depends. If it keeps up like this all day, the ground is going to be soaked for a week. You can't put wet tobacco in a barn — it'll mildew and mold. You don't just have to wait until you can get the equipment into the field through the mud, you got to wait until the leaves of the plants dry out." The man sat back and smiled. "Appears to me Bubba is going to be sitting on his hands for quite a spell."

"Right," Nick said. "And what does that mean for us? I can't see him as the kind of man who would let workers sit around doing nothing for a week."

Perhaps Bubba did have in mind something for them to occupy their time, something that would make him some money. But it apparently wasn't something he could whip out in an hour or two.

So as the rain beat down on the tin roof of the cafeteria, the people inside gathered in small groups and talked quietly. There were guards stationed at the door leading into the kitchen and the side door to outside, and the two big double doors in front. Two guards at each entrance sat on stools or in rockers, and as the day wore on Eagle Feather watched their attention wane. They left the doors open so there would be some ventilation in the building. The cafeteria had windows you couldn't raise because nails hammered into the frames prevented them from going up more than six inches. But there was a cross-breeze with the doors open, and since the rain had dropped the temperature outside, the room did not get insufferably hot.

Eagle Feather and Nick spent time together, pretending to be playing cards, when actually they were plotting their escape.

"I think we take this rain as a blessing and run with it," Nick said. "Those guards out there are not paying attention to anything. The ones in the back are smoking dope."

"When?" Eagle Feather asked.

"I'm thinking mid-afternoon," Nick said. "I'd like

to be able to get to that armory while it's still daylight."

Then they turned and exchanged meaningful glances with the others on the escape team. Eagle Feather would nod when it was showtime.

Chapter Fifty

STAR SAT in the cafeteria with the others, grateful the rain had stopped the work. She rubbed her hands together and winced from the pain of the scratches and sores where she had spent the day yesterday making the dry tobacco leaves handed to her into packets tied with twine.

There was a large group of people around her. And it occurred to her to wonder why that was. It seemed that everywhere she went, there were people gathered around her. It had not been that way any other time in her life. And maybe she was just imagining it. Still … she could feel a warmth from these people and she hadn't been able to sense a thing like that before she'd spent three months in the Astral mothership.

She couldn't have articulated even if she'd understood it — and she didn't — but somehow that warmth was *good*.

It was still raining outside, but not as hard as it had

been earlier. Papa Eagle Feather had only been gone for a short time, and the longer he was gone the more apprehensive she got. Beneath the general babble of low conversations around her she could hear another layer of sound. Not conversation, thoughts. They were whispers, and she could have attended to any one of the whispers, could have heard the words, if she had wanted to. But she didn't want to. She didn't want that part back with anybody except Noah.

What she couldn't turn off were the abilities that she'd come into the world with, that had nothing to do with Noah. She still saw flashes of images from people when she touched them. She didn't get to decide what it was she saw, didn't know if it was the present, the past or the future. Earlier today, she had tripped coming into the cafeteria.

"Yep, Stumbles is a good name, alright," said one of the guards. He grabbed her arm to steady her, then shoved her on her way. He had barely touched her, but in that brief encounter, she saw the flash of an image. The guard had been flattened up against a wall beside a closed door in some kind of storage room. He was holding a gun. There was another man — who had a Mohawk haircut — flattened against the wall on the other side of the door and his gun was drawn, too. That was it. That was all she saw. It told her nothing.

"Star, sugar, you sure you don't want something else to drink?" asked sweet Lottie Schwartz. 'I'd be glad to bring you something."

Before Star had a chance to answer, Selma Brentwood rushed up to the group of women and men seated around Star, agitated and upset. She whispered so the guards on the doors wouldn't hear — as if they cared. They were simply rocking back and forth in the rocking chairs paying no attention at all to the captives.

"You know what they're doing out there?" Selma whispered to Charlene Whitlock. "Did Ken tell you?"

"No, I just figured—"

Selma bowled right over her and continued whispering. "They're going to try to break out, try to overpower the guards and escape."

There was terror in the woman's voice, as well there should have been. Star remembered vividly what Bubba had said he would do to anyone who crossed him. And her words explained where Papa Eagle Feather had been going, why he had leaned over and told her softly that he'd be right back, and that everything would be alright.

He and the other men had some kind of plan. She'd told them where the armory was, and she was sure they planned to overpower the guards and get guns.

Star suddenly recalled the image she'd gotten when the guard had touched her earlier that day, the image of him standing with his gun drawn beside a door. When she examined her memory of the image she *saw* , she couldn't breathe. The boxes in the room, the word *"ammunition"* was stamped on the sides. That was the armory. And those guard were guarding it, waiting to ambush whoever came in. They *knew!* Somehow, they knew.

Star leapt to her feet, cried, "We have to stop them, they're walking into a trap."

But the sudden commotion outside made it clear her warning was too late. Whatever had been about to happen, happened. The people inside the cafeteria rushed to the open front doors, crowding around to look outside.

"That's Bill," Selma Brentwood cried, and there was a scuffle, as if others in the group had restrained her.

"He's not hurt bad."

"You can't go out there."

"You remember what Bubba did when ..." Charlene Whitlock couldn't finish, but she didn't need to.

There was a sudden hush, and dread blossomed in Star's chest.

"Out here, get everybody out here now!" came a loud voice from outside. Bubba. But his voice was colder now than it had been before, and there was a razor edge to it. He had not been anything like affable before, but he had been entertaining in his own demented way, enjoyed terrorizing the captives, was almost jovial. The voice that spoke now was anything but jovial.

It was only misting, but the ground was soaked and Star and the others splashed through puddles and gathered in the open area where Bubba had apparently indicated he wanted them to stand.

"You folks remember what I said would happen if you crossed me? You remember that, do you?"

Someone grunted in pain, so Bubba must have pushed or hit him.

"I asked you a question. Do you remember what I said would happen if you crossed me?"

"Yes," said a man. Star thought it might be Ken Whitlock. "I remember."

"Well, looks like you good people didn't hear me or didn't believe me. One or the other. Because if you'd heard me and believed me, you wouldn't a'done something so stupid as to try to break into my armory."

He paused. There was no sound except water dripping off the roofs into puddles.

"We are about to have an object lesson in staying in line."

Chapter Fifty-One

Eagle Feather lay in the mud where the guard had shoved him down, didn't move. The cold water soaked into his jeans, burned in the cut on his leg that was courtesy of his own Bowie knife. He recognized it in the hands of the red-mohawk monster who had jumped him and the others the minute they got the armory door open.

It had been a trap. A setup. Bubba had to have known they were coming because he had guards waiting for them right inside the door, got the drop on them, and hauled them away. The man who'd taken Eagle Feather's knife had cut him with it just for sport, muttering, "You kept this knife nice and sharp, Injun man. How you like the feel of your own cold steel?"

Eagle Feather studied the goons who stood with their guns covering the crowd of cowering humanity. He'd been looking them over since the group had first fallen into their clutches. As far as he could determine, there were only about half a dozen men in Bubba's inner circle, his real henchmen, the ones who kicked ass and took names at his command and enjoyed the bloodletting as much as he did.

The others … not so much. A couple of the motorcycle fiends who had descended on them in the woods hung back and said little. The guy in the demon helmet and the blond man wearing a dog muzzle did what they were told but that's all, seemed to take no interest in brutality for the joy of it. Eagle Feather noticed that the blond man always stationed himself between the children and the other goons, almost as if he were guarding them.

Beyond them was another layer of men who appeared to be as stupid as blocks of wood. It was from among their ranks that Bubba had selected the men who stood guard at the barracks at night, and paced back and forth down the rows of tobacco in the field when they were working. And beyond the stupids, rounding out his merry band of soldiers were the grunts, the hired help. At least half his army of thirty-five, maybe forty soldiers were those, seemed to be ordinary men who'd been pressed into service by the vicious drug lord. Eagle Feather could be wrong, of course. Maybe they had worked their way up from prisoner to guard by sucking up in some way. Maybe. But they didn't seem to be cut from the same ruthless cloth as the others.

Bubba had called the whole camp together. All his men stood behind him in a semicircle, facing the prisoners. Off to the right were the four men who'd been apprehended almost before they got started. The sun was setting behind where Bubba stood and the glow of sunset backlit his men, cast them as terrifying silhouettes.

It had been a simple plan. The best plans always were. They jumped the dope-smoking guards and made their way to the armory, dodging behind the garage into the bushes and brambles that had grown wild without the attention the grounds crew of the Boy Scout camp would surely have given them.

They were counting on the element of surprise. Take the armory. Secure the weapons. Take down the guards at each of the dormitories, hand out weapons to fellow prisoners and take over the rest of the camp by force.

It should have succeeded, would have succeeded, but it didn't.

Bubba was in a bad mood, occasioned by the weather and subsequent delay, which meant dollars lost to his operation every day the crews weren't working. And now there was a special glint to his eye, a downward turn to his mouth that spelled trouble if Eagle Feather had ever seen trouble.

Eagle Feather should have known better. He never should have gotten involved, should have let the younger men handle it. Nick and Bill were former military. Eagle Feather should have thought of Star instead of riding off to battle without considering the consequences to her if he failed.

And he *had* failed.

Bubba stepped out in front of the crowd and glared at them. Then he began to pace. Not so much like a general reviewing his troops as like a man who was trying very hard to hold onto his temper and only barely succeeding.

He let fly a string of colorful expletives, then just shook his head. "You assholes are dumber than dirt. Do you think *I'm* the one's stupid … that you could come up with a plan to escape and I won't know about it?"

They said nothing and he tapped his foot.

"I asked you people a question and I expect an answer. Do you think I'm so stupid you can get away with pulling off some half-assed escape plan right under my nose?"

Of course, the crowd didn't know what to do. Were they supposed to tell him no they didn't think he was that stupid, after they had just attempted to escape? Certainly, none of them was willing to tell him they *did* think he was stupid. So they said nothing. And he seemed to forget that he'd demanded they answer him.

"It cost me half a month's wages to install them little bitty microphones all over that cafeteria, and even more to get somebody who knew how to hide them so you wouldn't see them. Stuck them under the table with *chewing gum.* Ain't nobody surprised when they sit down at a table and there's gum stuck to the bottom of it, not a table where kids has been sitting. I been listening to everything you people been saying since you got here. I know when you fart."

Clearly, they had vastly underestimated Bubba

Blacksnake or whatever his real last name was and they were about to pay for that mistake.

Bubba was looking around the crowd, searching, and then his eye fell on Star, on the front row between two women. It struck Eagle Feather then that he had never seen her with other *children*, just "playing." Like a normal child. Star was always surrounded by adults. Adults who might not even realize that they'd been drawn to her by … yeah, by what?

Bubba leaned over and spoke softly to her. She jumped when she heard his voice, hadn't realized he was so close.

"Yo, Stumbles … what's all this shit I hear about how your dog can *smell* guns. And you can read his mind and know he's smelling them. What the fuck is that all about?"

Star had no answer so she said nothing.

Bubba turned to Eagle Feather and the other three men the guards had shoved down into the mud.

"Holy shit, man, you're willing to bet your lives on what some little blind kid heard from her imaginary dog? Run off on some hairbrained rescue mission like your pants was on fire just for that? Seriously?" He shook his head. "That is some *special* kind of stupid."

He straightened and continued to look at the men on the ground.

"But I would dearly like to know how it was you really *did* know there was guns in that building. And what else you know. And if you mighta figured out I got way more than guns stashed away in other hidey holes on this property. Let's start with the guns, though, and work our way up. Didn't nobody tell you they was there, so how did you find out?"

The question hung out there in the air. The silence swelled.

"You ain't gonna tell me, are you? Or at least not right now, you ain't. Right now you still think you can get away with *not* telling me. But you're going to find out how wrong you are. Time I get through with you, you're gonna be begging me to ask more questions so you can give me more answers."

He turned toward one of his men and Eagle Feather noticed that the man was holding a can. Bubba nodded and the man walked up to him and handed the can to him. It was a gasoline can with a spout. By the weight of it, it appeared to be full.

Eagle Feather's heart leapt into a gallop.

Bubba set the can down at his feet, reached into the breast pocket of his shirt and drew out a cigarette. No, a joint, rolled tight and thin. He put the joint between his lips, then reached into a pants pocket for an old-fashioned book of matches, grandparents to flipsticks, that were ignited with friction like matches, but there was no smoke and the sticks themselves were never consumed.

He tore off one of the little cardboard matches, closed the pack of them, then rubbed the bulbous head of the match across the rough strip on the bottom of the book. It instantly burst into flame, bright yellow and dancing around as it consumed the cardboard.

Then Bubba's face was lit by a wicked smile.

Chapter Fifty-Two

SAWYER SAT LOOKING at the images on the screens of the console in the security room. They were alive with activity.

Because it was almost dark outside, the shapes appeared in multi-colored hues. On the heat sensors, they appeared as fuzzy red dots, kind of outlined in orange. Like they were on fire. On the motion sensors, they appeared green. On the infrared cameras, they were a shade of turquoise. All the shapes were moving, as coordinated as a Russian dance troupe, coming through the woods all around the academy, across the fields to the north, through the trees and past the pond to the east, through the woods to the west and down the road leading to the facility from the south. There were probably fifty, maybe as many as seventy-five dots on the screens.

"Holy shit," Garson said in an awed whisper, leaning over Sawyer's shoulder. Sawyer hadn't seen the professor come in, but now the man was standing with

Brother Sebastian behind him, staring at the security cameras as the sea of dots approached them from all sides.

"Nothing holy about it," murmured Brother Sebastian and Sawyer could hear the fear in his voice.

Sawyer knew immediately they didn't have a chance. The resources at Sawyer's disposal were probably twice the number of spots on those screens, but that included deaf children and monks, both of which were useless in a fight. He and Brother Sebastian had roughed out a security plan just this morning, but right now, they didn't have the manpower to implement even ten percent of the measures Sawyer knew they needed. They had a hundred, maybe 150 grownup adults who were capable of firing a weapon. Brother Sebastian had gone to great lengths to explain that every man, woman and child — deaf children and monks included — had been required to take the marksmanship classes offered by Dr. Weiss. Every one of them knew their way around a weapon. But knowing how to hit the center of a paper target that sat perfectly still while you sighted on it and being able to hit a moving target were two different things. And even if they were physically capable of firing a gun properly, they were in no way psychologically prepared to defend themselves or anyone else.

The hodgepodge of people now living at Zion Academy had seen their whole worlds destroyed in the past three months. All of them were traumatized refugees, from as nearby as Jessup or as far away as Florida. Each had their own awful story of why they'd come and what had happened to them on the way — and none of it had prepared them to kill another human being. That took a special kind of training, a special kind of emergency, and Sawyer hadn't prepared any of them for something like that.

He had been on the job less than twenty-four hours.

Bottom line, he had three or four people he was reasonably convinced would actually shoot somebody if they had to. The rest of them would hold their guns and never pull the trigger, even if their lives depended on it.

Unfortunately, Dr. Weiss had already played the bluff card, so they couldn't make these people believe they were better armed or protected than they actually were. They could not hold off this many armed intruders. It was hopeless.

He shoved the chair back from the console.

"We're toast, right?" Brother Sebastian said before Sawyer had a chance to deliver the bad news himself.

"Pretty much. If we'd had a chance to train, get organized ..." He let the rest trail off. None of that mattered now. What mattered now was figuring out how to survive the assault with as few ... *casualties* as possible. And how to keep the intruders from taking everything they had.

"So what do we do?" Garson asked. "Run up a white flag or something? Is that the standard way to surrender?"

"We're not going to surrender."

"Surely, you can't be serious, Sawyer. Look at those

dots, fifty, sixty … probably seventy of them and every one of them has a gun and knows how to use it. They'll wipe us out."

"It comes down to deciding if this is a hill you're willing to die on," Sawyer said, iron in his voice. "We fight now to save our supplies, or we have nothing to eat this winter. The *kids* have nothing to eat this winter."

Garson and Brother Sebastian stood looking at him, saying nothing.

"I think they'll stop at the fence or the gate and make demands. I don't imagine they'll come barging in here with guns blazing. What we have to remember is these aren't trained soldiers we're facing, any more than we are. These are your friends and neighbors driven to this point by desperation. I don't imagine more than a handful of those little red dots has ever fired a gun at a person. The problem is their people who won't shoot way outnumber our people who won't shoot."

Sawyer turned to Brother Sebastian. "Where's the safest place for the children?"

"The wine cellars — stone walls, no windows."

"You see they all get there — except Reggie Hawthorne, Hank, Paul, Benjamin and Daniel."

"But—"

"They're sixteen and seventeen years old. Boys younger than that fought in the Civil War. We need the bodies. These were the boys Dr. Weiss used to help him bluff." Sawyer paused. "Except we're not going to bluff."

Brother Sebastian started to protest, but just looked at Sawyer instead. "I'll see the children are safe, and I'll send the older boys to you."

"And can you find somewhere safe, somewhere they wouldn't think to look, to hide the rest of the arsenal, the guns we're not using. If this goes south … I'd rather not arm the enemy."

The old monk nodded.

"Okay, then. Sound the alarm and let's get the children moved."

Chapter Fifty-Three

I**T WAS GETTING DARK.** The overcast sky, still pregnant with boiling rainclouds, admitted neither starlight nor moonlight. The lights on poles in the compound, apparently on timers, had switched on, a glaring glow that cast harsh shadows, all blacks and whites with no shades of gray. The puddles reflected the glow of the lights, making dozens of little spotlights on the ground.

The scene took on an unreal quality. Like Eagle Feather was watching some old horror movie — a vintage one not even in color. Though he had seen no more than half a dozen movies of any kind in his whole life, he'd seen something awful like this and his skin pebbled with gooseflesh. The darkness seemed to have taken on form and substance, no longer just the absence of light, but an entity of its own, an evil thing that had joined with the evil of the man monster who stood in front of the crowd of people slowly inhaling the smoke from a joint.

Something ugly was about to happen. Eagle Feather could feel it in his old bones, and the hair on the back of his neck stood on end. A cool breeze struck him and he shivered.

Bubba took another long drag, held his breath and looked at the joint squeezed between his thumb and index finger, an effeminate pose. Then he spoke as he exhaled the smoke from his lungs,

"Marijuana's a wonderful thing. Makes everything in life better. If you ain't never tried weed you's missing out on one of life's simple joys. Makes food taste better, makes everything *feel* better ..." He groaned an obscene groan and rubbed the front of his pants. "But what I bet you didn't know about weed was it makes *killing* better. True truth here, people. It is way more fun to kill somebody when you're high. It sorta slows down the process, you know, it's like you can see the blood splatter out in little drips, spray out in them heartbeat bursts if you cut an artery, and the drops shine in the light like red diamonds."

He took another drag and breathed it right back out.

"To make what's about to happen a truly memorable experience, I'd ought to let all of you get high, so you could appreciate like I do all the sights ... and smells, too. There's going to be a smell alright, and getting high would make it ever so much more enjoyable for you."

The joint had about burned down to his fingers and he pinched them together, almost delicately, and took one last long drag, held his breath and flicked the joint away. It flew in a lazy arc through the air — like a meteor, or an alien spaceship — and then plunked down into the mud where it sizzled briefly and went out.

He let out the breath of smoke he'd been holding, took in another deep breath and let it out, then fixed the crowd with a cold stare. The fake camaraderie was gone. The affability had vanished. This was a man-eater, looking over his prey, deciding which one he would feast on, which one he would devour.

Eagle Feather was afraid. He didn't like how Bubba was standing with his foot carelessly resting on the top of the gasoline can. Then Bubba picked up the can and took a couple of steps to where the four escapee wannabes lay in the mud with their hands bound behind their backs. He unscrewed the lid, then went from one man to the next splashing gasoline on their feet and legs, like a woman pouring water on her petunias.

The crowd almost groaned in fear, not an audible thing, but something you could feel passing from one person to another.

Eagle Feather had never been so terrified. He was ready to die, expected to die. But what ...? *Like your pants was on fire.* That was it.

Then Bubba turned and walked back to the spot where he'd been standing in front of the crowd. Right in front of Star. He stood there, holding the can, within grabbing distance.

"This ain't gonna take long. Real good object sessions are the best when they're short ... and brutal. Ruthless. I need every one of you, deep down in your heart of hearts, down in your soul where you live, I need that part of you to understand with absolute clarity that there is nothing, absolutely *nothing* I won't do to keep you in line. Once you get that part down, then we won't have to keep having these demonstrations. You'll just go to work in my fields, bring in my crop, saying 'yes sir' and 'no sir' and 'whatever you say, sir,' like good little doobies. Life will be a lot easier for both of us when that happens, so it really is in the best interests of all of us if I cut to the chase here, kill somebody, and get it over with."

He gestured toward the four men lying face down in the mud, their pants soaked in gasoline.

"Them fellas earned an object lesson in what it really feels like to have your pants on fire, doncha think?"

No one made a sound.

"You think I oughta show 'em?"

Silence.

"But see, that's the thing. Folks don't hardly ever get the punishment they deserve. Not in real life they don't. Ain't nothing fair about real life." He paused dramatically. "In *real life*, it's always innocent people who have to pay the price for the stupidity of others."

He struck with the speed of a rattlesnake, reached down and grabbed Star by the arm and flung her out into the mud in front of the crowd in a motion so quick it was hard to follow. She couldn't keep her balance, of course, tripped and slid on her side through the mud until she came to rest about ten feet from the front row of horrified onlookers.

A sound … a sound that wasn't quite a sound, something like a communal groan rumbled up out of the crowd, a painful, haunting moan that was not words, was too primeval for words, was an animal sound of pain and fear. It was so sudden, shocking and unexpected that Bubba's head snapped up and his eyes swept across the crowd, looking perhaps for the source of the sound, seeking to find it and silence it, but it came from everywhere and nowhere at once, from the throats and chests of every person in the crowd, unbidden and uncontrollable. And for a small moment, something like … was that *fear*? … flashed across Bubba's face, before it hardened again into the granite of evil.

Eagle Feather found that he had somehow managed to get to his knees with his hands bound behind his back, without being aware of willing his body to do so. It wasn't like he had some plan, like he intended to jump Bubba, it was a response, like hitting his knee with one of those rubber hammers and watching the reflex kick out. As he struggled to rise to his feet, Bubba whirled on him, took two steps and kicked him square in the chest. The blow sent Eagle Feather flying backward and he landed in the mud and slid. Looking at the guard nearest Eagle Feather, Bubba said, "He so much as blinks, shoot him in the head."

Then he turned and made eye contact with his men standing around with rifles or pistols drawn.

They had flinched away from the strange sound that had come from the crowd, moved away instinctively, looked uncertain.

"If any one of them people moves, takes a single step in my direction, shoot them, and shoot the people standing on both sides of them, too." His voice was harsh and cold, cutting through the darkness that boiled with his evil all around him.

He stepped back to where Star lay, grabbed her arm and hauled her up to a kneeling position.

"What's that imaginary dog of yours smell now, Stumbles?" he snarled into her face. "If he can smell guns … can he smell … fire, too?"

With drawn-out, unhurried, exaggerated leisure, he lifted up the can of gasoline and held it above her. He didn't look at the can or at Star as he did it, he glared out at the crowd in ruthless, hateful defiance, daring any one of them to oppose him, daring them to move a muscle so he could mow them down. The crowd stood as still as statues, casting a forest of harsh black shadows down onto the shiny puddles on the ground.

It began to rain again. Not a downpour. Just a gentle rain, the kind you'd want to fall on your flower bed after you planted all the daisy seeds.

Bubba's visage cowed them, every person, into terrified submission, his eyes darting from one person to the next, goading them, a twisted little smile curled on the edges of his mouth.

He never took his eyes off them as he began to pour the liquid onto her. She was bent forward at the waist and it landed on her back, drenching her shirt. Eagle Feather couldn't see her face, but she understood what the gasoline meant and she must have been terrified.

The crowd groaned again. Not painful this time, totally involuntarily a sound came from every throat that was somewhere between fear and rage. And the people standing there began to sway, like wheat struck with the wind and the volume of the sound intensified, and grew uglier.

"Shut up!" Bubba cried, and threw the can off into the darkness. "You hear me, I said shut up."

But there was no one to shoot for their disobedience. He'd have to kill them all because every one of them was contributing to the communal moan. There were no words, no movement of lips or jaws, and the unreadable looks on all their faces were identical.

Bubba's eyes grew large, so large the whites showed all around. The guards stepped backward, all of them, in a cringing-away movement, though they didn't lower their guns.

"You better shut the fuck up, all of you. You listenin' to me?"

Taking two steps back toward the crowd, Bubba grabbed hold of the woman who'd been standing on the right of Star, the one old enough to be her grandmother. He dragged her one step out of the crowd and punched her with his fist in the face. She collapsed in a bloodied heap on the ground, but the sound continued.

Bubba was not holding a gun. He had one

holstered at his side, though, and now he drew it and swept it in an arc across the crowd, back and forth.

"Who wants to eat a bullet? Huh? You? You want one?"

He put the gun to the forehead of a man Eagle Feather didn't know and pulled the trigger without hesitation. The gasp of surprise as the man collapsed interrupted the sound, but it returned on the next breath. Softer now, but somehow even more menacing. Though it didn't sound like, it did *feel* like the throaty growl of an angry bear. A big one.

Bubba shoved the gun back into his holster and pulled out the book of matches. With surprising speed, he pulled one free and rubbed it across the black strip on the back of the cardboard. A yellow flame leapt up off the tip, and in a voice that sounded frenzied and unnatural, he shouted at Star.

"Your imaginary dog smell fire, can he? Can he smell fried kid?"

Then he pitched the burning match toward where Star knelt, soaked in gasoline.

Chapter Fifty-Four

Noah was in his room, adding the finishing touches to a model building he wanted to show—

Suddenly, he smelled gasoline.

It was a stifling, gagging smell, like … like he was soaked in gasoline. The skin on his back, shoulders and arms burned from the touch of it.

Star's voice shrieked in his head, a cry of absolute terror.

It wasn't a word, only a scream, a wail of fear and under it was a rumbling roar unlike any sound Noah had ever heard.

His head jerked up and he dropped the piece of shaped-to-order balsa wood he was about to fit into the shaped-to-order space he had made for it on the side of the building. He was frozen, listening.

He hadn't heard Star's voice in his head since they were together in the mothership.

Something was terribly, horribly wrong.

Leaping to his feet, he raced to his door, opened it just as the school fire alarm sounded. Harsh strobe lights flashed in the hallways and behind him on the ceiling in his room and he gasped at the stench of ammonia. Hot air was spewing the eye-watering stench out the jets above all the doors. He could hear the vibration of the siren sounding, though no sound penetrated his silent world.

The children in the hallway were frightened, rushing as they had been trained to do to the cafeteria, their thoughts brushing through his mind as they passed.

"… really a fire this time …?"

"… just a drill …

"… if there's a fire, can a goldfish … burn?"

He ignored the passing thoughts, ignored the frantic people he met in the hallway. He had to find his father. Had to get his father to help—

He spotted his father coming toward him, rushing down the hallway with Brother Sebastian and Garson close behind.

Noah grabbed his father's hand and started signing frantically, but his father was too distracted to notice.

"Not now, Noah," he signed. "You need to go with the other children and Brother Sebastian to the wine cellar."

Noah tried to argue, tried to explain, but his father had already turned away before he had a chance and continued down the hall with Garson.

Noah took two steps to follow him, then stood still, trying to calm his panic and think. Dad said *panicked people always make bad decisions* and he couldn't make a bad decision now. Star was in trouble.

Think.

How could he have heard Star in his head? It had been as comfortably there in his mind as breathing out was a part of breathing in when they were together. Always with him. And then suddenly, it was gone and he was back on Earth, returned to where he'd been taken, with his father there beside the pond, so thrilled to see him it broke Noah's heart.

His father was there. But Star was gone.

Dad had said he heard on some spotty news report that all the people who had been abducted were returned. Noah clung to that, even though he was certain there were people taken nobody knew were gone, so nobody could be certain they'd come back. Paco said nobody knew or cared that he was gone, and Star said her grandfather wasn't likely to report that she was "missing."

So how did anybody *know* all those kidnapped had been returned?

He decided nobody did, no matter what they said, but he *believed,* believed with all his heart that Star was back, that she had been returned to where she was taken, which was a butte somewhere in New Mexico.

Noah had not heard from her since he returned. He had tried, stretched out his mind, sought hers out there somewhere, but it was useless. Star's place inside his head was hollow and vacant.

Until now. Until just a few seconds ago, when he'd

heard her cry out in his head. How could he hear her—

Star was close!

Of course.

He stood very still. Held his breath and "listened" in his mind with all his concentration.

He couldn't hear her voice anymore. But he could sense her, feel her with his mind in a way he hadn't for months. She had to be somewhere *nearby*.

The thought set his heart into a rhythm like a timpani drum, beating so fast he wasn't even aware of the individual beats.

Star was coming here, to him, *to join Noah*.

Suddenly, he knew that was true, though he had never even entertained such a thought before. It made sense. He'd told her and Paco about Zion, about the townies who'd tried to raid it for the supplies, about the monks and the farm … it was as good a place as any you'd find right now with Astral motherships hanging over the cities and shuttles zipping around through the sky.

They'd talked about that.

And Star had remembered. She had found a way — *some way* — to come to him. Even with the horrible lump of fear her cry of terror had placed in the pit of his stomach, he couldn't help a thrill of wonder and excitement. Star! Star was close.

Right, and Star was in *trouble*.

That's why he'd heard her. She must be nearby or he wouldn't have been able to, but it was the desperation, the terror in her cry that had carried it. That was what had powered her thought. She had been screaming inside her head like ... like she was afraid somebody was going to set her on fire.

He was so horrified by that prospect that he lost his breath for a moment, then an intention formed in his mind and he did nothing to dissuade it. Star was nearby and she was in trouble and he had to help her. He had to. And so he would.

He turned and went running to a side door of the building and slipped out into the darkness. He took a couple of steps, then crouched down low to the ground and ran bent-over toward the fence. He knew the heat detector sensors showed — what was it Dr. Weiss had said, "anything bigger than a raccoon" on the monitors in the security center. He believed that bent over, he might be mistaken for a big dog. It was the best he could do and he ran bent-over across the lawn and through the trees to the wall.

Brother Sebastian had told him about the passage-way, laughed that monks three hundred years ago must not have been as fat as monks today because nobody bigger than a child could crawl through it. And so, of course, at his first opportunity, Noah had gone exploring and found the entrance. It was over-grown with weeds and bushes, took him fifteen minutes to find it, but the tunnel through the wall still existed and there was still a bush in front of the exit on the other side. He'd not have been able of find it tonight if he hadn't marked its location by the mulberry tree. It was hard, still. Even with the bright lights out front spilling over into the side yards of the building, there was still not enough light to see where he was going. He had trouble finding the mulberry tree but finally did, then tried to walk directly to the wall from it, but he must have gotten it wrong somehow because the opening wasn't there. He felt frantically along the wall, crawling back behind the bushes, getting scratched and clawed, knew the wounds would itch like crazy for the rest of the night. He finally found the opening. It was a good thing Noah was used to dark caves because it would certainly have horrified any other little boy to pop down into a black hole, crawl through it and come out the other side in darkness. Noah didn't blink.

As he crawled through the dark, he considered the wisdom of this impetuous decision, but he didn't know what else he could have done. Star was near. She was in trouble, though he didn't know what he could possibly do to help her. He wasn't exactly a knight in shining armor on a white stallion. But his father would miss him. Whenever the current emergency was over, his father would come looking for him and he could lead his father to Star.

When he finally got to the end of the tunnel where it came out on the other side of the wall behind an azalea bush, he shoved his way through its limbs and stood, shaking off leaves and pieces of stems, dusting dirt off his hands and knees before he headed off into the woods. He stopped, well inside the tree line. Stood still. Concentrated. When he did, he felt a cold stone form in his belly. Oh, he could still feel the warmth of Star's presence. But it felt no different than it had felt inside the building. He thought it'd be stronger here. Like a fire that feels warmer and warmer as you approach it. He'd intended to follow the warmth, that it would lead him to Star. Nothing had changed. Clearly, he hadn't gone in the *wrong* direction because the warmth hadn't decreased. But it hadn't gotten any warmer, either.

Realization came slowly and Noah fought it. Wrestled with it, struggled not to see it. But he wasn't any good at that kind of thing. It was what it was. And reality was that he couldn't find Star by following her *warmth*. It was too diffuse. She might be a mile down the road or three hundred miles away. Noah couldn't lead his father to Star so his father could help her because Noah had no way to locate her.

His shoulders sagged in defeat. He had come running out here prepared to save Star … so excited to *be with Star again*, and it had been a foolish errand. He was turning around to make his way back to the azalea bush when he spotted a light coming toward him through the woods. Not just one light, several. People were out here with flashlights.

He remembered the attack of the townies, how they had come into the compound with big guns and would have stripped the whole place of supplies if Dr. Weiss hadn't shot that man, shot him right in the chest and then all the others ran away.

Was that what this was? Another attack by the townies?

Then he thought about his father who'd been running somewhere and the emergency fans had gone off. His father had been on his way to fight off these people in the woods!

But Noah had stood there too long. He'd be seen if he crossed the open area between the woods and the azalea bush. So he slowly circled the big tree he was behind, keeping it between him and the lights that were growing so bright he could see the forms of the men holding the flashlights. Could see that in their other hands they were carrying rifles.

Chapter Fifty-Five

IT WAS DUSK. Paco stood in the darkening puddle of shade beneath a juniper tree, hidden, out of sight from the big house across the street. It was Spade's house. The house he had commandeered as his Royal Palace when he took over the town after he took over the prison.

It was, of course, the finest house in town. Paco had walked the streets of the town, and he knew. This must have belonged to some uber-rich tycoon, some investment banker, or software developer, a techno-geek. Or just some lucky schmuck whose parents made a lot of money and he inherited it and never had to work a day in his life. The ornate house seemed fitting for Spade, Paco thought. It suited him. The man was a megalomaniac, someone who believed that he was a god, that whatever he wanted was the only thing that mattered in life. And that satisfying his desires was worth the lives, the very souls of the people around him.

Paco had stood across the street from the mansion looking at it for hours the day before, imagining what it must be like inside, how ornate and plush the furniture must be, beautiful hardwood floors or parquet floors or tile covered with Egyptian rugs that cost more money than Paco had ever had in his hands in his life.

He watched the windows, hoping to catch sight of Spade and hoping that he wouldn't with equal intensity. He wanted to see him, he wanted to reignite the hatred he had felt for the man, the boiling, curdling cancerous hatred that had sprung up in his heart as he ran away from the broken wall of the prison into the town, and into the shuttle that took him to the mothership. He wanted to see Spade, feel the intensity of that emotion again.

But on the other hand, he didn't want to see Spade. Was afraid of what he would do if he did. One part of him thought he would take one look at Spade's face, turn tail and run and not stop running until his heart stopped pumping blood through his veins. Another part of him thought that if he saw Spade's face at a window, he would be so outraged, so angry, so engorged with bloodlust that he would run across the street, knock down the guards around Spade's door, dash inside, grab Spade around the throat, and choke him until his eyes bugged out and his tongue turned black.

Making his way along the hedge that ran up the side of the lawn to the back of the house across the street from Spade's where Paco's men were waiting for him, he realized he wasn't afraid. He would either capture Spade or die in the attempt.

And he was certain he wasn't going to die this day.

Everything went according to plan at first. Greg Cox and Bill Lewis took out the guards at the front and back doors soundlessly, Angelo Russo picked the lock easily and within minutes the three of them were edging behind Paco down a dark hallway that led to the bedroom where Spade would either be asleep or having sex with someone, woman or man, consensual or rape.

Paco caught a whisper of thought — awake thoughts in the room off to their left and then in the one off to their right where no one should be awake at this hour. Paco had no time to concentrate on the thoughts, listen to them before the lights in the hallway came on, and two armed men leapt out of the rooms that opened onto it, guns drawn, pointed at Paco's chest. Paco and his three men were disarmed in seconds.

"Well, well, well, lookie here what we got," said a familiar voice and Paco looked up to see Spade standing in the open doorway of the room at the end of the hallway, a vicious grin on his face.

The sight of Spade ignited such an instant flash fire of rage in Paco's gut that if the man had been within grabbing distance, he'd have leaped at him and tried to choke him.

"When I heard you was back from wherever it was you went after the glorious night we spent together, I was delighted to hear it. I thought the reptars had gobbled you up. But it made me sad to learn that you's going to try to kill me and take over what's mine." He laughed then, a wide rumbling laugh that seemed to fill the whole space of the hallway. "Oh yes, my good friend Aasen Ivanov told me *everything* and he will be richly rewarded for his loyalty." Then Spade cocked his head to the side. "You've changed, boy." Paco watched Spade's eyes travel over his bearded face and muscled body. "How'd you do … *that* in just three months?" The man was genuinely surprised, and reluctantly impressed. "How does *anybody* go from boy to man in …? You must have some serious stones, son, working overtime to produce whatever it is does a thing like that. Some *serious* stones."

Then he was holding a knife, a long-bladed knife, like a butcher knife rather than a sporting knife. Paco hadn't seen him reach for it, but it was suddenly there. He turned it over in his hand and the overhead light sparkled bright on the metal shiny metal blade.

"You about to lose them stones, boy, and various other body parts, but not before I use you seven ways from Sunday. I'm gonna rip you a new one before I cut off your nuts. Then I'll just cut off pieces of you … an ear maybe, a toe, a couple of fingers. Nothing essential and nothing that'll take away from that pretty-boy face. You'll lose the beard, too. I liked you much better as a kid. Might be I can starve you so's you'll get skinny again, look like you used to. Yeah, I bet that'd do it. I'm gonna put me a collar around your neck and keep you like a dog on a leash. Make you a party favor to pass around to all the boys when we have backyard barbecues."

He gestured toward the back of the house.

"They's a backyard barbecue grill at this place, you b'lieve that? And a swimming pool. Fanciest house in town. We get together around the pool, drink beer and grill steaks. I'll lead you around to every one of my men, crawling like a dog on a leash, give ever one of them a piece of your ass. Won't that make a grand party."

Spade had approached Paco as he talked, turning the knife over and over in his hands.

Paco whispered softly into the minds of his three men.

I'm going to take Spade down! Get ready to grab the guards' guns when I do.

A quick sweep of their minds revealed they were scared ... *but they believed!*

Spade was wearing no shirt, and his feet were bare beneath his jeans. Paco had almost forgotten how huge and intimidating the man was. When he stood before Paco, he towered over him, grinning, the whole time grinning.

"You *mine*, sweet meat. I'm gonna—"

Paco *shrieked* into Spade's mind. Screamed. A wordless cry of rage and pain and humiliation and impotent fury that rose up from Paco's very soul, a sound that was not a sound ears could hear hammered Spade's mind. Paco remembered how Santoro had reacted the first time Paco had spoken inside his head. He'd merely spoken then. Now, Paco was yelling, *screeching,* pulling out all the stops. And he would pay for it, oh my yes, the migraine that was coming, packed up tight in freight cars barreling down the line at him would incapacitate him. He could feel the blood vessels swelling, feel the blood engorging them, stretching them. One of them might rupture and Paco would drop to the floor with Spade.

But if he survived, he would be ever so much stronger.

Paco didn't drop to the floor.

Spade did.

The knife clattered out of his suddenly numb fingers and hit the Moroccan tile a heartbeat before his whole body folded up, went as limp as a puppet when the puppeteer lets go the strings. He collapsed downward, then fell over on his side, his eyes open but staring sightlessly.

Paco's men had been ready. They took advantage of the surprise and shock to attack the two guards, knocked their weapons away. The fight didn't last long.

Paco would only be able to hold it together now for a few more minutes; the pain was already flooding into his temples.

"Shoot them," he said, indicating the men who'd moments before been holding guns on them. His men obeyed and the sound of the gunshots reverberated in the hallway, slicing a lightning bolt of pain through Paco's skull. "And tie him up." He nodded to Spade. "Tight, use the plastic zip ties, hands and feet." Russo pulled zip ties out of his pocket. "Haul him back into his bedroom and stay with him until morning. All three of you. Don't let him out of your sight. Don't take the zip ties off for anything."

Looking from one man's face to the next, Paco didn't dare tax himself with a peek into their minds to see their responses, but he didn't really need to. The looks on their faces told the story. Paco had designed a daring plan — kill a couple of guards and waltz into Spade's house — *surprise!* But that's not how it went down, thanks to Aasen Ivanov, and Paco would sooooo enjoy dealing with the traitor later.

The plan had not gone off without a hitch, but Paco had prevailed even when it looked hopeless. He'd been quick on his feet, improvised, saved them all. That earned him way more respect than a flawless plan. He saw admiration in the eyes of his men, compliance in their attitudes.

"Good job. Everything all set for the morning?"

"We'll have people out all night, knocking on doors, making sure everybody knows."

"I'll see you in the morning, then."

Paco turned and walked steadily out the front door of the house and across the yard in the cool velvet darkness, a vice of pain beginning to pinch his head in an ever-tightening grip. He'd made sure earlier that the house across the street was abandoned and he went around to the back door, where he'd used a polo mallet to break out the glass to let himself in. He didn't turn on the lights, just slipped through the darkness to the couch, the leather couch in the family room. He lay down on it carefully and waited for the tsunami to crash down on him.

He steeled himself for the coming agony, comforting himself even as the knife blades began to stab into his skull, with the understanding that on the other side of his suffering … he would be stronger.

Chapter Fifty-Six

THE LIGHTED MATCH Bubba flicked into the air toward Star seemed to Eagle Feather to travel in slow motion. It turned over and over, burning brighter and brighter as the flame crawled down the small piece of cardboard that had attached the match to the book.

Then Eagle Feather's view of the match was obscured. Something, he didn't know what, had rushed out of the darkness, knocking the match aside. A shape.

Though he was an old man, his eyesight was probably better than seventy-five percent of the people there, but even Eagle Feather couldn't tell what it was, the shape that had launched itself at Bubba with a low rumble like thunder, deflecting the match and slamming into the man's chest.

Pumpkin!

What happened after that was ... Eagle Feather was never able to describe it accurately, because he wasn't sure how much of what he was seeing was reality, in-this-world, you-can-touch-it reality and how much of it was … Yeah, was what? Was something more than what could be seen in the harsh glare from the light posts above the crowd. Their ugly yellow incandescence had created garish black shadows and those *shadows* had pooled and surged forward.

That's what it had looked like to Eagle Feather. A wave. An incoming tide of humanity moving as one. The crowd didn't decide to jump Bubba and his men. Nobody worked it out logically. Nobody's mind was saying "Now would be an opportune time to take over the camp." Not one of them was thinking "We should jump the men with guns while they're distracted."

All those things were true, of course, but nobody was thinking them.

That was the thing. No single person was thinking at all. The many had become one, communicating with each other as some kind of *hive mind*. No, it was more basic than that. More primitive and primeval. Every person there surged forward with no regard for their own well-being as an instinctual move *to protect Star.* Saving that child was all that mattered.

Much of what Papa Eagle Feather understood about the event came from putting pieces together in his head afterward. But there were missing pieces. Pumpkin had jumped out of the shadows at Bubba and the dog's assault had knocked aside the burning match so that it flopped into the mud and fizzled out. Had the dog *intended* to deflect the match? Eagle Feather did not know. What he *did* know … what he *came to believe afterward* … was that even if the dog had not knocked the match aside, it would not have ignited the gasoline-soaked little girl on her knees before the crowd.

The crowd had surged forward the instant Bubba struck the match, even before he flicked it away, swarmed over Star, protecting her with their bodies. And beyond that, a tsunami of humanity rose up like a sea monster and fell upon Bubba and his men and they had no chance of surviving its onslaught.

There were gunshots. Several. People cried out and fell. But nothing stopped their herd instinct. The former prisoners pushed forward over the bodies of the fallen and pounced on the guards.

Some in the crowd took guns away from the guards and shot them. Most used no weapon except their bare hands. They leapt en masse upon the guards, knocking them to the ground and then pummeling them with their hands, fists, and stomping them until they lay bloody masses unmoving in the mud.

Eagle Feather's assessment of the guards had proved mostly accurate. Only a handful were rotten to the core like Bubba. The prisoners had killed all of them, as if the herd of humanity could sense their evil, and had rooted it out and destroyed it. Others dropped their weapons and raised their hands in submission the instant the fight began.

Pumpkin remained cuddled next to Star as women poured buckets of water over the child to wash away the gasoline, then herded her into the women's dormitory to give her a soapy shower. Eagle Feather wasn't really aware of the passage of time, didn't know if the revolt of the prisoners took five minutes or thirty seconds or half an hour. Someone cut away the rope that bound his hands behind him. Someone else got a water hose and used it to wash off the gasoline that soaked his pants. Several guards made a break for it, until Nick Wilson picked up one of the rifles off the ground from a fallen guard and called out to those who were trying to escape to stop and drop their weapons.

Eagle Feather looked around, trying to find Bubba's body.

It wasn't there. Pumpkin was not trained to attack and kill like the Rottweiler Eagle Feather had shot. He'd leapt into action to save Star, but once the danger to her was over, he had not continued to attack until the enemy was dead. He had knocked Bubba down, and then left him lying in the mud. And in the pandemonium that followed, Bubba apparently had slipped away.

"He's not here," Nick said as he approached. He had obviously been of the same mind as Eagle Feather. "The son of a bitch got away into the darkness."

"Not dead, just hiding somewhere," Ken Whitlock said. His pants still smelled of gasoline, though Nick Wilson and Eagle Feather had gotten most of the gasoline out of theirs.

"Goody," said Fred Schwartz, who had joined them. "Such a comfort to an old man to know he's out there on the prowl, a monster like Bubba Blacksnake." He spit in the dirt. "*Blacksnake* … riiiiiight. His real last name's probably Rabinowitz. Or Schwartz."

Bill Brentwood, like Nick Wilson, had been a soldier and when the dust settled, leadership of the "freed prisoners" fell to the two of them by default. Bill had taken charge of the guards the crowd hadn't killed and he approached them now, holding two of the former guards at gunpoint. Both numbered among the bikers who had attacked Eagle Feather's caravan in the woods.

"This fella claims to have information you ought to have," said Brentwood, indicating the blond man whose bike had a cow skull mounted on the handlebars and wore a dog muzzle across his face.

"My name is Lars Carlsen," said the blond man. "Thanks for agreeing to talk to me, and for what you did here. You rescued some of us same's you did the other prisoners."

"Riiiiiight," said Fred Schwartz and rolled his eyes.

"I'm not asking for a thing!" Carlsen said. "Whatever happens to me now is better than working for Bubba." Then he addressed Nick. "I'm probably the only man still alive who knows where Bubba hid it in the woods, and the only reason I know is that he used me to put it there because I could drive a big rig — worked my way through college driving eighteen-wheelers."

Carlsen took a breath. "Gasoline. Bubba stashed a tanker truck full of it in the woods."

Nick was instantly interested. They'd abandoned

most of the RVs and doubled up in the others because they'd run out of gas.

"How big?" he asked.

Carlsen smiled. "*Big!* And it's full. Those suckers carry almost twelve thousand gallons."

"Show me," said Brentwood, waving his pistol at the man. The man turned to go with Brentwood when Eagle Feather stopped him.

"How'd you get mixed up with Bubba Whatever-hislastnamereallyis?" he asked.

The smile dropped off Carlsen's face. "I'm an architect …" He paused. "I *used to be* an architect and fixing up Harley Davidsons was my hobby. A friend of mine heard about this big bike rally in Virginia and he talked me into going. We decked out our bikes like real badasses — driving there and back was supposed to be a big adventure." He paused again. "We got to the rally the day before Astral Day."

The day the world fell apart.

"We tried to get back home but … I've got a wife and three little ones in Clarksburg. It's a small town next to a *prison,* Radcliffe Correctional Facility, and I can't imagine what must have happened there …" His voice trailed off. "Bubba caught us outside Bowling Green, wanted the bikes, and when Roger didn't get off his fast enough, Bubba shot him. Then Bubba told me, 'You're either on my side or you're dead.' I picked Door Number One."

Nick asked Eagle Feather after Brentwood led Carlsen away, "You believe him?"

Eagle Feather nodded. "Him and a couple of the

others. I watched. Didn't look to me like they'd volunteered."

"I suppose we could have him draw a house plan to prove it," Nick said, but he wasn't serious. His gaze scanned the darkness. "We need to do whatever we can to cripple Bubba." He gestured in the direction of the barns. "We need to spend tonight stripping this place, gathering up whatever we can use, and tomorrow morning when we leave … we burn the rest of it down — barns, equipment, weed, this camp. Everything."

"I'll bring the marshmallows," Eagle Feather said.

Chapter Fifty-Seven

In ADDITION to being smarter than Oscar Higgins, Harry Windom had the "dry run" of their disastrous raid on the academy as a "teachable moment" and he'd learned some valuable lessons from the encounter. His plan was far simpler and more direct. He knew it was futile to try to sneak up on the buildings. He didn't know where or how, but obviously there was all kinda fancy expensive surveillance equipment in the woods, alerting those inside of intruders way before they had a chance to stage a surprise attack. He wasn't counting on darkness and the element of surprise. In fact, his plan was just the opposite. He planned to surround the facility, lay siege to the place overnight. Let them stew in there, wondering what his plan was, waiting for the other shoe to fall. Then in the morning, he'd make one simple demand. He had secured a megaphone to use to do it. "Come out, drop your weapons and nobody gets hurt. Fight, fire a single shot, and we will kill every person inside."

Actually, he didn't have any qualms about killing a bunch of deaf children. What good were they and they were the progeny of a bunch of rich assholes from away-from-here who probably got rich off the sweat of some other man's brow. He didn't mind the thought of ridding the world of their progeny. But he knew that wouldn't sit well with the remainder of his troops, who were, by and large, just John Q. Citizens pressed into service and given a weapon and told that failure meant starvation for their children this winter.

After he made that announcement, he intended to pass it up and down the ranks of his men that it was a bluff, that he had no intention of killing innocent children. And after they surrendered … well, maybe he'd kill them, maybe he wouldn't. Depended on how he felt at the moment.

When his men had all gathered in the area in front of the gate of the academy, he dispatched them in teams of two to station themselves in a circle around the perimeter of the rock fence. They weren't to try to climb it. They were to wait for his signal and then they would use what Harry had had the foresight and good judgement to bring along. He'd removed the wooden doors from several abandoned houses. He intended to lay them on the top of the broken glass on the wall so his men wouldn't be injured climbing over. When he signaled, his men would pop these babies on the top of the wall, scramble over them and storm the building from all sides at once. The folks inside wouldn't have a chance.

But that was for in the morning. For now, let them stew.

SAWYER WATCHED the clump of heat-sensing dots disperse and arrange themselves in a circle around the outer wall of the monastery, the old one, the rock wall that Dr. Weiss had put broken glass on top of to deter the first round of armed invaders. Sawyer was sure these men knew the fate of the previous attackers, most likely had served in the ranks of the previous attackers. They would know about the broken glass and surely to goodness somebody had figured out a way to cross the fence without getting cut by the glass.

Sawyer had stationed his troops, such as they were, at the four corners of the main building, and then at two corners of the outer buildings, on the second and third floors. There weren't enough soldiers to put any on the ground floor, but Sawyer figured the better strategy was to pick them off from above while they were crossing the grounds. Joe would be on the ground-floor level, waiting for whatever mice made it through the trap alive and got to the cheese.

He waited for the leader of the group of marauders to make contact with him, but there was only silence. Whoever it was thought it would unnerve the people inside the monastery to be left waiting for someone to make contact with them. Idiot. The extra time just gave Sawyer time to hand out extra guns and ammunition to the snipers he had on the third floors. They wouldn't have to reload, just grab another rifle when they ran out of ammo and keep firing. And it gave Sawyer a chance to plan out what he would do and say once the demands came in the morning. And there'd be demands in the morning.

When they were ordered to turn over their supplies, what was he going to say, other than no, of course. He didn't think he had any other cards to play.

NOAH DIDN'T KNOW how it had happened. He'd seen the men coming through the woods and hidden from them, and they had passed him without spotting him hidden in the trees. But now they were between him and the wall. He had no way to get back inside the building. There were two men with guns stationed almost right in front of the entrance to the tunnel that led under the fence.

It was dark and late and getting cold. Noah hadn't had the sense to grab a jacket before he went running off on his insane mission to save Star. Now he was beginning to get genuinely chilled. And it occurred to him that it wasn't just likely, it was *certain* that he was going to have to stay here in the woods in the dark, alone, *all night long* He waited for the terror of that thought to punch him in the belly but it didn't. Worse things than this had happened to Noah Matheson in his short life.

He looked around for somewhere he could hide, somewhere he could spend the night that would be concealed and warmer than standing out here in the breeze, which wasn't cool — it was August in Kentucky, after all — but it would get chilly before morning.

He spotted another azalea bush nestled up against the wall and crept toward it. It was hard to be quiet when you couldn't hear. You could step on a stick that would crack … shoot, you could step on a whoopee cushion and not know it out here in the dark. He just trusted his senses the best he could, saw through the darkness the clustered limbs of the bush that drooped with blossoms all the way to the ground. He saw none of the men with lights anywhere around. In fact, the men who'd been stationed just outside the tunnel had turned off their flashlights, as had the others, so the velvet darkness was smooth and rough on his skin at the same time.

Squirming back into the undergrowth, Noah willed himself not to think about the possibilities that something truly heinous — a black widow spider, a skunk, a rattlesnake — had already claimed the spot and had taken up residence in it.

He leaned his back against the stem of the bush, pulled his knees up to his chest and stared out into the nothingness of the night. His father was likely missing him about now, probably looking for him. He had needlessly worried a man who already had enough matters of real concern to worry about. But there was no fix for that now, he'd be found missing and every-body would be frantic.

It had been a stupid thing to do, coming out here like this, racing out of the building because he could hear Star in his head. But he *had* heard her. He was certain that he had. Which meant she *was* close. No matter what else happened in the morning that was bad — and he was sure a showdown between the townies and the monastery wasn't going to end well — he would see Star soon. No, not soon — *tomorrow.* There was no way on earth he could possibly know a thing like that but he was certain of it. The hole in his heart, in his soul, would be filled tomorrow.

But between now and tomorrow were hours of darkness, hiding in the scratchy limbs of the bush, imaging every kind of creature was crawling on him. His butt was cold, sitting on the cold ground, but he didn't dare try to gather up a pile of leaves to sit on because he didn't know how noisy that might be. And so he sat. Cold and uncomfortable. Miserable. What an idiot!

At some point, he finally drifted off to sleep and stretched out under the bush … with his feet sticking out from beneath the branches. He was wearing bright red sneakers.

Chapter Fifty-Eight

THE MACHINE itself was covered with two big green plastic tarps. It was rolled into the gymnasium on a dolly. There was no way to tell what was under the tarps, only that whatever it was it was big and heavy. The wheels of the dolly dug into the floor of the basketball court, cut ugly grooves into the polished golden wood, damaged it beyond repair, not that anybody'd ever be playing basketball games in there again.

Paco wanted them all to see. Everyone. He wanted the bleachers full. He'd had men knocking on doors all night long ... had set it up even when nobody was sure he was gonna come out on top when he went after Spade.

You must have some serious stones, son. That's what Spade had said. And when he said it, he had no idea how right he was.

Paco's men had rounded up *everybody.* Every former prison inmate who had commandeered a home, and live-in servants in Clarksburg, and every one of those servants, too, every man, woman, and child for five miles in every direction. Paco wanted them all there. He wanted them all to see.

Spade had been locked up in the bedroom of the big fancy house he had appropriated for himself with his feet and hands held tight by plastic zip ties. When Paco sent his men to drag Spade out, he had been tied up all night with nothing to eat or drink. He had wet and crapped himself. *Good!*

People filed into the gymnasium by ones and twos. Not families come to watch their kids play basketball or volleyball, not cheering fans for the local team. No one said anything to anybody. They kept their eyes downcast, merely walked in and sat down in the bleachers because they'd been ordered to, and they knew if they didn't they would regret it.

There were only a few stragglers who showed up late, sneaking furtively in the door and up into a seat in the stands guiltily, like a dog that had been caught with his master's torn-up shoe in his mouth.

The silence in the big hollow room was deafening. There were no whispered conversations. No laughter. No clomping of little kids running up and down the steps of the bleachers. No squeak-squeak of sneakers on the polished floor, or thrum of a basketball dribbled, or the twang of a missed shot. Only silence.

Though there was no talking among the spectators, Paco could hear the low buzzing hum of their thoughts. It was an electric sound, more like a transformer than a hive of bees. He could attend to any one of them if he chose to, but he didn't. Not right now, anyway. He didn't give a shit right now what any of these people thought. He only cared what they would think after his little display.

He stopped for a moment, remembering the scared kid who was calculating how he was going to escape out of the Department of Corrections van when it returned the group of Scared Straight teenagers to the city. The van that never showed, leaving them stranded. He had been frightened, but he'd played it smart, kept his head down and minded his own business, made an ally out of Tiburon. His mind skittered away from those thoughts, from the shuttle that landed in the prison yard, from the reptars who ripped apart dozens of inmates confined in the yard, like foxes let loose in the chicken yard.

He tried to get inside the head of that boy, but he couldn't. It wasn't that it had been so long ago. Only three months or so, but those months had been years in his life. Decades. His time in the mothership had changed him in ways he wasn't even totally aware of unless he took the time to look. He had cowered in the white room of the ship after he was taken out of the alley, so scared he might have wet his pants if he'd had any piss in his belly. But he hadn't had anything to drink before he was abducted. He'd spent the night before servicing Spade, being repeatedly raped and brutalized and Spade hadn't thought to bring him a cup of hot chocolate and cookies the next morning.

At least being abducted had healed his injuries. Instantly. And he had been injured, though he'd had no time to determine how bad it was. He knew only that he had bled so much from the attacks that the sheet on Spade's bunk had been stiff with his blood the next morning. When he "came to" or whatever it was that happened between standing in that alley and standing in the all-white room in the mothership, he was fine. He noticed it immediately. The pain of what had happened to him had made it difficult to walk, he had been in agony running away from the inmates who found him in the abandoned house and planned to take him back to Spade.

"Ain't that Spade's bitch?" one of them had cried when they saw him.

Paco ground his teeth. Spade's bitch. Well, Spade was about to find out what it was like to be *Paco's bitch,* and there was nothing that could heal the injuries Paco was about to inflict.

When he decided the time was right, Paco walked out into the center of the basketball court. He didn't have to call for silence. There was no sound in the room but the clomp of his shoes on the gym floor. He stood for a moment surveying the crowd, sampling a few of their thoughts.

"… just a kid — what, maybe twenty, twenty-five? How come he's in charge?"

Twenty? Twenty-five? Try just turned sixteen!

"… show him who's boss …"

"… I could beat the shit out of him with one hand tied …"

"You're all thinking how could this guy be in charge, he's just a kid," Paco said.

There was an uneasy rustling as people squirmed a little in their seats. "I get that. But see, the thing you got to understand is age is irrelevant." He looked toward the ceiling. "The Astrals … don't even know how old they are and they don't care. They didn't care how old I was, either, when they put me in charge. It's not about age, it's about how big your cajones are, and I got a pair the size of Volkswagens. You're about to see that."

He paused.

"All of you, every one of you, I want you to think of the worst thing you ever did." He waited in uncomfortable silence. "Got it? Well, I am here to tell you that the Astrals know you did that. They know what color your lunchbox was when you started first grade, and the name of the boy you screwed in the backseat of your grandmother's old Honda. They know *everything* about you. You need to understand that the Astrals are not individuals. They are a hive mind … and *my* mind is connected to theirs."

He took a breath and spoke the next words softly, so the crowd had to strain to hear.

"And what *that* means, sports fans, is that whatever the Astrals know, *Paco knows*."

He picked out three people, concentrated — not too hard, not yet, that was for later. That would be for all the marbles and at the end of it, he would either be their undisputed master or he would be dead. He concentrated now on their thoughts, picked through their minds, not a deep dive, collected a few thoughts and then spoke.

Looking directly at a fat man wearing a yellow shirt and ridiculous white pants, like maybe he'd been a milkman and those had been uniform pants. They were so filthy and stained now it was hard to tell. He was seated beside an equally fat, equally slovenly man.

"You, Dominique Monteroya, you want to tell your brother there about how you tricked his little girl into riding home from school with you, how you raped her and beat her with a pipe for two days and then buried her body in the back yard?"

The man blanched much whiter than his pants had ever been on their best bleached day.

To his brother, Paco said, "You'll find her remains under his rose bushes. When you dig her up, you'll see he broke nearly every bone in her body."

The man turned to lunge at his brother and Paco said two words with an authority that was not to be denied.

"*Not. Now.*"

The man froze.

"Do whatever you want when you leave here, but right now you sit there and listen to me."

Paco pointed to a middle-aged woman seated beside her husband. "Does Malcom know you cheated on him with the best man at your wedding, screwed him in the coat closet with your white wedding dress all hiked up?"

The woman almost coughed out her dentures. She opened her mouth as if to protest, to argue or defend herself, but had the good judgement to close it again without speaking.

"And you," he said to a man he remembered from the prison. His name was Renaldo Santiago, and he'd been a member of the Escorpion gang, the scorpions, real hard-asses. "Every con in the joint says they're innocent, but you really are, aren't you, Naldo. You were nowhere near that liquor store when your stupid friends held it up. But nobody'd believe you."

The man's face brightened and something like a beatific smile planted itself on his lips. He opened his mouth to speak, but Paco cut him off. "Of course, you didn't get caught the time you broke into that garage, tried to steal the guy's golf clubs and when he came in, you beat him to death with a putter. And you didn't get caught when you broke that guy's kneecaps because he owed the Scorpions money, or threw acid in that woman's face because she screwed around on your boss, or that first one, your cherry, where you shot and killed a stranger to get into the gang."

The man sat dumfounded, had nothing to say now.

"The Astrals know everything because they have been collecting data on mankind for centuries."

"*Why?*" somebody called out belligerently. Scared, but demanding.

Paco and the others had discussed that when they were in the mothership, but nobody had any idea. Or why the Astrals did experiments on the people they abducted before returning them to Earth.

"I suspect if they wanted you to know that, they'd have told you, Joe," he said. "But you wouldn't want to go ask them. They don't like questions. The titans almost never speak. And the reptars ... I'm not sure they *can* talk, with that mouthful of teeth, and even if they could they'd be too busy ripping your face off to tell you what you wanted to know."

That silenced Joe.

"You only need to know two things: one, the Astrals sent me here to be in charge. And two, you don't want to cross them. No, make that three things. Three, if you dare to oppose me, I will summon a shuttle, wipe this whole miserable town off the map, leave nothing behind but little piles of black dust. Is that clear?"

No one spoke or breathed.

He waited a beat, then turned to Santoro.

"Bring Spade in now so I can show these fine folks what happens to people who displease Paco."

Chapter Fifty-Nine

HARRY WINDOM HAD SPENT an uncomfortable night snoozing in the cab of his pickup truck, trying to get comfortable leaning against the door. His wasn't no new fancy pickups like drove themselves. His was old, he liked to think of it as vintage, and it still had a handle that stuck out from the passenger side door to open it and it kept jabbing Harry in the back no matter how he squirmed around, kept him awake all night. Soon's he was in charge, soon as he was king of the mountain, he was gonna get him a brand new truck, one of them fancy kinds with the automatic driver and …

He stopped in mid-daydream. Yeah, and power it with what?

Truth of the matter was, they wasn't gonna be vehicles on the roads for very much longer, the way the world was going now. No gasoline for them. He had a storage tank on his farm they come by and filled up twice a week and he was lucky they'd come on the day before Astral Day. He'd been careful, conserved it, then him and Virgil broke into that Esso Station on Route Four and stole all the gasoline out of their underground tanks. He'd been using that ever since. But bottom line was, eventually wouldn't nobody have no gas. Then how in the hell was people supposed to get around?

He shook his head, now fully awake though he hadn't opened his eyes yet. Wasn't his problem to figure out how humanity went from cars back to … well, back to horses and buggies, he supposed. He had a job here today and when he done it right — and he would surely do it right — he'd have enough supplies, food and the like to barter with them that *did* have gasoline.

He had gas for the trucks that was gonna haul all the goods out of here. They was parked back from the gate, along with a handful of pickups driven by the men in his "army."

"Harry," somebody said right beside his ear and he liked to jumped out of his skin sitting up so fast.

Rob Jackson was standing beside his truck rapping on the glass.

"What in the hell do you think you're—"

"You wanna see this, boss, you do for sure."

Then he motioned and another one of his men come walking toward the truck dragging a kid.

Harry rubbed his eyes to get the sleep out of them, rubbed his hands over his face and watched Arthur Clark approach with the kid, dragging him. The kid looked scared enough to shit himself.

Soon's he got a good look at the boy, he threw his head back and laughed out loud, opened the door and got out of the truck.

"You know who this kid is?"

Clark shook his head.

"This here is Sawyer Matheson's son." He looked down at Noah. "Ain't you, boy. You're the sheriff's kid."

The kid just stared at him with eyes so clear blue they almost looked transparent.

He grabbed the kid by the arm.

"I asked you a question, son. You Sawyer Matheson's boy?"

He drew his hand back to smack the kid but Jackson stopped him.

"He can't hear you. Remember? The sheriff's kid's deaf."

Right. That was it.

"How do you talk to somebody can't hear?" he asked Clark. "I can't do that hand-signing shit."

Clark shrugged. Harry turned to the group of men who'd gathered around when they saw Clark dragging the boy to Harry's truck.

One of them said, "Lot of them deaf kids can read your lips. If you get right in front of them and talk slow."

Harry leaned toward the boy, who flinched away but Clark had a good hold on his arm.

"Are. You. The. Sheriff's kid?" he asked.

Noah nodded.

Harry looked at those gathered around and grinned.

"Well, lookie here what we found. We just got the key to all the locks."

"What you gonna do with him, Harry?" Jackson wanted to know but Harry waved him off. He needed a minute to think this one out. He'd just been dealt an ace, shit, he'd been dealt all four aces, but he still had to play the hand through to the end of the game to collect the pot and he needed to do it the way he could get the most mileage out of it.

He turned to Ed Davis, who was a painter.

"You got a ladder in your truck, a stand-up one?"

Davis said he did.

"Anybody got rope, don't need much, ten or fifteen—"

Vic Brown hauled a length of rope twice that long out of the back of his truck.

"Okay now, here's what we're gonna do," Harry said and the others gathered around like he was the quarterback about to name the play that was gonna win the game. Yes sir, Harry Windom was gonna like being the man in charge.

EAGLE FEATHER WAS up at first light, enjoyed a real breakfast for the first time since … eggs, bacon, ham, pancakes, syrup … the supplies provided from Bubba's stores and prepared by the women who'd been prisoners and who relished the opportunity to get into a real kitchen again.

When Eagle Feather finally located Nick, he was hunkered over one of the tables in the back of the cafeteria studying a map, and Eagle Feather would have bet everything he owned, which, granted, wasn't a whole lot, that the man hadn't even bothered to go to bed last night.

Eagle Feather shook his head. He'd spent his life responsible for nobody but himself. Then the aliens came, the prophesies he'd laughed at as a young man began to come true and he'd pledged himself to take care of Star *no matter what*.

Star. Only Star.

Then they'd met "the stranded" and in the blink of an eye, Eagle Feather found himself responsible for the lives of dozens of people.

And now . . .

Now there were enough people here to fill a whole village, and though he'd gratefully handed off to Nick Wilson the logistics of packing up, loading up, and moving several hundred people from Point A to Point B, Eagle Feather still felt the personal weight of responsibility. It was *his* job to get Star to Zion Academy, to Noah.

A man Eagle Feather didn't know was talking to Nick when he approached, pointing out things on the map. He was one of the prisoners, an old, toothless man named Farnley, and it was quickly clear that he knew every road, dirt path and rabbit trail for a hundred miles in every direction.

"It ain't that far to where you're goin'," the man said. "It mighta took a coupla hours back in the day. Pro'ly not that long."

"Show me," Nick said.

Pointing to a spot on the map within the Land Between the Lakes National Recreation Area the man dragged his finger across the map to the cave country of Kentucky, to a black dot labeled "Jessup."

"You say you been taking nothing but small country roads — and if you's travelin' alone, that's real smart." Then the man gestured around him, where people were stripping the cafeteria's industrial kitchen and outside others were loading the trucks with Bubba's treasure trove of firearms, ammunition and supplies. "This here ain't alone no more and the Western Kentucky Parkway is the best, the quickest, route."

Throughout their journey they had given cities a wide berth, even large small towns — it was just safer to go around. You never knew who might be there lying in wait, as Bubba had been.

Expressways were to be avoided for other reasons as well. There were abandoned vehicles everywhere. Three months after Astral Day, most people had been left afoot. People who'd been fleeing, going somewhere and ran out of fuel, there was nothing to do but leave their cars where they'd rolled to a stop and take out walking.

One of the bikers, the man in hockey pads wearing a helmet with a devil face and horns, had come forward last night. He was a dentist from

Atlanta who had set out for his parents' house in the mountains of Colorado on the decked-out, custom Harley Davidson motorcycle his neighbor had locked away in his garage. There had been no helmet or biker boots, so he'd donned his son's hockey gear for protection. The boy had played for the Cannonsburg Demons. Dr. Paul Balforth, DDM, said he'd threaded his way through ten solid miles of abandoned cars on Interstate 40 West outside Nashville before he abandoned the expressway for state roads and was snared by Bubba as soon as he crossed from Tennessee into Kentucky.

"Here's the thing," Farnley said. "The Western Kentucky Parkway goes *from* nowhere *through* nowhere *to* nowhere!" His cackle would have done a witch proud. "It was nothin' but pork belly." Eagle Feather had no idea what that meant and the confusion must have shown on his face. "You know, payback to some politician. There never was no traffic on the thing, didn't go nowhere anybody wanted to go. Course it's possible it's all clogged up with dead cars *now* same's every other highway. But I just don't see it."

There was a sudden commotion at the door and Star burst in.

"Papa Eagle Feather, we have to go, we have to go now!" Star was calling out to him as she ran, the hand not holding onto Pumpkin's lead waving out in front of her, searching the empty air for him.

Pumpkin brought her to a sliding stop in front of him.

"What's wrong?"

"Noah's in trouble. I can hear him."

"The boy who was in the mothership with you?" Nick confirmed. "Lives at this academy in Jessup?"

"Yes! We have to go, we have to help him. Please, now!"

Others had gathered around when Star cried out. When she sensed them, she turned to speak to them all, not just Eagle Feather.

"He's in trouble, men with guns … bad men, they're going to take over Zion Academy, steal … *everything*—" She stopped, cocked her head as if she were listening to something. "'Well, lookie here what we found. We just got ourselves the key to all the locks.' That's what the bad man said to Noah. The bad men have him, please …"

"Apparently, we aren't the only people looking to hole up at Zion Academy," Nick said. He looked at Eagle Feather. "The new world order."

"Fight or die," Eagle Feather said.

Chapter Sixty

Paco motioned for his men to bring Spade out. He came haltingly across the gym floor, leg irons from the prison around his legs, his hands handcuffed in front of him. He stank of piss and feces where he had wet and shit himself, but his face was set as hard and sharp as an ax blade.

When he got close enough, he lunged at Paco, but the men on either side holding his arms stopped him.

"You're so gonna regret this, motherfucker." Spade spewed the words at Paco, his voice hoarse and gravelly from having nothing to eat or drink. Paco took two steps toward him, spit in his face and then with all the strength he had, he slammed his knee in a vicious upper thrust into Spade's nuts. Spade cried out in pain and his legs buckled. The men on both sides of him held him upright.

"Payback's a bitch," Paco said.

A nylon rope had been stretched up over a ceiling beam in the center of the gym. One end of it dangled about six feet off the floor next to the tarp-covered thing on the dolly, the other was wound around a winch that could be cranked to lower or raise the rope. Paco nodded toward it and the men dragged Spade to the rope. Even trussed up in cuffs like he was, he fought like a caged bull. They had to call for help and three other men rushed out onto the court. They tied the rope to the link between the handcuffs on Spade's wrists, then one of them took a key out of his pocket and used it to unfasten the leg irons, first on his right leg, then on his left. Paco stepped over to the winch and began to tighten the rope on Spade's wrists and his hands lifted up in front of him and then over his head. Paco slowly winched him off the floor. A foot. Two feet. Three. Finally leaving him dangling with his feet about ten feet off the floor.

Spade was dressed in jeans as he'd been when Paco and his men had broken into his house last night. He wore no shoes and his chest was bare and the huge bicep and triceps muscles in his arms bulged under the strain of his own weight dangling from the slender rope over the beam in the ceiling.

Paco turned and addressed the crowd.

"No speech. Actions speak louder than words. Your 'fearless leader' fucked me over three months ago and I'm just returning the favor."

Then he nodded to his men and they rolled the dolly that held the huge mystery *thing* covered with a tarp and maneuvered it so that it was beneath Spade, only a few inches below his feet. He had recovered sufficiently from the blow to his nuts to recognize that something was about to happen to him.

"Hey, what is that thing? What you going to do, boy?"

"I'll show you what it is, give you a little demonstration." Paco had turned the machine on earlier that day and practiced using it so he knew how to operate it, though it required no more expertise than flipping a switch. Without removing the concealing tarp, he reached beneath it and turned the machine on. A sound erupted from it, a rumbling, grinding sound.

"What is that thing?" Spade's bravado was gone. He wasn't afraid yet, or if he was, he did a good job of hiding it, but he wasn't cocky anymore, either. "What you gonna do wid it?"

Paco reached up, grabbed the tarp and yanked and it fell away, revealing what was essentially a huge metal box. It had a tray in the front about halfway down and the top of it was open. Inside the top were grinding, whirling blades.

An involuntary groan rose up from the crowd when one after another of them realized what the machine was and then gasps as they connected the dots and realized what Paco intended to do with it.

"Hey, turn that thing off, man," Spade cried. He was scared now. Terrified. His eyes were huge, staring in horror at the whirling blades beneath him. He'd drawn up his knees to get his feet away from the open maw on the top even though there was still a couple of inches of clearance between them and the blades.

Paco nodded again, and two of his men hauled in

a tree stump about four feet tall and three across, about as big around as a drainage pipe. It took two men to lift the stump up and tumble it over the side of the top of the machine into the opening where the whirring sound of the blades instantly became a grinding sound. It was deafening, a high-pitched shriek as the wood chipper tore into the bark and the meat of the stump, chewing relentlessly at the wood, grinding it, *eating* it. Pieces of it began to blow out the slit in the front of the machine, but since there was no bin there to catch the wood chips they spewed out all over the surface of the gym floor and the smell of cut wood and a haze of sawdust hung over the machine.

The wood chipper had to chew on the stump for a while, its constantly revolving teeth and blades cutting into the bark and pulling it deeper and deeper into the machine. With a sudden crunching sound, it sawed through a final knothole and the rest of the tree trunk and roots disappeared into the guts of the machine to reappear seconds later as small chips, maybe the size of half a dollar, spewing out in a great stream onto the floor.

The shrieking stopped and a few seconds later the grinding noise silenced, along with the sound of the final pieces of wood blowing out onto the pile of wood chips on the gym floor. Then there was silence, broken only by the purr of the motor and the humming sound of the blades sharpening themselves against each other.

"Don't do this," Spade said. "You can't do this, man, come on. You want to kill me, do it, shoot me, go on ahead, shoot me, a big target like me hanging here, you can't——"

Paco had stepped over to the winch that held the rope where Spade was suspended, and he screamed, "Nooooo! Don't, please!" in a voice higher than his natural voice.

"I seem to remember saying the very same words — 'don't, please' — but you laughed in my face and ripped me open and you kept laughing while I screamed, begged and pleaded for you to stop. Over and over. For hours. So I'm going to extend to you exactly the same amount of mercy you extended to me."

"Look, I'm sorry, man. Oh, God, I didn't mean to — I'm sorry." When Paco's hand touched the crank on the winch, Spade cried, "I done it, so go on, kill me. Shoot me. You too chicken to shoot me, huh?"

Spade's face was wet, sweat mingled with the tears running down his cheeks. His bowels let loose with a kind of gurgling sound and a stream of liquid slid out the bottom of his jeans, over his bare feet, and dripped into the spinning blades of the machine. The front of his sweatpants darkened, too.

"Scared, are you, Spade?"

"Hell yeah, I'm scared. You can't do this, please, no, don't."

"I was scared, too, in the beginning. But after a while, the pain wiped all the scared away and all I could feel was how bad it hurt. It won't be long now before the pain takes all your scared away, too."

"No, dammit, no!" Spade writhed on the end of

the rope, making it swing to and fro, but never far enough so that his feet weren't still above the blades.

"Let's do six inches," Paco said affably and took hold of the handle of the winch. "No, make it eight. Just eight inches lower."

Paco cranked out eight inches of rope, lowered Spade eight inches closer to the wood chipper, which meant he had to draw his legs up to keep his feet out of the blades. If he relaxed, the wood chipper would chew up his feet about to the ankle and tug at the rest of him to drag him in, as it had the stump.

As Spade jerked on the end of the rope, trying to keep his feet away from the blades, Paco searched around inside himself for mercy, for pity. The boy who had been hauled with the other teenagers into Radcliffe Correctional for the Scared Straight Program might have had mercy. Probably would have pitied the poor man about to die an agonizing death. But no matter how hard Paco searched, he couldn't find that boy inside anymore. That boy had died, been murdered by a night of brutal rape ... and by a shuttle with reptars that ate his friend.

That boy was gone and the man who stood with his hand on the crank of the winch holding the rope had no pity in him, no mercy. Only hate. He was full to the brim with delicious hate.

Chapter Sixty-One

THE MEN who had laid siege to Zion Academy had remained silent all night. Sawyer had used the time well. He had reinforced the entrance door to the building. Nailed boards across the opening and then moved heavy furniture up against them. He thought it might even hold if somebody rammed a vehicle into it.

He'd done the same thing to all the other doors, made the place a fortress. Nobody would gain easy access to the facility.

When he was as ready as it was possible to be, he stationed himself in the window of the top floor laboratory facing the front gate. So far, nobody had tried to enter, but that ornate swinging gate wasn't going to stop anybody, just metal grill work under the arch that proclaimed Zion Academy.

He sat in a chair, the barrel of his rifle lying on the window sill. It was the deer rifle, the .30-06 XXX Springfield, loaded with the same .308-inch cartridges that had dropped the reptar. The rising sun in his eyes had lulled him into an uneasy doze when he heard a crashing sound from the front gate and was instantly on his feet, rifle sight to his eye. He'd once killed a buck in the woods five hundred yards away using that sight. At this range, he could see the buttons on a man's shirt.

Somebody had run a pickup truck through the gate, knocked it flying off the hinges. But then the pickup truck backed up and drove away, leaving the archway sans gate. But still no attack.

What he saw next made no sense at all.

A different pickup truck *backed* slowly out under the archway and stopped just beneath it. A passenger in the truck got out, dropped the tailgate and climbed up into the truck and opened a painter's ladder, moved it around until it was directly below the archway.

What in the Sam Hill …?

The man climbed up the ladder and tossed a rope over the top of the metal archway.

The bottom fell out of Sawyer's stomach when he saw the man toss one end of the rope to a man on the ground, who tied the rope around the door post of the truck and then slammed the door on it, holding it securely in place.

The other end of the rope dangled above the ladder. There was a hangman's noose on that end.

There was the screech and squawk of feedback from somebody keying a megaphone.

"You in there, sheriff? We need to talk."

And so it begins.

Sawyer keyed the switch on the microphone in his hand that sent his voice through speakers mounted on the front of the building. No screeching and squalling.

"We don't have anything to talk about. You are now trespassing on private property and you need to leave immediately."

"Now see, sheriff, that ain't the way of it at all. The way I see it, you's in possession of certain … items, food and supplies and such, and being neighborly like we are we knew you'd be willing to share what you got with us. So we come to pick up our share."

Sawyer didn't dignify the remark with a reply.

The man waited.

"We got trucks that we're going to bring in to load up the stuff in your warehouses. We need you to provide us the labor to do the loading because we figure there's a lot of stuff and … I got me a weak back and I don't need to be lifting heavy things, know what I mean. Soon's you get our trucks loaded, I'll give you an hour … shoot, a half hour's long enough, to gather up your personal belongs and vacate the premises so the new owners can take possession of the property." He stopped. "Leaving all firearms and ammunition behind, of course."

"That's quite a speech. Write it yourself, did you? Did you have to use all your crayons or do you have one of those fancy 64-count boxes?"

Sawyer was instantly sorry he'd said that. It had just slipped out. He had to remain cool and calm and not let this idiot goad him into doing something he'd regret.

"You think this is funny? You think we're joking, you—"

"I don't have anything to say to you but to order you off our property. And you won't be taking anything with you."

"You think you're so smart, Mr. Sheriff, do you? Think you got it all figured out. We got three times the manpower you got, unless you're giving guns to children. We could kill every man Jack of you with one hand tied behind our backs."

"Talk's cheap."

"Indeed it is, Mr. Sheriff. You're about to find out how cheap. See, we could get into a gunfight here. And we'd win eventually, but a bunch of you'd get shot and a bunch of us'd get shot and there really ain't no reason for nobody's blood to be spilled here today. So you're all going to lay down your arms and come walking out here with your hands in the air."

This guy was too cocky. Something was wrong. Off. He was playing with Sawyer. He was enjoying himself, was probably smiling a cat-that-ate-the-canary smile.

"Not happening, pal."

"If you're dead set on that course of action, Mr. Sheriff, sir, you need to be willing to pay what it's going to cost you."

"As are you."

"But you see, it ain't gonna cost me near as dear as it is you."

Two men approached, hauling something rolled up in a blanket between them. They laid it on the tailgate, then hopped up beside it and lifted one end, and whatever was wrapped in the blanket remained upright.

Oh, dear God no. There was *a person in that blanket* and they intended to …

His stomach lurched as he watched the men hold the blanket in place as they lifted whoever was inside it up onto the top of the painter's ladder, then maneuvered the rope around the person's neck, careful to keep the blanket in place.

The blanket was small. Whoever was up there was short. It had to be a … *child.*

"So here's the deal, Mr. Sheriff, sir, either you lay down your guns and walk out of there with your hands up right now, or …"

That was the cue for the men holding the blanket and they yanked it away, revealing a little boy standing on the top of the ladder with his hands tied behind his back and the noose around his neck.

The boy was Noah.

"… or Hank here is gonna put this truck in gear and drive right out from under him."

Chapter Sixty-Two

Paco threw his head back and laughed. It was not some hysterical giggle, or the laugh of someone unhinged, so pulled to the outside edges of himself that he'd lost his reason. No, this was the laugh of a man who was glad to be here right now at this moment. Glad to be breathing air and feeling the cold metal of the winch crank on his hand. Glad to be alive. Glad to be *in charge*. Glad to be giving back as good as he got. He hadn't thought about revenge the whole time he'd been on the mothership, had tried to wipe out all memory of what had happened to him. He should have been able to do that since the Astrals had healed his injuries as if they'd never happened. But the moment his feet touched earth again, he knew what he must do, what he was about. And this was it.

Now, it was Paco's turn.

But not just to kill Spade. That part would be easy. What Paco had to do as well was use Spade's death to bond the people in this room to him. He steadied himself, took a calming breath.

"Frightened are you, Spade? Legs getting tired?"

"Let me down off here, man, please, I'm begging you, please, let me down, kill me, shoot me, but let me down."

He was panting from the effort of keeping his knees bent to keep his feet from dropping into the blades.

"Don't, come on, please, let me down, let me down."

Paco took a deep breath and plunged in. Certainly what happened in the next few minutes would take Spade's life, but it could very well cost Paco his, too. But he was willing to chance it, to roll the dice, all or none. He would walk out of here the undisputed leader, the *ruler* over everything, or he would collapse from an aneurysm in his brain and they'd carry him out … or maybe not. Did they even bury people anymore? Of course, there wouldn't be a piece of Spade bigger than a gum wrapper to bury.

Paco turned and addressed the crowd.

"You tell me," he called out to them. "What should I do? Should I spare his life? Or should I let him die an agonizing death? What do you say?"

Then he cast out into their minds, swam with his mind through the sea of their thoughts. Some felt fear and uncertainty, revulsion for what they were looking at … but fascination with it, too. They were Lookie-Lous craning their necks to get a peek at the bloody bodies in a wreck on the side of the road.

No one spoke, but the sea of their thoughts settled from the turbulence he'd stirred up with the question. He put a thought out onto the crowd, pictured it as sailing a little paper boat out into the waters of a still pond.

Kill him.

Just two words. He said them softly into the minds in front of him, almost watched them melt into the collective mind the way butter melts and soaks into a biscuit.

"Kill him," someone said, didn't shout it out. Just spoke. If he hadn't been sitting in the second row of the bleachers, Paco wouldn't have heard him.

Spade had started to scream, a wandering wail, a banshee cry of fear and effort and out of the corner of his eye Paco watched his legs slowly lower toward the blades of the chipper. Then he'd jerk them away. And they'd lower again.

Kill him. Paco spoke into their minds, louder and more forceful now, and felt a little twinge of pain, just a tiny niggle behind his left eye.

"Kill him." A voice came from the back of the crowd.

"Do it, kill him." This was a shout, not a murmur. And it was a spark of flame in dry leaves, quickly igniting everything around it, growing bigger and brighter and hotter.

I want you to kill him. Paco put the thought out there, shoved it into the sea that was choppy now with the waves of thoughts and emotions.

"Kill him, let the bastard die."

That was a woman's voice and there was rage in it. If Paco had wanted, he could have followed it back to the source, found out what it was the woman had against Spade, but he had a pretty good idea without asking.

Spade's legs were trembling now from the effort of keeping them away from the blades. He had stopped screaming, used all his energy to concentrate on keeping his legs up. His whole body was slathered with sweat and the muscles in this thighs and calves bulged.

I want him dead. Kill him for me. Kill him.

Paco's thought was loud and forceful and the niggle of pain behind his eye burst into a white flare of agony. He couldn't stop now, though. He had to make these people a part of what he was doing, had to bond them to himself with this act. He had to make them see him as their leader, the man who carried the sword of their communal wrath, a man strong and courageous enough to bring that sword down on the outsider, down on the man who was not part of the new collective of minds Paco was forging here, now at this moment, melting their individual minds into a shape he could form and fashion with his will.

"Kill him!"

"Kill him, kill him, kill him, kill him! Kill!"

The words started out as single expletives from different parts of the crowd but quickly coalesced into a single chant that grew louder and louder as he loosed the power of his thoughts into the fire to feed the flames.

"Kill!"

"Him!"

"Kill!"

"Him!"

The room reverberated with sound, the shouted chant bouncing off the concrete block walls and returning to the source to be flung out there to mingle with the next chant and the next.

"Kill!"

"Him!"

"Another six inches, then," Paco said, but nobody heard him in the rumble of chanting that filled the gym. They saw him go to the winch, though, and some of the chanters broke into cheers. There was a manic, frenetic edge to their shouting and cheering, too fast and clipped, an insectile quality to the sound.

Paco turned the crank on the winch and slowly lowered Spade's body toward the blades. Spade had to extend his legs straight out to avoid losing a leg all the way up to the knee.

Paco could tell Spade was shrieking, wailing, his mouth open, his head thrown back, but he couldn't hear the sound over the roar of the crowd. Then Spade faltered. His left foot fell too low and a blade slashed a gash in his heel and he lifted it again, shaking, dripping blood. His eyes caught Paco's, pleading, begging. Paco's were as cold and hard as frozen marbles.

When the chipper finally grabbed hold of a foot and pulled it in, tugging on the leg behind it, Spade let out a bloodcurdling cry that sailed out over the roar of the crowd and the chanting faltered. He was shrieking, one leg ended in a bare bone and dangling flesh just below the knee and his other knee drawn up tight against him. But he couldn't hold it there for long. Paco let off the tension on the rope so that when the chipper got a grip—

And suddenly it did, grabbed his other leg and chewed it up to the knee. His face was so contorted in agony it was unrecognizable and when Paco let off all the tension on the rope, the chipper pulled in the rest of Spade in seconds, spewing out bloody debris, hunks of bone and skin and organs onto the pile of wood chips on the floor.

His screaming cut off in mid-scream and the room fell totally silent, every eye watching the few seconds it took the machine to chew Spade up. Then the end of the rope was swaying free above the machine. Paco waited until the ground-up gore no longer spewed out of the machine before he stepped over and flipped the switch to kill the motor.

The silence was so profound, Paco thought of Noah. For the flash of a moment, he thought: this is what Noah's world sounds like. Nothing. Nothing at all.

But he grabbed hold of the thought and choked it and stifled the rage at Noah that threatened to burst forth with it.

Paco's head was throbbing in bursts of pain inside his skull and he felt daggers stabbing into his temples with every heartbeat. But he hadn't gotten as close to the edge as he thought he might have to. Had pulled back well within the safe zone. He was getting stronger, more able to tolerate the mental processing, and tougher, able to endure the pain better. He could stand before the crowd and show nothing, not the faintest sign of weakness. But what he said would have to be brief, which he'd intended it to be all along.

He pushed through the pain and eased his mind out into the collective of thoughts, seeking. He searched for those in the crowd who had somehow not been sucked into the vortex of his thoughts, who still saw him as a weak boy, and found no one. To a person, every man, woman — there were no children — in the crowd had bonded to his leadership, accepted it, embraced it. That bond would grow with time, but it was strong enough right now to feel the cold pulsing off it, like he had opened the door to a freezer. He imagined his breath fogged in front of him when he spoke.

"This is the price of disloyalty," he said, and as he said the next words, he pushed them deep into their minds as well. "I'm in charge now. I rule."

He felt no pushback anywhere.

Chapter Sixty-Three

HARRY WINDOM LEANED over and spoke to Hank through the rolled-down truck window.

"When I give you the signal, I want you to pop the clutch and hit the gas and kick up dust so that ladder comes right …"

"You don't know yet whether they're going to—"

"Oh, they're going to surrender, alright."

"If they surrender, we don't have to bluff them with the kid—"

"Bluff? You think I'm bluffing." Harry turned and looked Hank full in the face and was instantly sorry he'd picked him to drive the pickup. He hadn't thought it through, really, just the first man he saw. That was a mistake. Leaders couldn't make mistakes like that. He should have thought through who would be willing to do whatever he said without argument, and he hadn't done that. Well, he'd just have to *make* Hank follow orders. He fixed the man with a penetrating glare.

"They're gonna surrender, like good little doobies, and I'm going to let them lay down their guns and come on out here in the open. Once they're about halfway to the gate, I'll give the signal and you hit the gas."

"But—"

Harry was prepared this time and had his pistol up and aimed into Hank's face before he could say another word. "We gonna hang that kid, right there in front of the whole bunch of them. And I'm gonna have my sights trained on the sheriff and soon's you hit the gas, I'm gonna take him out."

Hank said nothing, just looked at him.

"These people got to see we mean business, that we ain't just fucking around with them. We don't want to constantly have to watch our backs, waiting for a sneak attack when they get themselves some kinda plan to knock us off and make themselves king of the mountain again. It ends here. Today. Right now. I want the sheriff dead, laying on the dirt for all of them to see and his kid dangling from the gate. Take the fight right out of them and we'll never have to worry about any of them ever again."

Still Hank said nothing.

"I need an *amen, brother* to that," Harry said, and used his thumb to cock the big pistol.

"Alright," came the voice over the loudspeaker system in the front of the building. "We'll lay down our guns and come out. But first, you cut Noah down, get that rope off his neck."

Harry put the megaphone to his mouth with one hand and held the gun on Hank with the other.

"I'll tell you the same thing you just told me, Mr. Sheriff, sir. 'Not happenin', pal.' He stays where he is until you're out here standing in front of me unarmed."

There was no response from the building. Harry's men had congregated around the pickup truck at the front gate, probably thirty of them, all packing rifles they knew how to use. That included the leftovers from the previous aborted raid on the academy that had gotten Oscar Higgins killed, and the new men Harry had picked up by dragging Hungry all over town yesterday, before he took the leash off him and let him go. Might shoulda shot him, put him out of his misery, but he liked the idea of the skinny dog wandering around town, a constant daily reminder of what was coming.

These were Harry's "soldiers," but they had abandoned their posts and come here to the front gate to see what was happening and he'd heard a low rumble of disapproval from the group when he'd tied the rope around the kid's neck. Most of these men were farmers and store owners and they didn't have the stomach it took to make the hard decisions a leader had to make. He knew that when he ordered Hank to drive out from under the kid, leave him dangling by the noose, there'd be an uproar on *his* side of the fence as well as on the other.

He needed to nip that in the bud. A leader had to be ready to make the hard calls.

"You're either in or you're dead, Hank. Your choice."

"But Harry—"

Harry squeezed the trigger of the pistol two inches from Hank's face, blew a hole in it and splattered his brain all over the back windshield, the seat of the pickup. All his men jumped.

"What the fuck you do that for?" asked Eddy Davis, who'd provided the ladder and was standing so close might be he got some brain matter on his shirt.

Harry turned and surveyed his men.

"Either you in this to the end or you're dead. Those is the options you picked when you joined up. We gonna take what we need so's our families got food this winter, and if that means some people got to die … well, it's either their kids or *ours*."

He let that soak in for a beat.

"Just so we're clear. Anybody crosses me … *anybody* … gets a bullet in the face. I'll kill every man Jack here before I'll let my kids starve to death."

There were at least half a dozen of these men who knew Harry didn't have no kids to starve, that Betty Ann had scooped them up and bailed out on him 'cause he beat her. She'd called the sheriff on him once. That was his personal bone to pick with Sheriff Sawyer Matheson and he was gonna even that score before the sun set on another day. The men who knew had better sense than to say anything, and the ones who knew him *well* knew he'd hang one of his own kids up there on that ladder if it would get him what he wanted.

Opening the pickup door, Harry pulled on Hank's shoulder and he toppled out onto the ground.

"Get rid of this," he said and motioned to the nearest men. Then he turned to Carl. This was a strategic decision, this was thinking it through the way a leader was supposed to think things through. Carl wasn't the sharpest knife in the drawer but he was as loyal as an old hound dog and would do anything Harry told him to do. He's who Harry should have put in the truck in the first place instead of Hank. But part of being in charge was learning from your own mistakes and he was doing that, getting better as he went along.

"Carl, get behind the wheel and start the engine," he said, and Carl fell all over himself to do what he'd been told. Nobody else offered so much as a peep of opposition. Maybe selecting Hank, and then having to shoot him, had been for the best in the long run. Just like hanging the kid and killing the sheriff, it would serve as an object lesson to the troops: don't mess with Harry Windom.

A voice spoke through the speakers mounted on the tops of the academy buildings.

There was a buzzing sound this time through the speakers. No, it came from somewhere else.

"Alright. We're coming out."

"Bring your guns out with you, all of them," Harry called back, "and drop them in the grass. Then put your hands in the air and walk slowly this way. No funny business."

The buzzing sound grew louder.

Chapter Sixty-Four

THE IMAGE of Noah standing there with that noose around his neck was the single worst sight Sawyer had ever seen, and he'd have thought he had other candidates for that top spot, like cresting the hill and seeing a black pall of smoke rising up into the sky from the valley where his house sat, or watching Noah dissolve into a golden beam of light and disappear or seeing the boy balanced on the catwalk above the flour press at the mill. Or watching the reptar rip his deputies to shreds. But none of them had been as horrifying a sight as this — a noose around his neck!

He'd demanded that they cut Noah down but they'd refused. Nothing short of a full surrender would end this.

How had they gotten their hands on Noah?

The last time he'd seen the boy was in the hallway last night. Noah had been trying to tell him something then, but he'd rushed off. What was it?

None of that mattered, of course. Nothing mattered now but getting Noah down off that ladder.

… even if it meant all the people here suffered for it?

… *all* the children with nothing to eat this winter?

… *all* of them homeless?

… did he have a right to ask everyone to sacrifice to save one little boy?

There was a gunshot and Sawyer almost jumped out of his skin. It had come from the gate, from the group of men now gathered there. But he couldn't tell who had fired the shot. He could only see that Noah hadn't moved, was still standing there on the top of the ladder with the noose …

"If you're thinking what I think you're thinking, don't," said Brother Sebastian, who had come up unheard behind Sawyer. In those sandals and robes, the monks moved as silently through the hallways as ghosts.

"How can I ask—?"

"You can't. There's no question to answer. Everybody's already assembling downstairs ready to go out. They're clearing everything away from the front door. We're just waiting for you."

"But …"

"It ain't over 'til the fat lady sings, son," said the old monk. "They'll kick you guys out … but I'm assuming they want *us* to stay and run things, don't you?"

Sawyer just looked at him, unable to think of anything at all.

"We're only monks, after all. How dangerous can a bunch of old men in robes and sandals be?"

Sawyer felt like he was stuck in mud, his mind moving so slowly he was tripping over his own thoughts.

"But you wouldn't, you *couldn't* hurt …"

"Who said anything about *hurting* anybody? There's more than one way to skin a cat. There are waaaay more of us than there are of them. And we're a whole lot smarter."

He turned toward the door.

"Come along now, son, let's go get your boy. You let me and the other brothers handle the rest of it."

Sawyer keyed the microphone on the loud speaker.

"Alright, we're coming out."

When Sawyer stepped out onto the porch on the front of the building he heard a buzzing sound, not cicadas, something far off, almost sounded like a model airplane. He dismissed the sound, insisted on going first, in front of all the rest of the people. He walked out about fifteen feet from the building holding his rifle out in front of him and made a great show of laying it carefully on the grass. Then he took his pistol out of its holster and put that beside the rifle. While he was down on one knee, he lifted the leg of his pants and removed the spare gun from its strap.

Then he stood, raised his hands high over his head and began to walk slowly toward the assembly at the gate. There was a man leaned across the front of the truck next to the one where Noah was standing on a ladder in the back. He had a rifle, made his arms into a tripod and was sighted in on Sawyer, likely on the middle of his chest. But Sawyer kept walking. What else could he do?

The buzzing sound grew louder.

HARRY WAS LAID out across the hood of Arthur Clark's pickup truck, his rifle aimed at the approaching sheriff, sighted in on that fancy gold star on his chest. He was concentrating on the target, but the buzzing sound from behind him was getting louder and louder.

What the fuck …?

A couple of his men had turned and were looking up the road that led to the lane where the academy was located. Everyone could hear the sound now. Underneath the buzzing sound was a rumbling, too.

All the noise was getting louder and louder.

And louder.

It sounded like … a motorcycle, specifically a dirt bike. But no dirt bike could make a sound that loud.

Harry ignored the sound. He turned and made eye contact with Carl. Carl nodded. He was to wait for Harry's signal before he hit the accelerator and drove out from under the kid on the ladder. Harry wanted the sheriff to see that, wanted that to be the last thing he ever saw before Harry put a neat round hole in the center of that gold star on his chest.

Another step.

Just one more.

He turned his head to give Carl the signal.

Then the buzzing turned up a notch and *wailed.* Out the corner of his eye, Harry saw several of his men who'd been looking down the road jump backward in surprise.

He turned his head to see, reluctant to take his eye off the crosshairs on the sheriff's badge and—

Holy shit!

Motorcycles — dirt bikes like he'd thought but not just one. Three, five, *more* came screaming around the last corner of the road leading to the academy land and came flying down it. Behind them was the rumbling of street bikes, Harleys. Big ones and *lots of them.* It looked like a swarm of furious bees was hurtling down the road. Bikes, motorcycles, and behind them big trucks, two, three, four—

Shit!

Harry was too flabbergasted to do anything but gawk in shock as the first of the bikes careened into the academy's lane and came barreling right at them. The force of men on dirt bikes was on them in a heartbeat, roaring down the lane and skidding to a halt all around them. The cloud of dust their approach kicked up into the air obscured what came behind for a heartbeat and then the Harleys roared through the dust.

The lead Harley had a cow skull mounted between the handlebars, the tips of the horns painted blood red. The driver had long blond hair and wore something … it was a dog muzzle and it covered the whole bottom portion of his face.

The bike behind that one had long, jacked-up handlebars and held a rider wearing some kind of pads, like armor, and his helmet was painted with a monstrous devil face complete with fake horns attached to the top.

Too surprised to respond, none of Harry's men raised their weapons on the intruders, just stood there stupefied, watching the area behind them fill up with men.

The trucks skidded to a halt behind the motorcycles and out of the back of them flowed armed men, who *did* have the presence of mind to point their weapons at Harry's men, and in seconds an armed force five times their size had the drop on them. No one even ordered them to drop their weapons. They just slid out of their numb fingers to the ground.

Harry finally found his wits, but too late to do any good. If he lifted the rifle in his hands toward them, he'd be cut down before he could pull the trigger.

He only had a second to think.

Dropping the rifle, he took one big step, reached the truck that sat idling beneath the kid on the ladder. He flung open the driver's door, yanked Carl out of the vehicle and leapt in behind the wheel.

As he did so, he watched his men raise their hands into the air and nobody had said a word to them yet. Not one word.

Who were these motherfuckers?

He reached up to the gear shift to—

"Touch that gearshift and I will blow your face off."

Standing on the other side of the truck was Sawyer Matheson with a pistol pointed at his head.

He hesitated, weighing his … should he just …?

"After I slit your throat."

He turned and an Indian … a fucking *Indian* … was standing beside the door of his truck with a vicious-looking hunting knife inches from his neck.

He dropped his hand and relaxed back into the seat. Sawyer yanked the passenger side door open, reached across the gore-splattered front seat and snatched the keys out of the ignition, without once taking his eyes or his gun off Harry's face.

When he pulled back out of the cab, a bearded man, his black hair cropped close, military-style, took his place and pointed a pistol at Harry. The Indian turned to the post where the rope was tied and slit it in one stroke, it went limp, and the boy almost did, too, collapsing into the arms of his father, who'd climbed halfway up the ladder in the truck to get him.

The dark-haired man kept his gun pointed at Harry as the Indian turned back, grabbed Harry, dragged him out of the truck and threw him to the ground beside the still-warm body of Hank, the man Harry'd shot.

Lying on his back, Harry thought he saw a dog and a little girl … she looked like an Indian, too.

What was this, a fucking traveling circus?

NOAH FELT the rope holding the noose around his neck go limp and he swayed, but his father was there to steady him, had climbed a couple of steps up the ladder and was—

Noah! Noah, where are you?

Star!

He may have said the word out loud, he knew he thought it out loud, and he looked around frantically, trying to find her. His father was talking to him, hugging him as he pulled away the duct tape binding his hands behind him.

Star, I'm here. Where … How …?

He saw Pumpkin first, hopping down out of one of the trucks that had come roaring up out of nowhere full of men with guns. Star was behind him, and one of the men paused to lift her down to the ground.

Noah shook loose from his father, hardly seeing him as Pumpkin turned and started threading his way through the crowd of armed men who were disarming other men, leading Star to him.

Star!

Noah leapt off the tailgate of the truck and took off running toward her.

STAR HAD FELT HIM, his nearness growing, as the trucks rumbled along the parkway the Kentucky man had said would get them to Jessup *fast*.

She would never forget that … that all these

people had been willing to drop everything and rush off in a dangerous journey facing men with guns just because she'd said Noah was in danger.

She thought about all those things as they drove.

As they got nearer, and she could *feel* Noah.

She didn't speak into his mind, just sat there silent in the truck, bumping along, the engine rumbling. Noah was so frightened she didn't want to distract him. He was on a ladder with a rope around his neck, with armed men around and a man threatening to drive the truck out from under him if his father and the other people in the academy didn't surrender.

She was afraid to divert his attention with her presence, afraid he'd lose his balance and … So she had kept her mind silent, so frightened the nearer they got that she balled her hands into fists and discovered she had dug holes in the palms of her hand with her fingernails.

But he was safe now!

"Noah!" she cried out in his head, and let Pumpkin drag her off through the crowd to him.

"Star!" It was Noah's voice. Not in her head. Well, in her head, but also in her ears. He had spoken her name. Then the blob in front of her pulled her into a bear hug and she hung on.

She was so grateful to feel his nearness, his arms around her. But more grateful to feel him settle into the empty spot in her head, as she relaxed into the vacant place in his. They were together now, two halves of the apple made whole.

She didn't ever want to be away from Noah again.

Chapter Sixty-Five

THEY SEEMED an odd match for friends, the gangly professor with his pencil neck and social awkwardness and the old Indian with black braids lying on both shoulders. But from the moment Garson discovered that Eagle Feather's family had a special relationship with the aliens that had come to Earth before, he cornered the old man and peppered him with questions. Now, Sawyer often saw them together, deep in conversation. He knew they'd both talked to Star and Noah about their experiences in the mothership after they were abducted and he had to admit that he didn't much like it that the two men never looked like whatever they were talking about was a pleasant subject. They usually stopped talking altogether when anyone approached.

He finally decided it was time he found out their communal wisdom was about the Astrals' intent. Though he was pretty sure he wouldn't like what he heard, he'd decided to man up and seek them out today and take the bitter-tasting medicine he feared they'd give him if the asked.

He spotted Nick Wilson at the end of the hall and called out to him, "You seen Garson and Eagle Feather?"

"You mean Tweedledee and Tweedledum? Not this morning."

Nick stopped and waited for Sawyer to catch up. He was in muddy work boots and wearing a shirt covered in sawdust. He was in charge of the crews of workers building homes for the ever-growing population at the academy. They'd been able to build more than a dozen of them so far and given the multitude of "idiot labor" available to them, they would likely get twice that many more under roof before the weather turned cold.

"Not real sure I'd let Eagle Feather hear you say that. Have you seen that knife he carries?"

The smile fell off Nick's face like a bad memory had washed over him.

"I'm glad that old Indian is on our side."

Sawyer figured out where Nick's mind had gone. He had heard the horrifying tale of Bubba "Black-snake" and his marauders — who had at least provided the compound a huge arsenal of weapons and ammunition, a tanker truck full of gasoline and truckloads of supplies.

"And he's still out there somewhere," Nick said. "Not sure I'm ever gonna rest easy knowing that monster is still breathing."

The two men walked along together as they talked.

In the month since the arrival of Star and "the stranded," Nick and Sawyer had forged a friendship that didn't seem as odd as Garson and Eagle Feather's. Part of it was the common bond of being "ex-military." But mostly it was just that the two men respected and liked each other.

"I think Harry Windom was a Bubba in the making. Takes a special kind of evil to put a noose around a little kid's neck." Sawyer was surprised that he could still feel white hot rage in his chest at the thought of the man. "Now they're *both* still out there."

"What else could we do?"

It had been a matter of hot debate for days — what to do with Harry Windom and the other goons they'd captured. They'd had three options: execute Windom, hold him prisoner ... or let him go. In the end, they'd reached a simple conclusion. They couldn't shoot him down in cold blood, simply could *not* do it. And they were unwilling to operate a jail, to hold people there, prisoners. The best they could do was strip Windom and his soldiers of their weapons, ammunition and vehicles, and let all of them go. Most weren't soldiers anyway, just frightened, misguided civilians who'd been conned into doing something stupid to save their families.

The men stopped at the door leading to the kitchen where Nick had been headed to get jugs of cold water to take to the workers. They stared into each other's eyes.

"Maybe we should have killed him," Sawyer said quietly.

"Maybe we should have," Nick agreed.

They'd talked the point to death. It was what it was. Sawyer had at least spent some of his rage when he grabbed Windom by the shirt, hauled him to his feet and smashed his fist into his face that day, heard the satisfying pop when his nose broke.

When Nick pushed open the kitchen door, Sawyer spotted Ellie rinsing out baby bottles in the sink before loading them into the sterilizing dishwasher.

"Can I help you with any of that?"

"Just like a man. Show up when the job's ninety percent done and offer to help." But she smiled when she said it.

Ellie didn't look good. She'd returned from Ft. Knox in great spirits, bringing with her the orphan infant, Diana, to raise. Then something had happened. He didn't know what. She had walled off all questions about her "condition" and he respected her privacy. Her best hope had been snuffed out when the Astrals destroyed Jessup and killed the doctor who had promised to at least consider performing surgery on her. Unless some other doctor showed up on their doorstep — which wasn't outside the realm of possibility given the trickle that was slowly becoming a stream of people who did exactly that.

People from all over just ... showed up, with no plausible explanation for why they'd come, didn't appear to know themselves. They had nowhere else to go, of course, but that wasn't a unique circumstance in the world they lived in — what was it Nick and Eagle Feather called it? The new world order. And the motto of that order was "fight or die." But these people weren't the enemy. They'd been *drawn* here by … he pushed the thought away because even thinking it went against the grain of every practical, logical, grounded bone in his body. But in his more vulnerable moments, when he was tired, his defenses down, somewhere inside him admitted the truth that was evident to anybody with eyes to see it.

There was *something* about Star and Noah.

No way to put a name to it because it likely didn't have one. He'd sensed that something in Noah all his life, but it'd been dialed up after he was returned from the mothership. Once Star arrived, it was like she completed a circuit and what the two of them were together was far greater than either one of them was separately.

And what were they?

Sawyer had no idea, but whatever they were, the something *attracted* people, drew them like a magnet. And he didn't see any end in sight.

You can't save every puppy in the pound.

What would they do with the people who kept coming and coming?

He had absolutely no idea. Neither did anybody else. He'd cross that bridge when he got to it.

"You seen Garson and Eagle Feather?" Sawyer asked Ellie.

"They were headed to the orchard last I saw."

Sawyer found them there. Eagle Feather and Garson were seated at a picnic table under an apple tree. Noah had climbed up into the limbs and was tossing apples on the ground where Star was gathering them up and putting them in a basket. She went right to each apple, never wavered or had to feel around on the ground for it. Noah said that was because she could see what Pumpkin smelled.

That part, at least, had to be fantasy. *Had to be.*

When he'd passed the "construction workers" earlier, he heard music blaring out of one of them's juke. An old rock & roll song that put him in mind of the night he'd gone to Louisville to get Ellie, and he pushed that thought out of his mind, too. These days, he spent a considerable amount of emotional energy not thinking about things.

That couldn't be emotionally healthy.

But like everything else these days — children speaking inside each other's heads, Star's images of the future — even seeing what a dog smelled, for crying out loud!

It was what it was.

Garson and Eagle Feather stopped talking when Sawyer approached them. He thought Eagle Feather looked like the image on a buffalo nickel, the side view of the Indian there, and when he mentioned it to Noah, he said Star had always thought so, too.

"Talking about me, were you?" Sawyer asked as he approached.

"And we didn't have a single complimentary thing to say, so you best be on your way so we can continue our criticism," Garson said.

Instead, Sawyer lifted his leg up over the bench seat and sat down next to the professor.

"You ever plan to tell anybody what the two of you appear to know that the rest of us don't?"

"Oh, don't be ridiculous, Sawyer. If I had to tell you everything I know that you don't, it would take weeks."

"Heard from Dr. Bannister lately?" Bannister was an expert on Ancient Aliens, the spokesperson of the organization that Garson belonged to — scientists who'd been laughed at throughout their careers ... until little dots out by Jupiter proved they'd been right all along.

Garson looked uncomfortable.

"Only once in the past month, and I suspect that will be the last time."

"And Dr. Bannister said ...?"

"To tell you hello and that he hopes to get to meet you in person someday. He's a very friendly fellow. You'll like—"

"Cut the crap." Sawyer hadn't meant to sound harsh but it came out that way and maybe that's what it would take to get these guys to fess up. "I want to know what you know."

"We don't *know*—"

"What you suspect, then."

The two old men exchanged a glance and then Garson's shoulders sagged.

"Same old, same old. Nothing's changed. Just more confirmation of what we already deduced."

He waited, said nothing.

Garson sighed.

"Annihilation. Just like in the past, the Astrals

came here to judge humanity … and then they'll wipe us out and start over."

It wasn't the first time Sawyer had heard that death sentence, but it never got easier to hear. And he'd been hoping …

"So … there's nothing we can—?"

"No," Garson answered Sawyer's unasked question. "There's nothing *we* can do."

Eagle Feather spoke for the first time. He nodded toward Star, who was sitting on the ground giggling after Noah dropped an apple on her head. Then he sounded like he was quoting something he'd heard repeated again and again. "The child named for the heavens will go to the white giants and return with a gift that will save her people from destruction."

"What does *that* mean?"

Garson sighed and spoke slowly, as if addressing a small child.

"It means, my dear Sawyer, that that little girl is the only hope we have."

THE END

A Note from the Author

Thank you for reading *The Changed*.

If you enjoyed this book, you please consider writing a review on your favorite bookselling site so other readers might enjoy it too. Just a couple of sentences would mean a lot to me.

Thank you!

Ninie Hammon

About the Authors

Avery Blake doesn't want you to know where she lives, or what she does. She travels the world, moving from place to place quickly to ensure she can't be tracked. It's safer that way.

When she's not looking over her shoulder, you can find her in the corner of a cafe, facing the exit, typing as fast as she can.

Ninie Hammon (rhymes with shiny, not skinny) grew up in Muleshoe, Texas, got a BA in English and theatre from Texas Tech University and snagged a job as a newspaper reporter. She didn't know a thing about journalism, but her editor said if she could write he could teach her the rest of it and if she couldn't write the rest of it didn't matter. She hung in there for a 25-year career as a journalist. As soon as she figured out that making up the facts was a whole lot more fun than reporting them, she turned to fiction and never looked back.

Ninie now writes suspense--every flavor except pistachio: psychological suspense, inspirational suspense, suspense thrillers, paranormal suspense, suspense mysteries.

In every book she keeps this promise to her Loyal Reader: "I will tell you a story in a distinctive voice you'll always recognize, about people as ordinary as you are--people who have been slammed by something they didn't sign on for, and now they must fight for their lives. Then smack in the middle of their everyday worlds, those people encounter the unexplainable--and it's always the game-changer."

Also By Avery Blake

The Invasion Series

Longshot

Invasion

Contact

Colonization

Annihilation

Judgment

Extinction

Resurrection

Save The City Series

Save The City

Save The Girl

Save The World

Stonefall Series

Alienation

Stonefall

Snowfall

Downfall

The Taken Saga

The Taken

The Changed

The Hidden

The Saved

The Next Evolution

Transition

Convergence

Evolution

Stand-Alone Novels

Analog Heart

Family Royale

Ruthless Positivity

Vicarious Joe

Cornbread Mafia

Fire In The Hole

Blown' Up A Storm

Ridin' For A Fall

So Shall The Tree Grow

Nowhere, USA

The Jabberwock

Mad Dog

Trapped

The Hanging Judge

The Witch of Gideon

Blown Away

Nowhere People

Through The Canvas Series

Black Water

Red Web

Gold Promise

Blue Tears

The Taken Saga

The Taken

The Changed

The Hidden

The Saved

The Unexplainable Collection

Five Days in May

Black Sunshine

The Based on True Stories Collection

Home Grown

Sudan

When Butterflies Cry

The Knowing Series

The Knowing

The Deceiving

The Reckoning

The Fault

Stand-alone Psychological Thrillers

The Memory Closet

The Last Safe Place